PICTURE IMPERFECT

www.penguin.co.uk

Jacqueline Wilson

PICTURE IMAPERFECT

bantam

TRANSWORLD PUBLISHERS

UK | USA | Canada | Ireland | Australia
India | New Zealand | South Africa

Transworld is part of the Penguin Random House group of companies whose addresses can be found at global.penguinrandomhouse.com.

Penguin Random House UK, One Embassy Gardens,
8 Viaduct Gardens, London SW11 7BW

penguin.co.uk

First published in Great Britain in 2025 by Bantam
an imprint of Transworld Publishers

002

Copyright © Jacqueline Wilson 2025

The moral right of the author has been asserted

This book is a work of fiction and, except in the case of historical fact, any resemblance to actual persons, living or dead, is purely coincidental.

Every effort has been made to obtain the necessary permissions with reference to copyright material, both illustrative and quoted. We apologize for any omissions in this respect and will be pleased to make the appropriate acknowledgements in any future edition.

Penguin Random House values and supports copyright. Copyright fuels creativity, encourages diverse voices, promotes freedom of expression and supports a vibrant culture. Thank you for purchasing an authorized edition of this book and for respecting intellectual property laws by not reproducing, scanning or distributing any part of it by any means without permission. You are supporting authors and enabling Penguin Random House to continue to publish books for everyone. No part of this book may be used or reproduced in any manner for the purpose of training artificial intelligence technologies or systems. In accordance with Article 4(3) of the DSM Directive 2019/790, Penguin Random House expressly reserves this work from the text and data mining exception.

Typeset in 11.75/15.75 pt Sabon by Falcon Oast Graphic Art Ltd
Printed and bound in Great Britain by Clays Ltd, Elcograf S.p.A.

The authorized representative in the EEA is Penguin Random House Ireland, Morrison Chambers, 32 Nassau Street, Dublin D02 YH68

A CIP catalogue record for this book is available from the British Library

ISBNs:
9780857507631 (hb)
9780857507648 (tpb)

For Emma

1

I was designing a new custom piece, a dragon with gleaming green scales in a fiery tryst with a princess with red hair right down to her feet, when a jangling bell startled them apart. It took me a moment to realize I was dreaming – but the noise clamouring in my ears was all too real.

Feeling for my phone on the bedside table, I nearly sent it flying over the edge. Still bleary with sleep, I made a final, clumsy grab, and fumbled to press the green button. There was a voice in my ear.

'Are you . . . Dolphin?' a man asked uncertainly.

I started trembling. Very few people called me that now. Oh help, had Marigold created chaos again? I thought things were going so well.

'Yes,' I said, my voice husky.

'Sorry to wake you up in the middle of the night, but we have a lady here who's not very well and she's given us your number. She says she's called Marigold, Queen of the Sky?' He pronounced it solemnly, but I could hear a colleague spluttering in the background. Perhaps they thought they'd stepped into a parody of *Game of Thrones*.

I breathed out slowly, sagging in despair. She'd come off her medication again. Why wouldn't she ever learn?

'My mother really is called Marigold,' I said, trying to sound calm. 'She suffers from chronic mental illness, as you've probably gathered. Where is she – in a nightclub?'

'I'm a security officer at Gatwick Airport, North Terminal,' he said.

'What's she doing there?' I asked weakly.

'She's kicking up one hell of a fuss, that's what she's doing. She says she's missed her flight. She's had too much to drink, if you don't mind my saying, but we get a lot of passengers like this. We were going to let her sleep it off, but she started screaming to get through to Airside because she wants to go shopping in Hamleys, even though we've told her they closed at eight p.m.'

'I see,' I said, my mouth so dry I could barely get the words out.

'She's still kicking off, lashing out, falling over. We're concerned she might hurt herself more than anyone else. We've phoned a couple of hospitals but there aren't any beds going spare on the psych wards. I suppose the police could collect her and pop her in a cell for being drunk and disorderly, but she seems a nice lady, shame to give her a criminal record.'

The 'nice lady' actually had a criminal record as long as her illustrated arm, but I wasn't telling him that.

'So what do you want me to do?' I asked, though it was obvious.

'Could you come and collect her?' he asked. 'You should see the state she's in. And she is your mum, after all.'

She has another daughter! I'm her second daughter. Second by birth. And second best.

'Of course,' I said through a giant sigh. 'It'll take me quite a while to get to Gatwick, though.'

He'd already rung off. I stared at the glowing phone in the darkness and took in the time. Half past one! How in God's name was I going to get to Gatwick? I didn't have a car. I'd never even learnt to drive properly. A long-ago boyfriend tried giving me a few lessons and kept losing his temper, saying I was so stupid I'd likely kill myself and any passengers the first time I took to the road. I wanted to run *him* over then. I imagined a tattoo of me driving a giant steam roller, turning him into Flat Stanley.

I didn't persevere with our relationship or the driving lessons. So now I was stuck. There weren't any trains at this time of night. I wasn't even sure I'd be able to get a taxi – you mostly had to book a day or two ahead in Seahaven. I wouldn't be able to afford it anyway. It was at least £70 to Gatwick, and probably another £70 back again, though if Marigold was in a state the driver would probably refuse to take her. I didn't have £14 going spare, let alone £140.

Perhaps I could phone my dad to ask if he could possibly give me a lift? He'd helped me out with Marigold in the past. He'd always been kind to me, even though he didn't know I existed until we met when I was ten. He's tried to be in my life for the last twenty-odd years. Twenty-three years, to be exact.

I'm thirty-three, the same age as Marigold when she ended up in hospital for months. When she came out at last she seemed so different. We thought it was going to be all right. We'd be together again, Marigold and Star and me. But it didn't work out that way. She had so many ups and downs that Star and I were in and out of care until we turned eighteen. Star seemed to do well in the system, relieved she didn't have to look after me all the time. I never really coped, though. I just ached for Marigold. She meant all the world to me back then.

She still did now, in spite of everything. And I hated having to beg for help to sort her out, but there was no other way. I flipped through the contacts on my phone. Not that many. He's under D for Dad, because it feels good remembering that I have a father like anyone else. I pressed 'call', though I felt sick now, worried about contacting him so late.

He's always said, 'Get in touch any time, Dol, I'll always be there for you.'

I whispered this like a mantra as the phone rang and rang. Then suddenly there was a click and a voice. But not my dad's. My heart sank at the sound of his wife, Meg.

'Who is it? Is that *you*, Dolphin?' she whispered, though she must have seen my name flash up on the screen.

She always pronounces it Dol*pheen* as if I'm a character in a country and western song. I once tried calling her Meg*aaan* and she accused me of mocking her. Which I was, though I protested my innocence. She's technically my stepmother but I'm pretty sure she can't bear me. The feeling's reciprocal.

'Can I speak to Dad, please?' I mumbled.

'No, you can't!' she hissed.

I heard her moving around, a bed creaking, a door opening and shutting, and then the thump as she sat down on something hard. Oh God, was she in her bathroom? I really didn't want to talk to Meg while she was on the toilet.

'Do you have any idea what time it is?'

'I'm so sorry to wake you,' I replied, praying I wouldn't hear her weeing. 'But I need to speak to my dad.'

'Well, as I said, you can't! How could you disturb him in the middle of the night? You know he's not been very well!'

There'd been something wrong with his heart rhythm, but he had a pacemaker fitted and he promised he was fine now. 'The op wasn't serious, Dol. I just needed to be rebooted, like a computer,' he'd assured me.

'I'm really sorry. I just wondered if he could possibly give me a lift to Gatwick,' I said.

'*Gatwick?*' she exclaimed, as if I'd said Timbuktu.

'Yes, I know, but Marigold's been detained there and I have to collect her,' I said, steeling myself for her reaction.

'That effing woman!' she said. She's too genteel to come out with an honest 'fuck'. What's the matter with my parents? Why did they both choose horrible partners?

'Dad said I must call on him to help out if she gets ill again. I promise you, he did say that,' I gabbled.

'Yes, well, he would, wouldn't he, because he's such a mug. Your mother's nothing to do with him. He barely knew her.'

He lived with her for eleven months, and he loved her way more than he loves you. She was the one who left him and I'm not sure he ever got over it. So let me speak to him, you stupid bitch!

'If I could just talk to him and explain—' I started, but she'd already hung up.

I sighed despairingly. What was I going to do now? My head was thumping as well as my heart. I switched on the light and went to search the kitchen drawer. I haven't actually got a kitchen, it's a little recess in my bedsit containing a stove, a fridge and a three-drawer unit. If I had slightly longer arms, I could fry myself an egg sitting up in bed.

I found a packet of paracetamol and took a glass from the shelf. There was a sudden gushing sound *before* I turned on the tap. I stared at it in alarm – and then realized it was the tap the other side of the wall. The new guy, Lee, was obviously awake. Oh God, the Gatwick phone call probably woke him up too. The walls between our bedsits aren't even like cardboard – more like opaque tissue paper.

I hoped he wouldn't be too annoyed. He seemed a nice sort of man. I met him on the stairs last week when he moved in and helped him ease two dismantled beds round the bends. One was normal size, one was small.

'Have you got a child?' I'd asked hopefully. Unlike most renters, I love it if anyone has a small family. I've twice been an honorary Auntie Dolly, and I've babysat for free, played endless games and invented stories for various small people. I've always got on with children. Star says it's because I've never grown up properly myself.

'I've got a little girl – my Ava. She's the most amazing kid, four years old, perfect age, but I only get to see her occasionally,' he said. He attempted a shrug, as if to say it's no big deal, but he couldn't stop his face crumpling.

'Well, any time you need a babysitter, feel free to ask. I love kids,' I said.

'Thanks a lot,' he said, looking really touched. 'I take it you're up in bedsit world because you're on your own too. So if ever you need a hand, whatever, just let me know.'

He seemed lovely, though totally not my type: homely, fair curly hair, flushed cheeks, slightly tubby. The safe, teddy-bear type. Perhaps . . . the type to help out when you're in a tough spot? He's a gardener, so he had his van parked outside. Would he take me? But this wouldn't just be lending me a hand. It was asking for two hands, two feet, to drive me all the way to Gatwick and back again with my sick mother on board. It was way too much to ask when I hardly knew him.

I was desperate, though. He was my only option. I pulled on jeans and a jumper, stuffed my feet into trainers, grabbed the key and shuffled into the corridor. I knocked tentatively and the door opened almost straight away. He looked like a giant little boy in his old-fashioned blue-and-white-striped pyjamas, his curls sticking up all over the place.

'I'm so sorry, Lee – I think my phone must have woken you up,' I said.

'That's OK, Dol,' he said. I rarely told people my real name because it was so outlandish. 'I hope it's not an emergency?'

'Well, it is, actually,' I said, taking a deep breath. 'My mum's not very well. She's stuck at Gatwick Airport and I have to collect her. Um, you can't think of any way I could get there, can you? There's no public transport at this time and I haven't got a car,' I added, blushing at my sheer audacity.

I wouldn't have blamed him if he shut the door in my face. But he was a kind man.

'I'll take you in the van,' he said, smiling, as if it would somehow be a treat for him. 'I'll be ready in a tick,' he said. 'Hang on!'

'You're an angel,' I declared, weak with relief.

I rushed back into my own flat, had a wee, cleaned my teeth, and grabbed my phone and credit card – could there possibly be a fee to pay for collecting a drunken mother? I looked for something to eat in the van to keep us going and could only find half a pack of Jaffa Cakes, probably stale, but they were better than nothing.

I heard Lee's own front door opening and hurried back to mine. He was wearing jeans and a big scarlet sweater – a mistake with his ruddy cheeks, but he could have been wearing a sack for all I cared.

'Your carriage awaits, ma'am,' he proclaimed with a flamboyant gesture, as if he were a coachman and I was Cinderella. It was terribly cringy, but I smiled gratefully.

We went downstairs, tiptoeing in our trainers so as not to wake anyone else, and walked over to his minivan parked outside. I climbed into the front, sweet wrappers and crumpled fruit juice cartons crackling under my feet. I found myself sitting on a toy Alsatian.

'Sorry, sorry,' Lee said, bending to gather up the rubbish and shoving it all in a flowerpot at the back. He was gentler with the toy dog, placing him carefully on a sack of compost as if he was real, even giving him a quick pat.

'That's Fido,' he said, when he caught me staring. 'We got him from one of those arcade machines, Ava and me, and she insists I have him in the van to keep me company on journeys.'

'That's sweet of her,' I said, putting on my seat belt.

'Yes, she's the sweetest kid in the world,' he agreed. 'Though I would say that, wouldn't I?' He started up the engine. 'Right, Gatwick, here we come. Which terminal?'

'North,' I said. 'Shall I look up the postcode on my phone?'

'Don't worry, I'll find it. We go to Majorca every year – well, we used to . . .' His voice tailed off sadly.

It sounded as if he and his wife had split up recently, but it seemed rude to ask. There was a little silence as we drove. It grew longer. Lee switched on the radio and some through-the-night pop blared out.

'Sorry!' he said, turning it down.

'You don't have to keep saying sorry to me! I'm the one who should be apologizing to you,' I said. 'You're doing me such an enormous favour. You must at least let me give you some money for the petrol – though you might have to wait till I get paid.'

'So what do you do for a living?' he asked, sounding grateful for a topic of conversation.

'I work in a place called Artful Ink. A tattoo studio,' I told him.

'Really? So you're the receptionist?'

'No, a tattooist actually,' I said.

'Seriously? I thought tattooists were hulking great men covered in ink,' he said.

'That's the clients,' I said, bristling. 'Though they've changed nowadays as well. We often have professional people – and a lot of women too.'

'Have you got tattoos, Dol? Show me! If – if it's not in a difficult place,' he said, suddenly embarrassed.

'I haven't got any at all,' I said.

'Oh well. I'm a gardener and yet I haven't got a garden of my own at the moment,' he said, sighing. 'And to be honest, I don't really think tattoos look that great on a woman.'

'That's a bit sexist, isn't it?' He was really starting to annoy me now, even though he was doing me such a good turn.

'Sorry, sorry. I think *delicate* tattoos can look good on a woman – little daisies, bluebirds, that type of thing,' he said quickly. 'But you sometimes see women with tattoos all over, and that just looks, well, bizarre.'

'Bizarre?' I repeated.

He could tell by the tone of my voice that he'd said something deeply wrong. He glanced at me anxiously. I kept very still. If he said sorry one more time I'd start screaming.

'I didn't mean to offend you,' he said quietly instead. 'I should learn to keep my big mouth shut.'

'I suppose I'm just a bit tense at the moment.'

'Of course you are. You must be worried sick about your mum. I was just nattering on, trying to take your mind off things, and now I've ended up insulting your profession,' he said.

'Speaking of my mum,' I said, taking a deep breath, 'I think you'll find *her* bizarre.'

'What do you—? Oh God. Don't tell me *she's* got tattoos all over her?' he asked.

'She has. I didn't do them, she's had them since I was little. And added a lot more through the years. She's got at least twenty-five – maybe more. All over.'

He took one hand off the steering wheel and smacked the side of his head. 'I'm an idiot. How could I have been so flipping tactless?'

I sighed. He could be Meg's soulmate, with that weak substitute for 'fuck'. Then I felt terrible. I had to stop this. I have a habit of being antagonistic to kind people because they fluster me. Star says that's why I've always had such rubbish relationships. It's because I deliberately go for bad boys who will let me down. It's as if I'm outwitting my own gullibility. If I choose an obvious bastard then I won't break my heart. I know exactly what to expect.

Well, that's what she says. Anyone would think she was a psychiatrist instead of a GP. My sister, the doctor. I still can't get my head around it.

'You weren't to know. And actually, *I* think she looks bizarre, though I thought she was beautiful when I was a kid,' I said.

He murmured sympathetically, not risking saying anything else at all.

'She has bipolar disorder. She always gets another tattoo when she's in a manic phase,' I said. 'She's obviously in one now. I just hope she's not got an eagle flying across her forehead or a spider on both cheeks.'

He grunted, sounding appalled, but stayed heroically silent.

'I'm joking. Though the joke will be on me if she's done just that,' I said. 'You must think I'm dreadful, joking about my own mother. I know she can't help it, she's mentally ill. I'm just so sick of having to deal with it.' My voice wobbled dangerously.

'It must be an awful strain,' he said quietly.

His genuine sympathy was too much, and I turned to look out of the window so he couldn't see the tears spilling down my cheeks. I didn't see how I could keep on coping – but what choice did I have?

2

I felt totally unnerved when we'd parked the car at the airport. I'd only been abroad twice in my life and found it all entirely confusing. Lee steered me around and found the right place near Passport Control.

'Ah, you must be Dolphin,' the security man said, though he looked uncertain. Perhaps he'd been expecting someone as colourful as Marigold, not a little mouse in a jersey and jeans.

'*Dolphin?*' Lee muttered, staring at me. I gave him a rueful shrug.

'Are you her partner?' the security man asked Lee, looking relieved. Perhaps he thought I'd start kicking off too. Lee looked the sort of capable man, strong but kind, who could cope with hysterical women.

Lee shook the man's hand firmly.

'I'm a family friend,' he said.

'Well, come this way, both of you.' He beckoned us forward.

I'd imagined Marigold screaming in a cell but she was sitting at a table in an ordinary office. Another security man was with her, drinking a mug of tea. Marigold had a mug too, clasping it with both hands. She was shaking, and some of the tea had splashed down her white lacy top. It was very skimpy, displaying too much tattooed chest. Her skirt was very short too, though her long, bare legs were still shapely. She'd kicked off one high heel, revealing the green frog tattoo peeping out between her toes.

Her head was bent, her red hair hiding her face. I could see her white roots.

'Marigold!' I ran to her, took the mug from her and wrapped my arms tightly round her.

I breathed in her familiar smell of perfume and sweat and alcohol. When I was a little girl I'd snuggle against her and she'd hold me close, her long nails lightly tapping out a tune on my back. I was the one holding her close now.

'There now, Marigold. I'm here now. We'll get you home, don't you worry.'

She stiffened and pulled away from me. 'I don't want to go *home*! I'm getting the first plane to Scotland in the morning! I've got to see my grandchild!'

I froze. How in hell had she found out about Star's child? I'd solemnly sworn to Star that I'd keep it a secret. I hadn't breathed a word to anyone – oh God, except Steve.

I'd bumped into him at the tattoo fair at Olympia. Marigold used to work for him long ago, and though he looked like the tough, inked-all-over tattooist of Lee's imagination, he was like a jolly uncle to Star and me. I'd done my initial training with him. He'd always been sympathetic about Marigold, but that day he kept shaking his head and making tutting noises. I found myself boasting about Star to show that the family had one success story.

'Star's still up in Scotland. She's a fully qualified doctor now, would you believe? She's married to another doctor and they've just had a baby boy. I bet they've strung a tiny stethoscope round his neck for him to teethe on!'

I'd felt anxious as soon as the words were out of my mouth. Star had been so insistent that Marigold mustn't know – but I'd reasoned that the chances of Marigold herself bumping into Steve were minimal. She couldn't do any inking herself now because her hands shook too badly, and she knew Steve wouldn't touch her skin since she'd picked at a newly inked butterfly on her calf and it had turned septic. But clearly, I'd been wrong.

'Why didn't you *tell* me, Dol?' Marigold wailed, and started beating me on my shoulders, arms, chest.

She wasn't really hurting me, she was just hitting out feebly in frustration, but the security guard cried out, 'Hey, stop that!' and Lee grabbed Marigold's wrists, holding them firmly.

'Ah! Ah!' he said, like Graeme Hall taming a boisterous dog. 'Calm down, now! You don't want to hurt your daughter, she's trying to help you!'

Marigold tried beating at him too, but then collapsed against him, sobbing. Lee held her, patting her back, as if comforting a sadly befuddled woman in the middle of the night was an everyday occurrence. The security guards exchanged glances.

'That's it, mate. She obviously thinks a lot of you,' he said, as Marigold clung to Lee. 'So do you think you can take her home now?'

'Of course I can,' said Lee, kindly not telling them that he'd only met Marigold that minute. 'Come on now, Marigold, let's thank these guys for looking after you, and then we'll take you back home, OK?'

She looked up at him, grateful now, but still highly agitated.

'You'll bring me back, though? I have to see the baby! He's Micky's grandchild!' she garbled.

'When you're a bit better,' Lee said. 'Come on now! No need to cry!'

She was gasping now, choking on sobs, her eyes wet, her nose running, but he still hung on to her valiantly. I started sweating with embarrassment as we bundled Marigold away with us. A few stray travellers spread out on the seats gawped at us as if we were a freak show, but Lee ignored them and I tried to follow his lead. It was an enormous relief when we got back to his van.

'In you hop, Marigold,' Lee said.

Marigold pushed her tousled hair out of her eyes and peered at the van suspiciously.

'I'm not going in that!' she protested.

'Oh, for God's sake, Marigold!' I said, trying to get her to climb in the back.

'Not fucking likely!' Marigold yelled in the echoing car park, never a woman to bother with substitutes. She called Lee worse names as he tried to lever her in too.

'He's going to bung me back in hospital, isn't he!' she screamed. 'You can't fool me! You're egging him on, because you just want to be rid of me, Dol! I want Star! I want Star and her baby and my Micky!'

I felt like shaking her, though I knew she couldn't help it.

'He's not taking you to hospital, I swear it. He's my neighbour and he's being kind enough to help us. He has a van because he's a gardener. We're going to sit in the back and you're going to stop shouting and swearing and shut up!' I said fiercely.

It was the wrong tone, the wrong words, way too brutal – but it worked. Marigold and I sat in the back together, and I held her, and she stopped fighting me and subsided with her head on a sack of compost beside the toy dog.

'Are you all right back there?' Lee murmured.

'Yes, fine,' I said, though of course it was anything but. I was trying to make up my mind what on earth I should do. Could I ask Lee to take us all the way to Marigold's flat, which was miles past our own? And if he did, there was likely to be another fracas. Marigold's partner Rick particularly disliked me. His way of greeting me was always, 'Watch out! Here comes the killjoy!' His definition of joy was encouraging Marigold to spend her benefits on drink and dope, and suggesting she come off her Lithium because he said she was 'more fun' without it. No wonder I was a killjoy. I often felt like killing Rick myself.

The only other place she could go was back with me, and that made me feel sick with dread. I loved Marigold, I truly cared about her, but she was such hard work. Was I going to be stuck doing it for ever? I'd lost jobs before, because I hadn't been able to risk leaving her when she was in a psychotic phase. I'd lost flats. I'd lost friends. I'd lost my own life. It was so fucking unfair. Why wouldn't Star ever take a turn?

'Dol?' Lee must have seen me in his rear-view mirror.

'I'm OK,' I insisted.

'You poor thing,' he said softly.

Why couldn't I fall in love with someone like him, who'd always help me and try to understand?

Marigold moaned sleepily, half lifting her head.

'Shh now! Try to go to sleep,' I said, patting her back. I could feel her shoulder blades, sharp as little axes. She was obviously not eating properly. Not doing anything properly.

She wriggled, her hand going to her chest. Oh God, was she going to be sick? She'd certainly drunk enough. It would be the final horror if she was sick in Lee's van, and I'd have to mop it all up and scrub the floor.

'Hang on, Marigold,' I whispered sternly.

Thank God she did manage it, though the moment we got her out of the van she threw up. At least she did it neatly in the gutter while I held her head and kept her hair out of the way. Lee tactfully turned his back on us, but as soon as she'd finished he took her arm to help her along.

'I take it she's staying the night with you?' he asked.

'I suppose so,' I said.

'I'll be right next door if you need me for anything,' he reassured me.

'You're an absolute angel,' I said.

'Hardly,' he said, grinning. 'I wouldn't do this for anyone else, you know.'

What did he mean? Did he mean I was special? Did he fancy me? It didn't seem likely. I'd got very thin, my hair badly needed cutting into some sort of shape, and I was as pale as a ghost because I didn't bother with make-up any more.

I smiled at him uncertainly as he got the front door open, then we took Marigold's arms and helped her up the three flights of narrow stairs. The effort left us all panting. He helped me get her in my own front door and then looked round, momentarily distracted.

'Your room's so different!' he said.

Our bedsits were identical in shape and size, but I had made mine into the fairy grotto of my childhood dreams, with twinkly lights, miniature gardens in glass bottles and dolls sitting on the window sills. I'd covered the shabby furniture with embroidered throws, papered the cracked walls with pictures and posters and cards, and installed a vintage mannequin from a closing-down dress shop for company, buying her a long blonde wig and making her a Biba-type velvet dress so she'd feel glamorous.

I loved the way it looked, but, seeing it through Lee's eyes now, I was painfully conscious that it was a little girl's fantasy room, not a sensible home for a thirty-three-year-old woman. I felt my cheeks flush.

'It's all a bit childish,' I mumbled.

'I think it's amazing,' Lee breathed.

'That's my Dolly for you,' Marigold said, her voice slurring. 'Creative. You take after me, don't you, darling?'

I couldn't think of anything worse than taking after Marigold, but I knew she meant well, and I was so relieved she seemed to have stopped being angry with me.

'Come on then, Mum, let's get you to bed,' I said. I felt self-conscious calling her 'Mum', but I liked to do it when I felt really fond of her.

'My girl!' said Marigold, and gave me a clumsy hug. The lingering smell of sick made my nose wrinkle, but I didn't pull away.

'Well, I'll leave you two to catch up on your sleep,' said Lee. He looked at me, then back at her. 'Do knock again if you need me.'

'Thank you so much for everything. You've been a total . . .' I couldn't keep calling him an angel. 'A knight in shining armour,' I said instead, imagining him in medieval polished steel, with a purple plume flowing from his silver helmet. It was a popular tattoo for besotted young girls newly in love. The image suited Lee tonight, despite his homely face and sturdy body.

He grinned at me, nodded to Marigold, and left us to it.

'Are you two fucking?' Marigold asked before he'd properly shut the door.

'Shut *up*! No, we're not!' I hissed, fetching her a clean nightie.

'Why not? Is he a bit too dull? Mr Nicey Nicey?'

'That's a terrible thing to say, when he's been so kind,' I said, pulling her top off. I could see every rib. Her breasts were tiny puckers now – the python lasciviously coiling round them was going to have a very meagre meal. I pulled the nightdress over her head hurriedly, poking her arms through the sleeves. Then I hung on to one arm, horrified. Were these marks needle tracks?

'Oh my God, are you *injecting* now?'

'I'm not a fool,' she protested. 'Rick and I might smoke a little weed sometimes, but you know I'm squeamish with needles.'

'So how did you get these marks?'

'*I* don't know,' she said, shrugging.

'Look, this one's oozing! It's all infected. You should see a doctor!'

'Well, you can't get to see one for months nowadays so what's the point in trying? Oh, wait! I'll ask Star when I see her tomorrow!' she said, glowing at the idea.

'Don't start that again,' I said, trying to bundle her into bed.

'I'm going! First thing tomorrow!' she declared, struggling with me. 'Lee can drive me straight back to the airport!'

'Lee will be going to work, and so will I. And I don't know what *you'll* be doing, but it's certainly not going to Scotland. You haven't even got a ticket for a flight, have you?'

'I'm buying one. I've got a credit card, see,' she said, opening her bag, the stitching unravelling, the lining torn. She pulled out vapes, eyeliner, lipstick, a little brush with several missing bristles and, finally, a worn wallet.

'See!' she said, brandishing it.

I grabbed it from her and opened it. It contained a long-ago crumpled photo of Micky with his arm round Star, another photo of Star and me as little kids dressing up in Marigold's clothes, a voucher for a free cup of coffee and an old cinema ticket. It also had a credit card, but when I looked at it carefully it was months out of date and had someone else's name on it anyway.

'That's not going to buy you a ticket to Scotland, is it?' I said.

'It might,' she said. 'Or – or someone else might have dropped one by the ticket machine.'

'Oh, for Christ's sake, Marigold, stop playing silly games. You can't really be that stupid.'

'Then you lend me the money, Dol. Please! I have to go and see my grandson! That's not crazy, is it? Every grandma on earth wants to see her grandchild. *Why* didn't you tell me about him? How can you be so cruel?' she said, kicking at me feebly as I tried to haul her legs into bed.

'*I* haven't even seen him. Star never wants to come and see us.' I chose not to mention that Star had often invited me up to Scotland, though.

'She's my *daughter*! Micky's child!' Marigold shouted. 'My Micky – the love of my life.'

How often had I heard that? She meant it too, even when she was sober and sensible. But they'd parted so long ago I wasn't even sure she'd recognize him now if he walked straight past her. A fantasy Micky glowed in glorious Technicolor in her mind. Sometimes I wondered if she'd even know the glossy, grown-up Star in the photos she sent me.

If only she were here too, helping me cope.

'Star! Star, Star, Star!' Marigold called, as if summoning her.

'Shh! We've disturbed Lee enough for one night. And stop going on about Star. I miss her just as much as you do. She's my *sister*!'

She wasn't just a sister to me. She'd been like my mum when I was little, looking after me valiantly when Marigold was having an episode. She'd been my best friend too. No matter how scary life got, Star was always there for me. Well, most of the time. I was terrified when she went to live with Micky, thinking I'd lost her for ever, but thank God that didn't last long.

She came back and coped with Marigold, and I relied on her utterly. I found it very difficult when she went away to university. It was a shock when she chose to read medicine at St Andrews, almost as far away as she could go. She made one fleeting visit home the first Christmas, and after a few months Marigold managed somehow to raise the money for the two of us to make the complicated journey up there.

The visit wasn't a success. Marigold and I were both overwhelmed by the university, the entire town of St Andrews, Star's new boyfriend Charles and, most of all, Star herself. She didn't seem part of our family any more. She'd grown her hair longer, removed her nose stud, and wore soft, ladylike sweaters, smart jeans and bright white plimsolls. She didn't even sound like herself. Rather than picking up the soft Scottish lilt, she spoke posh English like most of the other students up there.

I felt uncomfortably in awe of her and became practically monosyllabic, unable to confide all the things I'd been bursting to tell her. Marigold went the other way, talking too loudly, wearing her brightest lipstick, her shortest skirt, her highest heels. She even called Star's posh boyfriend 'Charlie Boy'. He was smoothly polite, but he couldn't look at her without fractionally raising his eyebrows. She was so different from all the other visiting mothers – a squawking parrot in among a flight of doves.

I looked at Marigold now, so pitiful and bedraggled, her garish make-up smeared. I felt bad about not washing her face, but it was struggle enough to get her into bed. The moment I got her lying down she reared up again, words tumbling out of her smudged mouth in an incoherent babble. I'd been planning to sleep on the sofa, but the only way I could manage things was by wriggling out of my clothes and getting into bed beside her.

She still fought me, as if I was intruding in *her* bed, but I held her tight and felt her slowly relax. How long had she been awake? In a manic phase she often didn't sleep for days, and her voice got even higher until it sounded as if she'd been inhaling helium. She was still slurring too, drunker than I'd thought. Maybe she really had had money for a ticket but had bought herself too many double vodkas to give her the courage to go? I felt a pang of sorrow for her.

She'd started to shake again. I patted her and murmured all the soothing words I could think of. I even sang to her the way she'd crooned to me when I was little: *Hush little baby, don't you cry, Mama's going to sing you a lullaby.*

I sang it until her eyes closed and my own voice started slurring, and I fell asleep myself.

3

When I woke the next morning, I reached out for Marigold but just felt crumpled sheets. I swept my hand up and down, feeling with my feet too, as if she might be curled up at the bottom of my bed like a cat. I sat up and peered round the room. She wasn't anywhere.

I hurried to the little ensuite – a rather grand word for the toilet, basin and shower crammed together in their cupboard – but Marigold wasn't there. She wasn't in the corner kitchenette either. She wasn't anywhere.

Had she gone to find Lee? I pressed my ear against the communal wall but I couldn't hear any voices. I looked back to the bed where Marigold's clothes had been scattered. They were gone, even her high-heeled shoes.

I glanced at the clock. Half seven. Had she crept back to her own flat, and horrible Rick? I tried ringing her but a recorded voice told me no one could take my call right now. I knew it simply meant Marigold had switched her phone off, but it still sounded ominous. I was always so scared that Marigold might kill herself when she tipped from very high to very low. She'd already tried twice, once slashing her wrists, another time dashing in front of a car. What if last night drove her to try again?

I struggled into yesterday's clothes, had the quickest pee while pulling on my shoes, and then rushed from the flat without even cleaning my teeth or brushing my hair. I hesitated in the street, not knowing which way to run. Should I make for the cliffs? But there was no way Marigold would hurl herself into the sea. She was terrified of water. My swimming-coach father had never succeeded in coaxing her into even the shallow end of his leisure centre pool.

I ran the opposite way, towards the station. She'd once made a friend of a woman in her psychiatric wing who had set off at a run when the ward was unlocked. She made it out the hospital, ran half a mile in her medical gown and hurled herself off a railway bridge when the eight o'clock London train was rumbling underneath. I'd been horrified, but Marigold had seemed unmoved, remarking that at least it had been a quick death by all accounts. At the time I was shocked by her lack of empathy. Now I wondered if she was filing it away for future reference.

I couldn't think of any nearby bridges, but there were half-hourly trains from the station that quickly gathered speed along the track. My thoughts were gathering speed too, seeing Marigold running in her high heels, staggering up a grassy bank near the station, and then crouching, ready to leap.

I sped along, my heart pounding, a vile metallic taste in my mouth, not caring that people on their way to work were staring at me.

Then I saw her, standing at the top of the station steps, *singing*. A bemused crowd watched or edged past hurriedly. My mother, with her make-up still smeared, though she'd reapplied scarlet lipstick going way over the line of her mouth. She was wearing last night's clothes and those wretched high heels, and a hat lay on the ground in front of her. With a jolt, I realized it was *my* sunhat, upside down, clearly there to catch coins – although none were being proffered.

The song she was singing had a thumping rhythm and she was stamping her feet energetically. It was dimly familiar, an old Proclaimers song, something about walking five hundred miles, though she kept adding an extra riff: *to see my grandchild!*

For a split second I felt the urge to pretend I hadn't seen or heard her. I could scurry past and go about my ordinary life and not give her a second thought – like Star.

But I couldn't do it. I dashed up the steps towards her, pushing through the gathering crowd. Marigold gave a start when she saw me but kept on singing determinedly.

'Marigold. Stop it.'

'Just keep out of it. As you've taken my plane ticket and all my money I'm going to sing and sing until I've got enough to go by train, so there!' she said, still stamping her feet.

'I didn't take your ticket, I didn't take your money, you know I didn't. And this is all pointless, because even if you did get there, you don't know Star's address. You can walk your five hundred miles all over Scotland but you haven't got a clue where she lives,' I said steadily. 'Now come back with me.'

I tried to take Marigold's arm but she pulled away from me violently.

'Of course I know where my own daughter lives,' Marigold said furiously. 'You get the train to London, and then another train, and then another train, anothertrainanothertrainanother . . . heaps of trains to this little Saint place, I can't remember which, too many saints, oh dear God those nuns and their Saint Annes and Saint Michaels and Saint Jude the patron saint of lost causes and I suppose that's me, lost cause.'

She often talked about her childhood, the fierce nuns who ran the children's home, who rapped her on the head with their hard knuckles and slapped her whenever she wet the bed, as if it were the reason for her bad behaviour in adulthood.

Well, Star and I had had our fair share of taps and slaps from Marigold herself – though she *had* loved us too. I remembered all the games she played with me, the cakes she baked, the dances she taught us. I hero-worshipped her when I was little. It was so awful to see her now, manic, hungover, dishevelled, totally pitiful.

'Oh, Marigold,' I said softly, coming closer. 'I'm so sorry but—'

'Don't you dare feel sorry for me!' she hissed, so that several drops of spittle landed on my cheek. 'I'm not listening. I *know* how to get to Star, Star Light, Star Bright—'

'Stop it, Marigold! You're talking gibberish because you've come off your meds. And you *don't* know how to find Star – she left St Andrews years ago when she got her degree. It's true. I don't lie to you, do I?'

That was a lie in itself, though I wasn't lying about this. Star had lived in several different places as she and Charles climbed steadily up their medical ladders. He was already a consultant at the Dundee Royal Infirmary and Star worked in a big medical practice as their women's health expert. They lived in a four-bedroom house in the West End of Dundee. *Four* bedrooms! They obviously earned good money, and Charles's family were generous.

I'd never been there. Star had invited me several times, especially for Christmas, but I'd always made excuses. I didn't want to be Star's weird wee sister the tattooist, the odd one out among her genteel middle-class Scottish friends. The one who took after the unfortunate mother.

Perhaps I was just being paranoid. But that would mean I *was* taking after my mother. She was staring at me, shaking her head violently, though I could see from her eyes that she'd taken in what I was saying.

'I know an even better way to get to Star!' she declared, her chin up. 'I shan't bother with trains and planes. I'll fly there myself!'

Before I could take in what she was saying, she took a sudden huge leap. She spread her arms, her legs kicking, as if she were a cartoon character dangling in mid-air, but then she went crashing down the steps, her handbag bumping down behind her. She landed on her face, arms still outstretched, one foot sticking out sideways at a grotesque angle.

I hurtled down the steps, elbowing people out the way. Someone got to her first but I shouted, 'Let me! She's my *mother*!'

I crouched down by her side. I knew I shouldn't try to move her, I could see her ankle was broken, and her head was at a funny angle – oh God, don't let her neck be broken too! I was trembling so much I couldn't control my hand, but I managed to push her hair away from her face. Her eyes were half closed and there was blood coming from her nose, but I could see her lips moving.

'Oh, Marigold, it's all right,' I mumbled helplessly. 'I'm here. Your Dol's here. And we'll get you better, and I'll look after you, I promise I will.'

People around me were on their phones, calling an ambulance, and someone in station uniform was squatting down beside us, babbling something about a first aid course, trying to move her.

'Leave her alone!' I snapped, bending right over her like a lioness with her cub, trying to protect her from their touch, their gaze. I stroked her hair very gently, then bent even closer so I could sing the 'Hush Little Baby' song right into her ear. Her eyes fluttered and for one moment she looked straight at me, and I could see she knew I was there.

The wait could have been ten minutes or ten hours. We seemed suspended in time. The steps emptied because the station employee wasn't letting anyone else go past. I heard trains rumbling in and out of the station, and I thought about all the passengers. Were they having to miss their trains because of us?

Marigold's eyes were closed now, but I could feel her breath on my hand so I knew she was still alive. Perhaps she was flying in her head, out of the station, above the roofs, right up into the cloudy sky, all the way to Scotland. I hung on to her as hard as I could.

Someone patted me on the shoulder, trying to comfort me, and someone else asked if I'd like a cup of tea, which seemed a bizarre suggestion at such a moment, but I suppose they were simply trying to be kind. Then the paramedics arrived, and bent down beside Marigold, testing her methodically, murmuring to each other. I stood back to let them work, my eyes fixed on Marigold's face all the while.

It was a tricky job getting her on a stretcher and she groaned a lot. I tried to hang on to her hand to show her I was still there, and we went out of the station in an awkward procession. One of Marigold's heels fell off and I stopped to pick it up, and her bag too. It felt as if I was gathering up actual parts of her – a foot, a hand.

Then we were in the ambulance, and I was shaking so badly I couldn't speak properly. The woman monitoring Marigold was very patient and listened to my stutters carefully.

'She's bipolar, she's not been taking her Lithium, she thought she could fly, or maybe she was trying to kill herself, I don't know! She ran off while I was asleep, I had to rescue her from Gatwick in the night. I don't know how to keep her safe.'

'It sounds as if you've done your very best. They'll look after her in hospital. She's obviously hurt herself, and that ankle's definitely broken and she's smashed her nose, but let's hope she's not done any serious damage. They'll patch her up and put her on her meds and see if they can sort her out mentally as well as physically,' the woman said reassuringly. I wanted to cling to her like a little girl and beg her to keep saying it again and again.

She didn't once reproach me for not stopping Marigold, and I loved her for it. I was feeling desperately guilty. I kept replaying the whole scene – Marigold stamping her feet at the top of the steps, then suddenly leaping into thin air. Could I have caught her? Grabbed hold of her the moment I saw her? And why in God's name didn't I wake up when she crept out of bed?

Then we were at the hospital. I thought she'd be whisked out and dealt with straight away because this was definitely an emergency – but of course, we had to wait ages in a queue of ambulances, and then longer still to get her assessed in A&E, and by the time all her injuries had been checked and she'd been X-rayed, her broken ankle temporarily strapped into place and she'd been wheeled off to the psychiatric ward, it was late afternoon.

It was painted pale yellow, called Primrose Ward. It was kept locked, with a firm notice on the door that visiting hours were '2 to 4 ONLY' – but I tagged along with the porter and managed to talk the attending nurse into letting me stay to help calm my mother down. Marigold was beside herself by now, shouting and swearing, so the nurse readily agreed.

It was terrifying seeing her so wildly out of control, with her face smashed up. She'd been so pretty when she was younger. I remembered wishing hard that I could grow up to be just like her – yet now the thought frightened me.

'Can't you at least give her a proper painkiller?' I begged the nurse.

'I need to check with Dr Gibbon first,' she said.

Dr Gibbon? I was in such a state I pictured him swinging along the ward by the light fittings, long, hairy arms sticking out of his white doctor's coat, a stethoscope round his neck.

I'd always imagined weird stuff when I was a child and fell back into the habit when I was feeling intimidated. I was frightened of hectoring doctors, though Star always told me not to be such a fool.

But Dr Gibbon turned out to be a spindly youngish man with a lot of golden-brown hair and a friendly grin – more spider monkey than gibbon. Rather than the usual white coat he wore a crumpled blue shirt, baggy trousers and battered trainers.

'Hello. Are you my new patient's daughter? Tell you what – you pop into my office and wait while I examine your mum and try to make her more comfortable. Then I'll come and find you and we'll have a chat. OK?'

I felt the tightness in my chest loosen a little. I heard Marigold swearing at him from far away at the end of the ward, but gradually she seemed to calm down. I sat biting my nails, peering round the small room. I expected the walls to be plastered with medical charts and those weird drawings of heads coloured in different segments – but he had travel posters and photos of his wife and two small children sellotaped there instead.

I stared at his family until my eyes blurred, glad that they all seemed so smiley and ordinary. The sort of family I'd always longed to be part of.

Dr Gibbon actually knocked at his own office door before he came in.

'How are you coping?' he asked gently, as if he really cared.

I shrugged, so touched that I nearly burst into tears.

'I should imagine this scenario is relatively familiar?' he asked.

'Yes,' I said, sniffing.

'Your mum told me she's been locked up in effing hospitals half her life and she's effing fed up with it and she doesn't want to talk to an effing idiot like me. And I don't actually effing blame her.'

I couldn't help smiling. 'I bet she didn't quite say "effing" and "idiot".'

'She's got a way with words when she's fed up. She's very unhappy and frustrated at the moment. I expect she's off her medication?'

'I think so. She doesn't actually live with me.'

'I should imagine that's a relief,' he said.

I stared at him suspiciously, but he didn't seem to be saying it in an accusing manner.

'What do you mean?' I faltered.

'She's full-on at the moment. No reasoning with her,' he said.

'Well, she's got bipolar disorder,' I said, wondering if he hadn't realized this.

'I know that! But I don't actually think it helps sticking labels on people. I'd sooner see her as a spirited, intelligent woman whose brain's temporarily gone haywire. It's my job to calm her down a bit so she can leave hospital and live a normal life – until the next episode. Do you happen to know the name of her doctor and which hospital she was at last so I can access her records?'

I tried hard to remember but she'd had so many doctors, stayed in so many hospitals.

'I'll have to check with my sister. She keeps a record of everything.' Star had to, because I couldn't trust myself to read all the details correctly myself. 'She understands these things. She's a doctor,' I said.

'Well, that's useful,' said Dr Gibbon. He looked at me appraisingly. 'So she's in charge of all the medical details and you're stuck with the practical stuff?'

He'd got it in one! He was looking so sympathetic too. It was wonderful that he understood.

'More or less,' I said.

'Maybe more rather than less?' he prompted.

'Star does help out financially,' I said quickly, feeling guilty.

'Ah! So she's Star, is she? Marigold's been telling the entire hospital about her by all accounts,' said Dr Gibbon. 'And your name is . . . ?'

'Dol. Short for Dolphin,' I mumbled, embarrassed.

'Oh, I get it. Star and Dolphin. Tattoos!'

'That was quick! I suppose we're lucky not to be called Love and Hate,' I said.

I actually made him laugh.

'I'm known for being intuitive,' he said. 'It's the one thing I've got going for me. My senior colleagues don't always agree with the way I treat my patients. Though don't worry, I'm not too woo-woo. I do believe in medication for bipolar disorder. Do you know what your mum is usually prescribed?'

'She takes Lithium. But not all the time.'

'Has anyone ever tried cognitive therapy with Marigold? Or any kind of analysis? Perhaps we could give it a go. One last chance to help her manage her disorder? Perhaps there's something that triggers each episode and makes her self-medicate with alcohol and the wrong sort of drug?' he suggested.

'Well, she was in care, and hated the nuns looking after her,' I said.

'That's interesting. But whatever, she needs to take her prescribed antimanic drugs to keep her stable. If she has problems taking her medication every day, we could try her on one of the long-acting injectable drugs now. You start off with a monthly dose and then go on to three-monthly, so there's more chance of her staying on them. What do you think, Dol?'

'Maybe,' I said, not quite daring to hope it might make all the difference.

'Maybe is better than no,' he said. 'Well, I'm going to do my best to help your mum, I promise you.'

'Thank you so much!' I had a childish impulse to throw my arms round his neck in gratitude, but I managed to restrain myself.

I went down the ward to see Marigold. Perhaps she'd had some kind of tranquillizer because she seemed nearly asleep now, her eyes closed, but they flickered open when I kissed her cheek. 'You're safe now. Dr Gibbon will look after you. And I'll keep coming back, day after day until you're better,' I promised her, though I wasn't sure how I could manage it.

4

I took out my phone on my way to the bus stop and saw a flurry of fierce messages from my boss Brian, plus concerned enquiries from my friends Jo and Big Al. I texted *So sorry, mum ill* and then dialled Star's number. It rang for quite a while before she answered.

'Dol?' Star's voice was lowered. She sounded rather irritated. 'Dol, we've got people round for dinner. Can you ring back tomorrow? Unless it's a total emergency?'

'Yes, it *is* a total emergency. It's Marigold,' I told her.

Star breathed in hard, as if she were about to jump into a swimming pool. 'OK, OK. Just a moment,' she murmured, and I imagined her edging out of her dining room, mouthing apologies, waiting to be safely shut away in the kitchen before talking properly.

'What is it now?' she said. 'And be quick – I'm in the middle of serving.'

'Oh, I'm so sorry interrupting you and your posh friends at your dinner party! It's nothing important – just that our mother tried to kill herself today and she very nearly succeeded.' The image of Marigold leaping kept replaying in my head.

There was a pause.

'Seriously?' Star said, her voice wobbling.

'Well, how serious is it, to jump from the top of a huge flight of steps all the way to the bottom?' I said.

'So what has she done to herself?' Star asked, and I heard the fear in her voice.

'She's broken her ankle and—'

'Is that *all*?' Star said, more confidently now.

'No, she's smashed up her whole face and she's in the middle of a manic episode. I had to sign all the stuff to have her sectioned and she spent the whole day yelling your name, desperate to find you.' I didn't feel guilty at all about laying it on thick.

'Oh Christ,' said Star. 'But she's in hospital now, and they're looking after her?'

'*Yes!* Aren't you worried about it in the slightest?'

'She's just making a pathetic bid for attention. Remember that time she covered herself in white paint?'

'And I was the one left to deal with it, when I was just a kid. You'd cleared off to live with your precious father. Though that didn't last long, did it?' I said spitefully. I felt like the sister in the fairy tale spitting toads but I couldn't stop myself.

'Look, let's talk about this in the morning. I've got to get back to our friends. And, oh God, I think that's Chrissie crying now,' Star said, as if it was all my fault.

'Oh, the blessed Christopher. Why do you and your precious family and la-di-da friends always have to come before your own mother and sister?' I shouted, more toads dribbling down my chin and leaping about my chest. Passers-by glanced at me nervously.

'Stop it!' Star hissed.

'You don't think *I'd* love to have a baby? But how can I, when I have to look after Marigold on my own? Why are you so much more important than me?' I said furiously.

'Oh, Dol! Of course you're just as important as me. And when you find the right person and get properly settled, you'll make a wonderful mother.'

'Is that the sort of patronizing nonsense you spout to all your anxious patients?' I snapped. 'I don't need a wretched partner or a posh home to be a good mother!'

'I tell you what you *do* need to do – and that's to grow up a bit,' said Star, losing her temper too. 'You're like a child, forever working yourself into a terrible state.'

'Of course I'm in a fucking state! Don't you even *care* that Marigold's in hospital and she's really hurt?' I cried.

'Of course I care! I spent my entire childhood worrying myself sick about her. I tried so hard to look after her, to look after *you*. But we're both adults now. We have to make our own lives. Can't you see she's a hopeless case? She refuses to take her medication regularly. She's never going to manage her bipolar successfully, and I am done taking responsibility for that.'

'This new doctor is going to try some new treatments, and—'

'There isn't going to be a happy ever after, Dol. She's in her fifties – you can't believe she's going to learn to be responsible now. I'm sorry, of course I'm sorry, but mostly for you, because you care so much.'

'You're such a hypocrite!' I spat, clutching my phone so hard it's a wonder it didn't shatter in my hand. 'You're happy that I *do* care and try to look after Marigold, because it means you don't have to do anything. You stop yourself feeling guilty by pretending I'm somehow made that way, that it's my *choice* to take on the role of martyr and give up on my own life.'

A deeper voice sounded in the background, along with a baby's cries. I heard Star catch her breath and then she said in a sweetie-pie voice – 'So sorry, darling, no, it's not an emergency. You carry on serving and I'll settle Chrissie.'

'So you *don't* think our mother nearly killing herself is an emergency?' I shouted down the phone.

'Dol, please. I've got to go. Look, we can talk about this in the morning – no, wait, I've got a nine o'clock surgery—'

'That's right, put all these other sick people before your own mother! That's what's so fucking ironic!'

'Do you have to swear continuously?' Star asked coldly.

If she was there in front of me, I'd have slapped her. 'Yes, I do, as a matter of fact. Because it's so unfair. So *fucking* unfair! Because Marigold doesn't give a damn about me. It's you she's desperate to see, you and your precious baby. She went to Gatwick to try to fly up to Scotland, she was at the station to get the train to Scotland, she stood on those station steps singing to try to raise the money to get the ticket.'

'Oh God.' Star's voice was suddenly desperate. 'You haven't given her my address, have you?'

'No, I haven't. But when she found out you've had a baby—'

'You *told* her? You swore you wouldn't!'

'I *didn't* tell her,' I said hotly. 'Someone else did and now she's so desperate to see him and keeps going on about being a grandma. She seemed so thrilled. I know she's not really in her right mind when she's manic, but for goodness' sake, why is it so terrible to want to see your grandson? Why can't you—' Then I realized she'd hung up, and I was talking to my lock screen.

Standing there in the darkness, I dithered about ringing her straight back, but I could see there was no point. I took the bus home, trying not to make an exhibition of myself by crying.

There was no light on in Lee's bedsit when I got back. I opened and closed the front door as quietly as I could and crept up the stairs until I was on the top floor. When I let myself in I found a note had been pushed under my door.

I sat down, smoothed it out on the table, and held my hands

either side of my eyes so I could concentrate properly. It took me a long time to read it and I had to guess some of the words.

Dear Doll,

I hope you and your mum are OK. I knocked this morning and tried again when I got back from work. Going to turn in early now but do get in touch if you need anything. I really mean that.

Yours,

Lee

I tried knocking on his door in the morning, but he'd already left for work. I was touched by his note and felt I should write him one back – somehow! I was OK using a computer because every time I made a spelling mistake a red line wiggled under the word so I could correct it. I was on my own when it came to writing with a pen.

I'm hopelessly dyslexic. Such an utterly stupid word to describe the condition – anyone would have problems spelling it correctly. I could draw intricate lines for my custom tattoos without so much as a wobble but when it came to writing words my hand dithered across the page and started shaking.

Trying to write brought back all those awful memories of school, and Miss Hill and the girls in my class who made my life a misery. Still, Lee had been so kind. I wanted to thank him properly. I drew a picture instead, of me holding my hands together making that 'thank you' gesture celebrities do on television. I wrote *Dol* at the end, with one kiss.

I wanted to add *Thank you for being my friend* but I always had trouble with the word 'friend' because of that tricky i and e, and I could never remember which way round the d should go. I always had trouble with friends full stop. I was the odd one out at all my schools. It was even worse when I left without a single GCSE.

I got taken on as an apprentice hairdresser because I was good at hairstyling. The owner, Patrick, was kind to me, but the other girls were a bit of a nightmare. They kept teasing me and calling me thick when I didn't know what to say to the clients, let alone write their names correctly in the appointment book. They nattered away so easily to all the posh ladies who swanned into the salon, whereas I never knew what to talk about. Patrick told me to relax and chat about the weather and ask if they were going on holiday and general stuff like that, but I was hopeless.

Then Marigold came into the salon one day saying she wanted her hair styled.

'I want *her* to do it!' she said, pointing at me.

I just about died, though I knew she was trying to help me out. I was sure she didn't have enough money to pay our prices for a start – and in her sleeveless vest, signature short skirt and high heels, showing off her tattoos, she looked so out of place among all the other clients with their blonde bobs and their designer clothes.

The other girls raised their eyebrows at each other, smirking. Patrick was lovely and let me style Marigold's hair, even though I wasn't qualified. When she told him proudly that she was my mother, he insisted she had her hairdo on the house.

The moment she'd waltzed out the door, flipping her hair about happily, the other girls all started giggling.

'What are you laughing at?' I demanded fiercely, though of course it was obvious.

But Patrick showed me some of his own tattoos on his upper arms and said he thought Marigold's were very original and decorative, especially her newest, a green dragon with wings flying up her leg.

'*I* designed that one!' I said truthfully.

'Then being a tattoo artist might be the perfect career for you,' Patrick said. 'You've got the makings of a good little stylist, but I think you might be happier in a different kind of environment, Dolly.'

He was being very kind. It was the most sensitive dismissal I could wish for. But although I liked designing tattoos for fun, I didn't want to be a professional tattooist – it was Marigold's world, not mine! But what else could I do, with no qualifications and barely able to read and write? I went to train with Steve and worked for him for a while, though I felt half stuck in my childhood, still living with my mum.

So I went to a different studio altogether where nobody knew me. They weren't sure at first, because I looked so young for my age, and nobody wants to let a scrappy little kid ink them permanently, but I knew so much already from watching Marigold and designs seemed to come to me naturally, so they gave me a chance. I moved around every couple of years – new studios, new bedsits, new boyfriends, never really settling. I could never seem to find the sort of life I wanted to be living.

I've made quite a name for myself, even so. People often ring up now asking specifically for Dol Westward to work on them. I love doing intricate custom designs – but like most tattooists, the flash work, girly roses and hearts and cutesie-pie teddies and kittens, is my bread and butter. I'm always a bit wary if they want names, their best friend forever, their boyfriend, their babies. I can make mistakes even if I get them to write it down for me and I copy it carefully. I always get Big Al or Jo to check it for me now before I start inking.

Drawing my message to Lee had taken up time. I was going to be late for work. The train along the coast was my quickest bet to get to town, but I couldn't face those station steps again.

Marigold's fall was still playing in my head like the world's grimmest GIF.

I took the bus instead, hoping Brian would be in a reasonable mood when he turned up. He generally lounged in late, checked a few emails, drank a lot of coffee, maybe gave an old mate a tattoo as a favour, then sloped off about three – but he liked Big Al and Jo and me to be in the studio at ten sharp, and stay till seven or even longer. I dreaded him having a rant at me – but when he came in and saw my white face and the dark circles under my eyes, he gave me a little nod of sympathy. Big Al and Jo hugged me, sat me down and gave me cups of tea, making a fuss of me.

Brian called me into his office when he was finishing off his sausage roll and starting on a spicy bean flatbread. I hadn't had any breakfast because I was feeling sick – and the smell didn't help.

'You don't look too chirpy, kid,' he said. 'I thought you said it was your mum who was ill, not you?'

'She's in hospital.' I took a deep breath. 'I've got a flash booked in this morning, but nothing else. Could I possibly get time to go and take some stuff in for my mum after that?'

I was freelance, working for myself, but putting my takings through the till for Brian to take off his fifty per cent for my chair in the studio. Theoretically I could please myself when I worked, but Brian liked to be in charge.

'Yeah, but there could be any number of potentials popping in,' Brian said, chewing with his mouth open, overwhelming me with the smell of spicy beans. The office would smell even worse when they'd descended to his digestive system. 'What if they're after some arty-farty custom bollocks – you know you're the girl for that.'

'I've thought of a new design that should go down well with all the TikTok girls who like romantasy novels,' I said quickly, diverting him. 'Here, let me sketch it out for you.'

I tried hard to remember my weird dream and managed a reasonable representation of it in ten minutes, though I hated Brian standing over me, pressing too close against me. It wasn't personal – he rubbed himself against any nearby female, whatever type, age, sexuality. He was the sort of Neanderthal who thought women were the equivalent of sofas, simply there for his comfort and convenience.

'Hey, that's not bad,' Brian said. 'In fact, it's fucking fabulous! I'll put it on TikTok straight away.'

'Thanks,' I said meekly. He hadn't actually given me permission to disappear for most of the day, but it was clear he wouldn't object now.

My flash booking came in at half past ten, a woman in an Indian embroidered smock and jingling silver bangles. She already had the yin and yang signs and a bluebird but now she wanted a dolphin, because she said it symbolized peace and harmony. I hadn't had much of either in my life so far, but I just nodded and got on with it.

I'd just finished sterilizing when a guy came wandering into the studio – one of those cocky, good-looking men with longish dark hair. He had tight jeans and wore a silky floral jacket over his black teeshirt, the kind of feminine Harry Styles look.

'Hi,' he said confidently. 'Can one of you give me a tattoo of theatrical masks? You know, there's a smiley one and a sad one, signifying comedy and drama?'

Jo had a client due in soon and shook her head but Big Al spoke up eagerly.

'Sure thing!' he said. 'Come and sit down and I'll show you several designs so you can take your pick.'

But the dark-haired guy wanted to take his pick of us too.

'Thanks, mate – but maybe I'll go with you,' he said, nodding at me.

Oh, for God's sake! I need to pick up stuff for Marigold and take it to the hospital. And why are you looking at me like that? Are you expecting me to be thrilled you've chosen me? (Though, actually, I was. I'm always attracted to this kind of guy. You'd think I'd have learnt my lesson by now.)

'OK, fine,' I said, giving Al an apologetic glance. At least it wouldn't take too long. Those masks were easy – and such a corny choice. Was he some kind of actor? He had that air of easy arrogance about him.

'Where are you thinking of having the tattoo, sir?' I asked primly, determined not to give him any encouragement.

'My chest. Above my heart,' he said, raising his eyebrows and grinning.

'OK,' I said, and started preparing.

He lay back on the couch and took off his flimsy jacket and teeshirt as casually as if he was in his own bedroom. Big Al couldn't take his eyes off him. I suppose his chest did look quite good, lightly tanned with just the right amount of dark hair, and it was clear he worked out a lot. I'm used to touching bodies, but when I got started on his flash I felt a little shiver run through me. He was looking straight at me and to my horror I started blushing.

What was the *matter* with me? All right, he was gorgeous, and his eyes were that deep blue I loved, but I was determined not to let him see the effect he was having on me. Thank God I kept my hand steady. I usually chatted to clients but I felt so distracted I couldn't think of a thing to say. He just lay there, looking amused. He didn't wince once, though he seemed to be a first-timer as I couldn't see any other tattoos.

Big Al came and chatted instead, blethering on about going to the gym and his different workouts. The guy was polite – friendly, even – but I could tell he wasn't really into the conversation.

'I wish Dol here would come along to the gym,' Big Al said. 'See her little matchstick arms?'

'Yes, I see them,' said the guy. He looked at me. 'Have you given it a try?'

'Gyms aren't really my thing, all those sweaty guys grunting away,' I said shortly.

Jo was listening and laughed. She seemed fascinated by the guy too, though she's not usually into men at all.

'What is your thing, then?' he asked.

I shrugged. 'Art, I suppose.'

'She does incredible custom designs,' Jo said. 'I thought *I* was good, but Dol's really great. You should get her to do you one sometime.'

'Maybe I will,' he said. He looked at me enquiringly. 'Would you?'

'If you like,' I said off-handedly – but I couldn't help hoping he'd take me up on the idea.

Jo was staring at him now, her eyes narrowed.

'Do I know you?' she asked.

'I don't think so,' he said, but his eyes gleamed.

He seemed pleased with his masks and gave me a generous tip.

'See you again soon, Dol,' he said, shaking my hand, rubbing his thumb across the gap between my thumb and forefinger in a strangely intimate way. Then he sauntered out, giving me one last look.

'He really fancies you, Dol,' Big Al said enviously.

'Well, I certainly don't fancy *him*,' I said.

That wasn't entirely true, but surely I knew enough now to steer clear of men like that? I'd learnt from bitter experience that they just wanted another quick conquest, especially with odd, shy girls like me. Then they were off, barely bothering to say goodbye, while I was still day-dreaming about loving words and soft kisses and walking hand in hand.

Jo peered at the name he'd signed in my accounts book.

'Oh my God! I knew he looked familiar. He's Joel Fortune.'

'Who?'

'You know, he played the bad guy in that soap – what was it called? *Heartbreak!*' said Jo. 'Wow! And he seemed really keen on you, Dol!'

'No, he wasn't,' I protested. 'And he's not my type anyway. Too full of himself.'

'You're crazy,' said Big Al.

I simply smiled, though I get a bit touchy whenever anyone uses that word. Marigold herself used it, but I wished she wouldn't.

5

I got away quickly afterwards, unsettled by the actor guy. Were Big Al and Jo right – did he fancy me? But I had other things to think about now. My stomach churned at the idea of going to Marigold's flat. I didn't want another awful confrontation with Rick, but I had to collect her clothes, toiletries and all her make-up. She wore it like armour now, layer upon layer. I had her spare key but I knocked hard on the door first to warn Rick I was coming. I waited a couple of minutes and then let myself in.

It smelt stuffy and sour inside, of old takeaways and sweat and spilled booze. I had to squeeze my eyes shut for a moment to stop my tears. Marigold always used to keep everything in our old home so fresh and pretty even when she was in the depths of despair. It was clear that Rick had taken over.

The curtains were drawn in the living room, but I could make out bottles on the floor and some makeshift cooking apparatus on the coffee table – but it clearly wasn't for food. Why in God's name did she take all this dangerous rubbish and yet 'forget' to take the Lithium that would keep her on an even keel?

I stomped angrily to her bedroom to collect her stuff – and stopped short. It was gloomy in there too, but I could see enough to spot Rick in bed, spread-eagled on his back, snoring heavily – and some youngish girl was curled up beside him, wearing a skimpy vest and nothing else.

'For Christ's sake!' I cried, snapping on the light. The girl sat up, gasping, struggling to cover herself with the greyish sheet. Her eyes were circled with smudged liner, and one of her front teeth was missing. She was at least half Rick's age.

'Are you Marigold?' she whispered.

'No, I'm her daughter. And you're sleeping with her partner, so I'd get your stuff and fuck off sharpish,' I said forcefully.

I was probably smaller and skinnier than she was, and I'm generally as intimidating as a bunny rabbit, but I was so angry that she shot out of bed, dressed in a flash, grabbed her bag, and stuffed her grubby feet in her trainers without pulling them on properly. She'd shuffled out of the flat in less than a minute, while Rick was still seemingly comatose, though his snoring had stopped.

'How dare you bring that girl back here!' I growled, shoving his shoulder.

'Dol? What are you talking about? What girl?' he rasped.

'The girl who's just left! You brought her to my mother's flat?' I poked him hard on his back. He rolled over and sat up, squinting at me.

'Here, lay off! Don't you get on your high horse with me! Marigold's sodded off. She got some bee in her bonnet about your sister and she's gone to Scotland or Wales or wherever to see her. Who knows if she's ever coming back?' he blurted, trying to catch me by the wrists.

'Get off! She's in a serious state in hospital because she very nearly killed herself!' I yelled at him.

'Silly bitch,' he muttered.

'How dare you!' I slapped him about the head now, and the big glass 'engagement' ring Oli gave me when we left primary school nicked his temple.

'For God's sake!' he said, cowering from me pathetically. He touched the little cut. 'I'm bleeding!'

'If I had a knife, I'd be stabbing you,' I hissed. 'Marigold is *not* a silly bitch. But as you well know, if she doesn't take her meds every day, she becomes manic and reckless and does dangerous things, *especially* if she gets high on drink or drugs. You're supposed to be her partner. Don't you care about her even in the most basic way?'

'Shut it, Dol, you're doing my head in,' he whined. 'How was I to know she's in hospital? Look, I'll go and visit her today, see if I can cheer her up.'

'Actually, I'd sooner you kept right away from her. It's time you moved on. I want you out of here. Get all your gear together and push off,' I said, whisking round the room, gathering a handful of clothes from Marigold's wardrobe and stuffing her make-up into one of her bags.

'You can't throw me out my own home!'

'It's not your home, Rick, it's Marigold's, and you're going to have to find some other poor fool to give you a bed,' I said, breathing heavily as I bundled everything together.

'You can't make me,' Rick said, getting off the bed, fists clenched, doing his best to look menacing.

Don't be scared! It's only stupid old Rick. He's always so fuddled he'd fall flat if he tried to swing a punch.

But I hated the way he was looking at me. He was much taller than me, and stronger too. I took a step backwards and I saw the triumph in his eyes.

No, stand your ground. It's not his flat!

'Maybe I can't make you, but the police can,' I said, whipping out my phone. 'I'll give them a call right now.'

'They won't give a monkey's,' he scoffed. 'They don't go round evicting people, not if they've done nothing.'

'They'd be interested in all that drug stuff in the living room,' I said. 'How *could* you let Marigold start injecting? I've seen those tracks on her arm. They're going to be after you, Rick. Now, get out. I'll be back later to check – and I'll bring my mate Big Al with me.'

He'd come nosing round the studio once and met Big Al. Rick might not be bothered by the thought of police after him – but Big Al was a serious threat. Rick started sweating now, blinking nervously. I could see I'd got through to him. I stuffed Marigold's meagre belongings in an already splitting bag-for-life and stormed out of the flat.

I actually did a fist-pump, thrilled to have stood my ground and got the better of him for once. It felt so great. But as I got nearer the hospital I started worrying that he'd maybe trash the flat now – or call some of his druggy mates and come round to my place. It didn't seem likely, but it kept nagging at me.

Why did I find myself in these sorts of situations?

The answer was simple: Marigold.

I had to fight to stop snivelling with self-pity.

Pull yourself together!

I dug my nails into my palms and set out in search of Primrose Ward.

You had to ring the bell to be admitted, just like a prison. I tried twice, but no one came. I waited, wondering if I dared try a third time. Then a porter came out with a limp elderly lady in a wheelchair.

'Can I please go in to see my mother?' I asked.

'Visiting hours don't start till two,' he said.

'But she's only just been admitted and she needs some clothes and personal belongings,' I pleaded.

The elderly lady started fumbling with the straps keeping her upright.

'No, don't do that, Maggie!' he said, sighing. 'OK, pop in quick and leave your mum's things at the nursing station.'

There was no one there, though. I peered through the window of the tiny cubicle opposite. They usually put the suicide-risk patients near the station so they could be easily observed. Marigold was huddled on the bed, arms over her head to blot out the light. She didn't have a pillow. Perhaps they thought she'd try to smother herself. She looked pathetic curled up like that, her newly plastered leg sticking out of the sheets. I hurried to her, and gently touched the little mound of her under the bedcovers.

'Marigold? It's Dol. Oh, you poor love,' I whispered, trying to pull her hands away from her head.

'No! No!' she mumbled urgently. 'You mustn't see! I look like a monster! I'll have to wear a mask!'

'Don't be silly, Marigold. You look lovely, you always do,' I insisted, but when I managed a proper look at her face, I was horrified. Her eyes were purple, her nose swollen, her lip split.

'See!' Marigold said, clamping her hands back.

'Yes, you've got some nasty cuts and bruises, but they'll all be better in a week, you wait and see,' I said as soothingly as I could.

'And I can't move my leg. They've spoilt my whole leg, made it so heavy I can't even move it,' she wailed.

'It's just your ankle, it's in a cast so it can heal. You broke it, remember, when you fell down the stairs,' I said.

A returning nurse burst into the cubicle and took me firmly by the arm. 'What are you doing here? Visitors aren't allowed in until two,' she said, pulling me towards the open door.

'But I need to see my mother!' I protested, trying to keep my feet firmly planted beside the bed.

'I don't think you'll get much sense out of her at the moment,' she said. 'They fixed that ankle this morning. She's still dozy from the procedure – and not at all well besides.' She tapped her head to indicate Marigold's mental health, which I thought truly unprofessional. 'Are you her carer?'

'I'm her daughter,' I said firmly. 'Marigold lives independently, though. She's been managing really well recently.'

'But she's come off her medication, hasn't she? Isn't there anyone to supervise her, make sure she takes it?' she persisted. 'It looks like this was a pretty serious suicide attempt.'

She might as well bellow it from a megaphone: *This girl neglected her mentally ill mother so she tried to kill herself!*

I felt as if everyone was staring at me accusingly, though I could see the patients with their cubicle doors open were lolling lethargically, taking no interest.

'I don't think my mother was actually trying to kill herself,' I said, trying to sound in control.

Please don't let it be a serious suicide attempt! It makes me feel so much more guilty.

'That's what it says on her notes,' the nurse insisted.

'Can I see them?' I asked. Surely dear Dr Gibbon hadn't written any such thing?

Marigold reared up suddenly and tried to scramble out of bed. She hopped towards the door, groaning when she tried to put her plastered leg to the floor.

'I'm not having any fucking treatment!' she growled. 'Dol, get me out of here!'

'I'll get you out as soon as you're well enough,' I said, rushing to her to give her support.

'I've heard that before!'

'Back to bed with you, Marigold,' said the nurse.

'Fuck off!' barked Marigold, swaying dangerously, half exposed in her hospital gown.

'Now, now. No need for bad language,' said the nurse, taking hold of Marigold's lurid arm and steering her by the armpit.

Marigold wasn't strong enough to resist and flopped back on the bed, grabbing at her leg and rocking with despair.

'Can you give her more medication to help with the pain?' I asked, turning to the nurse.

'She can't have anything until it's prescribed. Now, please leave – it's clear you're upsetting her,' she said.

'Can I just put her things in her locker?' I asked meekly, though I felt like killing her.

She sighed extravagantly, but nodded. She stood beside me, policing my every move because she insisted Marigold was a suicide risk. She confiscated her Oud perfume – in case she drank it! Marigold was undeniably not in her right mind, but she'd never swallow such an expensive scent. She wasn't allowed her badly needed hair dye, either, in case she squirted it down her throat. The nurse even banned her make-up – in case Marigold poked her own eyes out with a mascara wand? She wasn't allowed her long cowgirl belt in case she hanged herself from a light fitting in the toilet. She wasn't even allowed the bag holding all these items in case she rammed it over her head and suffocated.

She'd already confiscated Marigold's jewellery, locking it away in her office.

Marigold kept rubbing the finger that still bore the indent from her so-called wedding ring. She'd always insisted Micky had given it to her, although we didn't believe her.

'She'll keep it very safe for you,' I promised, as she rubbed her empty finger furiously, trying to manifest her ring back into place. 'I'll try hard to make her give it back to you straight away. What do they think you're going to do – swallow it?'

'As if! You're a good girl, Dol,' Marigold said tearfully.

'What else can I bring you? Chocolate? Grapes? Magazines?'

She shook her head, slumping back down the bed and trying to pull the meagre covers up over her head.

'Marigold?'

'Want to sleep,' she muttered.

'No, wait a minute. Listen.' I needed to ask her again. '*Did you try to kill yourself – or did you really think you could fly?*'

I was terrified it was all my fault. I should have heard her getting out of bed that morning. And why hadn't I caught hold of her when I was standing beside her on those station steps?

'I was just popping up to see Star and my little grandson,' said Marigold, evading the question. She choked on her words now, rocking again.

'Couldn't you try very hard to forget about Star for the moment?' I pleaded.

She's done her very best to forget about you!

'Star, Star, Star, Star, Star!' Marigold began mumbling defiantly.

'Oh, for God's sake, stop that. I think you're putting it on deliberately.'

'You don't know what it's like to be me,' she moaned, outraged. 'I can't *help* it.'

I *knew* she couldn't help it, and yet I was so sick of it. And sick of feeling guilty and resentful and unhappy.

'I want to see my grandson,' Marigold started up. 'What does he look like? Is he blond? Is he like my Micky?'

Please don't let her start on Micky too. She always insisted he was the love of her life. They'd met at some wild gig, started an affair, started living together, started Star – and then Micky started to feel trapped, and left her, left them both. Oldest story in the book.

'*Is* he like Micky?' she repeated.

'No, he's a baby, he doesn't really look like anyone but himself,' I said without thinking.

'So you've seen him?' Marigold sat bolt upright and clutched my shoulders. '*You've* been to see him but you wouldn't let me?'

'I haven't seen him in the flesh, I swear I haven't. Star just sent a photo,' I admitted reluctantly.

'Let me see it! *Let me!*' Marigold demanded, shaking me.

I cursed myself silently. I had to show her now, though I'd promised Star I wouldn't.

'Then try to calm down. You're hurting me,' I said, prising her hands away. 'Let me get my phone.'

'You're going to phone Star!' Marigold cried.

'No, I told you, I don't know her number now,' I lied. 'But she sent a photo when he was born. I'll find it for you.'

I got my phone out of my pocket and started flicking through the photos stored there. I didn't have as many as most people. I'd deleted the ones of past boyfriends. They were mostly photos of clients showing off their specially designed tattoos, and Oli and Ross's civil partnership. Plus one baby.

'Here!' I held the phone towards her. She grabbed it, peering at the screen. She's needed reading glasses for years but won't wear them because she says they're ageing – not realizing that the wrinkles round her eyes and across her forehead from years of squinting make her look far older than she is anyway.

Then her face softened and she breathed out, transfixed.

'He's gorgeous,' she murmured. 'The very spit of his grandad. Micky, a grandfather! I bet *he* gets to see his grandchild!'

'I'm pretty sure Star hasn't been in touch with him for ages,' I said, this time truthfully.

'What is the *matter* with Star?' said Marigold. Then her head snapped up from the phone and she looked at me directly, her green eyes piercing. 'Is she ashamed of us?'

She asked as if it had only just occurred to her.

'Of course not,' I said hurriedly, but I knew I didn't sound convincing.

'It's me, isn't it?' said Marigold. 'But listen, Dol, I'll dress myself up, I'll wear granny clothes, a suit, sensible shoes, whatever they wear. I won't touch a drop of drink, I'll be a perfect frump, I swear. Just take me to see Star and this gorgeous little boy. I won't let you down, I won't let anyone down.'

I felt as if my heart was tearing in two.

'And you'll take your Lithium?' I had to ask.

'It's poisoning me, Dol. Look at my hands!' She held them out and showed me her tremor. 'And I feel sick half the time. My eyes are getting worse. My voice slurs even though I don't drink any more – well, not often. It's doing me in, I know it is. So let me see the baby before I die.'

I held her hands tight. I longed to help her, but knew I couldn't trust her. She couldn't control herself. She was lying here all smashed up because of my lack of vigilance, and I had to protect her from hurting herself again.

'Let's see what Dr Gibbon says tomorrow,' I hedged.

'Who cares what that monkey doctor says!' she said, and she made stupid gibbering noises like a silly schoolgirl.

'Stop that,' I said curtly.

'Why should I? Aren't I shut up here because I've gone off my head?' She tried to get out of bed, so busy making monkey noises and scratching herself that she forgot her broken ankle. I caught her just in time as she tried to stand and then swayed alarmingly, screaming.

There was a sudden squeak of footsteps back up the ward, and the nurse appeared in the doorway, glaring.

'What are you doing, letting your mother get out of bed? Do you want her to break her other leg?'

'Not her fault!' Marigold shouted. 'I need the toilet and she was helping me, that's all, you silly bitch.'

I gaped at the nurse, whose expression had turned steely. I was touched that Marigold was protecting me, impressed that she could think so quickly, exasperated that she was swearing at the nurse because she'd antagonize her further. In manic phases she speeded up astonishingly, as if she was fast forwarding, outwitting everyone – but outwitting herself too.

The nurse made her sit on a bedpan with her door still open, which seemed a deliberate humiliation, though no one bothered watching. I wondered if they were all heavily sedated. When I came back tomorrow would Marigold be dulled into a stupor too, barely bothering to blink?

'Now, are you going to lie down sensibly and stay in bed?' the nurse asked when Marigold had finished. 'Or am I going to have to use the restraints?'

I winced. I knew they were simply wide straps that tied round her wrists but there was a touch of medieval torture about them and just that one word made Marigold cower. I saw the little flicker of a smile on the nurse's lips and loathed her. She *was* a bitch, and I hated that she had power over Marigold. She was wearing a different-coloured uniform to the others so I prayed she was an agency nurse and would only be here temporarily.

'Please be kind to my mother,' I said, trying to sound calm and reasonable. 'Imagine if you were the one in bed suffering with a mental illness.'

The nurse looked at me, a vein throbbing in her forehead.

'Imagine if you were the one dealing with the patients who need watching all the time, and all those others in the day room heaving their jigsaws off the table, and more of them outside having a smoke when it's strictly forbidden – and my only help this shift is a girl scared out of her wits sobbing in the kitchen because this isn't at all like her Peppa Pig book about doctors and nurses,' she snapped, her voice harsh and raw. Then she smoothly segued into a professional tone. 'A good nurse always feels compassion and empathy for her patients. But they have to lay down the law too.'

I shut up, and mercifully so did Marigold, scared by the threat of restraints. She said the nuns used to tie her to her chair long ago and she's never got over the horror. She's got a scalding cauldron of childhood memories that she stirs endlessly. Sometimes the stories contradicted themselves. She was in care as a little girl, just like Star and me, but were the dreaded nuns running a convent school or a children's home? Was the nameless man who did awful things to her a teacher, a foster father, her own father? And what about her mother? She's never once mentioned her.

Was she mentally ill, this missing mother? If some mental disorders could be hereditary then did all the Westward womenfolk slot inside each other like identical Russian dolls: my grandmother, my mother . . . me?

6

When I left the hospital at four, I hurried back to the studio. I wondered if the dark-haired actor might have come sauntering back to book a custom appointment – but of course he hadn't. And wouldn't. He'd just been idly flirting.

However, because Brian had been as good as his word and posted my new romantasy design on TikTok, there were already three girls at the studio wanting it inked on their arms! They wanted the full deal: dragon, girl, flames, flowers. One girl saw the design and had come immediately, all the way from suburban Surbiton.

'Do you know how much a really elaborate tattoo could cost?' I asked.

'I've got heaps of cash,' she said, unzipping her shoulder bag and showing me a wad of twenty-pound notes stuffed inside. I hoped she hadn't nicked it.

She seemed to think I could do the whole design, with colour and shading, in a couple of hours. I wearily explained that it would take many sessions and tried to talk her into having just one baby dragon coming out of an egg, which I could feasibly manage before she returned home.

I offered to make appointments for the other girls later in the week. They weren't happy, but they saw reason. But the Surbiton girl begged me to do her arm there and then, adult dragon and maiden, and she'd like the baby dragon too. She said she didn't care how long it took, and how late into the night. Brian suggested I do the whole outline now, princess, adult dragon and baby, leaving me to lock up around nine or ten, but thankfully both Jo and Big Al protested on my behalf.

'Dol looks exhausted already, poor kid. She's just had her mum admitted to hospital. You can't possibly expect her to do a new complicated design in one go! We should send the girl home now,' Jo said furiously.

'You're just jealous because Dol's getting all the work,' Brian sneered.

'Don't stir that kind of shit, Brian,' Big Al said. 'Jo just cares about our Dolly. And so do I. You'd better watch it or she'll walk – and you know full well she's the real draw. I reckon she's ready to set up in her own studio now.'

I smiled at them gratefully. It was so wonderful to have loyal friends after the hell of my schooldays. I don't know what I'd have done if I hadn't had Oli. I took the desperate Surbiton girl into the cubicle and sat her down.

'What's your name, sweetheart?' I said, yawning.

'Kate,' she said.

'And how old are you?'

'Eighteen,' she said.

I looked at her. She wore heavy make-up and was trying to appear ultra confident, but she kept twisting her hands together anxiously. I hoped I hadn't looked like that with the actor. Maybe he thought I was pathetic and was just flirting with me for a laugh? Or even worse, could it have been a pity-flirt? He likely hadn't given me a second thought the minute he walked out of the studio.

You forget him too and get on with your job! The girl's come all this way!

'I'm sorry, I'm going to have to ask for proof of your age,' I said.

'I've got my passport, see.' She produced it triumphantly from her bag. I glanced at her photo, checked her age.

'Don't you believe me?' she said indignantly.

'We have to check. I'd lose my job if I gave you a tattoo under age,' I told her. She'd only had her eighteenth birthday a fortnight ago. 'Do your parents know you're getting a tattoo?'

'It's nothing to do with them. It's my body, and you can see there I'm legally an adult. I'll do what I want with it,' she said defiantly.

'And it's your money?'

'Yes, all my birthday money,' she said. 'Now, let's get on. I want it on my upper arm, here, really big, shoulder to elbow,' she said, rolling up her sleeve and showing me. 'And all coloured in too.'

'Oh, Kate, I already told you. I can't possibly do the whole tattoo in one go,' I said, shaking my head at her. 'The design's way too intricate. It'll take fifteen hours, maybe even longer.'

'I don't care,' she said determinedly, though her eyes widened when I said 'fifteen'.

'You'd care if I fell asleep on the job and you ended up with me piercing your vein,' I said. 'Why do you want this so badly?'

I thought it would be because she wanted to look like some tattooed influencer. She was looking suddenly starstruck.

'I'm in love, see,' she said.

'With a boyfriend?'

'No!' she said crossly. 'With dragons.'

I blinked at her. I'd had clients who wanted a cat tattoo because they loved cats but this was something else.

'With actual dragons?'

'They're so cool,' she swooned. 'Imagine having sex with one!'

'I'd have thought they'd be pretty hot,' I said. 'Especially when they started heavy breathing.'

She nodded at me earnestly. 'They say you burst into flames when you have an orgasm. That's what I want on my tattoo, see. The girl and the dragon. Can you make him actually penetrating her so her head's back like this, in ecstasy?' She demonstrated.

'Stop it! I don't do that sort of stuff!'

'No need to be so uptight. Fine, it can be just like your design, barely touching each other, OK?'

'No, not OK. I'll do you a small dragon emerging from its egg, like I said – and then you go back home and think very carefully about it, and if you really want to go through with the maiden and dragon idea, you can phone up and make a series of appointments. Final offer.'

She backed down and I gave her my standard baby dragon on her left arm. She didn't get nervous and start making a fuss. She just sat there stoically, and when she saw the baby dragon's face she started smiling.

'He looks so cute,' she said. 'If only I could find a dragon's egg! It would be so magical to have a baby dragon as a pet.'

She said it as if it was actually a possibility. We certainly had some weird clients at times. She was thrilled with the tattoo when I'd finished it. I coloured it pale green, the egg a darker green, and was pleased with the result.

'Studio Ghibli, eat your heart out,' I said.

'You what?'

'It's a Japanese animation studio that . . . Oh, never mind. Right, let's cover it up and get you ready to go.'

I took her money, gave her a card so she could contact the studio, and shooed her out the door. The others had long gone. I took a deep breath, suddenly feeling sick and dizzy. When was the last time I'd eaten? I had a long drink of water and snaffled the last couple of squares of Jo's Chocolonely bar she'd left on her shelf, sterilized my stuff, then locked up and made for home.

I was so tired I fell asleep on the bus, but jerked awake just in time for my stop. I trailed up the street and saw Lee just getting out of his van.

'Hi, Dol!' he called, then gave me a second look. 'You look really tired. Have you been with your mum?'

'Earlier today. She's in hospital,' I said.

His eyes widened. 'I'm so sorry.'

'She's broken her ankle and hurt her face. And she's in a psych ward now.' I saw Marigold leaping again and again, and screwed up my face. 'Do you mind if we don't talk about it?'

'But she'll be OK eventually?' he pressed.

I shrugged. 'She'll get better, physically.' I was too tired to go into the chronic aspect of bipolar disorder.

We walked to the front door, struggled up all the stairs to our attic rooms and hovered between our two front doors. Lee looked tired too, his tanned face sallow in the dim light, dark smudges under his eyes, and he smelt slightly of warm, healthy sweat, the sort you get from digging in a garden all day long.

'Do you usually work this late?' I asked, trying to start small talk so he wouldn't ask more about Marigold. I knew he'd be kind and sympathetic but I couldn't bear to talk about her. She'd stopped endlessly leaping in my head and was instead huddled under her sheets now, scarcely moving, only the tip of her plastered foot visible.

'Not usually, but I've got this new job, a posh old lady living in a massive house with a huge garden. Her last gardener said it was too much for him and packed it in last winter, and it's practically wilderness now. I've never seen such brambles and nettles and ivy. The more it's chopped down the more it grows, like a Hydra.'

'A what?'

'That monster snake that Hercules had to fight,' he said. 'I loved this book when I was a boy, *Ancient Myths and Legends*. I'll show you.'

He led the way into his flat, knelt by a still-unpacked box and brought out a greenish-grey story book, very old and battered. He opened it up to a colour plate of a man battling with a monster with multiple snakey necks with fork-tongued heads. 'Did you ever read about Hercules?'

I shook my head, feeling the sweat break out under my fringe. I didn't want him to know I could barely struggle through *Spot the Dog* when I was little. I'd missed out on most children's books as a child but I'd made up for it now, listening to endless audiobooks to help me get to sleep.

Poor Lee. He was simply trying to be nice to me, and I was barely responding. I made a supreme effort.

'How long have you been a gardener?' I asked, pulling a smile on to my face. 'It must be a very rewarding job.'

I didn't think it could possibly be rewarding, battling with weeds all day long, spreading manure and dealing with slugs and worms. But Lee's eyes positively shone.

'It *is*,' he said. He started to tell me more about how he was determined to get this old lady's herbaceous borders back into condition. I didn't have a clue what they were – something to do with basil and rosemary and coriander?

I kept nodding politely when all I wanted to do was rush next door to my own flat and go straight to bed – though no, no, the new Marigold image was taking over, and the smell of her Oud perfume was probably still on my sheets and my only other set was waiting to be dragged to the launderette.

'You look done in,' said Lee. 'Here's me going on about gardening when what you need is a good meal and a proper night's sleep.'

I smiled wanly. 'I'm not sure I've got anything in,' I mumbled. I'd left the Jaffa Cakes in his van, and they were probably hard as rocks by now. I didn't really care. I'd gone past being hungry, but he was beaming at me eagerly.

'Well, I've got more than enough. In you come! I'll have dinner for two ready in a jiffy.'

I stared at him, mortified. 'Oh no! Please! It's very kind of you, but I don't really want any dinner,' I protested, but he pulled me across the room and sat me firmly on his small sofa. It was rigidly upright and the upholstery cushion was lumpy, but I was so tired I slumped on it gratefully.

'Would you like a drink?' he asked, going to his fridge. 'I'm afraid I haven't got any wine, but how about a cold beer?'

I didn't drink much at all, scared that I might get addicted like Marigold, but he seemed desperate to be hospitable.

'That would be lovely,' I said.

'I haven't even got myself proper glasses yet. Is it OK to drink it out the bottle – or shall I pour yours into a coffee mug?'

'Out the bottle is fine,' I said, peering around. His room was very basic compared to mine. He didn't have any pictures or ornaments and was making do with the most rudimentary furniture. The only colour in the drab room came from the miniature pram stuffed with two naked baby dolls, a neon pink scooter, and several indeterminate fluffy creatures that looked like they came from an amusement arcade crane, probably siblings of Fido the Van Dog.

'Ava's toys?' I said, nodding to them as we clinked bottles.

'You remembered her name!' he said, delighted. 'I'm going to collect her on Saturday morning and she's staying overnight. I wish she didn't live so far away now. My ex-wife's moved to the other side of London where it's all high-rise flats and hardly any gardens – I'd never get enough work round there. Part of me thinks she did it deliberately to spite me. I can't afford the rent by myself at our old house – so here I am!' He gestured wryly round his stark little room.

'It must be hard for you,' I said.

'It is what it is,' he replied. It was a hackneyed phrase I usually hated, and yet somehow the simple way he said it gave it a dignity. He seemed such a genuine man.

Tired though he was, he whirled into action, peeling potatoes, cutting up onions, setting sausages to sizzle in the pan.

'Let me help,' I said, though I knew next to nothing about cooking. We'd relied on takeaways and frozen meals when I was small, and now I mostly made do with soups, toasted sandwiches and the odd stir fry because they were easy and fast – and, most importantly, cheap.

'You can keep an eye on things while I have a quick shower,' he said.

'Sure,' I said, but my heart started thumping. It was going to be a bit weird him having a shower in the same room. I worried he was getting clean and spruced up because he hoped we might end up having sex. I liked him and he'd been very kind but I didn't want to start another disastrous romance, especially not now, when I had to deal with Marigold. I wasn't even sure I wanted to be with a man at all.

The memory of the dark-haired actor looking at me quizzically from the studio doorway popped into my head, but I pushed it out. No, no, no! I wasn't going to fall for his type ever again.

I heard Lee now in the small shower cubicle, tactfully taking off his clothes inside it and throwing them outside, only exposing one tanned arm. He turned on the water and had a thorough scrub.

'You're supposed to be over in the kitchenette, stirring the onion sauce with your back to me,' he announced, opening the shower door and releasing a waft of steam into the main room. 'Stare at that stove as if your life depends on it, until you hear a cheery whistle.'

I did as I was told, relieved. He certainly didn't sound as if this was an overture to sex. I heard elastic snapping at a waist, little hops as he put on clean socks, a grunt or two as he pulled up his jeans, a tugging sound as he did up the laces on his trainers. He whistled and presented himself fully dressed in a clean blue teeshirt and good jeans, his hair sticking up and his face red from his exertions.

'Are you going out?' I asked, surprised.

'No! I just wanted to look decent, not a total scruff,' he said. His face was even redder now, so perhaps he was blushing.

'Oh, I see,' I said awkwardly. Why would he feel the need to scrub up for me? I had to find some polite way to stop him coming on to me. I took a deep breath. 'Lee . . .' I started tentatively, and then floundered.

Luckily he was quick on the uptake. 'I had a shower because I was embarrassed about being whiffy after a day's work. Don't worry, Dol, I'm not about to make any clumsy passes, I promise. I mean, I find you very attractive, but as I've just come out of a failed relationship I'm not in a hurry to mess up anyone else's life, especially not yours.'

'The relationship with Ava's mother?' I asked gently.

'Here, give me that,' he said, taking the spoon from my hand and stirring properly. He checked the sausages in the pan, turned them over, glanced at the bubbling potatoes, and nodded. 'Yep, my wife. We're getting a divorce.'

He seemed such a steady family man. I couldn't imagine he was the type to risk having an affair. 'Why?' I asked, and then worried I was being too nosey.

He hesitated. His eyelid started twitching, and he rubbed it fiercely. 'Because I'm too boring, I suppose,' he said.

'You're not the slightest bit boring,' I protested.

'Ali thinks I am. She wants excitement, surprises, fancy meals out, late nights, wild sex – sorry, I'm oversharing now! It's not that I'm against all that – fine every now and then. But if you're getting up early with a kid and then working eight or nine hours getting gardens into shape, you're a bit knackered in the evenings. You just want a good meal, a cuddle on the sofa watching telly and an early night. See – boring!'

He was sending himself up in a rather endearing way. I'd never known a man do that before.

'So now she's scarpered with some guy she's met,' Lee said, breathing out heavily.

'And she gets to keep Ava?' I asked. 'That doesn't seem fair.'

Lee's face tightened. 'Well, I work really long hours, and I can't take her with me, not to other people's gardens.' He switched topic abruptly. 'How are these potatoes getting on? I wish they were home-grown. My dad had a veg plot and grew all our own vegetables.'

'Does he still garden now?'

'He died of a heart attack just after Ava was born. It was such a shame – I'd have loved her to know her grandad, he was a lovely guy,' said Lee, taking milk and butter out of the fridge.

'And your mum?'

'She died of breast cancer when I was a kid. She was lovely too. Not striking-looking like your mum – more plump and cosy.' He paused. 'I know you don't want to talk about it, Dol, and I won't press you, but is she seriously hurt?'

'She's smashed up her face and broken her ankle, like I said, but she'll get better. She's been sectioned, though. Again.' I tried to sound world-weary, but he must have seen how much it still tore me apart because he left the meal preparation and opened his arms.

'I think you need a hug,' he said.

I gave in to the urge to be held, laid my head on his chest and wept.

7

Lee must be the last man alive who still used cotton hankies. I snuffled into one after my sobs had died down while he served the meal. It was simple enough – sausages, creamy mash, onion sauce, washed down with beer – but dinner at the Ritz couldn't have tasted better. It felt wonderful to have a warm meal inside me, and great to have this lovely man cosseting me.

Marigold was still there in my head, though, and I teared up again whenever I imagined her shut in that tiny cubicle in the bleak ward, calling for Star, for the baby, for bloody Micky, for me to come and rescue her. But I knew she was safe there, even though she hated hospitals. She'd be staying for a while so I had a little breathing space, time to think about myself.

My eyelids felt heavy and I knew I was in danger of falling asleep.

'I'd better go back to my own room now,' I mumbled.

'You can sleep on my sofa if you need company. No, *I'll* sleep on the sofa, you can sleep in my bed. I can make it up with clean sheets in no time,' Lee offered.

'You're the kindest man in all the world, Lee. Your Ali must be mad wanting to leave you. But it's fine, I'll go back to my place now. It's not as if I've got far to go,' I said.

'Well, I'll walk you to your door, then,' said Lee. He was joking, but he really did come out of his bedsit, walk five steps and wait while I fished out my key. 'Night then, Dol,' he said, giving me a pat on my shoulder before going back to his own place.

I breathed in the familiar rose and dried-lavender smell of my own room, used the tiny bathroom, stepped out of my clothes and huddled down in my bed. It still smelt faintly of Marigold's perfume but I had kept Lee's handkerchief to launder it, and I used it like a damp comfort blanket. I fell asleep quickly and didn't wake up until dawn.

I still had the keys to the studio so I went in early to make sure everything was clean and tidy, and checked the takings and our individual earnings, writing it all down neatly in our respective account books. I needed Brian to be pleased with me, because I was hoping to get more time off this morning.

He swanned in very late. I'd already done a heart flash and outlined a dragon for one of the girls wanting my new romantasy tattoo, so I thought he'd be pleased. I wanted to go and check on Marigold again, but he wouldn't let me this time.

'It doesn't look good when there's an empty couch for hours. Don't think you can keep skiving off like this, Dol,' he said irritably.

'I'm not *skiving*! My mum's very ill,' I insisted, but I couldn't sweet talk him this time. I wondered about ignoring him and simply walking out, but Brian could turn nasty. I needed this job. And Marigold would probably be dozing through the day as depression sank in. Maybe I didn't really need to go back so soon.

So I stayed and worked hard on the wretched princess/dragon tattoo, leaving various arms and legs with outlines, and making appointments for the colouring-in process.

I was heartily sick of the design now, and practically begged the last girl to try a little variation – maybe a unicorn? – but she wasn't having it. My eyes kept blurring and I told her I'd have to stop, but she begged me to carry on. I prayed my hand would stay steady. Brian insisted I finish the last outline, saying it was only fair.

It wasn't fair to me. It wasn't fair to Marigold. She was on my mind all the time. I fancied her cries of *Star! Star! Star!* were still ringing in my ears. But at long last I finished the dragon with the last flick of his scaly tail, made an appointment for the client to start the colouring process, and finished sterilizing . . .

My phone rang as Brian let me go at last. I felt sick, clutching my chest, my mind racing. No one rang nowadays except in an emergency. What was wrong? Had Marigold made another scene, escaped from the hospital, tried to kill herself . . . ? Then I made out the name on the screen.

Star!

'What is it?' I asked in a panic.

'Where *are* you?'

'At work!'

'Still?'

'Yes, well, I'm working late because I've been going backwards and forwards to the hospital to see our sick mother,' I said, laying it on thick again. I could get cross with her now she sounded perfectly all right.

'Well, get yourself home, girl. I'm sitting on the stairs at the top of your building, waiting to see you,' she said.

'What?' I said weakly. 'Seriously?'

'I cut my afternoon clinic, got on a plane, in a taxi – and here I am, as requested,' she said. 'Come back as quick as you can, Dolly!'

All my fury blew away like smoke.

'Oh, Star – I'm coming!' I cried.

I ran all the way to the bus stop, jumped on the bus and sat on the edge of the seat, willing it to go faster. I kept checking my phone to see if she'd left any further message.

When I finally got back, I charged in the front door, panting, and thundered up the endless steps.

'Star!' I gasped, as I turned the last twist of the staircase. Then I stopped abruptly. There was no one sitting at the top of the steps. No one leaning against my door. Where on earth was she? Surely she hadn't got fed up and wandered off? Had she gone to the hospital? Or had she simply changed her mind and was now halfway to Gatwick for a return flight? I clutched my head, trying to think straight.

Then Lee's door opened and he stood there, smiling, still in his muddy gardening teeshirt and torn jeans.

'I thought I heard you charging up the stairs!' he said. 'Come in!'

'No, it's my sister, I've got to find her—' I gabbled, and then she was standing there, behind Lee, immaculate in a cream jacket and black trousers, holding a baby in her arms.

'Star!' I cried, and pushing past Lee I flew to her. I couldn't hug her tight because of the baby and she couldn't hug me back properly, but we did our best, little Christopher wriggling in surprise that he had four arms cradling him.

'Meet your Auntie Dol, Chrissie,' said Star, holding him up.

He was beautiful, of course he was. Not one of those sallow scowling babies, not a big ruddy-faced bruiser, not a tiny shrimp – he was delicately pink and perfect, with downy hair as white as milk. He stared at me intently with his blue-green eyes, then his small, pursed mouth widened, softened, and he smiled at me.

'Look!' I breathed. 'Oh, Star, he's smiling at me! Or is it just wind?'

'It's a smile, silly.'

'Oh, Star, I've missed you.'

'And I've missed you, Dol. Why do you insist on mouldering here?' she exclaimed.

I screwed up my face. Why did she always have to insult me and the way I lived?

'Hey, there's not a speck of mould in this particular bedsit,' Lee said quickly, deliberately misunderstanding. 'I scrubbed it down with so much vinegar and water it smelt like a fish and chip shop for days.'

We'd both momentarily forgotten him. I smiled at him gratefully. Star very slightly raised her eyebrows, as if she thought he was being a bit thick. I could have killed her. I felt dizzy with all these violently opposing emotions.

'Here, sit down, Dol, and I'll make you a cup of tea,' Lee said. 'You look all done in.'

He started moving towards the kettle to plug it in, and Star looked at me. 'Are you two an item?' she mouthed.

'He's my friend!' I wasn't quite as good at silent-mouthing as Star. Perhaps Lee heard me, because his back stiffened slightly.

'Would you like a cuppa now, Star?' he asked.

So he'd offered her one already and she'd refused. What was up with her? Was PG Tips not classy enough for her nowadays? My sister, the snobby cow. But she was also my sister Star, who'd practically brought me up, who'd always been there for me, until she wasn't. Who'd come when I'd given her that desperate call.

'No, thank you,' she said to Lee. She sat down on his sofa after giving it a swift brush with her hand, as if it might have crumbs on it.

Lee was looking in his fridge now. I spotted a bottle of Prosecco, which surprised me. 'I'll make you a sandwich, Dol. I bet you've missed out on lunch again,' he said. 'Cheese or ham?'

'No, it's very sweet of you, but I'm taking Dolly out for supper,' Star said smoothly.

'What about the baby?' said Lee.

'Oh, I daresay he'll fall asleep on my lap,' said Star. 'Babies are very adaptable.'

'I know,' he said. 'My own daughter curls up like a kitten on the floor whenever she's tired, bless her.'

'Oh, you've got a daughter!' She looked round and took in the toys. 'She lives with you?'

'Sadly not, but she'll be visiting,' said Lee. 'There, Dol, here's your tea.'

'It was good of you to invite my sister in,' I said, frowning at Star.

'Yes, it was really kind of you,' said Star sincerely. 'I suppose I was making a bit of a row, yelling and banging on Dol's door.'

'Lucky I left work early tonight,' said Lee.

'Put your tea down, Dol, and give Chrissie a cuddle,' Star suggested.

I held out my arms tentatively. I'd never held such a young baby before. He was heavier than I expected, and reassuringly sturdy. I thought he might start crying when Star handed him over but he lolled against me without protest. I held him close, his warm head resting against my chest. I sat very still, scarcely breathing. It felt so good to hold him. I gently rocked him, murmuring meaningless phrases, blowing him little kisses. Star watched me, smiling. Lee was looking too.

'You'd make a lovely mother, Dol,' he said softly.

I imagined my own baby, and a sudden physical ache overwhelmed me, taking me by surprise. I wanted to sit there holding Christopher all evening, but Star was already standing up.

'I'll have him back now, Dol,' she said. 'We'd better pop next door, have a little tidy up, and then go out for our meal. Thank you so much for your hospitality, Lee.'

'You're welcome. Enjoy yourselves, girls.'

For a moment I wondered about asking if Lee could come too as he'd been so friendly and welcoming – but I wanted proper sister-time too much to be polite.

I went next door with Star and Christopher, keen to see what she thought of my room. She looked round appraisingly. She'd actually lent me the hefty deposit and then refused to let me pay her back, which embarrassed me terribly.

'Oh, Dol, this is so like all the places we lived when we were children,' she said, looking amused. 'Fairy lights, postcards and posters, Indian throws, little plants in jars, toys in every nook and cranny!' She wandered round the small room, shaking her head.

'Look, this is my home. Do you have to criticize it?' I said hotly.

'I'm not! I'm just saying, you're a loyal follower of the Marigold school of decoration,' she said, holding Christopher up to see the crystals hanging in the window. They made a soft rainbow pattern on his face, and he crowed, dazzled.

'I am not copying Marigold!' I insisted. 'I'm just trying to make it look pretty, that's all. On a budget! It's all right for you, with two hefty wages coming in. You can afford all manner of chic cream sofas and pale wood and fine art – though wait till Christopher is crawling all over the sofas with sticky fingers and scribbling all over your paintings with wax crayons—'

'What's the matter with you, Dol? You asked me to come and here I am. Quit acting as if Charles and I are bloody millionaires. We're hard-working doctors, not hedge fund managers! By the time we've paid tax and the mortgage and soon the amazingly expensive nursery fees, we really won't have much left over,' she said.

'Oh yes, poor you, having to put up with your measly fortnight in the Seychelles and your skiing trips and your weekends in Europe, and your three-hundred-quid dinners in fancy restaurants,' I sneered, seemingly unable to stop myself. I didn't give a fuck about her fancy lifestyle, didn't envy her posh Charles with his trainer-trim body and big ears like his regal namesake. But I did envy her Christopher, who was starting to squirm and grizzle, alarmed by our raised voices.

'Hush, darling. It's all right, I promise. Auntie Dolly isn't cross with you, it's just me she resents,' Star said infuriatingly.

'I *do* resent you,' I cried. 'I resent you not going near Marigold when it's you she's longing to see, not me. It's Star this, Star that, and now it's Star's baby too. Surely to God she's got a right to see her own grandson?'

Star wouldn't quite look me in the eyes. I saw the little pulse in her smooth forehead. Was she feeling guilty at last? She was biting her knuckle the way she used to do when we were both kids.

Then she took a deep breath and looked at me properly. 'I know it's hard on you, Dol. But I did my fair share when we were young.'

'You couldn't wait to leave home, though,' I said.

'I know,' she said. 'And I hardly ever came back, because I wasn't going to let her drag me down. She might say she loved us, but she never put us first, did she? I spent my entire childhood with my stomach clenched, wondering what was going to happen next. I kept on believing that maybe she'd change, try harder to be a proper mother, stay on her medication. Remember when we visited her in hospital after the paint incident and she promised it would all be different, we'd be a proper family together again – how long did that last? Six months, if that! So I put my head down and worked really hard, and got all the exam results I needed and headed off to try to make something of myself. I worked and worked and worked and escaped altogether. You could have done that too, Dol – you just chose not to.'

If she hadn't been holding Christopher, I would have shaken her.

'How exactly could I have escaped? I could work twenty-four hours a day but I still couldn't pass an exam to save my life. It's not a question of trying hard when you're severely dyslexic. You can stare at all those stupid squiggles till you're blue in the face but they still don't make fucking sense! You've no idea how frustrating it is. How could I ever have swanned off to university like you?' I was shouting now, forgetting all about Lee the other side of the wall.

'Yes, OK, but you could have still tried harder at that hairdressing salon. You were so good at styling hair. You might have had your own salon by this time, instead of working in a grotty tattoo studio and living in a little bedsit surrounded by saddos.'

'Shut up!' I hissed, remembering Lee at last. 'He's a lovely guy and he's been so kind to me – and to Marigold too. And there's nothing wrong with working in a tattoo studio.'

'Dol, we always hated it when Marigold got a new one. I suppose she's got heaps more now?' Star asked. 'Oh God, do you tattoo her?'

'No, I don't.' She'd asked, many times, but I couldn't do it. It would be too pathetic. She'd stopped looking exotically beautiful and had more and more random tattoos here and there that totally destroyed the overall picture. I'd seen people shaking their heads and goggling over their shoulders after she'd walked past, as if she was a sideshow.

Christopher was still fussing, so Star shrugged off her jacket, unbuttoned her shirt and started feeding him. I couldn't help staring. They looked so beautiful, Star smiling and murmuring at him, and Christopher sucking intently, his tiny hand on her breast.

I gave a deep sigh.

'Don't let's quarrel. It upsets Christopher. It upsets me,' said Star. 'I love you, Dol. I'm really here for *you*, not Marigold, because I can't bear to hear you in such a state.'

'But you will stay and see her, won't you?' I begged.

'Yes. Tomorrow morning.'

'But visiting is two till four on her ward,' I told her.

'Dol, I'm a doctor as well as a daughter. I'm pretty sure they'll let me see her. Now, go and get ready while I finish feeding his lordship. I'm taking you out for supper at my hotel. I've booked a room at the Grange – do you know it?'

Of course I knew it. It was a stunning hotel, Art Deco style, overlooking the sea. Jo and her wife Steph had been there to celebrate their fifth anniversary and said it was incredible – stylish, expensive, but relaxed and friendly. Trust Star to find the best hotel in the neighbourhood.

'But why aren't you staying with me?' I asked.

'Oh, come on, Dol. It's too small, and there's nowhere for Christopher. I thought you might like to stay with me for the night,' she said, sitting Christopher up and rubbing his back.

She kept her shirt open. Her breasts were so full now. I looked at them enviously. She used to be as meagre as me.

'Don't be silly,' I snapped. I knew I was cutting off my nose to spite my face, but I hated her always acting like Lady Bountiful. 'It's pointless paying for me too when I live here.'

'I just thought you might like a little treat. And we could lie awake and talk the way we used to,' said Star.

Christopher gave a cute little burp, which made us both giggle – and it seemed to reset things between us.

'Well . . . OK,' I conceded. 'I'd love a night at the Grange!'

'Brilliant!' beamed Star.

I had a whistlestop shower and washed my hair. I heard Lee's shower running too. It was weird thinking we were both naked, just a few feet from each other. I hoped like hell he hadn't heard too much, especially Star calling him a saddo. And he wasn't at all, he was a lovely man, simply actually sad because his marriage was over and he missed his daughter. A much better parent than either of our fathers.

I dried myself and changed into my one posh outfit. It was a black satin Ghost dress I'd found in a vintage shop while rummaging for a winter coat. I knew I'd hardly ever have an occasion to wear it, but I couldn't resist it all the same. It reminded me a little of the witchy dress Marigold had made me when I was ten. She'd embroidered moons and stars on it. I'd stitched just one crescent moon in silver thread at the neck of my Ghost dress in tribute to it.

I didn't have any unladdered tights but it was a warm night. I did have heels, though – an electric-blue strappy suede pair.

I put make-up on too: grey eyeshadow, mascara, a pale lipstick. I thought of Marigold's garish red smeared past her lips and felt a swoop of sadness. What the hell was I doing, going out with Star while she was imprisoned in that ward? But there was nothing I could do for her just now. I found I was shaking my head to my own self in the mirror. It was scary seeing how mad I could look at times.

Star was absorbed in feeding Christopher on the other breast but when she momentarily looked up, she smiled. 'You look lovely, Dol!' she said.

'I think I look a bit . . . strange. Star, if I ask you something, will you swear you'll tell me the absolute truth?'

'OK. I swear. What do you want to know?' she asked.

I took a deep breath. 'Do you think I might be a bit mad?' I asked.

'Definitely!' she said, grinning, and then when she saw my reaction she straightened her face. 'Oh, Dol, I'm joking! Of course you're not even the slightest bit mentally ill. You're the toughest little cookie ever. You cope no matter what.'

'But don't you think I'm a bit weird compared to other people?'

'Yes, but so what? You're creative and unusual and original and intense and infuriating and stubborn as a mule, my totally weird sister, and there's nothing wrong with that. I love you just the way you are.' She propped Christopher gently against a cushion and came and gave me a hug. I burrowed my wet hair against her shoulder and hugged her back as hard as I could.

She tucked Christopher into his sling while I seized her silver wheelie case and hitched my own canvas knapsack over my shoulders. Halfway down the stairs I suddenly turned and started running back up again.

'What have you forgotten?' Star asked, tutting in a big-sisterly manner.

'Nothing. I just need to tell Lee I'll be staying at the Grange with you,' I said.

'Oh, for God's sake, Dol. He's just a neighbour!'

'He's my friend,' I insisted, and rushed up to his door.

He answered it immediately and then looked me up and down.

'Wow! You look amazing!' he said.

'No, I don't,' I said self-consciously. My cheeks were very hot and I prayed I wasn't blushing. I wasn't used to compliments and felt awkward. But pleased too. He was looking quite good himself, in his white teeshirt and clean jeans. He might be stocky, but he was obviously very fit from his gardening work. His hair was wet but brushed into submission.

I wondered if I should compliment him back, but maybe that would give him the wrong idea.

'I just wanted to thank you again and say sorry if we were making a bit of a row just then,' I mumbled. 'You know – sisters!'

'I didn't hear a thing,' he said stoutly.

'And to tell you I'm staying at Star's hotel tonight in case – in case you were worried about me,' I explained, though now I said it out loud it sounded presumptuous. Why on earth should he worry? He was just a neighbour, after all.

'Thanks for letting me know. I would have worried,' he said reassuringly. 'Well, have a lovely time.'

'Thank you. Oh God, we can't stop thanking each other,' I said.

'Well, it's better than swearing at each other, surely,' he said.

'Dol!' Star called from downstairs.

'She's a bit bossy, your sister, isn't she?' Lee whispered.

'Not half,' I said, and we grinned like conspirators.

8

The Grange Hotel was even grander than I'd imagined, but Star didn't turn a hair, calmly telling reception that I was sharing her double room and would require breakfast in the morning. She asked if we could put back our reservation for dinner by an hour, and then tipped the guy who took us up to our room, carrying the suitcase and my pathetic canvas bag as if they were Louis Vuitton.

'So this is what it feels like to be rich,' I said, whirling round the large green and cream bedroom with its blond-wood bedside tables and huge black-and-white photos of twenties and thirties movie stars on the walls. I threw myself on one of the two enormous beds.

'Watch those shoes on the coverlet! And for the thousandth time, I'm not rich. Just comfortable.' She lay Christopher down on a blanket on the floor, tickling his tummy while he thumped his little pink feet up and down in delight.

'Well, I'm comfortable too,' I said, kicking off my shoes and lying spread-eagled on the bed. I couldn't help thinking how Marigold would enjoy it if she were here with us. But I also knew it wouldn't work. She'd be too hyped up with excitement, and start ordering room service, bottles of champagne to celebrate, flirting with the hotel staff, laughing too loudly, and everyone would stare and murmur to each other. Did that matter if she was having a wonderful time? Whether it should or not, it did.

She couldn't have come anyway, not hobbling on a broken ankle. I was worried it would take ages to heal, but I couldn't help being relieved too, because it meant she was tethered in the hospital ward for the moment, being kept safe.

'You absolutely promise you'll come and visit Marigold tomorrow?' I asked Star.

'Yes! But don't let's talk about her endlessly now,' said Star, taking her clothes off and walking into the bathroom. I looked at her carefully.

'How on earth have you kept your figure after having a baby?' I asked.

'I go to the gym whenever I can fit it in and see a personal trainer once a week. You should just see him, Dol. He's called Piotr and he's a cartoon cliché – fair, tanned, gorgeous eyes, ultra fit, speaks with a cute accent and flirts, but in a subtle, respectful way. Almost too respectful, actually. I wouldn't mind if he went a bit further,' said Star, running water into the sunken bath and ladling in bath foam.

'Seriously?'

Star had always been a bit of a flirt herself, kissing in corners with much older boys when we were children, but I'd thought that side of her had disappeared now she was Dr Westward married to Mr Charles Renton, Consultant. She hadn't taken his name because it would be confusing to have two doctors with the same name – and because she never wanted to be thought of as just a doctor's wife when she was a doctor herself.

'What would Charles say if he could hear you?' I asked admonishingly.

'Well, he can't, can he?' said Star. 'And I'm not sure he'd care that much either. He's gone off sex a bit now, maybe because he spent too long peering at Christopher being born. Gynaecology was never his chosen subject. Most new mothers go off sex temporarily too, but not me. I'd have sex every day if I could – wouldn't you?'

'No!' I cried.

'Haven't any of those bad-boy boyfriends been any good at it?' Star asked, lounging in the bubbles complacently. 'I was sure that had to be their only attraction because they didn't seem to have much else going for them.'

'You're so snooty. Though you're right. Some of them were hopeless, only concerned about their own pleasure,' I said, sighing.

'What, just a few thrusts and that's it?' Star sounded appalled.

'Well, some wanted all kinds of weird stuff, but for their benefit, not mine. The one I liked most did try harder with his foreplay, but he just kept pressing with his finger like it was a lift button,' I said to make her laugh, though it was true enough.

'Oh, my poor Dol,' said Star, stifling a giggle. 'Hey, I know you're all glammed up but why don't you take your dress off – fabulous, by the way – and come and have a bath too?'

'But we might be late for supper, and we've already rearranged it,' I said anxiously.

'Oh, we'll be twenty minutes tops. They won't mind. And sod it if they do. We can always eat elsewhere, even if it's fish and chips. Go on, Dol, you'll feel like a movie star.'

I was tempted to rip my clothes off and jump in with her, so we could splash and sing and lark about the way we used to when we were kids – but it would feel a bit odd now as adults. I played with Christopher instead while Star luxuriated, taking her time.

When she'd dried herself at last, she wriggled into a glorious slinky green dress that showed off her newly large breasts.

'Let's hope to God Chrissie doesn't start yelling, or I'll have dark milk patches on both boobs,' said Star. 'Nothing like motherhood to show we're all basically animals.'

Christopher seemed blissfully peaceful, gurgling away to himself.

'I don't think your Charles can possibly be his father,' I said, scooping him up and cradling him in my arms. 'The angel Gabriel himself descended from heaven and impregnated you.'

'Well, if he looked anything like Piotr then I hope he comes back,' said Star, busy styling her hair. She watched me hold Christopher under his armpits and dance him up and down in the mirror.

'You're a great auntie, Dol,' she said. 'Hey! I've had the best idea. It's hell on earth finding a good nanny and I'm not that thrilled with the nursery idea. It costs a bloody fortune but there's no individual care for the babies. How about you becoming Chrissie's nanny?'

I gaped at her. 'We live hundreds of miles apart.'

'Yes, but you could move in with us,' she said.

'In Scotland?'

'It's not bloody Outer Mongolia,' said Star, rapidly applying make-up now.

'But I'm a tattooist, not a nanny!' I protested.

'Well, I do believe there are tattoo studios in Dundee, surprising though it might seem. You could work at one part time and be Chrissie's nanny whenever I have a surgery. How about it? I'm serious, Dol.'

I stared at her. She wasn't being serious, was she? I couldn't give up my life here, could I? Though what was my life? Did I really enjoy working in Brian's studio? Did I want to stay in my cramped bedsit for the rest of my life?

'What about Marigold?' I asked.

'Dol. You're . . . how old are you? Thirty-three! For Christ's sake, you've given up the best years of your life worrying about Marigold,' she said.

'I can't just abandon her,' I said automatically.

'Look, you didn't ask to be born her child. You don't have to take care of her your whole life. Has she ever seriously tried to help herself? Has she ever even been bloody grateful for all you've done for her?'

'She's ill. You're a doctor, you know she can't help the way she is.'

'If I was your doctor, I'd tell you to put yourself first, for once. Marigold's a tough old cookie, she'll manage somehow – but if she doesn't, that's her responsibility, not yours. Mothers are meant to look out for their children, not the other way round. And listen, Dol,' she said, changing her tone. She spoke softly now, putting her arm round me and pressing her cheek against mine. 'Maybe, just maybe, you've been using her as an excuse all these years because you haven't had the nerve to start living your own life.'

I started trembling. Was she right? Or was she just trying to excuse her own selfishness? I pulled away from her.

'Don't be like that – I'm saying it because I love you. We're not going to have another row. Just park the idea and think about it. Come on, girl, we're going down to eat now, and have a fabulous time, OK?' she said, stepping into jade-green high heels.

We did have a fabulous time, too, helped by the champagne Star ordered. She only had a few sips, like a good nursing mother, so most of it was left to me. We had glorious seafood starters, an amazing chicken dish then an elaborate deconstruction of banoffee pie, followed by tiny ice-cream cornets with our coffee.

'This has been the best meal of my life!' I said, sitting back completely stuffed, thankful that my dress wasn't belted.

'I don't know – it's nothing special. It's just like we had at home, remember – fish fingers, chicken nuggets, mashed banana with brown sugar and a Whippy ice cream for a treat,' said Star.

'My specialities when Marigold couldn't be bothered to cook.' She bent her head to look at Chrissie, fast asleep in his thoughtfully provided carrier. 'Imagine a mummy who can't even make her babies their din-dins,' she murmured to him.

'But remember that time when Marigold was into baking cakes and she did hundreds – sponges and lemon drizzles and fairy cakes and Swiss rolls and cherry Bakewells, and even birthday cakes though it wasn't our birthdays,' I said, still in awe.

'And remember when we had to keep eating them even when they started to go mouldy, because we didn't have any money left for any proper food, and Marigold came over all Marie Antoinette and said, "Let them eat cake",' said Star.

'Still, they were amazing when she first made them. I remember cramming a carrier full of cake to share with Oliver at playtime and all the other kids suddenly tried to be my friend because they wanted some too,' I said. 'Oli was the best friend ever. I wish he didn't live so far away now. Have you kept up with any of your friends from the old days, Star?'

'Not really. I've got new friends now. We take it in turns having supper parties, and before I got pregnant with Chrissie I used to go to Pilates with a couple of women down the road from us. Then there's all my book group – they call themselves the "book group buddies",' said Star, wrinkling her nose. 'And we go on holiday sometimes with Charles's two best mates from his schooldays and their wives – and there's all the old uni crowd . . .'

'So heaps of friends,' I said, my voice hollow.

'But none of them are actually *friend* friends,' said Star thoughtfully. 'I never really tell them stuff. I always feel an odd one out, though I cover it up well.'

'Oh, Star, I feel exactly the same! Even with Jo and Big Al at work. I was proper friends with Oliver until he moved to the country with Ross.'

'Imagine little Owly with chickens and sheep and a donkey! I'd have thought he'd be terrified of all of them,' said Star. She looked at me, head on one side. 'Still, you have a new friend now, don't you? Lee?'

'Well, yes,' I agreed. 'I haven't known him long but he dragged himself out in the middle of the night so I could collect Marigold from Gatwick. So don't you dare be a snobby cow about him. I don't especially like your Charles, but I'm always polite to him,' I said.

'I sometimes feel exactly like you do about Charles,' said Star. 'There are times I look at him and think he's a ridiculous, pompous git.'

'Are you serious?' I asked.

'Yes. No. I don't know,' she said, throwing up her hands. 'Don't worry, I'm not going to rock the boat. I've got everything I've ever wished for, and now I have to live with it. Don't look so shocked, Dol. Maybe I'm just a bit maudlin on three sips of champagne.'

She looked totally poised and in control as always, but when we got up to go to our room upstairs there was a wild gleam in her eye. She found a nineties music channel on the huge TV and started dancing about, shaking her blonde hair and bouncing Christopher around.

He woke up and protested, so she tucked him up in the hotel cot. He grizzled for a bit, so she sat down and gave him another feed, another change, then he settled straight away. He was soon giving very soft baby-snores.

'Just like his dad,' said Star, wriggling out of her green dress. I peered down at Chrissie.

'Why are you staring at him like that?' Star asked.

'I'm trying to work out who he looks like,' I said.

'Well, he doesn't look like Marigold in the slightest,' Star said firmly.

'No,' I agreed. 'But I think he might look just a little like his grandad.'

'No, he doesn't. He's a bit of a pompous git too, forever laying down the law and putting Charles down,' Star said, bending over Christopher protectively.

'No, his other grandad.'

'What? Oh, for God's sake, Micky?' She straightened up, laughing. 'I'm not sure how he'd feel if he knew he was a grandfather.'

'Haven't you even told him?' I asked, astonished.

'We haven't been in touch for ages. I'm not even sure where he lives now. He and Charles didn't really get along.'

'I can imagine,' I said.

'I suppose Marigold is hoping my Chrissie is the spitting image of Micky,' Star said, sighing. 'Probably the only reason she's so desperate to see him.'

'She's desperate to see you too,' I said. 'She keeps on saying your name, Star Star Star, over and over again. Wait till you see her!'

'Yes, wait,' said Star darkly, stepping out of her beautiful underwear and reaching into her suitcase for her nightdress.

I'd thought she would wear something similarly silky and sexy, but she pulled a white cotton nightgown over her head, the sort she'd worn when we were children, the sort I still wore now. I held my own nightie up and we burst out laughing.

'Dear God, we look like two little nuns!' Star spluttered.

'Fancy you still wearing one of these too!' I said. 'Doesn't Charles mind? It's not exactly sexy.'

'I think it actually turns him on,' said Star. 'Which isn't the reason I wear it.'

'Is it because it reminds you of home long ago?' I asked.

'Not exactly. Home was quite scary. I suppose it's because it reminds me of you,' she said.

I gave her a hug, and when we were in bed we held our arms out of our individual beds and held hands. It usually took me ages to get to sleep, but now I didn't even have time to think about it, I just closed my eyes and passed out. I just woke once, to see Star sitting up in bed feeding Christopher, whispering to him tenderly, and I remembered the way she used to whisper to me when Marigold was staying out late and I was scared she'd never come back.

'Love you, Star,' I mumbled.

'Love you, Dol,' she whispered back.

'I wish you could stay another day or so,' I told her the next morning at breakfast.

'I wish so too,' she said. 'But I've got to go back this afternoon. Plane booked.'

'You will still see Marigold, won't you?' I said anxiously.

'Yes, I keep telling you. This morning,' Star insisted. 'I've cancelled my surgery for today.'

'Well, I've had to cancel all my work too,' I said.

Star stared at me. 'Of course, it's truly life-threatening if you have to make someone do without their skull and crossbones tattoo,' she said.

I glared at her. 'I'm perfectly well aware that I'm not a doctor saving people's lives, but I'm actually quite good at my job and I need to keep it,' I said huffily.

'No, you don't,' said Star, suddenly earnest. 'Come and live with us. Christopher, you want your Auntie Dol to look after you, don't you?'

He gave a little burp that sounded remarkably like a grunt of approval. It made us both smile. *Would* it be a good idea to go to Scotland and start a whole new life with Christopher and Star? And Charles. And all their posh friends. Would it really be *my* life then?

My head was aching after so much champagne. I massaged my forehead, unable to think clearly enough to make a decision. I texted Brian to say I wouldn't be in until this afternoon and then switched my phone off before he could text back, moaning. I looked over at the vast display of food, wondering whether to try one of the pastries or a bowl of strawberries or a simple slice of toast with honey, but my stomach was churning too much.

Star took her time, going into the hotel lounge with her coffee and flicking through the papers while I held Christopher for her. I played peek-a-boo with him, marvelling that he smiled and chuckled every single time. He really seemed to like me. He caught hold of a lock of my hair, twisting it in his tiny fingers, his grip really fierce, as if he wanted me to stay with him for ever. He'd known me for less than a day but we seemed to have bonded completely. Perhaps the other people in the lounge were thinking he was my baby.

I held him close, images of a possible future flickering in my head. I saw me building castles with him, playing ball, taking him swimming, telling him stories, holding his hand as I took him to school – though it wasn't likely that I'd ever be able to help with his homework.

Christopher started fidgeting, pouting his lips, giving little wails.

'Feeding time again,' said Star, with a sigh. 'I'd better nip up to our room.'

After a while I went upstairs too, using my own key to let myself in the room. Star was lounging in a chair by the window, Christopher at her breast. The sun shone on her face, the golden cane of the chair a circle behind her head, almost like a halo. Mother and child. A beautiful tattoo for a proud new father.

I fumbled in my knapsack for a pen and pad and started sketching.

9

Star became a different person altogether when we went to the hospital. It was as if her cream jacket was a white hospital gown, her gold bee pendant necklace a small stethoscope, her wheelie suitcase a medical trolley. She handed me Christopher and marched along confidently, rang the bell outside Primrose with purpose, and spoke with such authority to the nurse on duty that she agreed at once that Star could see Dr Gibbon as soon as possible.

'I'll go to check on Ms Westward while we wait,' Star announced, and swept into the ward.

She kept up her stride as I steered her to Marigold's room, but I could see by the tension in her jaw that she was gritting her teeth. Marigold was curled up again, the sheet over her head.

'Marigold?' said Star, and she eased the sheet away. Then she gasped in shock. I think she'd forgotten that Marigold had smashed her face when she jumped. The bruises were a livid purple now, there were plasters on her nose, and her lip was still very swollen. 'Oh my God, you're in such a mess!' Star said, and she burst into tears.

'Star?' Marigold murmured blearily. 'Are you Star?' She looked at me for confirmation and saw Christopher in my arms. Her hands went up and covered her face. Then she peered above her fingertips, blinking hard, trying to focus. 'Is – is it the baby? Micky's baby?'

'Oh, for God's sake, Marigold, Micky's my *dad*! This is Christopher, my husband's child – *my* child, *your* grandson,' Star said, recovering almost instantly.

I thought Marigold would sit up and beg to hold the baby, but she was shaking her head.

'He doesn't look right,' Marigold said, though she could only see Christopher's downy head, the curve of his peachy cheek, the squiggle of his small pink ear. She continued to shake her head vehemently, her wild red hair on end, and then she flopped back down and pulled the sheet over herself again.

Star blew out her cheeks and then started laughing shakily. 'Well, this was clearly a waste of time and trouble!' Her voice was shrill.

'Marigold, it really is Star and this is baby Christopher. Isn't he gorgeous? They've come all this way from Scotland to see you. Why don't I help you sit up and we can all have a lovely time together,' I said, but Marigold pulled away from me, wriggling down the bed until even the tips of her hair were out of sight.

I looked at Star, shaking my head helplessly.

'I don't know why she's being like this. She was so desperate to see you,' I gabbled.

'Ah well,' said Star, fighting to recover her professional self. 'Bipolar disorder patients can suffer psychotic episodes. Perhaps she's been having hallucinations and thinks this is one of them. Or maybe she's gone into such an overwhelming depression that nothing makes any impact on her at the moment. Don't worry, I'm not taking this personally.' She was saying all this as matter-of-factly as she could but I knew Star too well to be convinced. She didn't look like a medical professional any more. She'd stopped crying but her fists were clenched and she looked desolate.

'Marigold, please. It really is Star, please talk to her, please hold Christopher, this is all you've dreamt of, it's actually happening, please *look*!' I begged.

'Shut up, Dol,' Marigold murmured from beneath her sheet.

'Yes, stop going on about it. I *knew* this was going to be a waste of time,' snapped Star. 'Don't let's upset her more. We'll wait to see Dr Gibbon and then I'll have to get going.'

'Let's *try*!' I suggested desperately. 'If we sit on the bed and talk to her, maybe she'll start talking back to us.'

Star sighed and shook her head, but she waited ten more minutes with me. She told Marigold all about Christopher and what an easy baby he was, really quite advanced for his age, and she talked about her job and how she enjoyed treating her women patients. She even spoke about the past, reminding Marigold of the time Micky came back and bought us all cuddly toys in Hamleys and then we went on a carousel.

I remembered that day so vividly too: how I clutched the barley sugar rail and threw my head back as we went up and down and round and round, making myself so dizzy I could barely walk when we clambered off. Marigold was dizzy too, delirious with happiness, too ecstatic, talking too loudly, dancing, singing, and people were staring. Micky was staring at her too, realizing she was ill, worrying about her, worrying about his newly found daughter most of all.

Marigold was very still under the sheets. She was obviously listening, though, making odd little sounds under her breath. I tried convincing myself she was laughing with happiness at the memory, but I think she was sobbing.

'I'm sorry, I didn't mean to upset you, Marigold,' said Star, her voice wavering. She bent and kissed the shape of her head. 'Please take your medication and you'll start to feel better soon. Come on, Dol. We'll wait for Dr Gibbon in his office.'

I kissed Marigold too, and tried lying Christopher against

her, hoping that Marigold's colourful arms would slide out the sheet and cuddle him close – but she didn't move. So I picked the baby up again and we walked away. I kept looking back over my shoulder, hoping she might have a peep at us as we retreated, but she stayed hunched up, hidden.

The nurse looked at us sympathetically as we came out of Marigold's room.

'I'm afraid she's not very communicative today,' she murmured.

'Don't worry, it's only to be expected in her condition,' Star said, her voice clipped, trying to sound professional. When we were in Dr Gibbon's office she sat down heavily and reached for Christopher. She rubbed her cheek against his downy head to comfort herself.

'I don't know why she's acting like this. She was absolutely desperate to see you and the baby. That's why she's ended up here,' I said. 'You do believe me, don't you, Star?'

I touched her elbow, wondering if I should put my arms round her. She shrugged slightly to show she'd rather I didn't. She was still struggling to stay in control.

'Of course I believe you,' Star said. 'I knew this would turn out to be a total anti-climax. You're such a romantic, hoping we'd have this happy-ever-after ending, all of us cooing over Chrissie, our special little family.'

'But that's what she *wants*,' I cried.

'I truly don't think *she* even knows what she wants any more,' said Star.

'I just feel so awful, your coming all this way when she won't talk to you or even *look* at the baby,' I said, unable to sit still, pacing round and round the small room. I dug my nails into my palms, trying to think of ways I could have made Marigold behave the way I wanted. 'It's all been such a waste of time,' I said, and I kicked the leg of Dr Gibbon's desk.

'Hey, what's my desk done to deserve that?' said Dr Gibbon, coming in through the door.

'I'm so sorry! I didn't mean to. I was just feeling so frustrated,' I said, hot with embarrassment.

'Don't worry. I know the feeling. I've kicked that poor desk enough times myself. It's a wonder it's still standing. Hello again, Miss Westward. And *Dr* Westward?' He smiled at Star, his head on one side. He'd obviously talked to the nurse.

'I *am* a doctor, but I'm not a psychiatrist,' said Star, holding out her hand. 'How do you do, Dr Gibbon. I'm Dol's sister.'

Dr Gibbon shook hands with her and gave me a nod and a smile. Then he looked at Christopher. 'And this lovely little chap is part of the family too?'

'He's Marigold's grandson. She wanted to see him so desperately,' I said mournfully. 'I thought if she could meet him, and see Star, she'd be so happy.'

'My sister still hopes our mother will suddenly recover,' Star said, her voice brittle. 'Even after all this time. Here, I've printed out some of Marigold's medical records and the different medication she's been on.'

'That's very helpful,' said Dr Gibbon.

They started talking about Lithobid and Depakene and Depakote and Fluoxetine. It sounded as if they were talking gobbledygook, the way Star and I did when we were children pretending to be from a faraway land. It was pointless anyway, because I knew that all these drugs had been tried, and now Marigold was back where she started on Lithium – though what use was it if she chose not to take it?

Dr Gibbon talked about Abilify Maintena, the once-monthly injection, but admitted it could cause restlessness, anxiety and weight gain.

'But Marigold's already desperately restless and anxious

and she'd get terribly depressed if she put on a lot of weight,' I interrupted.

'You're so right, Miss Westward,' said Dr Gibbon. 'I'm afraid there's no miracle drug out there, no matter how hard the pharmaceutical companies try. In Marigold's case I think we'll just have to keep plugging away with Lithium. At least we can make sure she's taking it while she's here in the ward.'

'But why won't she keep taking it when she's not here?' I asked. 'She can't want to feel like this, so sad and mixed-up she won't even look at Star and the baby when it's what she wanted most in the world.'

'This is the terrible downside of her condition. But haven't there been times when she's all lit up and laughing and utterly joyful?' Dr Gibbon said.

I thought of all those times, saw Marigold's green eyes glittering, shrieking with laughter, whirling around, dancing as if in a magical trance.

'Yes, there have been times like that,' I said.

'Part of the manic phase, when she's high as a kite,' said Star.

'But it obviously feels good,' said Dr Gibbon. 'Perhaps if we ever felt like that we'd want to keep experiencing it, no matter the consequences.'

Star sniffed slightly, though she didn't contradict him.

'I can see you're not a fan of my non-scientific approach?' Dr Gibbon said cheerfully. 'You're quite right too. It doesn't do much to change the situations of my poor patients. It must be hell on earth to have a severe mental disorder. And equally hellish if you're the person doing the caring.' He looked at me with such sympathy that I wanted to hug him.

When we left his office I begged Star to have one more try with Marigold.

'There's no point, Dol,' she said wearily, but I persisted.

'For God's sake,' Star barked, but she let me lead her back to Marigold's bed. She hadn't changed her position, still a ghost mother under the white sheet.

'Marigold,' I whispered, bending over her. 'Star and little Christopher are going now. If I untuck just this little bit of sheet, you'll be able to see them to say goodbye. Is that OK?'

Marigold didn't answer but she didn't try to stop me. I pulled the sheet to one side but she kept her eyes tightly shut. She was like a toddler, maybe thinking if she couldn't see us then we couldn't see her. There were tear tracks down her cheeks. Her poor nose and lip were still in a horrible state but she seemed slightly better, just very tired. I reached over and gently kissed her cheek.

'Star?' she murmured.

'Star's still here!' I reached behind me, pulling her to the side of the bed.

'I love you, Marigold,' Star whispered, and she gave me Christopher to hold while she bent down too and kissed her.

'And – and the baby?' Marigold whispered.

'Here he is, come to see his grandma,' I said, and held him out.

He gave a little startled cry, perhaps frightened of her cut face, maybe just alarmed to be held at an angle like that.

Marigold opened one eye. She peered at him. Then she spread her sore lips in a glimmer of a smile.

'Hello, baby.'

I hoped she might sit up properly, but she simply shut her eyes again, too exhausted to take any further interest.

We waited, but after a minute Star took Christopher from me and turned to go.

'I think she's actually gone to sleep on us,' she said, trying to keep her voice expressionless.

'It's not her fault. They've probably given her some kind of tranquillizer.'

'They'd have to give an elephant's dose to make Marigold tranquil,' Star said.

'She's just in a dark place now – and she'll be minding terribly about her face. Her ankle's probably hurting too,' I said breathlessly, because Star was walking at a tremendous pace now in spite of holding Christopher and pulling her case along. She pressed the button for the lift when we were outside the ward, and when it didn't come immediately she thrust Christopher at me again and started bumping the case down the stairs.

'Go easy, Star!' I called.

It was obvious she wanted to get out of the hospital as soon as she possibly could. She misjudged the stairs and lost her footing on the last three and tumbled down, her case almost landing on top of her.

'Oh my God, Star!' I said, rushing to her while still holding the baby tight.

Star groaned, sitting at the bottom of the stairs, examining the silver finish on the case.

'Bloody hell, it's horribly scratched,' she groaned.

'Never mind the case, what about *you*? Please God you haven't broken your ankle too!' I gasped.

'Don't be daft, I'm fine.' She stood up gingerly and tried walking. 'I might have twisted it just a little bit, that's all. It's just these stupid heels.' She looked at them furiously, as if she wanted to kick them off and hurl them down the long corridor.

'I know it must be very upsetting for Marigold to hardly take any notice of you or Christopher—' I started, but Star cut me short.

'Could you stop the amateur psychoanalysing?' she snapped. 'You're obviously channelling Dr Gibbon.'

She marched on, out of the exit, and started stomping her way around the long circular route to get to the road. Christopher was wailing now, clearly picking up on the tension.

'He sounds really upset,' I said timidly.

'He's just hungry, that's all,' said Star. 'There now, Chrissie!'

She stood still and rocked him but Christopher cried harder now, turning his head, opening his mouth wide, obviously looking for a breast.

'Oh God. He won't stop until I feed him,' she groaned, looking around. She spotted a bench, but it was chilly now, and there were cars and ambulances screeching past. 'I suppose it will have to be the ladies' room.'

So she went back into the building and struggled to feed Christopher sitting on a toilet because they didn't have any other facilities for a nursing mother. I hovered outside, guarding her case, wishing I'd never phoned her because it had all gone so horribly wrong. But feeding and changing the baby calmed Star down too, and she kissed me on the cheek when they emerged from the cubicle.

'Sorry, Dol. I was being a right cow.' She glanced at her little gold watch. 'I've got heaps of time. Shall we go and have a coffee? They're bound to have a Costa somewhere.'

We found an M&S café right at the other end of the hospital site so we had iced currant buns with our coffee, and on impulse Star added a packet of Percy Pigs, which we munched through like little kids.

Christopher took no notice while we had our coffee and buns, dozing contentedly in Star's arms, but he woke up when he heard the rustle of the packet and reached out hopefully.

'We're corrupting him already,' I said. 'If I really *were* his nanny, I'd let him have just one sweet if he ate all his vegetables like a good boy.'

Star was staring at me. 'You mean you'll give it a try?' she said eagerly.

'No, I was just joking,' I said hurriedly.

'Well, I'm serious. You *must* come, Dol. I can't bear to see you throwing your life away. You can see for yourself, Marigold doesn't really want either of us looking after her. Didn't you say she's got some kind of boyfriend living with her anyway?'

'Oh God, Rick. He's total pond life. I tried to send him packing but I don't know what I'm going to do if he's still hanging out there,' I said, cramming another couple of Percys into my mouth.

'But it's not your responsibility, Dol, I keep telling you that. Come with me. Not right now – you'll have to pack up and give notice to your landlord and that bloke with the tattoo place – but when you're all sorted I'll send you a ticket and you can come and stay and I promise you'll love it,' Star said, talking fast.

She went on trying to persuade me until we'd emptied the packet of sweets and she'd found an Uber driver willing to take her all the way to Gatwick. And I was tempted. It would be such a relief in so many ways. I loved Star, I loved little Chrissie – and I could put up with Charles. If I was so far away from Marigold, maybe I could stop worrying about her so much?

'Look, I'll think about it,' I said.

'You promise? You're so lovely with Chrissie, much better than any nanny could be,' said Star. 'And you're the only person in the world who really gets me. You're like my best friend as well as my sister. We have such fun together. I've got everything I've ever wanted – a good husband, sort of, a gorgeous son, a great career, and yet I get so lonely sometimes without you.'

'I miss you so much too,' I said, my heart aching that my proud sister could let herself sound so vulnerable. 'Let me think about it. I don't think I can just leave Marigold to cope by herself. And it's not just because of her. I wouldn't be leading my life any more. I'd just be part of yours, don't you get it?'

'I just don't *understand*,' Star said.

I didn't really understand myself. *I* was lonely – and I didn't have the husband, the child, the career. I was good at my job, and no one else could design a custom tattoo like mine. It was a niche talent, but I was proud of it. I didn't have anyone special in my life but at least I wasn't living with anyone cruel or controlling or downright scary, like most of my ex-boyfriends. The important thing was that this imperfect, cobbled-together life was all *mine*. There were things I wanted to change about it, and perhaps one day I would. But was the answer to give it all up and try to slot into Star's world?

I wavered desperately while we waited for Star's car – and when it drove off I shouted after them, 'I'll think about it – I promise!'

I wondered about running after them, catching up at the traffic lights, jumping in the taxi with them, flying off to Scotland straight away – but turned my back and trudged along to work instead.

Brian was very angry with me, telling me there had been a couple of people coming into the studio and most put out that I wasn't there.

'Was one of them that actor guy, Joel someone?' I asked as casually as I could, but Jo looked up and shook her head. I shrugged, an *oh well, as if I care* gesture, but I'm not sure I convinced anyone. It turned out the potential customers were two more girls wanting the dragon-and-princess tattoo.

I felt so down that I treated myself to a punnet of strawberries on the way home, even adding a carton of cream, but I didn't really fancy them when I got back and just picked at them. I could hear Lee bustling about next door, obviously busy, whistling as he wandered about, sounding happy. I wondered about knocking, but didn't want him to get the wrong idea.

I had a message from Star much later saying she was safely back at home, but Chrissie wouldn't settle and kept moving his head around as if he was looking for his auntie. I wasn't sure I believed her. She could be so artful at times. And it worked. I was starting to wonder why I hadn't agreed straight away.

I had a headache now from all the drama of the day, so decided to go to bed early. I pulled the duvet up over my head to shut out the rest of the world. Was that why Marigold hid under her sheet? I thought of her now, in the ward that was never properly dark, lying alone. Would her thoughts be racing until her head felt like it was going to burst – or would they have slowed down, so sluggish that she couldn't put two words together to save her life? Would she even remember that Star and the baby had come to see her?

I turned this way and that, trying to stop obsessing about her. I could still hear Lee's footsteps from next door. It sounded as if he was doing a bit of spring cleaning, though it seemed a strange time to be doing it. There were a few thumps too, and once I heard a stifled *Christ*. It was comforting rather than annoying, reminding me that I wasn't completely alone. But then there was a shout and another big thump, almost like a body falling from a height. And then silence.

10

I charged out of my room and hammered on his door, scared he'd had a serious accident.

'*Lee!*' I shouted. He opened the door, looking sheepish but a hundred per cent alive in a faded lumberjack shirt and torn jeans. Relief made me dizzy and I clutched at the door frame for support.

'I'm so sorry, I must have been making a bit of a row. I was balancing on a box and a case trying to reach up to attach some fairy twinkles to the main light fitting and I slipped and ended up on the floor,' he said.

'I thought you might have killed yourself!' I said, screwing up my face and feeling ridiculous.

He gaped at me. 'Are you pulling that face because I'm still alive?' he asked.

'I'm relieved, you idiot!' I blurted. After several calming breaths, I added, 'Fairy twinkles?'

'Come in and see,' he said.

I let him lead me in, and gasped. He'd been turning his stark bedsit into a fairy grotto as bizarre as mine. He'd made up the little bed with a Tinkerbell-patterned pillow and mini-duvet and tucked two plastic fairy dolls between the covers. Fido the dog lay at the foot of the bed, flower-fairy postcards were stuck all over one wall, and a Christmas tree fairy was attached to the tip of a green shrub with creamy flowers the colour of her net skirt. A long line of fairy lights drooped from the light fitting and pooled on the floor.

I smiled at Lee. 'I take it Ava's coming on a visit?'

'That's right! I'm driving up to get her tomorrow. I've given up the Saturday gardening – I'm quitting all those suburban gardens with their perfect lawns and privet hedges.'

'So you're not going to be a gardener any more?'

'I'm still going to be gardening – wonderful gardening. The old lady I've started working for, Mrs Knight, was so impressed with the work I've done for her so far that she wants me to come full time.' He beamed. 'I asked if I could have weekends off if I worked my guts out Monday to Friday and she's happy with that. So I can see my Ava! That's why I'm prettying up my room – well, trying, anyway. You wouldn't help me, would you, Dol?'

'Of course, though you've made it lovely already. I've got kitchen steps – I'll go and get them. And I'll see if I can find any other decorative bits too.'

'I'll stick the kettle on. No, tell you what.' He opened his fridge door. 'I bought a bottle of Prosecco to celebrate – well, I hoped you'd have a drink with me, but your sister came with the baby and – anyway. Fancy celebrating now?'

I didn't feel like it in the slightest given my sore head from last night's champagne, but it would be rude to turn him down when he was so happy and he'd been so kind to me.

'Great idea,' I said determinedly. 'See you in a minute. And don't go clambering on that box and case again. I expect you'll be black and blue as it is.'

I remembered I had some arnica in my kitchen drawer, and then prowled around my room, trying to find a present for Ava. I'd bought myself various little toys when I was especially down and lonely. I wasn't buying things for a real child. I was buying them for the child I once was, because Star and I mostly had grubby jumble-sale stuff when we were small, dolls with shorn hair or a teddy without any eyes. I'd bought a little striped zebra with a wistful expression and a musical box with a twirling ballerina and a tiny wooden doll's house with a family of carved mice tucked up inside.

I didn't play with them – I hadn't gone completely off my head. I just treasured them, stroking them gently whenever I was feeling blue. Maybe I could give Ava the zebra and the picture book I'd made to go with him. There weren't any words – I just drew him having adventures. Or I could offer her the music box. She'd like the *Sugar Plum Fairy* music and she could twirl round keeping time with the miniature ballerina. But perhaps she'd prefer the little wooden house with the mouse family. It was the one I liked best, myself.

I wrapped the mouse house in tissue paper and put it in my knapsack with the arnica and the strawberries and cream, dragged the kitchen steps along too, and lumbered them all next door.

'My goodness, it's Dolly Christmas,' said Lee, taking them all from me. 'Strawberries and cream!'

'I thought we could have them with the Prosecco,' I said shyly.

'Perfect! And this is . . .'

'Arnica, for your bruises. You rub it on,' I said. 'Here, I'll do it for you.'

He grinned. 'Dolly, I landed on my bum.'

'Oh! Well, you'll have to do it yourself, then,' I said, laughing. 'Do it now before the bruises start forming.'

'All right, Nursey. But what's this in the tissue paper?'

'It's – it's just a little present for Ava,' I muttered.

'But you didn't know she was coming!'

'Maybe I'm clairvoyant,' I said. 'Go and rub the arnica on. It really helps, honestly.'

I've got good balance so I managed to stand at the very top of the kitchen steps, reach up and attach the fairy lights properly. Then I looked at the fairy wall. A four-year-old girl would adore it. I smiled at Lee as he came out of his bathroom, wiping his hands on his jeans.

'I can't feel any difference,' he said.

'That's the point. Your bum would be starting to feel really sore and tender otherwise,' I said. It seemed bizarre discussing his bottom, and I found my eyes flicking down to it. It wasn't too bad a bum actually. He was a sturdy man but his bum was relatively small, not at all saggy. I gave myself a mental shake. What was I doing, thinking about him like that?

'You should wash your hands, you'll get your jeans all mucky,' I said, forcing my eyes back to the fairy wall.

'It's OK, they're hardly designer,' he said, though he went to soap his hands obediently at his kitchen sink.

'I don't know – ripped jeans are still considered cool,' I said.

'That's good, because after a few weeks of trying to tame Mrs Knight's wilderness every pair will be ripped. Here, let me finish the fairy lights, Dol – you're way too small to reach safely.'

We finished hanging them between us. Lee turned off the main light and the room glowed softly and looked beautiful.

'Do you think she'll like it?' Lee asked.

'She'll love it, you know she will.'

'Can I open your present to her?'

I nodded. He sat down on the sofa, not switching the main light back on. It was easy enough to see by the fairy lights. He unwrapped the tissue paper carefully and I waited, holding my breath. When he gingerly took the house out of the wrappings, he breathed in deeply. He ran his hands over the smooth sloping wood, the tiny windows and door, the little chimney.

'It's beautiful,' he said, his voice hushed.

'Pull the roof off and look inside,' I prompted.

He did so gently and felt for the mice. There were four: one small, one smaller, one really tiny, and one minute, the size of a child's fingernail. He held up each one very carefully.

'But I can't possibly accept such a wonderful gift,' Lee said, placing each mouse back in the house as delicately as if they were real.

'Don't you think Ava would like it?'

'She'd love it. And she's a very careful kid, she'd look after it beautifully, but you must keep it. Save it for when you have children of your own,' Lee said.

'I don't know if that will ever happen,' I said, though I felt that tug now whenever I thought of Christopher. I was starting to long for a child of my own, practical or not. But it would be years before they'd be ready to treasure a little mouse house. 'I'd like Ava to have it,' I insisted.

'I'm overwhelmed,' said Lee. He put the little wooden house down on the sofa beside him and came over to where I was sitting cross-legged on the floor. He knelt down beside me.

'Thank you so much,' he whispered, and then he kissed me. Not on the lips. It was a sweet shy kiss on my cheek. I was suddenly conscious of the fact that I was wearing my white cotton nightdress and nothing else. I wondered if he would try to go any further, unsure whether I wanted him to or not. I liked the feel of him close to me. It might be good. Very good. He hesitated, but then he straightened up.

'I'll open the Prosecco,' he said quickly.

He'd bought two flutes specially. We clinked glasses and then sipped Prosecco and dipped our strawberries in the cream carton, as if we were on a picnic.

'I take it your sister's gone back home now?' Lee asked tentatively.

'Yes. Flying visit. Literally – she lives in Scotland.'

'You're so different, you two,' he said.

'I know. She's a doctor, the clever one. And she's obviously the pretty one too!' I said it jokingly, but Lee looked at me seriously.

'I think you're just as pretty, just not so made-up and immaculate. And I'm sure you're just as clever,' he insisted.

'No, I'm not.' And then I said in a rush, 'As a matter of fact I can't even read fluently.' I'd never told anyone before, unless forced to. I felt my blood flooding my face and put my hand to my cheek. 'Oh God, I must be as red as the strawberries.'

'You can't read?' Lee repeated gently.

'Well, I can, sort of, but only simple stuff, and it takes me ages. I'm severely dyslexic,' I explained, wishing I hadn't told him now, because he was shaking his head. I prayed he wouldn't look down on me.

'Didn't they try and help you at school?'

'I sometimes had to do extra reading at playtimes with a teaching assistant – but she didn't really help me. And the stories I had to read with her were deadly boring anyway,' I said.

'And your mother didn't try to help?'

I raised my eyebrows at him. 'You've met my mother. Can you see Marigold sitting down with a book with me, or taking me to a specialist? She's not exactly a keen reader herself.'

'How is your mum? How did she react to the family visit?'

'She wouldn't even talk to Star properly or hold Christopher, and yet she was desperate to see them before,' I said, sighing. 'So they've gone back and it's all down to me again now.'

Lee's forehead was creased with concern. 'I don't suppose your dad's on the scene now?'

'Not in any meaningful way,' I said.

'Sorry,' Lee said awkwardly. 'Well, you come to me whenever you need help, promise? Especially when your mother's unwell. I take it she'll be in hospital a while?'

'Yes, they've got to sort out her medication and the psychiatrist is maybe going to try some therapy with her too. I like him. I think Marigold will like him as well when she gets a bit better.' I had another few sips of Prosecco and Lee filled my glass again. I felt as if the bubbles were inside my head. I had to go easy now. I couldn't get carried away two days running.

I looked round Lee's room. 'Your room is nicer than mine now!'

'Never!' he scoffed.

'It is so. Ava will love it.'

'You will come and meet her, won't you?' he asked. 'I know she'll really like you.'

'How on earth do you know that?'

'Because *I* do,' he said, looking at me.

He had lovely brown eyes, direct and honest. I smiled back at him and we sat there together. I wondered about shifting a little nearer, maybe nestling against him, but didn't want to risk spoiling our budding friendship. He'd said he wasn't ready for any new relationship. And if we had no-strings sex and it didn't work out, wouldn't it make things awkward when we lived right next door to each other?

So I headed back to my room not long after that, congratulating myself for being sensible. I heard Lee setting off bright and early on Saturday to make the long journey to Ava's new home. I went to work early too, and had coffee and pastries waiting when Jo and Big Al arrived. I did several flashes and drew a new romantasy design – a grinning devil coiling his tail round a hypnotized girl.

'Yuck!' said Jo.

'I know – but it's right up Brian's street and I need him to let me visit Marigold again.'

'But you've only just seen her,' said Big Al.

'I know. But – she's my *mum*,' I said.

Would I feel so compelled to check on her constantly if I lived up in Scotland and it was physically impossible to do so? Star sent me a photo of Chrissie as I hurried to the hospital. His eyes were wide open, staring directly at me, looking so cute. Star had written underneath *I miss you, Auntie Dolly! Please come and live with me.*

'Oh, Star, stop it!' I muttered, even as I stood still and touched Christopher's little button nose and the soft curve of his cheeks. I ached to hold him in my arms again.

'Maybe I will come, Chrissie!' I whispered, and then hurried on to Marigold.

I almost wanted her to be hiding under the bedclothes again, sullenly uncommunicative to prove that it was pointless visiting just now – but she was sitting up in bed when I went into her cubicle. She waved to me lethargically and gave me the glimmer of a smile.

'Oh, Marigold, you look so much better!'

She shrugged. 'Liar,' she murmured, but fondly.

'If only you'd been sitting up when Star came,' I couldn't help saying.

'She really came?' said Marigold. 'I thought that was a dream.'

'She brought little Christopher too,' I said.

'She never did,' said Marigold, shaking her head.

'Yes, I laid the baby down beside you,' I insisted.

'It's all a bit vague,' said Marigold. 'There was a baby, but he didn't look right. Not a bit like Micky.'

'Well, I don't suppose I look much like *my* grandfather, whoever he is,' I said.

'Yeah, we don't have many relations, do we,' Marigold said. She yawned hugely. Her teeth were still white and not a single one was missing. For someone who had spent time living on the streets, I thought she didn't look too bad. Her face was washed clean of make-up, the gashes were starting to heal, and someone had given her a wide Alice band so that her roots didn't show so badly.

'I'll do your hair for you sometime, if you'd like,' I offered.

'Yeah. Bit sleepy now, though.' She yawned again, and burped in the process. 'Sorry. The food's rubbish here.'

'I'll bring you some treats to eat next time,' I promised.

'And drink. Wine? And my vapes.'

I eyed her suspiciously, unsure if she was being serious.

'You're not allowed, not in hospital,' I said.

'Only kidding,' Marigold murmured, and then she sank back on her pillow and shut her eyes, falling asleep instantly.

Dr Gibbon's medication seemed to be working already, though I was experienced enough with Marigold to know that she could switch wildly from one mood to another. The one thing I'd learnt not to expect was consistency.

I waited five minutes in case she might wake up again and then kissed her forehead and left the ward. It seemed so sad that Marigold had not been in any kind of state to appreciate Star's visit when it had been what she wanted most in the world. Still, she'd made an effort to talk to *me*. I wasn't ever going to be the favourite daughter, but I was the one she'd grown to rely on.

It was obvious that Ava had arrived when I went home after work. I could hear peals of laughter through the wall, and a joyous cry of 'Daddy, you're so funny!' There were regular thuds, too, and a high-pitched whinnying sound. It sounded as if Lee was pretending to be a horse, galloping round and round the tiny room with Ava on his back.

I wished I had a spy hole so I could watch them. I could just nip next door and see them properly, of course, but I didn't want to intrude on their precious time together. I couldn't be bothered to start cooking anything. I made a quick coffee and then began designing more tattoos. I drew another princess, looking rather haughty. I gave the dragons a rest and sketched a humble peasant guy pursuing her.

I heard more giggling and movement next door – and then a knock on mine.

11

I opened the door to see Lee standing there, of course, holding Ava's hand.

She was enchanting, though not quite what I'd expected. I'd thought she'd be fair like her father, with his brown eyes and pink cheeks, but her hair was the silky sort, little wisps escaping her plaits. She had big hazel eyes with long lashes, and was very pale. I suppose she seemed a little like me when I was her age, though she was squeaky clean and wearing a blue-and-white-checked dress, white socks and red polished Mary-Jane shoes, whereas I'd been a scruff, frequently needing a bath and wearing the same black home-made dress week after week. Perhaps it was no wonder the other kids steered clear of me in those days.

She was gripping Lee's hand tightly, and hung back, trying to hide behind him.

'This is Ava,' Lee said proudly.

I bent down to her height and said, 'Hello, Ava.'

She blinked at me. She opened and closed her lips but didn't make any sound.

'Say hello to Daddy's friend Dol,' Lee prompted.

Ava mouthed the word but no sound came out. Lee mouthed to me too, 'She's just a bit shy.' Then he said in his normal voice,

'We're having Ava's favourite supper: sausage faces. We'd love you to join us.'

'Oh, yes, please, I love sausage faces,' I said, though I didn't have a clue what they were.

I went with them to Lee's newly refurbished room and saw there were three plates on the table, two big and one smaller one. He'd put a large circle of mash on each plate, with a chipolata sticking up as a nose. There were baked beans for eyes, and more for a smiley mouth.

'I promise I can cook more dishes than sausage and mash, but this is Ava's treat,' Lee murmured.

I burst out laughing. 'It looks great but you only get one sausage this way.'

'Oh no you don't!' said Lee, whipping a cloth off a dish full of extra chipolatas. 'What do you have to do, Ava?'

He waited, his eyebrows raised, head on one side.

'Eat the nose first!' Ava giggled.

It turned out you ate the sausage, then Lee made the mashed face cry because it didn't have a nose any more. Then Ava would say, 'Here you are,' and fork another sausage from the dish on to the mash, and then Lee would say, 'Oh thank you, thank you, thank you!'

'I know it's totally daft but we like our little game, don't we, Ava?' said Lee.

It *was* totally daft, but the moment Ava started roaring with laughter replacing a sausage, I couldn't help joining in. We had lemonade to drink, and then traffic-lights jelly for dessert, a circle of red, yellow and green on each dish. It's the easiest thing in the world to make packet jelly, but I was charmed that Lee had gone to the trouble to make each colour and then use a cutter to make up the traffic lights.

'Ava's very lucky to have a dad like you,' I said softly.

'It's such a shame you didn't have a dad around when you were little,' said Lee. 'And I don't suppose your mum was the sort to play daft games with your food.'

'Well, to be fair, she once made fifteen different cakes for us,' I said.

Ava blinked. 'Really?' she gasped. '*Fifteen?*'

'Truly. Different sponges, and chocolate cake, and jam tarts and brownies and fairy cakes, all sorts,' I said. 'Perhaps you and your dad could make fairy cakes one day? This is a lovely fairy room, isn't it?'

She nodded enthusiastically, and I glanced around too. There was no sign of the mouse house – it wasn't on the window sill, or on a shelf or with her other toys. Perhaps Lee thought she wouldn't like it after all and had hidden it away. I tried not to feel too disappointed.

Ava took care eating her traffic lights, one mouthful of red, one of yellow and a bite of green in meticulous order. She didn't say any more to me until supper was finished and washed up (Ava standing on a chair at the sink and giving each plate and dish a thorough swipe). Lee gave her a drawing pad and a set of wax crayons and she lay on the floor and carefully drew a stick man with a smiley face. She didn't have a pink crayon and stuck her lip out mournfully when she tried using red for the man's face.

'It's come out wrong!' she wailed, tearing the page out.

'Hang on, I've got some felt tips,' I said. 'They've got a splendid pink. I'll nip next door and fetch them.'

It took less than a minute to do just that. I brought my drawing pad too, wondering if she'd like to see my princess tattoo designs. Lee's forehead wrinkled when he saw my huge set of Caran d'Ache colours.

'Those are special ones. I don't think Ava should have them, she might break the tips by accident,' he said anxiously.

'No, I won't, Daddy,' Ava promised. 'Can I draw a new picture using all her colours?'

'My friend's called Dol, not "her". You ask Dol, then,' said Lee.

Ava swallowed, peering at me through her wispy fringe. Her mouth moved but she still couldn't quite manage to say it out loud.

'Is that a little mouse squeaking?' I said, cupping my hand around my ear. 'Do you know what I think it said? It squeaked, "Please may I use all your crayons on a lovely new picture, Dol?"'

Ava giggled, her hand over her mouth.

'Of course you can,' I said.

She lay down again, ran her finger lightly along all the colours, lost in admiration – and eventually selected a black one to do the outlines of her new picture. She drew the stick man again, giving him brown eyes and golden curls, and then she found the precious pink and coloured in his face, her tongue sticking out with concentration.

'That's your daddy, isn't it? It's a beautiful picture,' I said.

'Dol draws pictures on people's arms and legs,' said Lee. 'Tattoos!'

Ava blinked at me.

'I draw pictures on paper too,' I said. I leafed through pages of dragons and werewolves and bats, clearly not suitable for small girls, and found the princess page.

'Oh!' said Ava. She sat up and looked at them very carefully, a big smile on her face. 'They're lovely!'

'I'll draw you as a princess, if you like,' I said, flipping over the page. I was going to turn the next page too, the one with the princess and her cheery peasant suitor, but Ava stuck her finger out, stopping me. She peered at the picture, and then pointed.

'You've drawn Daddy!' she said.

'What? No, I haven't!' I said, staring at my peasant guy. I took in his curls, his eyes, his build, his entire stance, and gulped. Ava was right. I had drawn Lee.

'Let me see!' he said curiously.

'It's not you – it's just—' I snapped my mouth shut before I said 'a peasant boy', because it sounded insulting, even though one ended up the hero of many a fairy story.

Lee took the drawing pad and chuckled. 'Wow, it's quite flattering. But how come I don't get to be all dressed up in fancy clothes like the other men?'

'Because they looked silly and you don't,' I said quickly. 'Shall I draw you next to the man who looks like Daddy, Ava?'

'Yes, please,' she said.

She watched, so absorbed her mouth hung open a little, and her own hand copied mine, drawing in thin air.

'Teach me how to draw like you, Dol!' she begged.

'You'll probably draw much better than me when you grow up,' I said. 'Have you decided what you want to be when you're a lady?'

Ava thought about it solemnly. 'I want to be a lady who does make-up,' she said.

Lee groaned. 'Her mum lets her look at all those young women demonstrating make-up on TikTok and Instagram,' he explained.

'But I also want to have my own stable of unicorns,' Ava said solemnly. 'And a garden with heaps and heaps of roses. And I want to marry you, Daddy.'

'Little girls don't marry their daddies,' said Lee, though he looked enormously pleased.

'But then we could be together all the time,' Ava explained, her voice slow and deliberate, because he wasn't being very quick on the uptake.

'Well, that would be wonderful,' said Lee. 'But I need you to be my special little girl, not my wife.'

'Oh,' said Ava. She looked at me sideways. 'Is Dol your wife now?'

'No!' Lee said hurriedly. Then he looked worried because he'd sounded so adamant. 'I mean, Dol would be a lovely wife, but she's my new *friend*.'

'I used to have one, two, three friends at nursery – Asma and Becky and Daniel,' said Ava. 'But now I don't go to nursery any more, I just stay with Mummy and my other daddy and sometimes Granny, and we don't paint and play in the sandpit and sing.'

'You'll be going to proper school in September,' Lee said. 'And Phil isn't actually your daddy, he's just Mummy's boyfriend.' He was clearly making an effort to keep his voice matter of fact but he said the word 'boyfriend' as if it was a synonym for 'evil, wife-stealing bastard'.

'What would you like to be wearing in the picture, Ava?' I said quickly. 'Princess clothes or dungarees like the man who looks a bit like Daddy? No, *I* know! We'll give you fairy clothes. Look at all the fairy postcards on the wall and choose which sort of fairy you'd like to be.'

She ran to the wall eagerly and scrutinized them, row by row. It took her a long time. While she was absorbed in choosing, I whispered to Lee, 'I bet Phil-my-other-daddy is a total prick.'

'You're dead right. Cock of the walk, skin-tight suit, flash car, pinky ring,' said Lee disdainfully. 'They met at this wedding we all went to. My wife's friend Laura was getting married again. Her brother Phil was best man. Ava was actually the flower girl. It's all like a sitcom: sort of cringe-funny, unless you happen to be part of it.'

I reached out and patted his arm. 'Still, you've got Ava and she obviously hero-worships you. I've had totally rubbish relationships, and no daughter at all,' I said.

'But you like being a tattooist, don't you?' he asked.

'It's OK. Especially when I can make up a new design. It gets a bit samey, though. But I suppose everything does. Do you like gardening?'

'I love it,' he said, his face relaxing, his eyes bright again. 'I used to be an electrician, and it was good money – but I hated it. I loved gardening, though – read up about it, did a course, and I've gardened ever since.'

'And this new gardening job for the old lady?'

'It's going to be hard work for a year or more, getting it back into shape, but it'll be worth it seeing it all come back to life,' he said, spreading his fingers wide.

'You sound like Mary in *The Secret Garden*,' I said. 'It's a book,' I added, when he looked blank.

'I thought you said you didn't read much?'

'I listen on audio. It's fantastic. I often listen to a story when I'm doing a boring old flash design. The clients don't mind when they see my ear pods, they think I'm listening to music to get me in the right mood. Heavy metal for the bikers wanting something dark, Taylor Swift for the girly daisy brigade,' I say.

'So what music would you pretend to be listening to if you were tattooing me?' he asked.

I thought hard. 'Maybe . . . country? Or classic rock – Queen?'

'Spot on! And what kind of tattoo would I choose?'

'That's simple. You'd have a little heart inside your wrist with "Ava" written on it,' I said.

'Maybe I'll get you to do it for me, if I can pluck up the courage. I'm not a great fan of needles,' he said.

'Oh, I'd be very gentle,' I said. 'You'd hardly feel it.' He held out his arm and with the tip of my finger I gave his wrist little feathery taps.

'What are you two doing?' Ava asked, turning round.

I blushed scarlet. We were flirting, that's what we were doing. We pulled apart, not meeting each other's gaze.

'Have you chosen your fairy outfit, Ava?' I asked.

'I think so. It's this one,' she said, pointing.

'Sweet pea!' I said, making a lucky guess. 'I love her pink dress and her pale-green tights.'

'And she has a baby sister,' Ava said delightedly.

Lee went still. He swallowed. 'Mummy's not having another baby, is she?' he asked, trying to sound nonchalant.

Ava wrinkled her nose. 'No!'

'Oh,' said Lee, breathing out. 'That's good.'

'*I'm* her baby!' said Ava. 'And I'm your baby too, Daddy!'

'Yep, my little baby,' said Lee, and he gave her a big hug and sat her on his lap. 'Oh darling, I've missed you so much.'

'I've missed you too,' said Ava. She craned her neck, checking that I'd started drawing her fairy outfit. 'Can I colour in my dress, Dol?'

'Yes, of course you can,' I said.

'I won't go over the lines,' she promised.

She did her best, taking her time, breathing heavily. She was doing well until her hand shook and the pink suddenly wiggled downwards beneath the hem of the fairy outfit.

'I've spoilt it!' she wailed, nearly in tears.

'No, you haven't! That pink line can be your fairy tail,' I said.

'Fairies don't have tails,' she said, frowning at me.

'Yes, they do,' I insisted. 'They're a very important part of fairies. It helps them balance when they perch anywhere.'

'I've never seen a fairy tail,' said Ava, clearly suspicious.

'That's because they keep them tucked in their knickers most of the time, all neatly coiled up. But when they're sure no one's watching they take their tails out and wave them around,' I said.

'I think you're teasing me,' said Ava.

'No, she's not,' said Lee. 'Remember that big red book I read to you sometimes – what was it called? *The Big Book of Fairy Tales*!'

I laughed at the joke and Ava laughed too.

'Oh yes, I've got a fairy mouse toy with a tail!' she said, grinning.

'Ah! You've reminded me, Ava. Dol has brought you a very special present,' Lee said. He went to his cupboard and took out my tissue-wrapped wooden house. He'd added a red ribbon and heart stickers to make it look even more special.

I was really touched. Lee *did* like it, then. I so hoped Ava would too.

'Here we are, Dol. You give it to her.'

Ava clapped her hands. 'Is it really a present for me?' she asked eagerly.

'Don't get too excited, now,' I said. The house was quite plain, smooth pale wood rather than the bright plastic most kids preferred nowadays. It didn't have any proper furniture to arrange inside, just the four little carved mice. They weren't cartoon-style animals, wearing clothes – just a quartet of simple brown mice.

If Ava had been any other child, she'd have torn the paper off, peered at the house, shaken it, taken the lid off and scooped up the mice and then dropped them back where they came from. She might have given me a cursory thanks, or she might not even have bothered.

But Ava wasn't any other child. She undid the ribbon, then wound it round her hand tidily, like a little old lady. Then she unwrapped the tissue paper, her small teeth tucked over her bottom lip in anticipation.

She gave a gasp as she saw the house, and ran one hand over its smooth surface.

'It's beautiful,' she said solemnly. She lifted it up and heard the mice moving – it was almost a scuffling sound. 'There's someone inside!' she whispered.

'Why don't you take the roof off and have a peep?' said Lee.

She wasn't quite sure how to do it so he helped her.

'See who you can find,' he said.

Ava felt and then held up the smallest mouse.

'Oh, he's so little! And he has a wiggly tail just like the fairy!' she exclaimed.

'I think you'll find he's got several friends,' said Lee.

Ava found the other three and stood them in size order on the table.

'I love them all! Especially the teeny-tiny one! Oh, Daddy, are they really mine?'

'Yes, all for you. But don't thank me, thank Dol.'

Ava gently put the mice back in their house and ran to me.

'Thank you, thank you!' she cried, and gave me a big hug.

I hugged her back, now glad a hundred times over that I'd given her the mouse house.

Ava knelt down and played with the mice, making them scuttle round the tray looking for cheese. Lee sprinkled a few crumbs of real cheddar for them to enjoy. She turned the mice into four friends, Asma, Becky, Daniel and Ava. She'd named the tiniest mouse after herself.

'Don't you want to be the biggest one?' Lee asked her.

'Don't worry. Teeny-tiny Ava bosses the others around and they have to do what she says,' Ava said serenely.

I wasn't sure this was the case in real life but I was glad she could make it happen when she was pretending. It was the sort of thing I'd done as a child. It was so strange. I loved baby Christopher, of course, my beautiful little nephew, but I identified much more with this girl. She was like the daughter I'd never had.

12

When I woke up on Sunday I could hear Lee and Ava playing together. I reached for my drawing pad and started inventing parent-and-child designs: a father cradling a baby in his arms; a father holding hands with a small child; a father and a small daughter dancing together. The back of my neck tingled as I drew. I knew I was on to another winner. There were so many proud dads wanting to celebrate new fatherhood by marking it in some way. A Dol Westward special tattoo would be just the trick.

After a while, I heard Lee and Ava having breakfast, getting washed and dressed for the day. I stayed drawing in bed, thinking they'd want some precious time together, but I heard Ava pleading.

Then there was a tentative tap on my door, and I jumped out of bed, heart racing. Why hadn't I showered and spruced myself up a bit? At the very least washed my face and brushed my hair – and I didn't even have a proper dressing gown. In the end, I had no choice but to answer the door in my nightie *again*, feeling desperately self-conscious – and there they were, Lee and Ava, fully dressed and ready for the morning.

'Oh God, Dol, I'm so sorry. We've woken you up!' Lee said, looking stricken. 'There, Ava, I told you it was too early!'

Ava bit her lip and ducked her head.

'No, it's fine, honestly. I wasn't asleep. I was in bed, drawing,' I said, keen to reassure her.

'Have you done another picture of Daddy and me?' Ava asked, not at all shy now. 'Oh, let me see, please!'

She went running past me towards my bed.

'Ava! Come back here!' Lee said, trying to sound stern. 'Say sorry to Dol for disturbing her!'

'Sorry,' Ava said over her shoulder, but she'd found my drawing pad. She flipped through all the gothic stuff, totally uninterested, smiled at the princesses and then stopped at the new father-and-daughter page in delight.

'Look, Daddy! It's lots of daddies and their little girls, just like you and me!' Ava declared.

'I was trying out new designs for tattoos,' I said, looking at Lee. 'They're not portraits of you and Ava, they're more generic, obviously.'

I meant it, and yet when I looked at them now, I realized they were how I'd imagined Lee caring for Ava when she was a baby.

'They're beautiful,' said Lee. 'Can I have a copy of this?'

'Where? On your chest? Back?' I teased him. 'A full sleeve?'

Lee grinned ruefully and ran his hand through his curls. 'A picture on the page, not on me, thanks.'

'*I* want a picture on me!' said Ava. 'On my arm so I can look at it whenever I want.'

'Little girls don't have tattoos,' said Lee.

'But you said I'm a big girl now,' Ava argued.

'I'll do you a felt-pen tattoo on your arm and then you can wash it off when you get fed up with it,' I offered.

'Oh, yes, please. One of me and Daddy!' Ava asked. 'That would be lovely, wouldn't it?' She looked at Lee for confirmation.

'Yes, it would, but maybe Mummy wouldn't like it,' Lee said

awkwardly. 'Tell you what, why don't you choose a little animal, seeing as we're going to the zoo?'

'Good idea! Which animal would you like, Ava? Let me see . . . I can do a very cute baby dragon. Or maybe a baby unicorn with just a tiny stub of horn?'

'Oh, a unicorn!' Ava cried, enchanted by the idea.

'Now she's going to expect to see unicorns at the zoo,' said Lee. 'Would you like to come with us, Dol?'

'It's lovely of you to invite me, but I'm sure you'll have much more fun just the two of you,' I said quickly, not wanting to intrude on their time together.

Lee misunderstood. 'I know the whole zoo concept is a bit dodgy nowadays, but this is a really well-run children's zoo. No large animals, no stark cages. We've been loads of times, and the animals all seem healthy and happy,' he assured me.

'I'm sure it is. Actually, I've never been to a zoo before,' I admitted, feeling foolish. Marigold never took us because she hated the thought of anything being kept in confinement. I suppose this was understandable, because the nuns of her childhood had apparently locked her in a cupboard when she misbehaved, and certainly as an adult she'd been shut up in enough psychiatric hospitals to give her a phobia about it.

The image of her cowering under the sheets threatened to overwhelm me for a moment – but Primrose Ward seemed better than most, and Dr Gibbon was gentle and understanding. And she'd seemed surprisingly lucid yesterday, so their treatment might be helping already.

Star had said I should start thinking about myself now, not Marigold. I'd be visiting her this afternoon anyway. I'd always longed to see what zoos were like, but didn't want to go by myself in case I looked odd without a child in tow.

'I'd love to come,' I found myself saying.

I drew a little silvery-white unicorn on Ava's wrist so she could look at it properly all day. It had a twisted silver horn with matching hooves, dark blue eyes and light blue shading. He looked adorable. I thought of a new design for work: a baby lion cub and infant unicorn as a heraldic device, holding up a crest with the name of a newborn baby in fancy writing. I seemed to be on a roll, thinking up new designs every day.

Lee and Ava popped back next door while I showered and dressed in my best jeans and a blue teeshirt with silver moons, a Christmas present from Star. I didn't have a proper mirror, just a small glass rectangle above the washbasin, but I felt I didn't look too bad. I tried putting my hair up with a scrunchie, but I couldn't get it to look right so I wore it loose instead.

Lee had decided not to bother with Ava's plaits either, so her hair bounced on her shoulders too. I couldn't help wondering if anyone might think us a real family, with Ava my own daughter.

The zoo was only half an hour's drive away in Lee's van. Ava ran around, greeting her favourite animals as if they were old friends. She particularly loved the capybaras. They looked like huge guinea pigs and I felt a little wary of them, but Ava knew them by name and seemed ready to leap the barrier to give them all a cuddle. She adored the meercats too, especially as there was a special tunnel you could crawl through so you bobbed up with your head right in the middle of their enclosure, safely inside in transparent plastic. There was no stopping Ava, who bounced up in the bubble and chatted animatedly to all the meercats, even though they ignored her.

The zoo had its fair share of rides and novelties too. Ava begged to try an enclosed climbing tower and battled her way to the very top, though she was the smallest of all the children and some of them tried to push her out the way. It didn't look at all safe and I found myself gripping Lee's arm tightly as we sat watching – but Ava triumphed and we gave her a big cheer when she eventually emerged, grinning.

We had pizza slices and salad for lunch, and then Lee let Ava have a huge iced bun for pudding – 'Though don't you dare tell your mum!'

Inevitably Ava could only manage a few mouthfuls and then started furtively putting little chunks into her jeans pocket. Lee gently stopped her.

'It's OK, Ava, Dol and I will share it,' he said.

I was full myself, but I loved the idea of sharing, and found I was eating up my share heartily.

'I can't believe it's nearly time to take Ava back,' Lee sighed. 'The time's gone so quickly! Still, at least I'll be seeing her regularly now, every weekend.'

'Your wife – ex, whatever – won't try to stop you seeing her so much?' I whispered, as Ava gathered up our plates and cleared our table, playing at being waitress.

'I think she's glad, to be honest. It gives her more time alone with lover-boy,' said Lee.

'Still, that's good if you get to see Ava.'

'Absolutely,' he said, brightening. 'This has been a fantastic weekend.'

'I hope I haven't got in the way too much,' I said anxiously.

'You're part of the reason it's been fantastic,' he said.

I couldn't help twitching because it sounded so cheesy, but I could see he was being sincere.

'It's been fantastic for me too,' I said.

We went back home so that Lee could help Ava pack her bag.

'What are we going to do about your lovely mouse house?' he asked her.

He said she could take it away with her as she liked it so much, but she shook her head.

'No, you look after it for me, Daddy,' she said. 'I want to keep it special here. Oh, I forgot!' She searched the pocket of her jeans and pulled out several pieces of squashed iced bun – and the smallest of the wooden mice.

'*My* mouse wanted to come to the zoo with us. She liked it a lot, especially being fed,' said Ava. 'But I'll put her back in her house with her friends now.'

'Well, I'll feed her for you till you come back next weekend. Only six days, Ava! Not too long at all,' said Lee, trying to stay upbeat, but he said it as if it was six months.

He gave me a lift to the hospital in the van, insisting it was on his way. Ava gave me a big hug goodbye, winding her arms tightly round my neck, and I felt a tug of love for her, even though I'd only met her yesterday. If it felt like that for me, Lee must be going through agonies, though he was smiling bravely, and as the van drove off I could see they'd started a sing-song.

It had been such a happy time. I wished I could just sit at home and draw some more and mull everything over. But I had to go to the hospital.

Marigold wasn't out in the ward, and her cubicle door was shut. When I looked through the window, I saw that the sheet was up over her head again. I started shaking. I'd let myself relax and be happy, but now I had to pay for it.

'Marigold?' I whispered, walking into her cubicle. 'It's me, Dol.'

She murmured something indistinct.

'I can't quite hear you. Can I move your sheet just a little bit so we can talk?'

She reached up and pulled it down herself. Her eyes were hazy, not focusing properly, but she murmured, 'Hello, Dol.'

'That's better,' I said.

'That's worse,' she said. 'I look like fuck. I *feel* like fuck.'

'I expect that's the drugs kicking in now, calming you down.

But you actually look much better,' I said, really meaning it. Her nose still looked odd, but less swollen. Her black eyes and bruises were still dramatic, but perhaps they were starting to fade. Her lip was healing now, just cracking a little as she tried to smile.

'You're such a liar, Dol,' she said. 'So where's your sister and my grandson?'

'Star's had to go home to Scotland, remember?'

'She was only here two minutes!' Marigold complained.

'But you wouldn't speak to her!'

'Yeah, well, why should I? She's ashamed of me, isn't she?' Marigold stuck her chin in the air defiantly, but she looked upset. 'My eldest daughter the fucking doctor.'

'You're a bit too fucky this afternoon,' I said brightly. I sounded like a gently disapproving nanny and fidgeted, embarrassed.

'She looks down on you too, Dol,' said Marigold, her tone darkening.

'I know.'

'And that baby gave me a look, like he didn't reckon me for a grandma.'

I tutted. 'You didn't see him! All that fuss about him and yet when he's here you wouldn't even give him a cuddle!' I said. 'You're the most contrary woman in the world.'

'I can't help it. I have a severe mental disorder,' Marigold said shirtily.

'Mostly because you won't take your medicine,' I nagged.

'Oh, fuck off,' said Marigold, and pulled her bedclothes back over her head.

It was banal and blackly comical. Sometimes I even wondered if she was pretending to be ill. It didn't really matter. I still had to put up with her.

'I've come specially to visit you. You could at least look at me properly,' I said, trying to keep my temper.

'I've got X-ray eyes. I can see right through the sheets,' said Marigold.

'For God's sake, how old are you? Six – or fifty-six?'

'Better than six six six, the sign of Beelzebub.'

'Don't start all that crappy Black Arts stuff. You know it's all complete bollocks,' I said.

Marigold pulled the covers down a bit so she could peer at me.

'You're a bit full of yourself today, Madam. What have you been up to?'

'I've been to the zoo with Lee and Ava,' I said.

'Who the fuck is he?'

'*Lee!* The lovely guy who picked you up from Gatwick!'

'Oh, *him*!' Marigold said disparagingly. 'And Ava? Don't like that name!'

'It's a lovely name. She's Lee's little girl,' I said.

'I see! He's just after someone to look after her,' said Marigold.

'That's ridiculous!' I said furiously.

Surely she can't be right? Why do people keep mistaking me for a nanny?

'He's the loveliest, kindest guy and looks after Ava beautifully himself,' I said. 'I'm going now if you're just going to be hateful.'

'Push off then,' she said, but her arm snaked out of the sheet and she grabbed my wrist to show she really wanted me to stay.

I melted a little then, but it turned out it was mostly because she wanted me to go to her flat to get her some more clothes and some flat shoes for her physio session, though both she and I knew she'd never owned a flat pair of shoes since she was twelve.

'You find them for me, but that lazy bastard Rick can bring them. Why hasn't he come to visit me?'

'Perhaps because he *isn't* the loveliest, kindest guy?' I suggested.

'Who wants Mr Nicey Nicey anyway? They're not likely to give you a thrill,' said Marigold.

'A thrill?' I repeated, with contempt. 'You've gone out of your way to find men who will let you down.'

'But they give me a good time too. You wait, Dol. Maybe one day you'll fall heavily for someone and then you'll know you don't give a damn how they treat you, you'll put up with anything just to get that high when you're with them.'

'I suppose that's the way it was with Micky?'

'That's the way it was,' said Marigold, and she shut her eyes tight to stop the tears leaking down her cheeks.

I sat beside her on the hard hospital chair, holding her hand, not trying to talk any more. It was difficult to keep feeling angry with her when she looked so sad.

When visiting hours finished I leant forward and kissed her and then slipped my hand out of her grasp. She didn't try to hang on to me this time. Maybe she was asleep.

The thought of going back to her flat was daunting to say the least. What if Rick was still there? I wondered if I should ask Lee to come with me when he got back from delivering Ava to her mother. It seemed one request too far, though. I couldn't keep begging him to do these awful things for me. And I wasn't sure how he'd manage if it all turned ugly. He was strong and could probably hold his own in a fist fight, but Rick was the type to fight dirty – maybe he had a knife. Better to wait till tomorrow and beg Big Al to help me, though it wasn't really fair of me to involve him either.

I wished I'd told Star and asked her to come to the flat with me. But then she had Christopher, and we couldn't risk a baby being around that man. Should I go to the police? But I didn't think they'd be willing to get involved, especially as Marigold had invited him to stay with her and given him a key. It struck me that if I *did* manage to get him out, I'd have to get the lock changed. Would I even be able to do that if my name wasn't on the lease?

I dithered outside the hospital, clenching my fists, helpless – and then hit myself hard on the thigh. What was the matter with me, still acting like a frightened little kid when I was in my thirties? It was time I grew up.

I caught the bus to Marigold's road and walked along it, planting one foot determinedly in front of the other. My hand was shaking as I put the key in the lock. It didn't turn properly at first, and I wondered if Rick had got there before me and changed the lock himself. But then it clicked into place and the door opened.

I held my breath, bracing myself for Rick's whining voice. Or had he left but trashed the place? There was a smell, but it seemed to be just stale air and rotting food in the bin. Greasy dishes were heaped in the sink, a tap left dripping – but that was probably the usual state of the kitchen.

I checked the bathroom for Rick's stuff, though he didn't seem to wash or shave too regularly. I looked in the living room: used coffee cups, glasses, a couple of bottles on their sides, a cushion flung on the floor. I went next door to the bedroom. The bed was unmade, the sheets tumbled and grubby, the pillows stained, one faintly orange from hair dye. I looked in the wardrobe but it just contained Marigold's skimpy clothes, dangling pathetically from their hangers. I looked in both bedside cabinets but there was no drug gear, no packets of weed.

Rick really had cleared off! I'd actually got rid of him! I punched the air in triumph and then set to, trying to clean up the flat so it wasn't so seedy and depressing. I scrubbed and vacuumed, changed the sheets, put a wash on, and after an hour's hard work the flat was still shabby but immaculate. Then I foraged for suitable outfits for Marigold's hospital stay, feeling bad that I hadn't got this organized before, though she was still mostly confined to bed in a hospital gown.

Some of her clothes dated back many years. I found a flimsy summer dress I'd loved when I was a child because it had a mermaid design with mother-of-pearl buttons down the front. I'd often dressed up in it when Marigold was out or asleep, wafting around the flat making breaststroke gestures with my arms, pretending to be a mermaid myself. It wasn't as wonderful as I remembered – it was very limp and crumpled, and the mermaids looked grotesque, with over-developed breasts and the wide-open lips of a porn doll. But on a whim I took off my clothes and pulled it on over my head.

I peered at myself in the spotted wardrobe mirror. The dress fitted me now, but I still looked like a child dressing up in my mother's clothes. The pearl buttons didn't go high enough, exposing too much flat white chest, and my small bottom didn't fill out the back properly, so that the material puckered.

I sighed, wriggled out of the dress and returned it to the back of the wardrobe. I tried to find three outfits that looked relatively suitable for the day ward in a hospital but was hard-pressed to find anything to fit the bill. In the end I made do with a pair of skin-tight pale-denim jeans, a miniskirt, a striped shirt and two tight teeshirts. None of them were appropriate for a sick woman in her fifties, but it couldn't be helped.

I went down on my knees and fumbled in the darkness at the bottom of her wardrobe among a forest of high-heeled shoes, and managed to find a pair of flat silver sandals that would have to do for now. By some miracle, Marigold had a roll of black plastic rubbish bags in among a clutter of cutlery in her kitchen drawer. I used one for her clothes, emptied all the greasy rubbish into another, and then locked up the flat, wondering how long it would be before Marigold would be back living in it. I couldn't help hoping it would be a good long while. I wanted her to get better, of course, but when she was locked up in hospital I didn't have to worry about her coming to harm. Getting her to still pay the rent might be a problem, but I could get on with my own life, just about.

When I got back to my own home there was no sign of life coming from Lee's room. He didn't return until much later. I was disappointed when I heard him trudge past my door, not bothering to knock. I wondered if I should knock at *his* door – but perhaps he didn't feel like company. I heard him having a shower but there was no whistling. It didn't sound as if he was making himself a meal. Perhaps he was going straight to bed. He was probably tired out from the journey. Or very down because he was missing Ava already. He'd turned his room into a child's fairyland, but it must be painful being inside it when his little girl wasn't there.

I found I was pressing my hand against the wall in sympathy. I imagined him pressing his own palm back on the other side. Then I went to bed myself. I couldn't help wishing our friendship had gone one step further. It wasn't that I really wanted to have sex with him. It would just be so good to be curled up together, and not feel so alone.

13

The first thing I heard when I woke next morning was Lee bustling about, getting ready to go to his new full-time gardening job. When I heard him opening his door, I plucked up the courage to stick my head around my own. He was used to seeing me in my nightie now.

'Good luck with the new job,' I said.

'Thanks, Dol,' he said warmly. He was wearing a fresh checked shirt, still with the creases from the package, clean dark jeans, and newish-looking workman boots instead of his usual scruffy trainers. He was clearly making an effort, and I was amazed what a difference it made. He looked surprisingly good – kind of sexy, in a big lumberjack sort of way.

'How did the hospital visit go?' he asked.

'Not too badly,' I said. 'And your journey back with Ava?'

'OK,' he said flatly, sighing wearily. 'Though it's always bloody painful saying goodbye to her. She cried when she got to her new home, clinging to me, and Phil the Prick had the cheek to tell her to stop being so naughty. I nearly punched him, but didn't want to worry Ava.'

'Awful for you, and for Ava too,' I said, aching for her.

'Anyway, the weekends together are still going to happen, and Ava will get used to the routine, even though it must be a struggle for her,' Lee said.

'And a struggle for you too.' I felt so sorry for him I gave him a hug.

For a second he seemed startled – I certainly was. But then his arms went around me too and we stayed like that, pressed close together, for a good half-minute. He felt so steady and strong. I breathed in his warm smell of coconut shampoo and toast and new shirt. I could feel his heart beating fast against my cheek. I wanted to press even closer but I made myself pull away gently.

'You'd better get going. You'll be late for work,' I said.

'You're right. But I wish I could stay,' he said. Then he kissed me quickly on the cheek, just a friendly brush of his lips again.

What would it feel like if he kissed me properly? Did I really want to know? Or was I just confused, because he was the most decent man I'd met in years? Not the sexiest. I still couldn't forget the dark actor with his mask tattoo – but I had to avoid that sort of guy. Lee would never hurt me, never break my heart.

I hung over the banisters, watching him go down all the stairs. He peered up and saw me and waved. Then he was out the front door and I went back into my room to get ready for my own work, taking my drawing pad with me.

I showed Brian all the new designs, hoping he'd be impressed. He looked at them for a long time, pursing his lips, considering.

'Mm, quite promising!' he said eventually. 'Though a tad sentimental?'

'Come on, Brian, they're bloody brilliant,' said Jo.

'You're a genius, Dolly,' said Big Al, clapping me on the back.

I murmured that they were really nothing special, I was just doodling to amuse a little girl, but I was thrilled they were treating me like Michelangelo. I got to work on a big tough guy who wanted a portrait of his pet dog on his calf. He showed me a photo: I'd expected a German Shepherd or a Staffie – but she was a dainty little Bichon Frisé.

'Her name's Blossom,' he told me proudly.

I managed a reasonable likeness and he went away delighted.

'I've got portraits of all the dogs I've ever had on my legs,' Big Al confided unexpectedly. 'It's a way of remembering them.'

'Come on then, show us,' said Jo.

He unzipped his jeans and pulled them down to his knees while we gazed at the little troupe of dogs dancing round his burly thighs. It was oddly moving.

'What on earth are you doing?' A scowling blonde woman stamped into the studio in kitten heels. She had a fluffy kitten on her sweater too, but there was nothing remotely fluffy about her. She had her hands on her hips, looking outraged.

'Al, pull your kecks up!' Brian said sharply. 'I'm so sorry, madam. Just a bit of tomfoolery. How can we help you?'

'Are you the owner of this place?' she demanded.

'I am,' said Brian.

'Well, I don't think you will be much longer!' she said, eyeing him balefully. 'I'm going to do my damnedest to close your shop down. You're breaking the law!'

Brian rolled his eyes. Just occasionally, Artful Ink attracted crazy people who thought tattoo studios were dens of iniquity. The popularity of the Satan flash didn't help. 'It's not illegal to run a fully licensed, immaculately hygienic tattoo studio,' he said.

'But it *is* illegal to tattoo a child!' she growled.

'I assure you no children have ever been given a tattoo here,' said Brian, outraged.

'My thirteen-year-old daughter – *thirteen!* – came here a few days ago and came home with a ludicrous tattoo on her arm!' she said furiously.

We all stared at her. Jo crinkled her nose at me and Big Al mouthed, *'Nuts!'*

Brian shook his head at her. 'Are you sure it's not some kind of transfer?' he asked.

'Are you suggesting I'm simple? It's a tattoo, a real tattoo from this establishment. Look!' She took a card out of her handbag. It was our own black-and-white card, designed by me.

Brian frowned when he saw it. 'I don't know where you got that from or what it signifies, but I can promise you, hand on heart, we would never in a million years tattoo a child. I don't know how your daughter acquired her tattoo, but it's simply not possible it came from here.'

'Are you calling me a liar?' she asked.

'I'm suggesting you're mistaken. We always require proof of age from younger clients and document it,' said Brian, going to the record book. 'What's your daughter's name? And why haven't you brought her with you?'

'Her name's Sarah Bentley – and I'm not dragging her out of school and bringing her all the way here from Surbiton!' she said.

Surbiton! My heart started thumping. Oh my God, not the girl I'd fobbed off with a baby dragon? But I'd seen her passport, looked at her photo, checked her date of birth. She was eighteen.

'There's no Sarah Bentley here,' Brian said. 'There's a *Kate* Bentley, but definitely no Sarah. And we have her passport details, take a look!'

'You fools!' said the mother. 'Sarah obviously took her sister's passport, the crafty little monkey. But surely you realized she's only a kid? She could never pass for eighteen! Which of you was the idiot who tattooed her?'

I swallowed hard. My mouth was so dry I could hardly speak. 'I'm afraid it was me,' I said hoarsely. 'But I didn't dream she was so young. She had the money and everything and, as Brian says, I checked her ID.'

'*My* money, that I keep in my dressing-table drawer to give to the cleaning lady!' she spat. 'It's been a nightmare weekend of revelations. First I spotted the dreadful mark on her arm when I accidentally walked in on her in the bathroom. She'd kept it carefully covered up for days. And then I discovered she was a little thief on top of everything else.' She was nearly in tears now, and I couldn't help feeling sorry for her, as well as scared for myself.

'Well, I'm afraid we can't take responsibility if your daughter lied to us, Mrs Bentley,' Brian said firmly.

'Oh yes you can, and you will! We've looked it all up on the internet! We're going to get you fined good and proper. Hopefully you'll lose your licence and have to close down your wretched place. And we're thinking of going to the press too, telling them how you lured silly young girls to come for these ugly tattoos, advertising on social media.'

Brian's smooth expression didn't change but I saw the fear in his eyes.

'I think that's rather an extreme reaction, especially as your daughter went out of her way to hoodwink us. These young girls, eh? And she obviously comes from a good home. I can see why you're distressed, but I'm sure you can take Sarah for lasering treatment. Two or three sessions and the tattoo will be gone without trace. And although it's not our responsibility, as a gesture of goodwill, we will offer to pay for the lasering,' he said. 'So would you like the treatment to be in Surbiton? As soon as possible, I presume?'

'She's not having any lasering "as soon as possible"! Then we'll have lost our evidence, won't we? You must think I'm a fool, Mr Smart Arse. You're not going to get away with this! You're a danger to foolish young girls. I made my daughter show me how she found out about you. I *saw* the pornographic dragon-and-girl tattoo you posted on TikTok.'

I was starting to feel so sick I could hardly stand.

'It's not pornographic,' I protested weakly. 'There's no . . . sexual congress. They're just embracing.' It sounded so ridiculous that I couldn't stop my lip twitching.

'It's no laughing matter!' Mrs Bentley said, outraged. 'So did *you* do that dreadful design?'

'Well – well, yes, I did. It's because of this craze for romantasy, about dragon-riders. I expect your daughter reads the books, but anyway, I didn't do *that* design on her arm.'

'Because you saw she was a child – so you did her a childish little baby dragon!'

'No, because there wasn't time to do the design she wanted. I thought she looked young for her age, but she had her passport – the photo looked like her, and it never occurred to me that it was her sister's,' I stammered. It was the truth and yet I knew I didn't sound convincing. I tended to be able to pull off a lie, but I somehow sounded shifty when I was being totally honest.

'You deserve to be locked up! It's abuse, tattooing a child, whether she asked you to do it or not. I'm going to close down this hell-hole if it's the last thing I do!' Mrs Bentley declared, her face distorted with rage. Even the kitten on her jumper seemed to be scowling like a tiger now.

Everyone was staring at me. Jo looked near to tears, Big Al was wringing his hands helplessly – but Brian had his lip snagged in his teeth as he eyed me up and down, pondering.

'I can understand you taking this attitude, Mrs Bentley. I assure you it's all been a dreadful mistake. Dol here must have been totally convinced your daughter was eighteen. Perhaps she's a little gullible, who knows. Won't you forgive her and let me make amends?' Brian asked.

I was surprised he was sticking up for me, but hugely relieved all the same. I flashed him a little smile, but he didn't meet my eyes.

'No, I'm absolutely not going to forgive her! She's a disgrace – and so are you!' she declared.

'Well, not me, Mrs Bentley. I own the property, but the tattooists don't work for me. They simply pay me a percentage of their earnings as rent. They are freelance. Isn't that right?' said Brian, looking at Big Al and Jo.

'Well, I suppose you could say that, technically,' Big Al blundered.

'Exactly. So although it breaks my heart, because I'm very fond of little Dol here, I shall have to terminate our arrangement,' said Brian.

'What?' I gasped, reeling. I couldn't believe what he was saying.

'Plus, my offer of laser treatment still stands, Mrs Bentley. And you have my word I won't let her work here any more. Plus, I'll repay the fee charged to your daughter and obviously cover your expenses for your trip here, and a little extra as compensation for the shock you've suffered.'

'You can't do that!' said Jo, appalled.

Brian raised his eyebrows at her meaningfully. Perhaps he was trying to tell her it was all a bluff to get rid of Mrs Bentley? She was wavering, but then Brian opened up the till, stuffed full of twenties because many of our clients were the sort who liked to deal in cash. He took out a whole wad, enough to fill a large envelope, and handed it over.

I thought she was going to fling each note into his face like giant confetti, but she fingered it instead, counting it with nimble fingers, like a bank teller. She seemed satisfied by the total, squeezed the envelope into her handbag, gave Brian a curt nod, me a fierce glare, and went to the door.

'Don't think you can pull a fast one on me! I shall check to see if this evil little creature is still in your employment,' was her parting shot as she flounced out the door.

'What a cow!' said Jo, the moment she'd slammed it shut. 'As if it was poor Dol's fault. I saw that girl handing over that passport! How could a thirteen-year-old be such a scheming minx?'

'Takes after her mother,' said Big Al. He put his muscly arm round me, feeling me trembling. 'Don't you worry, Dol, Brian was just bluffing to get rid of her. Weren't you, Brian?'

He was taking out another much smaller wad of money, not bothering with an envelope this time. He held it out, not quite looking at me still.

'Here you are, Dol. You actually owe me for my percentage of your current takings but I want to be generous. This should keep you going for a few weeks.'

'You're really sacking me?' I cried. 'But it wasn't my fault! How was I to know it was her sister's passport?'

'That's as may be, girl, but I can't risk keeping you on after that. Now, off you go. That Bentley woman is probably watching at the end of the road.'

'You're not serious, Brian! You can't get rid of Dol! She's better than Big Al and me put together, and you know it!' cried Jo.

'Steady now,' said Big Al, waggling his eyebrows in protest, though he added, 'But you're right. It's not fair, Brian, and you know it.'

'Of course I fucking know it. But I can't risk that bitch making trouble if I don't. You're a lovely little worker, Dol, and we'll miss you,' said Brian with an air of finality.

'We're not standing for that,' said Jo. 'If you get rid of her then we'll walk too, won't we, Al? Then where will you be, Brian?'

Big Al held his hands up. 'Hang on a minute, Jo. I can't just down tools and bugger off into the wide blue yonder! I doubt I'd find another job. Guys like me have gone out of fashion. I know when I'm well off. The old bikers know I'm here, but all these rinky-dinky modern tattoo studios would never take me on.'

'You disloyal bastard,' said Jo indignantly. 'Well, *I'm* walking. We'll set up our own studio, you and me, Dol! It'll be fantastic.'

My heart leapt. Could we really do that?

But Brian was actually laughing. 'Oh yes? Do you two girls know how much it costs to rent a decent gaff, get it all set up and decorated, and get the licence? You're living in dreamland.'

Jo's mouth twisted sideways. I knew she'd just taken on a tiny flat with her wife and was forever worrying how they were going to pay the mortgage.

I couldn't let her make such a crazy sacrifice.

'You're so lovely, Jo, but actually I think Brian's right. It wouldn't work. And as a matter of fact, I've been thinking of chucking it all in anyway. My heart's not really in tattooing any more.' The last sentence was a downright lie. I'd been suddenly brimming over with enthusiasm, loving making up new custom designs. But I had to save face.

'Are you sure, Dol?' Jo asked anxiously.

'Certain,' I said as firmly as I could.

'Yeah, I sensed that,' Brian said. 'What with all this to-do about your mum and having to bunk off work – I've been good about that, now, haven't I? But if she's in hospital a while and you're visiting her every day, it's not going to be viable. I wouldn't have been able to let you keep your spot anyway. So take your money, girl.'

I took it and then shuffled to get my drawing pad from his desk.

'What are you doing?' Brian asked. His voice suddenly shifted from false compassion to sharp query.

'I'm taking my pad,' I said, astonished.

'Oh no. You gave it to me this morning. I approved all the designs. They're mine now,' said Brian.

I felt as if he'd punched me. 'I didn't *give* you them! You can't keep them!' I shouted. 'And there's all my private stuff too!'

'Here, Dolly,' said Jo, snatching the pad herself and thrusting it into my arms.

'Thanks, Jo. Love you so much,' I gabbled, and then I ran out the studio, stuffing the money down my bra and clasping the pad under my arm. I didn't dare loiter. Brian was quite capable of snatching it back. He was much bigger and heavier than me – but I was speedy. I ran full tilt, down the road, round the corner, down a lane, out on to the main road, then dodged down an alleyway, zig-zagging madly for a few minutes until I was certain he couldn't catch up with me.

I leant against a wall, panting so hard I thought I was going to be sick. I cradled my drawing pad like a baby. I started crying, and bent my head so no one could see. I struggled to make sense of everything. It had all happened so quickly. How could Brian have chucked me out just like that, after all the work I'd brought to the studio?

It wasn't my fault! It wasn't my fault! It wasn't my fault!

Or was it? I'd checked the passport, but had I asked her for any further proof? I suppose she *had* looked surprisingly young. Was I concentrating properly? Was I still caught up with worrying about Marigold? And oh God, was I also wondering whether Joel the actor would come back? It didn't really matter. I'd lost my job and I knew Brian would never back down now.

'What am I going to do?' I asked myself helplessly.

It's easy! You take Star up on her offer. You love that little baby. He's family. And so is Star.

But I didn't want to go running to her like this. I couldn't bear to tell her that I'd got the sack. It would be just too pathetic. I was *good* at my job, everyone said so. My tattoos were really in demand now. Fuck Brian. I'd go somewhere else. I'd show him!

I went to the two other tattoo studios in Seahaven, trying to act as confident as possible, waltzing in as if I was doing them a favour. But it didn't work. They both knew me, liked my work – but were dead suspicious about my leaving Artful Ink.

'I've had a row with Brian,' I said, insisting he'd got rid of me unfairly.

One owner suggested I might have been a bit lax with sterilizing, which infuriated me because I always took such pains to be hygienic. I walked out and tried the other studio instead. The second guy actually rang Brian to hear his side of the story – and I heard him talking about under-age clients and the vengeful Mrs Bentley. He shook his head at me.

'Sorry, Dol. It's probably not your fault – but basically, you're stuffed. I can't take you on.'

I decided to try further along the coast, clutching my drawing pad under my arm. Brighton would be my best bet, but I thought I'd better fit in a quick visit to Marigold first. If I *did* get a new job, I couldn't keep asking for time off straight away. I didn't have time to go all the way home again to fetch the clothes I'd retrieved from her flat.

She was sitting up sideways in bed, swinging her bare legs. I'd always envied their shapeliness, and her feet were beautiful, with a very high arch and perfectly straight toes. Dancers' feet. She loved to dance and insisted she'd been on the stage long ago in several musicals. I'd fully believed her when I was a little girl, but was less gullible now.

'Hello, Marigold,' I said wearily.

'Hello, darling Dol,' she said. She looked at me properly. 'Hey, you look a bit of a droopy-drawers. What's up?'

I took a deep breath, but found I couldn't bear to recount it all. I remembered how pointless it had been telling her I was having a hard time at school. She was always on my side but wanted to make a terrible fuss on my behalf, which generally made things worse.

'Just a bit of bother at work,' I mumbled.

'That Brian kicking off?' she asked, surprising me by remembering his name. 'He sounds a total wanker. Take no notice of him, Dol. Anyway, where are they?'

'Where are what?' I asked, sitting beside her.

'My clothes! You haven't forgotten them, have you?'

'No, I've found you some, but they're still at home,' I said.

Her mouth opened wide in agony, like Munch's *The Scream* — a weirdly popular flash design. 'Well, why didn't you bring them with you?' she demanded. 'I *need* them! For God's sake, is it too much to ask you to fetch me a few decent clothes?' She pulled at her skimpy teeshirt in disgust. 'I'm fed up of wearing this, but you should have seen the old-lady rags they offered me! You haven't even bothered to go round to my flat, have you?'

'Yes, I did! I chose some clothes, but they were all a bit manky, you know that stale wardrobe smell, so I washed them, but they were still damp this morning. I'll bring them tomorrow,' I promised.

'Yes, and tomorrow you'll say you'll bring them tomorrow, and then when it's another tomorrow you'll say you'll bring them tomorrow and—'

'All *right*!' I snapped. 'I swear I'll bring them tomorrow. Now I have to go.'

'But you've only just got here!' Marigold wailed.

'Marigold, I've got a job to do,' I said, although my problem now was the exact opposite.

'Isn't anyone else going to come and visit me?' Marigold complained, sitting cross-legged now and staring at me, her chin jutting. 'Where's your sister and that baby?'

'I told you, they've gone back to Scotland.'

'Well, tell them to come back!' Marigold commanded, and then had the grace to burst out laughing, hearing how ridiculous she sounded.

'You should have made the most of them when they came all the way to visit you,' I said.

'I didn't know what to say to them,' Marigold said, her wide smile fading. 'That Star isn't like *my* Star. Is that me being crazy?'

'No, she's not really my Star either,' I admitted.

'Thank God you haven't gone all posh and given yourself airs,' said Marigold. 'You're not going to run off and be a doctor too, are you?'

'As if! I couldn't write a prescription to save my life.'

I thought of all those red circles around the misspelt words in my school exercise books.

'Why didn't they give me extra help at school?' I asked Marigold. 'And aren't there special schools just for dyslexic pupils?'

'Don't ask me,' said Marigold, shrugging.

'Couldn't you have taken me to some educational specialist or something?' I persisted. 'Then I might have learnt to read properly and I could have studied and got a proper qualification.'

'Don't be daft, Dol. You were always a bit thick,' she said.

'Thanks!' I said, stung. 'Many highly intelligent people have dyslexia. It's nothing to do with intellect. Oli told me that. He actually studied it when he was doing his English degree.'

'Oh, well, if Oli says so!' Marigold said disparagingly. 'And I'm not meaning to be horrid, just truthful. *I'm* thick. And I didn't just get told off, those nuns whipped me savagely every time I made a mistake.'

Those bloody nuns again! Their brutality had escalated over the years. First it was shouting. Then smacking. Now they were flicking their whips. Doubtless next year they'd be punching her senseless. Why did she have to keep on and on whining about the past? Oh God, why did *I* keep on about my own past? I buried my head in my hands and we sat in silence for a minute until I couldn't stand it any more.

'I have to go now,' I said, getting off the bed. 'See you tomorrow.'

'Why doesn't Rick drag his lazy arse here? Doesn't he care about me?' Marigold wailed.

'I think he's pushed off,' I said gently.

Marigold called him a sharp, ugly word. She said it so vehemently that a passing visitor glared at her and another patient heard and said it too, again and again, setting up a chant.

'Now look what you've started,' I scolded, but Marigold didn't seem to care. She was moaning to herself about Rick, but she didn't sound truly upset.

'You don't really love him, do you?' I asked. I hoped not, seeing as he'd taken that young girl back to his bed the moment Marigold disappeared. Should I tell her? No, it might make her even angrier.

She thought about it. 'Nah,' she said. 'I suppose he's just company. I get so lonely, Dol.'

'I know. I'm sorry.' I squeezed her hand.

'If only Micky would come back,' she whispered.

'But he's not going to. You know that, don't you?'

'Yes, but it doesn't stop me wanting it,' she said, and started crying, genuinely this time.

An incredibly thin girl in a huge sweater and baggy jeans appeared at the door, looking concerned. I thought she was a child at first, then realized she was in her late teens or early twenties.

'You all right, Marigold?' she asked.

Marigold shook her head sadly. I suddenly noticed she was back to being properly red-haired, no grey roots at all.

'You've managed to dye your hair!' I exclaimed, holding her at arms' length.

'She helped me,' Marigold sniffed.

The girl nodded. 'I'm training as a hairdresser,' she said. Her own long hair was extremely fine, so that her scalp was visible. She brushed it over her shoulders self-consciously with her skeleton fingers. Her wrists were so thin they seemed ready to snap if you touched them. She looked as if she had terminal cancer, but if she was in Primrose then she was probably anorexic.

'It was very kind of you,' I said, and she ducked her head shyly.

'We look after each other, Lettie and me,' said Marigold. 'Don't we, girlie?'

'Yes, we do,' said Lettie.

They smiled at each other and then *held hands*! I gaped at them. I knew people formed close relationships very quickly in hospitals out of camaraderie, but Marigold rarely made any friends, especially not with women. What was going on with her and this little ghost girl? They seemed almost like mother and daughter.

I found I was shaking, really upset. I wanted to reach out and chop their hands apart. Was I *jealous*? Marigold had never been much of a mother to me, though she'd tried in her own way. We'd always had an intense relationship, but it was more like *I* was the mother, Marigold my wayward child.

I was being ridiculous. It was probably very good for both of them to be friends. I was pathetic for resenting it. Even so, their little-girly clasped hands were making me feel sick.

'I really have to go now, Marigold.' I tucked my drawing pad under my arm, and rushed away.

14

There was a flower stall near the entrance to the hospital, mostly bouquets of roses – cheerful gifts for the patients, though a nuisance for the nurses. Maybe I should have bought a bunch for Marigold. I remembered an elaborate card I made for her on her thirty-third birthday. I'd done my best to draw her thirty-three favourite things: Micky, Star and me, Marigold's favourite clubs and pubs, a CD player, high heels, a bikini, jeans, various tight tops, a jangle of jewellery, and when I ran out of ideas I did garlands of roses to add up to the right number. (I'd wanted them to be marigolds, but the orange felt tip had run out.) I'd tried so hard but Marigold barely glanced at it and used the back of the paper to design herself a new tattoo to celebrate her birthday. The ink came through and blurred all my drawings.

'Stop it!' I shouted out loud, not caring who heard or saw. What was the *matter* with me? Why was I so stuck in the past, with all these pathetic childish resentments, when I was the same age now as Marigold had been then? I couldn't help it, though. What did I have to show for my life? I'd always taken pride in being a good tattooist, especially when I'd thought up a new custom design and everyone praised it – but now it looked as if I didn't even have my profession any more.

I was nothing. A nobody. People's eyes slid past me as I hurried along the streets. Had Marigold ever felt like that? She'd often said she hated having to wear the same uniform as every other child when she was in the convent school. Hadn't she said there'd been one of those giant photographs taken one year? She'd pored over it and had been alarmed to find she couldn't spot herself among all the other little girls with pale faces, pudding-bowl haircuts and checked smocks.

Is that why she'd had her first tattoo the moment she left the home? She must only have been sixteen, but she could have tattooed herself all over and no one would have cared. She always glowed when she got another tattoo – and another and another and another . . .

I was sounding like her again. I stopped walking so suddenly someone bumped into me from behind and told me to watch out. I stood still, clenching my hands, wanting to yell back at them. I breathed in deeply. I had to calm down. I wasn't going to make a scene in public. I was not going to let Brian and Mrs Bentley and her deceitful daughter wreck my life. I was going to get a new fucking job if it killed me.

I got the train to Brighton. I googled all the tattoo studios and then tramped round the town, trying to follow the map on my phone. It was such a struggle that I gave up trying to find tattoo studios systematically. I came across one that was beautiful, with wonderful, award-winning designs. The guy in charge was kind, totally understanding when I told him what had happened, but he shook his head sorrowfully.

'It might still be a risk if this mother knows your name. And we already have a top designer, as you can see. I really can't help you – but maybe one of the other studios might be willing to take a chance.'

I went to every one I could find, though it was getting late and they were about to close. There was just one person who seemed vaguely interested, running a one-man operation in a decrepit shop in a back street. He was a huge guy, heavily tattooed himself. He looked a bit like Big Al, but very crude and rough. He barely glanced at my designs.

'We don't do that type of fancy stuff. My customers want basic designs. Very basic, if you get my drift,' he said, and he actually licked his lips.

I knew what he meant. Horny ink. The thought of working on porn in that dark cubby hole with him made me feel nauseous. I shot out of there and trudged miserably uphill towards the station. There was no point trying to get the train to anywhere else. All the studios would be shut.

You need a job! How else are you going to pay your rent? Try harder! Get any kind of job, just to tide you over!

I went into the next pub I saw and asked if they needed any more staff.

'You're not really the right type, dear,' said the man behind the bar.

'What do you mean?' I asked. 'I can take orders, I can serve drinks, I can add up.'

'I'm sure you can. But if you don't mind my saying, you've not really got the bit of oomph we're looking for,' he said.

'You mean you want a bouncy blonde with big tits?' I said bitterly.

He just shrugged.

'Well, I wouldn't work for a dinosaur like you if you offered me a million pounds,' I retorted, but I spoilt the effect by bursting into tears as I reached the door. I couldn't stop crying on the train going back. A woman came and sat beside me and asked quietly, 'Anything I can do to help?'

I shook my head but managed to smile at her gratefully. I tried my hardest to calm down on the walk home. I didn't want Lee to see me crying all over again. I crept up the stairs and opened my front door as quietly as I could. There was a note on the floor.

Dear Doll,
  Give me a knock when you get home. We're celebrating!!!
  Lee x

He'd written it in big painstaking print, clearly thinking it might be easier for me to read, and his thoughtfulness brought on a new round of sobs. It took me a while to work out *knock* and *celebrating*, the words insisting on turning themselves round and being incomprehensible, but I got the general message anyway. I just couldn't bear to do what he suggested. He'd be so happy about his new job and I'd be so miserable because I didn't *have* a job. It would be so unfair if I put a damper on everything. I couldn't face any company, no matter how kindly they were. I just wanted to go to bed and pull the covers up over my head—

Pull the covers up over my head? Marigold again.

I stumbled over to my bed, kicked off my shoes and crawled under the covers fully dressed. I lay there on my stomach and heard general noises next door: the shower running, then cupboards being opened and music playing softly. Then they stopped. There was silence my side, his side. Minutes ticked slowly past.

I kept thinking about the girl from Surbiton. I could picture her face vividly. It was getting younger and younger. How could I have been taken in so easily? Why was I such a fool? I replayed my hands inking out that tiny dragon again and again, and then I rewound, so that my indelible green line disappeared and her wrist was bare.

I'd often pretended I was a witch to the mean kids at school. Even Oli believed I had magical powers. I could sometimes even convince myself that I could manifest whatever I desired if I only concentrated hard enough. I tried erasing that dragon tattoo in my mind, squeezing my eyes shut and holding my breath, willing it desperately, but of course I couldn't turn back time. I wasn't a child any more, when anything seemed possible. I was a woman of thirty-three, who had messed up her life royally in every respect.

I turned on my side, curled in a tight ball now, knees under my chin. It seemed important that I hold myself tightly to stop myself falling apart. When I closed my eyes, I didn't feel anchored to my own body. I seemed to be floating this way and that, up and down, in every corner, diminishing until I was just little wisps of smoke.

There were footsteps, a door opening and closing, and then a tentative knock on my door. Clearly from Lee. I ignored it, figuring he'd think I was sleeping and go away. Another knock.

Go away, Lee. I don't want to see you. Believe me, you don't want to see me either. I left you alone last night. Leave me alone now. Please.

A much louder knock now.

'Dol?' Lee's voice made me start. It was almost loud enough for him to be in the room with me. I had to pull my head up to check my door was actually closed. I let it thump back down again on the pillow.

'Dol, I know you're in there. Are you all right?' he called.

'Please go away!' I mumbled.

'I can't quite hear you. You're frightening me.'

'Go *away*!' I yelled.

'What's happened? Come on, let me in and tell me!' he demanded.

I imagined the tenants on the floor below listening, smirking, shaking their heads. It must sound as if we were having a lover's tiff. I started burning all over.

'Please, Dol. Just let me see you're all right and then I'll go away again, I promise,' he begged.

'Why can't you simply leave me in peace? I didn't come banging at *your* door yesterday evening!'

'Is that what this is all about?' He sounded bewildered. 'Have I hurt your feelings?'

'No, you haven't hurt my fucking feelings!' I shouted, angry now. 'I just want to have an early night because my life is crap at the moment and I want to blot everything out.'

'What do you mean? You haven't done anything stupid, have you?' His voice was sharp now.

Did he seriously think I was slicing my wrists open or gobbling painkillers, trying to do myself in? I was finding him infuriating, but I couldn't leave him worrying like that. I'd been in agony enough times over Marigold's attempts that I couldn't do it to him.

'Wait!' I dragged myself out of bed and made my way wearily to the door.

I opened it – and there was Lee, pink-cheeked and smelling of his coconut shower gel, in another clean, white teeshirt and dark jeans. His face was very pink, his damp curls tangled. He held out his arms, and I couldn't resist falling into them again.

He held me there in the doorway, not saying anything, rocking me slightly, so that we swayed in a very slow dance, my tears trickling against his teeshirt.

'There, now,' he said eventually, and led me to my sofa, still holding me, and sat us down together.

He lifted the edge of his shirt and brought it up to wipe my eyes.

'No, it looks clean on!' I said jerkily, still in that awful hiccupping, snorty stage.

'Well, you can wash it for me later,' he joked. 'You've already got it all wet.'

He straightened up and plucked at the teeshirt. He might have a bit of a tummy but his arms were firm and muscular.

'Do you go to the gym?' I asked.

'Course I don't. It would bore me silly. Gardening keeps me fit. Good, honest work in the fresh air,' he said.

'So you enjoyed your good, honest work in the fresh air today?' I asked.

'It was wonderful. Now I know I'm there permanently I can get really stuck in, not fanny about putting in a few bedding plants near the house. I've been tramping round working out a proper clearance plan. Can you make nettle soup?' he asked.

'What? No!'

'They say it's very good for you. Can't say I really fancy the idea, but you never know. Anyway, there are about twenty billion nettles rampaging round the grounds, and enough brambles to have snared Sleeping Beauty for a hundred years. That's Ava's favourite story. I have to pretend to be the handsome prince, of course, and wake her with a kiss on her nose and she always squeals with laughter.' His face softened as he said it, and he smiled wistfully.

'Are you missing her horribly?' I asked.

'Yes,' he said shortly. 'So what about blackberries? My mum used to make a marvellous blackberry and apple crumble. Judging by the brambles, we'll have twenty billion blackberries as well.'

'I suppose I could try. At least they taste better than nettles,' I said.

'Or *I* could try. I'm probably a better cook than you,' he said.

'You're probably a better everything,' I said, and pressed my lips together hard to stop myself bursting into fresh tears.

'What is it, Dol?' he asked, pulling me closer, so that I was nestled up on his damp chest again.

It felt really good, so comforting, even though I was in the depths of despair.

'I don't want to talk about it,' I murmured. I just wanted to lie pressed up against him, breathing in his warm, clean smell, feeling his arm around me, his hand cupped round my shoulder.

'Is it your mum?'

I shook my head. 'She's actually getting a bit better. And she's made a friend there. This young girl – Lottie, Lettie, whatever.'

'That's good,' Lee said.

'I suppose.'

'So what's upsetting you, lovie?'

Lovie? It was an unexpected endearment, quaintly old-fashioned, and probably considered irritating and patronizing by most women. But it sounded so tender to me, so perfect for the moment, that I wriggled even closer and found myself kissing his neck almost without thinking. I felt him quiver. With surprise? With wanting? I felt a little drag of desire inside me.

'Mm,' he said. 'Don't tell me if you don't want to. But go on kissing me like that.'

I wanted to kiss him deeply on his soft mouth now but I pulled back a moment. 'Lee, if you were the manager of a pub . . . would you say I was the wrong type to work behind the bar?'

'Yes,' he said, without even thinking it over.

'Oh!' I said, stung. 'So you think I'm so dull and mousey no one would want to buy a drink from me?' I tried to sit up but he pulled me back against him.

'Hang on. I don't know what this is all about, but I think you're the most interesting woman I've ever met. And I wouldn't call you a mousey type. I reckon you could be as fierce as a ferret if you wanted,' he said.

'So now I'm like a *ferret?*'

'You know what I mean. I'm not good with words – apparently

I'm rubbish at compliments, according to my ex,' he said ruefully. 'I mean you know how to stand up for yourself. You've got spirit. You're sparky.'

'Keep going,' I said, snuggling against him again. 'You're not doing too badly now.'

'And very responsible about your mum. And fantastic with my daughter. And you look brilliant so I don't like to think about you being chatted up by a load of drunken blokes in a pub,' he said.

I knew perfectly well I didn't look brilliant. I *did* look dull and mousey, but I liked him saying it.

'Anyway, why on earth would you want to work in a pub when you design marvellous tattoos?' Lee asked.

'Because I got the sack this morning,' I blurted out, and then I hid my face in his chest, because those seven words were now flapping about my head like bats, tangling in my hair, biting me with their fangs.

'Why on earth would anyone sack you?' Lee said indignantly. 'They must be crazy!'

I explained in a monotone, and Lee became more and more furious on my behalf.

'That bastard! He's the one who should be taking full responsibility! How dare he act like this? And it's hardly likely this awful mother is seriously going to sue. It's all the daughter's fault for conning you! Don't you worry, Dol, I'll go there tomorrow and have it out with this Brian creep,' he said.

'No! You mustn't! I don't want to work there any more anyway.'

'Well, don't worry, there are lots of tattoo studios who'd be desperate to give you a job,' he argued.

'No, they won't. I've been round heaps already. They all turned me down. And I even tried a pub – that's why I was going on about it – and they turned me down too. I don't know what I'm going to do. I seem to be fucking useless at everything,' I said miserably.

'No, you're not. You're great at caring. Look at you with your mum. You're the one she depends on, not your fancy sister. And my Ava's fallen in love with you. You should have heard her in the van going on about you. She thinks you're the bee's knees.'

Another old-fashioned phrase, one I liked even more.

'Do bees even *have* knees?' I asked, diverted.

'No idea,' said Lee. 'Do you like honey, Dol? I'm thinking of encouraging Mrs Knight to have some beehives. And a strawberry bed. And an apple orchard. And plums, greengages, maybe even a mulberry bush. Who knows, we might be feasting on fruit in a year or two. I'll make sure my girl gets the pick of the bunch.'

'Your girl Ava?'

'She will too. But I was meaning my girl Dol,' he said, his cheeks pinker than ever. 'Is – is it all right if I call you that?'

'Well . . . yes,' I mumbled. I wasn't at all sure, we weren't actually even dating, but I knew he was meaning to be sweet.

'Is it all right if I kiss you properly?' he whispered.

I nodded, touched that he'd asked, and yet wishing he'd just gone for it. I wasn't used to lovely guys like Lee. None of my other boyfriends (or the quick hook-ups) had ever been polite or considerate. Lee and I would be dancing a quadrille if we didn't watch out.

He leant in and kissed my lips, so softly, so gently, so tentatively. I reached up and put my hand on the back of his neck. We kissed more – still lightly at first, but then deeply, hungrily. Then he pulled me on top of him and very carefully took off my teeshirt. He asked if he could touch my breasts and I wondered if we were going to go through seeking permission for every single body part.

'You can touch anything, do anything,' I murmured into his ear, and that made everything so much easier.

I longed for it to be so arousing and involving that the amused commentator inside my head packed her bags and vanished, but she hung around so long I couldn't quite live in the moment. We hitched ourselves over to the bed because it was marginally more roomy, and we didn't have to keep our voices down because there was no one next door, we were in mine, squeezed up together. It should have worked, but it didn't quite. Well, not for me.

I rested my head on Lee's chest again, and he played with my hair.

'That was incredible,' he said.

I wasn't sure if he really meant it or was simply being polite. I felt him tense a little, waiting for my reply.

'Yes, it was,' I said quickly. He had been so careful, so concerned, that it was almost off-putting. I wasn't used to such tenderness. But he'd tried so hard to please me that I did my best to reassure him.

'And I didn't hurt you at all? You're so petite,' he said, stroking my back, feeling down the small knobs of my spine.

'You were very gentle,' I said. Almost too gentle, as if he was scared I might actually break. 'You mustn't worry. I'm quite tough and bendy.'

'I know that,' he said, chuckling. 'You're amazing, Dol.'

I thought I should return the compliment in some way, but I wasn't used to such sweet post-sex chit-chat. Some of my brief encounters had been barely monosyllabic. I rehearsed a few phrases in my head but they all sounded too cringy or too pornographic.

I ended up mumbling, 'So are you. But I thought we were going to be friends *without* benefits.'

'I said it, yes. But I fantasized about the benefits,' Lee said.

'Really?'

'Of course I did. You're exactly my kind of girl,' he said, giving me another kiss.

I wriggled away this time. 'You mean . . . I'm like your *wife*?'

'No! Good grief, you're nothing like Ali,' he protested.

'What does she look like?'

'Well, I suppose she's darkish naturally, but she's sort of honey blonde now. She's forever at the hairdressers. And she's more . . .' He moved his hands ineffectually.

'Curvy?'

'What's that word – vol, something?'

'Voluptuous,' I suggested.

'That's the one. For a girl who doesn't read, you've got an amazing vocabulary,' he said.

'I told you, I listen to books. Though I couldn't spell "voluptuous" or indeed "vocabulary" to save my life.'

'Do you know how to spell "Lee"?' he asked, leaning up on one elbow and looking down at me.

'For God's sake, are you mocking me?'

He looked horrified. 'No, I was just – I don't know what the hell I was doing. I'll shut up now.'

'It's OK. I'm just ultra prickly about it. I got teased a lot at school. I was the grubby little kid at the back of the class who did colouring while everyone else read – the weirdo who didn't have any friends. Poor little Dolly.' I was deliberately mocking myself now.

'Really? I'd have been desperate to be your friend,' said Lee.

'Well, I did have one friend,' I said. 'A boy.'

'I hope he punched any kid who was mean to you,' said Lee.

'Hardly! They were mean to him too. Dear Oli. They all called him Owly because he had to wear these enormous glasses. But we were good mates and he did stick up for me as best he could. He was even lovely about Marigold. He thought she was great!'

'Did the two of you ever go out together as adults?' Lee asked.

'No. Oliver realized he was gay in his teens and now he's happily married to a lovely guy called Ross,' I said. 'I haven't seen them for ages because they moved to Norfolk. I do miss him a lot, though.'

'Well, maybe we could—' Lee started, and then gave a little cough and just told me I had lovely shiny green eyes.

'Witchy eyes,' I said, and told him how I used to pretend I could cast spells, but my head was reeling. Had he been going to suggest driving me all the way to Norfolk to see Oli? To have a holiday with them? Surely one sexual encounter hadn't sent him galloping into the realms of relationships?

'You've certainly cast a spell on me,' said Lee. 'Shall we drink to that?'

'I don't think I've even got a can of beer,' I said, frowning. 'There might be a Coke in the fridge. We could share it.'

'Shall we just nip next door? I've got a bottle of wine in the fridge and there's a chicken in the oven. I thought we'd celebrate my new job – and now we can not only commiserate the loss of yours, but drink to our very special friendship too,' said Lee.

'I should be treating *you*,' I said guiltily. 'I was so wrapped up in my troubles I forgot it was your first day. I'm not really much of a friend, am I?'

'You're the best,' he said.

I started to worry. It felt good that he seemed so keen on me, reassuring that at least someone fancied me – but I didn't want him to get too serious.

I started putting my clothes back on, but he stopped me.

'Don't. You look so lovely. Come just like that. Who's to see?'

'Someone from downstairs might come knocking, complaining about the bedsprings creaking.'

'We won't answer the door. Come on,' said Lee, grabbing his own clothes but making no attempt to put them on either.

I giggled, feeling like a teenager again. I remembered the first time I had sex, when I was in the last year at secondary school. It was with a boy called Rory Maxwell. He was a handsome bully, brilliant at sports, popular with everyone, even the teachers. He was forever larking around, saying mean things to all us nerdy kids, but then pretending it was just harmless banter. But sometimes he'd give me a quick smile or a little nod, as if he secretly liked me. I was overwhelmed when he asked me to go for a walk down by the river after school one time.

I was such an idiot. Rory and I walked along holding hands and he kept up this stream of chatter, telling me he'd always thought I was special. I believed every word of it.

It was late autumn and getting dark, and I knew what was likely to happen when we got to the wilder part of the riverside, in the woods, but I didn't care, I *wanted* it to happen. I was so happy when he kissed me and untucked my blouse and felt my barely-there breasts. I felt shy but didn't protest too much when he suggested we lie down and I take my clothes off. He said he wanted to see me properly and he didn't want me to get my uniform all muddy. He sounded so caring, so concerned.

We did have sex, very quickly, so that I wasn't certain it had actually happened, but then he pulled his trousers up, took a great handful of my clothes and yelled, 'Fooled you!' There were whoops from behind us and two of his mates were there, falling about laughing, and then they all ran off into the dark.

I was left, shivering and sobbing. I still shake when I remember how awful it felt. I didn't know what to do. I didn't dare move away for a long while, hiding miserably in the bushes. How could I get home? Was I going to have to walk along the pavements stark naked? And I only had the one school skirt and blazer. How was I ever going to replace them? I was still wearing my school shoes and socks, but that made me look even more ridiculous.

I was crying loudly now, practically wailing. I don't know how long I hid there. It felt like the entire night, but I think it was probably only an hour or so. And then I heard someone coming along the nearby path and I huddled down, horrified.

'Dol? Where are you?' It was Rory, coming back. 'Hey, no need to cry! It was just a joke. I left all your clothes up there, where they were easy to find – but you didn't come looking for them. We were waiting to see you, and then the others got fed up and went home. So I've come looking for you, see?' He sounded as if he were proud of himself for being gentlemanly.

'You bastard,' I muttered.

'Hey, no need to be like that! Look, I've brought your clothes back for you.' He offered them to me as if they were a special gift.

'What am I meant to say, "thank you"?'

'Well, yes – most girls are bloody grateful to get a fuck from me,' he said, practically crowing.

'You hateful prick!' I said, snatching my clothes and trying to take a swing at him.

'Hey! I was joking, but you *should* be grateful. You don't think I actually *fancied* you? It was a pity-fuck because you're such a loser,' he said.

I stared at him, trembling. Then I stopped feebly hitting out at him. I stood up straight.

'What if I don't put my clothes back on, and run screaming along the river, and go straight to the police completely naked and tell them what you did,' I said.

'I didn't rape you! You wanted to do it!' he blustered.

I heard the panic in his voice. He paused, breathing heavily, obviously thinking it through. Rory already had a reputation locally and looked like a fully grown man – whereas I knew I still looked like a child.

'Look, please don't go to the police, Dol,' he said, in a different tone altogether. 'I didn't mean that. I do really like you and I thought you liked me. The police could easily get it all wrong and think I forced you. For God's sake, I could get charged and sent to prison!'

I waited, listening to him. Then I started hastily tugging on my clothes.

'Only joking!' I spat. 'Not so funny now that you're the butt of the joke, is it?' I ran off, making sure I was properly dressed before I got to the path. He didn't try to follow.

We avoided each other at school, not making eye contact when we passed each other in the corridors. I tried to blot him out altogether, although at night I couldn't help thinking about him and what we'd done. Not what had actually happened. I imagined Rory whispering to me tenderly, taking the trouble to kiss and caress me, making love slowly and beautifully. When I was sure Star was fast asleep I'd touch myself until I came, as the phantom Rory breathed in my ear that he loved me.

I knew it was sick, I knew it was stupid, but I couldn't help it. I dithered in my room now, wondering whether to tell Lee an edited version of this woeful tale, but decided to shut up. It was time I stopped harking back to my wretched childhood. The days of the bastards were over. From now on, I wouldn't give the Rory types the time of day. I'd found a steady, gentle man who cared about me. And he came with the daughter of my dreams. Never mind getting sacked from work. Perhaps I'd found my fairy-tale ending now.

15

Lee woke me by kissing my neck and shaking me gently.

'Hey, Dol!'

'Hey,' I murmured. It felt so good to be lying curled up with someone. I cuddled against him sleepily and then realized it was still dark, that intense blackness of two in the morning when it seems as if it will never be light again.

'What is it?' I said anxiously, rearing up.

'Don't sound so worried! It's just I've suddenly had a great idea and I couldn't wait to tell you. I know a job you'd be absolutely brilliant at!' He sounded wide awake, excited.

'What is it?' I muttered.

'You could look after children. Like a nanny or a childminder or a nursery school teacher. You'd be marvellous. You're a total natural, Dolly.'

'Funny you should say that. Star wants me to be her baby's nanny,' I told him, voice still foggy with sleep.

'Well, there you are,' said Lee triumphantly.

'Being bossed around by my sister? Having to get on with her patronizing husband and her fancy friends in Scotland?'

'What? I forgot! No, you can't possibly go to Scotland! But you could be anyone else's nanny,' he insisted.

I wasn't so sure. I didn't look or act like a proper nanny. I could try a nursery instead, but you probably needed proper qualifications to work in one. You even needed to pass exams to be a childminder and I couldn't look after several little kids at home because there wasn't room. It was all too complicated, and I was still half asleep.

'Let's talk about it in the morning,' I mumbled.

'OK, OK. I'm sorry, I shouldn't have woken you up. I was just lying awake, thinking about you, and it suddenly came to me,' he said, kissing me apologetically.

'Haven't you been to sleep yet?'

'Not properly. I'm too excited. Feel my heart, it's still thumping. This has really happened, you and me, together,' he said. 'I just can't believe it's true.'

I liked it that I meant so much to him already, but it worried me too. Lee and I had only just got together. We didn't really know each other properly yet. He'd said he wasn't ready for any kind of relationship. Was he jumping in feet first now just to show his wife he could find someone too?

Though he certainly seemed keen enough. He was kissing me more now, first my lips, then my breasts, then kiss by kiss all the way down to where I wanted to be kissed most, and I was wide awake now too, and the sex was better this time – more urgent, less careful. I was aware that Lee had to get up early to go to his new job and I had to try hard to find any job at all, but we stayed whispering together in each other's arms for a long time afterwards.

Lee can't have got much sleep at all. I was dimly aware of him creeping out of bed into his shower, and then pulling on his clothes. I tried to stumble out of bed too, but he gently pushed me back.

'You get some more sleep, Dol,' he murmured, giving me a kiss.

He must have brought me a cup of tea, but when I woke up

hours later it was stone cold. I wondered how on earth he was going to manage to work hard all day long. My eyes were heavy as lead, and it took me ages to get up.

I'd left my clothes behind in my own flat so I put on Lee's towelling dressing gown. It was a long time since I'd woken up in someone else's room. I enjoyed making myself a fresh cup of tea and popped a couple of slices of bread in his toaster. I found butter and some Bonne Maman apricot jam, which was delicious. I hooked out a whole apricot with my finger and ate it with guilty pleasure.

I had been a duffer at French because words in a foreign language were even more baffling for me, but I knew that '*bonne maman*' meant 'grandmother'. It didn't seem likely that Marigold was going to be a good grandma, for all she'd been so desperate to see Christopher. She'd never really managed to be a conventional good mother, though we knew she always loved us. She just wasn't that great at looking after us.

Lee thought I was great at looking after Ava. Star felt I'd make a good nanny for Christopher. *Could* I wangle myself into an informal nanny job round here too? Suddenly, anything seemed possible. I went and had a shower in Lee's cramped cubicle, smiling at the two plastic dolls splashing at the edge, clearly put there by Ava.

I used his soap and coconut shampoo, I used his hairbrush, I even used his toothbrush because what difference did it make when we'd shared so many kisses? I wandered round his room drying myself on his towel, smiling at all the little touches he'd added, and then wrapped the towel around me to go to my own room just in case anyone came up the stairs, though that seemed highly unlikely. I barely knew the other people in the house, and all post and delivery parcels were left downstairs in the porch.

I put on a summer dress with a short jacket and ballet

flats – hoping I looked relatively smart but sensibly dressed for running around after toddlers. I wore make-up for once and tried tying my hair up into a neat chignon, but wisps escaped every time I turned my head, so I gave up and simply brushed it straight.

There was a playschool a few streets away from Artful Ink beside the park where I sometimes went for an ice cream at lunchtime.

I paused as I passed the studio, wondering if it might be simpler just to go in and beg Brian to risk taking me back. The windows were deliberately darkened so I couldn't see if they were busy inside or not. I lurked a while on the other side of the road and saw one of my dragon-and-princess clients go in the front door. I waited, hoping she might come out again in a couple of minutes, looking upset that I wasn't there. After fifteen long minutes I crossed over and peered through a crack in the glass. With my neck craned on one side I could just make out Jo's couch. She was bending over my client, applying colour to my design. Jo was good at standard work, though she didn't have the skill for subtle shading – but the client was smiling at the starkness of the green dragon scales, obviously exclaiming in delight.

It felt as if the needles were stabbing my own skin. I felt betrayed, though I knew it wasn't Jo's fault. I didn't seem to be missed at all. I'd just provided a few designs – and they'd prove popular for a year, maybe more. Then they'd go out of fashion and I'd be forgotten altogether. They were all fine without me.

'Well, sod the lot of you,' I muttered fiercely, and marched off towards the playschool. It was called Duckies and had cartoon yellow birds on the noticeboard. The children were in the yard, playing on toddler trikes and poking each other with plastic spades in the sandpit. Two young women wearing aprons with the playschool's duck logo on the front were standing chatting to each other, mildly tutting at any child getting too boisterous, but not really getting involved.

Why weren't they helping the boy getting frustrated because he couldn't get his bike to move? Or kneeling beside the sandpit showing the children how to make a sandcastle? Or organizing a game, wiping a runny nose, taking the child clutching the crotch of her dungarees to the toilets before it was too late?

The dawning awareness that I could look after these kids much better than them gave me the courage to ring the bell at the locked gate. When a disembodied voice asked me if they could help me, I asked if I could see the head of the nursery school, trying to sound polite and professional.

The gate unlocked and I walked up the path. The two apron girls exchanged glances. They were a good ten or more years younger than me, but I hoped that didn't matter. I walked through the door at reception and a woman behind the window said, 'Wait here while I check if Mrs Harris is free,' and reached for her phone.

I was pointed along the corridor to the head's office in a matter of minutes. The walls were covered in lovely poster-paint pictures, colourful daubs, with the sky a blue strip at the top, the ground another green strip of grass, and various stick people with big bellies seemingly suspended in mid-air, apparently unperturbed, given their wide smiles. I clutched my thumbs, excited. I'd love to organize an art session for these kids. I could show them how to make animals out of dough and families out of pipe cleaners and furniture out of conkers. We could make a Hydra out of lots of old tights and then cut off all the heads with plastic scissors. I was breathless at the thought of it all. I knew I could do this job if they'd only give me a chance.

I knocked on the door in front of me, seeing the big H and a few letters that obviously spelt 'Harris', and went in confidently enough. And then quivered. Mrs Harris looked formidable, wearing an immaculate navy suit with a silk scarf at the neck, with a perfectly cut, shiny brown bob. She was professional to her manicured fingertips. Hardly likely to take a chance on a woman like me without any qualifications.

I wanted to run away but I managed a timid smile.

'Good morning. Do sit down. How can I help?' she asked.

I tried hard to think of something to say.

'Do you have a child attending Duckies?' she said helpfully.

'No, no, I – I'm here because – because I'd like to work here,' I said.

She looked a little surprised.

'Oh, I see. Well, I'm not sure we have a vacancy at the moment – but do tell me your details. What's your name?'

'It's Dol Westward,' I said.

'Dol is short for . . . ?'

I took a deep breath. 'Dolores,' I improvised, sure she'd think Dolphin too outlandish.

'Which pre-schools have you worked at previously?'

'I – I haven't actually worked at a pre-school as such, but I'm very experienced at looking after children,' I lied.

'You've been employed as a nanny?'

'Well, I've been offered a job as one, by a doctor actually, but – but I thought it would be more . . . more stimulating to work with a whole group of children,' I suggested.

'What sort of training do you have in childcare? Do you have an NVQ?'

I couldn't risk lying, when I knew nothing about it – not even what the initials stood for. I shook my head.

'Mm,' she said, as if she expected as much. 'Did you study childcare at school?'

I shook my head again. 'It's just – just I know how to get on with children,' I said. 'I do, truly.'

'I'm sure you do, Miss Westward, but I'm afraid I couldn't possibly employ anyone without qualifications. I have to insist on Level One at the very least,' she said.

I was clearly Level Zero – and always would be.

'Oh, well,' I mumbled inadequately, and started to get up.

'I tell you what, I always welcome volunteers into the school to help out in an informal manner. Would you be interested?' Mrs Harris asked. 'How about a little storytelling session once or twice a week?'

I hesitated. I needed to earn some money – but making up stories was one of my few skills. I had often kept Star spellbound when we were children, even though she was three years older than me. Maybe I could fit in a few sessions while I job-searched.

'Perhaps I could,' I said uncertainly.

She reached for some picture books on a bookshelf beside her desk.

'How about reading me one of these? Julia Donaldson always goes down well with the children. Try this one,' she said, pressing a book on me.

My heart started banging so hard I felt I'd drop down dead any minute. I didn't listen to picture books because there didn't seem much point without the pictures. I peered at the title of this one. It was in spindly capitals. They danced around on the cover, defeating me. I started sweating, trying to keep calm. I looked at the shape of the word. It started with a G and I could see two ffs. That was surely a word I knew from an old Animal ABC book.

'*The Giraffe!*' I read out as confidently as I could.

She gave a little gasp. I looked up and saw the stricken expression on her face. I'd clearly got that wrong. I felt my face burning, and the awful, helpless churning in my stomach I always got when asked to read aloud at school.

'I don't think you're really the right person for the reading sessions,' Mrs Harris said tactfully. 'But thank you so much for coming in today.'

It was clear my interview was over. I slunk out, wondering how I could have been such a fool to think I could ever work there.

I staggered out of the playschool, my legs shaking, so hot and damp my dress was sticking to my back. I scurried to the park, wanting to hide myself in the trees until I calmed down. My stomach still churned and once inside the gates I threw up as neatly as I could in a rubbish bin. Then I washed my mouth out at the drinking fountain and made my way to a bench in the shade.

I sat there for a while, barely taking in my surroundings, breathing deeply to try to calm myself. I still had a bad taste in my mouth and longed for something to freshen it. It was past lunchtime so I went into the park café and bought myself a mango ice lolly. There was a big noticeboard with various flyers and adverts pinned to it. They could mostly have been written in Arabic for all the sense they made to me – any scrap of reading confidence had vanished now.

Several seemed to be adverts for summer camps, because they had photos of children risking their lives racing BMX bikes, flying on zip wires and abseiling down cliffs. The ones who'd somehow survived were sitting cross-legged around a camp-fire cooking sausages. Oliver and I had always declared activity summer camps our idea of hell.

But there was one summer camp that seemed much more attractive. There were photos of children in dressing-up clothes, acting, dancing, singing, playing, painting scenery. *Painting!* I looked at the heading on the flyer. I knew the first two words, both beginning with S. *Summer School*. There were two more words. One unfamiliar, beginning with P. But the last word was easy: *Art*! Though there was an s on the end for some reason.

I squinted at the small print at the bottom but couldn't work out what it meant. I glanced around the café. There was a woman about my age near by, with two lively little boys blowing bubbles in their lemonade with straws. The smaller one was too enthusiastic and his lemonade bubbled out on to the tabletop.

'Oh, Jack!' his mum said, mopping him up with a paper napkin. She raised her eyes at me. 'Kids! How am I going to cope all through the summer holidays? I can't wait till they're old enough to go to one of those camps.'

'Ah, yes. I'm considering one too,' I said, thinking rapidly. 'Actually, I've got dreadful eyesight and I've left my glasses at home. Could you possibly read out the bit at the bottom of this one, please?'

'Sure!' She pointed a finger at her sons, who were now aiming at each other with the straws. 'Cut that out!' she commanded ineffectually and came over to read out all the blotchy squiggle words. It said there were two-week courses, each ten to four, five days per week, and there were still a few vacancies.

Then she added, 'Terms and conditions, website, blah blah blah, tuition, vacancies, etc.'

'Vacancies? Like, jobs?'

'Yep. There's a phone number if you're interested,' she said.

'Could you possibly read it out?' I swallowed the last of my lolly, took my battered old phone from my knapsack and carefully typed in each digit as she announced it. I got her to check it for me just in case. Then I thanked her fervently and left her mopping up more lemonade puddles on the floor.

I walked off into the trees where I could enjoy relative privacy. I stared at the number, psyching myself up to ring it. I kept telling myself it was pointless – that flyer had probably been pinned there for months. They'd have had heaps of people applying, all younger than me, with experience and confidence and tip-top reading ability. Still, nothing ventured, nothing gained, I told myself.

My mouth was dry again even though my tongue was still coated with mango juice, but I swallowed hard and pressed the dial key. It rang for a long time and I was about to give up when a fruity voice said, 'Good morning. You've dialled Lavender Hall. How can I help you?'

I had to swallow again before I could summon up any voice whatsoever. 'I was wondering about your job vacancies for the summer school,' I mumbled.

'Could you possibly speak up? It's a bad line,' she said. Or perhaps she was a little deaf. She sounded quite old but still very dynamic. 'Were you asking about vacancies for the summer school? I'm afraid I have nearly all my tutors in place now, especially on the drama side.'

'I was really wanting to teach art.' I swallowed. 'I'm very good at it – and good with children too,' I added desperately.

'I like your attitude,' she said, chuckling. 'Still, we don't actually have an art course.'

'But it says art on your flyer,' I protested.

'No, dear, it's *Performing Arts*,' she said, hissing like a snake when she said the s. 'It's a generic term, encompassing drama, music, singing, dancing, do you see?'

'Well, isn't art part of "arts"?' I said.

'Good question. Probably it is,' she said.

'And wasn't there a photo of some children painting pictures on a wall?' I persisted.

'They were painting scenery for the play they put on at the end of each fortnight. However, if you're a professional artist they could certainly do with some help. And some of the children might enjoy a little recreational painting and drawing when the leading cast are busy rehearsing. The children get the chance to try out every activity, and then, with a little tactful help from the staff, choose one or two specialities. Every child is given a part performing in the play at the end of the second week.'

'That sounds brilliant,' I gushed, daring to wonder if she might actually employ me. I took a deep breath. 'I'm sorry to ask, but it wouldn't just be voluntary, would it?'

'That's right, dear, always check the salary situation. We pay top rates, starting at twelve pounds an hour.' She said it proudly, as if it was a huge sum. It sounded more like a bottom rate to me – but it would be good as a temporary job and would give me experience working with kids. It sounded as if it might actually be fun.

'I'll take it!' I said eagerly.

'Hang on, you haven't been offered the job yet!' she said, but she was cackling in a wonderfully posh way, sounding like a broody hen. 'Pop in tomorrow morning – Lavender Hall, the full address is on the flyer. Do you drive? If not, Purfield Station is about half a mile away. What's your name?'

'Dolphin Westward,' I said recklessly, hoping that a theatrical old biddy might not mind an unusual name.

'Oh my goodness, what a wonderful name! Lucky you. I'm Henrietta Yewtree. Perhaps you've heard of me?' she said.

'Oh – oh yes!' I lied, hoping to please.

'Retired now, of course, since – well, you know.' She gave a brave sigh.

I didn't know at all, but made a little 'ooh' sound to be sympathetic.

'See you tomorrow morning, then. Any time will do. I'm always here. Bye-bye, Dolphin.' She chuckled again as she hung up.

I did my best to type in relevant names in my phone: *Lav Hall*; *Hen Yootree*; *Perfeeld Sta*. I hurried back to the café to see if the kind woman with the unruly boys was still there. They'd gone but there was an old man sitting at the same table having a cup of tea and feeding his dog most of his biscuit. The dog took a shine to me and nuzzled at my hips, hoping there might be further treats in my pocket. I tried the lost-glasses trick again, and the man was kind enough to write the full address on the back of an envelope for me.

I thanked him fervently, patted the dog, and bounced out of the café. I couldn't help putting a finger up at Artful Ink when I passed it. I still didn't have a proper job, I might not even get this holiday position if Henrietta Yewtree took an instant dislike to me face to face, but I'd done my best, and it felt great.

16

I didn't visit Marigold in the afternoon as I didn't want her to get used to my coming every single day, especially as I might well soon be working weekdays. She had Lettie for company now anyway. And I suppose I had Lee.

I decided to make an effort that evening. It was clearly my turn to make a meal but I'd never really learnt proper cooking. We'd mostly existed on takeaway food when we lived with Marigold, though she sometimes did a quick shopping trip to Iceland. Star learnt a few simple recipes at secondary school, and macaroni cheese became our quick, easy favourite. I could make it for Lee – he seemed a guy who liked simple food. I already had a packet of cheddar in the fridge to nibble whenever I got hungry. I didn't have much spare cash for a good bottle of wine, but found one on a half-price offer in the supermarket and hoped for the best.

I wanted to find a dessert too. Star and I used to love Angel Delight and would often share a whole bowl between us. Did they still make it? Yes, they did – and I needed to buy milk anyway for the macaroni cheese. There! It was hardly haute cuisine, whatever that was, but it was better than nothing.

When I got home I drew a picture of myself stark naked, balancing a big plateful of food in one hand, and holding a bottle in the other. I wrote my flat number 3a with a question mark, hoping I wasn't writing the wrong way round. Star used to call me Alice through the Looking Glass because I often did mirror writing by mistake.

I slipped it under Lee's door and then came back to mine for a shower. I put my summer dress in the washing basket and wore jeans with a silky camisole top, hoping I might look a little bit sexy.

Then I settled down with my pad and drew things children might like: a desert island, a treehouse, a castle with a moat, a jungle with all kinds of animals, a meadow with a herd of unicorns, a sea with mermaids swimming, dolphins leaping, and a whale blowing bubbles in the background. I was thrilled to see how quickly the ideas were coming, and delighted to be doing something very different from stylized tattoos.

My phone started ringing, making me jump. No! Surely not another Marigold emergency? She was surely safe in that locked ward – and she couldn't walk far with a broken ankle. Was it my dad? I'd tried leaving him a message, saying I was sorry he wasn't very well, so that he'd know I'd tried to get in contact. He hadn't replied. Maybe Meg had deleted it. Or maybe he wasn't really that bothered to get in touch.

I squinted at the name of the caller. Star!

'Oh, Star, it's you!' I said joyfully.

'Marigold's not done something else, has she?' Star asked, sounding anxious. 'I'm just checking up.'

'No, she's fine – well, of course she's not fine, but I think she's a little bit better,' I said. 'Maybe it was seeing you and Christopher.'

'Don't be so daft, she didn't give a damn about seeing either of us!' said Star. '*I told* you how it would be.'

'Well, *I* loved seeing you. I'm so glad you came. You do really care about Marigold, don't you?' I asked.

'Of course I do,' Star said irritably. 'But I care about you more, Dol.'

'I'm fine,' I said. 'Hey, listen, Star, I'm going to be a tutor at this summer school for the performing arts – I'll be teaching children art, me!'

'What? No, you've got to come and be Chrissie's nanny!' said Star. 'You said you would!'

'I didn't, not definitely,' I said. 'I mean, I might after the holidays are over. This teaching job is just for six weeks.'

'Oh, phew! So have you packed in your tattooing job at that weird Brian's place at long last?'

'To be honest, he packed *me* in, actually.'

'*What?*'

I told Star the whole story about the Surbiton girl. She was outraged that Brian would jettison me just like that.

'Still, it's worked out well, because I'm really keen to start this summer thing,' I insisted. 'I want to do it, Star. I think I might be quite good at it.'

'But it's not like it's a proper job. Oh, Dol, for God's sake, why do you have to be so stubborn? Please come and be Chrissie's nanny. You'd be brilliant and it would be so great if we could be together. I really miss you!' Star said.

'And I miss you too, dreadfully, but I can't rush up to Scotland just like that,' I told her.

'Why not?' Star demanded.

'Well, Marigold, obviously,' I said.

'Look, you can't give up on your own life watching out for her! How many times do I have to say it?' Star said forcefully.

'She needs me, Star.'

'*I* need you!' she said. 'Please just think about it!'

'I will, I promise, but it's not really possible,' I said.

'Oh God. You're not sticking around just because of Lee, are you?' Star asked.

'No! Of course not!' Though I wasn't as sure as that sounded. I loved it that Lee seemed so keen on me. And I loved his daughter wholeheartedly.

'He makes me feel so wanted, so special,' I added shyly, wanting Star to understand.

'Oh, for Christ's sake, are you that desperate?' Star said.

I was so shocked I couldn't even reply. I simply ended the call. How dare she! She wasn't really concerned about me or Marigold. She just wanted a cheap nanny for her precious baby.

To hell with you, Star! I'll do what I want!

So *did* I want Lee? Yes, I bloody well did. It seemed he cared about me way more than my sister or my mother.

I started cooking supper for us – and after twenty minutes or so I heard him climbing the stairs, going into his own room, then standing still a few moments. I hoped he was smiling at my picture. Then his shower started spluttering, and in ten minutes he was knocking at my door. He had a bunch of pink and white roses in his hand.

'For my girl,' he said, giving them to me. 'Mrs Knight's garden is a tangle of old roses. I picked her a big bunch too.'

'They're lovely,' I said, beaming. 'I don't think anybody's ever given me flowers before!'

'Well, nobody's ever drawn me a naked picture before. What a lovely surprise!' said Lee, taking me in his arms.

He was still damp from his shower, and the flowers got a bit squashed between us, and I didn't even get a chance to open the bargain wine for a long time. Lee admired the silkiness of my camisole, fondling me, and then carefully pulled it off over my head. I unzipped my jeans and pulled everything else off, while he tore off the clothes he'd just that moment put on. We made do with my single bed again.

'Open your eyes,' Lee murmured, after a minute or so.

It was only then that I realized I always shut them when I had sex, staying in my own dark world. I opened them obediently. It was hard to make proper eye contact with him but I managed to look at his honest face flushed with effort and his soft mouth whispering lovely words. It was much more romantic, but now I couldn't fantasize a much wilder scenario. What was the matter with me? Why was it so hard for me to respond to care and tenderness?

Afterwards, I didn't tell Lee that Star had phoned, but I told him about the promising call with Henrietta Yewtree while I was cooking. He whipped up the Angel Delight for me, grinning.

'Henrietta Yewtree? Isn't she that actress?' Lee said. 'She was in one of the soaps for ages – the posh old girl who liked a drink?'

'Well, that's exactly what she sounds like on the phone. Did something happen to her?'

'They decided she was getting a bit past it, so they dumped her. It must have come as a horrible shock to her.'

'Well, she sounded sharp as a tack when she was talking to me. We really got on together. It sounds as if she might actually take me on to paint some scenery and teach art.'

'You'll be absolutely great at that,' said Lee, dipping his finger in the pudding. 'I haven't had this since I was a kid. It still tastes amazing!'

The macaroni cheese went down well, and we had two helpings of Angel Delight – and polished off the whole bowl with the last glass of wine. Lee gave a great yawn and stretched.

'I think we'd both better have an early night,' he said. 'Your bed or mine?'

'Yours,' I said, though I was disconcerted again. Were we going to sleep together every single night? But I was glad of his warm hug because I couldn't nod off in spite of all the wine, worrying about the journey to Lavender Hall tomorrow, and whether I'd be able to find my way from the station.

Lee fell asleep straight away, but my tossing and turning woke him up again.

'What's up, Dol?' he murmured.

'Nothing. I'm just being pathetic,' I said.

'Come on, tell me,' he said gently.

I couldn't believe his patience. Star had done her best to comfort me when we were little and I got scared, but she could get very ratty if I woke her too often. I learnt not to run to Marigold if I had a nightmare. She was generally so out of it I couldn't wake her, or so hyped up she'd suggest crazy things like singing songs at the tops of our voices or going out to count the stars. The few boyfriends I'd lived with weren't the tender sort. They'd generally think a quick fuck might help and then roll off and fall instantly asleep.

'I know it's totally pathetic, but I'm worrying about finding this Lavender Hall place tomorrow,' I whispered.

'It's OK. I'll drive you and we'll find it together. I don't think Mrs Knight will mind too much if I'm a bit late, I can choose my own hours. There now. Cuddle up.'

He stroked me sleepily and I fell asleep at last. His alarm went off early and while he was in his shower I stayed huddled in a ball in his bed, wondering if I really wanted to go through with the whole Lavender Hall idea now. It wasn't just my worry about finding it. Maybe Henrietta Yewtree would thrust some kind of contract at me to read and sign and I'd be stuck.

I'd had enough humiliations over the last few days that I wasn't sure I could take any more. I felt the little courage I had left seeping into the sheets. Why didn't I just accept the fact that I was totally useless? Useless daughter, useless sister, useless employee . . .

But then Lee came whistling out of his shower, pulled down the duvet, and gave each of my breasts a kiss.

'I want to kiss every little bit of you but we're going to be late if you don't get up now,' he said softly, handing me a clean towel.

I looked up into his earnest face. He was so kind, so gentle, so helpful. He was the one person in the world who had faith in me. Perhaps it was time I had faith in myself instead of acting like a helpless child all the time.

Star was always eager to analyse me, telling me that I hadn't been able to act like a child when I was little, because I was too busy trying to cope with Marigold, so now I found it really hard to act like an adult.

'Well, you couldn't be more adult and yet you had to cope with Marigold *and* me,' I'd retorted.

She'd looked me in the eye. 'Or maybe I just act all calm and collected but inside I'm scared most of the time too.'

Was that true? Or had she just said it to make me feel better? Was everyone secretly scared?

'Lee, do you ever feel scared about anything?' I asked, as I rolled out of bed and stretched.

'Of course I get scared. I worry about Ava continuously, I worry about the bastard who lives with her and whether she'll think he's more her dad than I am. I worry about my job and whether I've made the right decision giving up my other work – and I worry about you and how soon you'll realize I'm just a boring old fart and get sick of me,' he said.

'Don't be daft,' I said, and gave him a hug. He lifted me up easily and I wound my legs round his hips, and we found ourselves having sex again after all.

I couldn't decide what to wear after I'd had a shower too. I went back to my room and had a peer round. My dress was sweaty and crumpled, the camisole too sexy. Best jeans, then – and maybe the black teeshirt with my own design on the front, the one I often wore in the studio. It was a picture of a woman with astonishing hair, skimpy clothes and many amazing tattoos.

'Good God, that's your mother, isn't it?' said Lee, peering round my door to hurry me up.

'No, it's just an imaginary woman. Marigold's hair isn't as long as that – and she's much older,' I protested. Then I looked at it again and realized Lee was right. Consciously or not, I'd depicted Marigold in her heyday. Why was I *still* so obsessed with her? If she'd been around more when I was a child, would I be able to move on? 'I'll take it off, it's a bit too extreme,' I said hastily.

'Don't take it off, it's very eye-catching. Probably the sort of thing Henrietta Thingy would appreciate, if she's the actress I'm thinking of,' said Lee. 'Come on then, let's get cracking.'

I shoved my sketch pad in my knapsack so that I could show Henrietta my work.

We nibbled at peanut butter sandwiches and took swigs of thermos coffee in the car. It was further than I'd realized to Purfield, and Lavender Hall didn't correspond exactly to its postcode, but at last we found it down a lane, through imposing metal gates, and up a long pebbly driveway that made the van bounce about. Lavender Hall was ultra impressive, a very large, mellowed brick house with gables and domes and an ancient wooden door with iron studs.

'It must be hundreds of years old!' I said in awe. 'Medieval?'

'I think it's Arts and Crafts, early twentieth century. She must have earned a hell of a lot as an actress if Henrietta actually owns it – though it looks like it needs a lot of work done. See those loose tiles on that roof? I bet she has to have bowls and buckets all over the attic whenever it rains,' said Lee. 'I like the garden at the front, though. Actual lavender!'

There were unruly bushes of it everywhere in different shades of purple. The moment we got out the van, their gorgeous scent hit us in the face.

'Beautiful! Though they could all do with a good pruning,' said Lee. He looked round. 'She needs another big soap part sharpish because it's all a bit dilapidated everywhere.'

'Shh! She might hear you,' I whispered, though there was no sign of anyone. I looked at my watch. It was only quarter past nine, for all our panicking that I'd be late. Perhaps she wasn't even up yet.

'I think I'm much too early,' I said.

'Well, I'm going to have to leave you here even so,' said Lee, glancing at his watch. 'I'm going to be much later than I thought for Mrs Knight. Will you be OK?'

'I'll be fine. I'll just loiter for a bit,' I said. I gave him a kiss. 'Thanks so much for bringing me.'

'And you think you'll be able to find your way back to the station?'

'Easy. Down the drive, down the lane, and then turn . . . right?'

'Left! Think L for Lee, L for left.' Then he bit his lip, looking awkward.

'I do know the alphabet!' I said, slightly irritably. 'I just can't spell properly. Or read that much. I was always in the R for Remedial class.'

'Sorry,' Lee said, abashed.

'That's OK,' I said. 'Lee, you don't think Henrietta will ask me to read anything out loud, do you?'

'Of course not,' said Lee, though he didn't look certain. 'Well, I must go. Good luck!'

I waved him off. The van made such a crunching sound on the drive I thought someone would surely come rushing to the windows, but they all remained blank. I waited a few minutes, feeling horribly prominent, and then walked on the grass verge to the side of the house. There was a kitchen garden at the back, with squashes and cabbages and runner beans twining up canes, and several apple trees with small clusters of fruit.

I dared to pluck one but it wasn't ripe yet and was so sour my eyes watered. I threw it on the grass where there were other windfalls, turning it with my foot to cover up the nibbled part. I wandered on, through longer grass and ox-eye daisies and poppies and ragwort, admiring the colours, wondering if children might like to have a go at painting them.

I was suddenly aware of faint splashing sounds. A tap . . . a hosepipe? No, it sounded as if someone was swimming. I passed a clump of trees and discovered a pool. Not a proper turquoise chlorinated one, more a murky pond. There was a head bobbing along with a topknot of garish orange, an eerily familiar shade. For one bizarre moment I thought it was Marigold – but when I blinked the swimmer into focus I saw she had a large, pale body without a single tattoo.

She saw me, spluttered in surprise, but then swam to the muddy edge and hauled herself out. She was wearing an old-style swimming costume, the sort with a skirt. She had a substantial body but scrawny legs, very white and veiny.

'You're early! I'm Henrietta Yewtree – and you must be Dolphin, my arty candidate. Well, my dear, do you want to live up to your name and have a little splash?' she said, enveloping herself in a long towelling coat like a tent. 'Go on, be a devil. Don't you think it looks wonderfully inviting?'

I wondered if she'd take against me if I answered honestly. The pond looked filthy, and full of those long, wavering weeds that would feel like eels if they curled themselves round your legs.

'I'm afraid I'm not much of a swimmer,' I said, which was a downright lie. My dad had taught me a reasonable breaststroke and crawl – one of the few father-and-daughter activities we'd done together.

'Well, you're missing out. It's delightfully refreshing,' she insisted, though she was shivering in spite of her towelling coat. She had a strand of pondweed caught in her hair. I wondered if I should flick it away for her, but didn't dare.

'Anyway, why are you so extraordinarily early? Are you simply very keen – or desperate for a job?' she asked, sensing the pondweed and removing it herself without any hint of embarrassment.

'I suppose you could say it's a bit of both, plus my friend gave me a lift here in his van and he couldn't be too late for his own job,' I said.

'He must be a very good friend,' she said, with a hint of innuendo.

A bit taken aback, I chose not to answer and gave a little shrug that could mean yes, no, or mind your own business. I realized she was older than I'd imagined, in her seventies or maybe even eighties. Her face was reasonably unlined but her neck was skinny and puckered, and her feet sticking out of her long coat looked ancient, with bad bunions that gave her an odd gait as she started walking back to the house.

I scurried along beside her as she lurched towards a back door.

'Tell Glad to get the breakfast on,' she commanded, when we'd made our way to a long dark corridor. 'Won't be a mo!'

She disappeared up the steep backstairs, counting as she went: 'One and two, and *one* and two, and cockadoodle doodly do!'

Perhaps she wasn't simply eccentric. She might well be totally bananas. I wondered whether to give up on the whole idea and make a break for it out the back door while I could. But although I was wary of her now, I also liked her. I obediently went off in search of this Glad. Presumably Gladys?

I imagined another eccentric old lady acting as a companion, but instead found a plump fifty-something blonde lady in the kitchen in a striped tee-shirt and trackie bottoms. She was called Nina – 'Nina the Cleaner, that's me,' she said, laughing. 'And the cook and the secretary and the driver and the shopper and general bleeding dogsbody.'

'I'm Dolphin,' I said. 'Why does Henrietta call you Glad?'

'Oh, I sing hymns a lot when I'm dashing about with our Henry,' she said.

I thought she meant a real guy called Henry, but it was only their vacuum cleaner. Henrietta had nicknamed her Glad because her favourite hymn was 'Glad That I Live Am I'.

My own name seemed relatively normal in this sort of household and I relaxed a little. I saw Glad/Nina had a little bluebird on her ankle and I told her that I'd been a tattoo artist. She was fascinated.

'Oh my, a tattooist! My granddaughter talked me into getting mine. She's only eighteen and she's already got three tattoos – a high-heeled shoe, a Taylor Swift portrait and a heart with "I love Nan", bless her,' she said. 'She's thinking of getting her boyfriend's name on her shoulder but there's always a danger they'll split up, so I'm trying to talk her out of it. Show us *your* tattoos, then,' she said, cracking eggs. 'Scrambled or fried?'

I felt quite hungry now despite the peanut butter sandwich, so I asked for scrambled. 'I haven't got any tattoos myself. My mum has, though. Many.'

'Really!' said Nina, sounding interested. 'So did you do them for her?'

'No, she started getting them when I was just a kid.' I began telling her about Marigold's snake down her spine, the seeing eye at the back of her neck, the Celtic swirls on her arms, the bats on her thigh, the daisies garlanding her foot, the tiny frog between her toes, and of course the star and the dolphin.

'Oh my!' said Nina, marvelling.

Henrietta came in at the tail end of my mapping Marigold's body and nodded approvingly.

'I have one myself, dears, a butterfly emerging from a rather private place,' she said. 'Want to see?'

'It might put us off our breakfast,' Nina said briskly. 'Sit yourselves down and tuck in.'

Henrietta raised her eyebrows at me but sat down at the kitchen table obediently. Her hair was still wet in its untidy topknot, but she'd managed to apply a lot of make-up with rather a shaky hand, and she was wearing a long gown that could have been evening dress or an elaborate nightie.

'Excuse Glad – she's a little uppity for a servant,' she said. I gasped at her rudeness, expecting Nina to storm out, but she just laughed, not at all offended.

They bickered lightly all the way through breakfast just like sisters, while my eyes flicked from one to the other as if I was watching tennis. Eventually, Nina interrupted one of Henrietta's long anecdotes about an unlikely liaison with a famous actor.

'Aren't you supposed to be interviewing this young lady instead of rattling on about your love affairs?' she asked.

Henrietta chewed on her mouthful of eggs, dabbed her lips with a lacy hankie, and turned to me.

'So, Dolphin Westward, tell me why you think I should employ you this summer,' she said imperiously. 'Have you ever painted scenery before?'

I took a deep breath.

'I think you'll find me very versatile, no matter what the play is,' I said. 'And I seem to have the knack of creating images that children like. Shall I show you?'

I opened my knapsack and revealed the recent pages.

'Oh my! Come and have a look at these, Glad,' cried Henrietta.

She seemed to like them! Nina did too, smiling at each image. 'Dragons!' she said happily.

What was it with dragons?

'There's a most excellent dragon costume we kept from last year,' Nina explained. 'With coil after coil for its tail, all hand sewn. It would be a shame not to use it.'

'Can you sew, Dolphin? Our costume creator Linda could do with an extra pair of hands.'

'Yes, I'm used to sewing,' I said, because I often made my own clothes out of necessity.

'I think you're an excellent find, Dolphin Westward. Consider yourself hired!' said Henrietta. 'Starting Monday week. Nine o'clock. The children don't start till ten, but we'll have a staff meeting first and get organized,' she added, beaming.

'Brilliant!' I said, smiling broadly. Oh, it was more than brilliant! It was gloriously bright and beautiful. And I'd done it all myself!

'I'll see you out, dear,' said Nina.

I wondered if there was going to be any further confirmation of my pay. *When* was I going to be paid? I wouldn't have to wait till the end of the course, would I? I'd have to ask Star if she could possibly help me out and that would be so awful.

'Excuse me, Nina – Miss Yewtree mentioned that I'd be paid twelve pounds an hour. Is that right?' I blurted out when we'd got halfway down the corridor.

'That's right. It's a bit meagre but it's because you're inexperienced. If you prove popular, it'll go up to fourteen pounds, maybe more. Of course the beloved boy gets more – but Nina has to bribe him somehow. And he still has a soft spot for her. Your money will be paid into your bank account every week, just give me the details – or you can have cash if you prefer. You just come to me any time you've got questions. I'm the one who sorts everything out. I've been looking after Henrietta ever since she was on the West End stage and a big star. Gawd knows why I put up with it. Perhaps it's because I just love the old tart.'

I thanked her and shook her hand, in a very professional sort of way – but when I was down the long drive out of sight of the windows, I actually started dancing. Things were suddenly so great! The job seemed fantastic, and I'd have cash in hand. I'd have to fork out for the train fare but maybe Lee would give me a lift occasionally. I might end up being Christopher's nanny eventually but I'd bought myself a few weeks to think about it.

17

I had a new routine now I didn't have to leave early to go to Artful Ink.

I stayed in bed long after Lee left for work. He worried about waking me up too early every day, which made it easy to have some nights alone in my own bed. I liked curling up with him, I liked the sex, but it was good to have time to stretch out by myself and think my own thoughts. I'd prop myself up on the pillow and draw compulsively, planning lessons for all the different age groups and abilities attending summer school at Lavender Hall.

I tried out the simplest ideas on Ava at the weekend. She loved drawing unicorns, insisting on equipping them with wings too. She coloured each one in bright Caran d'Ache colours, adding spots and stripes and rainbows to her favourites. She liked drawing mermaids too, though she chortled when she drew their bare chests.

We had to room hop when she was asleep so she didn't see my own bare chest if we got carried away. We could hear her through the paper-thin walls if she woke up and called out. We tried very hard not to make any noise at all. Even so, she seemed to have a sixth sense, and occasionally acted as our own effective contraceptive. We used real ones too, obviously, except when it was a safe time of the month.

'No babies for us, right?' said Lee.

'Absolutely,' I replied, though my new nephew and little Ava herself had triggered this fierce longing inside me.

'Is Dol your girlfriend now, Daddy?' she asked on Sunday morning.

'Yes, she is,' said Lee, without hesitation.

'Good,' said Ava, and went on playing with her mouse house.

I sensed Lee looking at me, and I determinedly avoided his eyes. I was thrilled that Ava was happy for me to be her dad's girlfriend but I wasn't at all sure that was what I actually wanted. I'd have much preferred it if he had talked to me in private first, rather than saying 'yes' to Ava like that. And surely you saw someone for many months before you actually committed to each other so concretely? I'd never got that far with any of the other guys in my life. I hadn't even minded too terribly when several dumped me. It saved me the bother of trying to slide out of a relationship that didn't feel right.

I suppose when it came down to it, I'd never properly fallen in love with anyone. I'd fancied some of them, the bad ones who didn't treat me well, but had never felt I'd met The One. I almost envied Marigold's obsession with Star's father, Micky. I'd never forgotten her wild happiness when she found him again when Star and I were children – and her despair when he explained he couldn't stay with her.

I'd always thought Star really loved her Charles, but now I'd changed my mind. Perhaps she just needed to be part of his world. Oliver told me he was head over heels in love with Ross when they had their civil partnership – but somehow there didn't seem much passion between them. They were just two sweet cardigan boys who loved cooking together and listening to Adele albums and stroking their cat Moonface. Maybe that's what true love really was?

I was starting to worry that Lee might tell me he loved me. There were moments when we were about to have sex, his eyes blurry with wanting me, when I thought he might say it. Or perhaps afterwards, when my head was on his chest and his arm round me, and he suddenly took a deep breath as if he was about to murmur it – but thank God he didn't. Because then I'd feel obliged to say it back to him, and it would probably sound horribly false and cringy. Yet I didn't think I could bear to say I didn't love him. I didn't want to hurt him because he was so kind to me.

I wished I had someone to discuss it with. I didn't want to see Jo again, at least not yet. I couldn't tell Star because she'd try to talk me into breaking it off with him altogether and jetting off to Scotland. I certainly wasn't going to breathe a word to Marigold.

However, she was in a surprisingly affable mood when I visited mid-week, so when little ghost Lettie was marched off to be weighed, I found myself asking her what it felt like to be in love.

'Are *you* in love, Dol?' she asked, her eyes crinkling up with amusement. 'It's not that Lee-with-the-white-van, is it?'

'It isn't a white van, it's a blue van with all his gardening tools in it, and what does it matter what fucking colour it is?' I said, furious with myself for starting the conversation. 'And if it wasn't for Lee and his van you'd probably still be banged up in Gatwick.'

'Oh Jesus, it *is* him!'

'I'm going,' I said, getting up.

'No, don't go,' said Marigold, and she hung on to me. Her nails were beautifully filed and painted a subtle, pearly green.

'They don't have a nail bar in the hospital, do they?' I asked incredulously.

'Lettie did my nails for me. She's a little gem,' said Marigold. 'Just like a daughter to me.'

'Well, this actual daughter, who has been there for you through thick and thin, is going to fuck off right now,' I said, peeling her hands off me.

'Language! Saints preserve us, two fucks in less than a minute!' she said, shaking a finger at me in mock disapproval.

'What would all those scary nuns say if they heard you taking God's name and all his retinue in vain?' I retaliated childishly.

'They'd smack me hard on the back of my legs – but they'll all be very shaky old ladies by now, or dead in their coffins so they can't hurt me now, can they? I don't have to keep harping on about them because it's over now. I don't need to be unhappy and upset. I can live in the present,' Marigold declared.

'Oh, hark at the therapy speak!' I said cruelly, though I was actually impressed. 'So why this sudden attachment to Lettie, letting her hang around you like a little dog with separation anxiety? Is she a substitute daughter now, to make you feel better about being such a rubbish mum to Star and me?'

'Was I really a rubbish mum?' Marigold asked, her eyes filling with tears.

I felt my own eyes prickling with shame. It was a terrible thing to say to her, especially now, when she was so vulnerable.

'I'm sorry. You were a lovely mum in lots of ways,' I said. 'And even when you weren't, you couldn't help it. It was just your illness.' I gave her a hug.

Marigold had a little weep, burrowing her head into my chest, and when she was through I found a tissue and mopped her face tenderly.

'Dr Gibbon said I need to take responsibility for managing my bipolar,' she sniffed. 'I have to take my medication and avoid all the triggers that turn me into a nutjob.'

'I don't think that was quite the terminology he used,' I said. 'He's lovely, isn't he?'

'Yes, he is, bless him. Why don't you fall for a man like him, Dol?'

'There are too many medical people in the family already,' I said.

'True!' said Marigold. 'OK, stick to your gardener, Lee Lover-Boy.'

'He's a *friend*.'

'So you don't fancy him? Why not see what he's like in bed?'

'I *have* done, actually. We have lots of fun,' I said, willing myself not to blush.

'Good for you, darling,' said Marigold. For once, she seemed sincere.

To stop her asking for details, I rapidly changed the subject, telling her about my new summer-holiday job. She was quite impressed when I told her about Henrietta, who had once been much more famous than I'd realized.

We were still discussing her when Lettie returned, red-eyed and subdued, because the nurse had found keys, a phone and a couple of stolen spoons hidden in her knickers as a desperate attempt to bluff about her weight. I felt truly sorry for her.

'Oh, Letts, how could you be so silly,' said Marigold, but she sounded comforting, not critical, and put her arm round Lettie's bony shoulder.

I murmured sympathetically too, but found it difficult watching Marigold be more of a mum to this girl she barely knew than she had ever been to me. I waited an endless ten minutes to be polite and then stood up.

'Well, I really have to go now. Bye, Lettie. Bye, Marigold,' I said.

'It feels like flying,' said Marigold, as I reached the door.

I turned back. 'What does?'

'Falling in love. It's this huge, powerful, soaring sensation that makes you feel you're flying up in the sky, way over everything. Everything's in Technicolor and it doesn't matter about anything else in the whole world,' said Marigold, her eyes shining. 'You can't mistake it, Dol. It takes you over and everything else is grey and boring but you're the golden ones, you and your lover, and the whole world spins around much faster and nothing else matters.'

Lettie listened, open-mouthed.

'I've never loved like that,' she said, her voice filled with awe.

'Neither have I,' I said lamely.

As I walked home, I compared Marigold's description to my feelings for Lee. There was no flying at all. We kept our feet on the ground and sometimes it was like strolling along the pavement, other times wandering through daisy meadows hand in hand. Pleasant, but quite prosaic. Was I just kidding myself that I fancied him because it was a relief not to feel lonely any more?

I felt guilty even thinking it. Lee was the sweetest, kindest guy I'd ever met. I loved being with him. Well, most of the time. I couldn't help finding it a bit boring when he talked endlessly about his job with Mrs Knight and his plans for her garden.

I paid attention at first, but when he went on and on about it I just murmured every so often, not listening to a word, concentrating on my drawing instead. He even took me to a plant nursery, asking my advice on what to choose.

'Oh, Lee, to be honest I don't really know anything about gardening!' I told him.

'You've got those lovely miniature gardens in your room,' he said.

I rolled my eyes. 'I bought them ready-made. All I have to do is water them occasionally. I can't do real gardening.'

'But you're the artistic one. I want to make a big herbaceous border near the house so Mrs Knight can peer out the window and see a mass of colour to light up her day. Help me choose the right sort of seeds and bulbs, so that they'll set each other off and look perfect for her,' he said.

I enjoyed running here and there at first, choosing pink and purple and blue flowers, while Lee made careful notes on his phone. Then I planned a great bank of yellow flowers like giant daisies, imagining them interspersed with red poppies, thinking we'd gather them all up so that Lee could plant them straight away. When I said as much to Lee, he smiled at me fondly.

'But that would cost an absolute fortune,' he said. 'And it wouldn't be the same as sowing the seeds in trays and nurturing them along, planting the bulbs and watching them all come up next year, seeing them slowly filling in all the gaps.' His hands made gestures in the air as if he was actually sowing and planting. He explained how important it was to know the right kind of soil where the plants would thrive, and my mind started to drift the way it had always done in school, though I nodded now and again as if absorbed.

He looked at me carefully.

'You're bored stiff, aren't you, Dol?' But he didn't seem to mind. 'Oh well, maybe I'll be able to turn Ava into a gardener one day.'

'Sorry,' I said sheepishly.

He bought several presents for Ava in the shop: a child's watering can, a spider plant, and a picture book about a girl who enjoys gardening with her daddy. When Ava arrived the next weekend she loved all three gifts, though she wanted to keep watering the spider plant until it was in danger of drowning.

She loved the book too. Lee read it patiently to her over and over again, and when he started cooking our tea Ava pressed it into my hands.

'You read it to me, Dolly,' she said pleadingly.

Lee glanced over his shoulder anxiously, but I managed to stay calm.

'OK,' I said, as casually as I could.

After all, I'd heard Lee reading the story so many times I'd practically learnt it by heart. I knew the little girl was called Sophie, whereas if I'd just come across the word on the page I might well have pronounced her Sop-he. She *was* soppy too, forever saying, 'Oh, Daddy, let me, let me, let me,' which was easy to read, and I made Sophie talk in a high-pitched silly little voice that made Ava laugh.

There were still a few sentences I had to guess so I made them up. One time, Ava looked at me sideways as if to say, 'Are you sure it says that?' but luckily she seemed to think my amendments amusing.

'I can't wait till I can read properly,' said Ava. 'I can read *bits*, though. Listen!' She did her best to read a passage to me, pointing along gamely, trying hard to spell out the words and roaring with laughter when she got it completely wrong.

Lee left the stir fry on the stove to look after itself for a few minutes and sat and helped her. He never once told her off or got the slightest bit impatient when she repeatedly got a word wrong. He just gently reminded her again and again. He glanced at me once or twice and I knew he was doing it for my benefit too.

'You're a very good teacher, Lee,' I said, after Ava had been put to bed.

'I could try teaching you if you like,' he said eagerly.

It was well meaning of him, but I didn't like the idea at all. He was picking up Ava's silly story book now, opening it at the first page.

'Try reading it to me now,' he said. 'I just want to try to understand what you find difficult, that's all. Please!'

He handed me the wretched book. I sighed. I knew the first two pages off by heart so I 'read' them in a bored sing-song.

'Happy now?' I asked.

'What about the last few pages? Have a go at them,' Lee persisted.

I sighed even more heavily and glanced at them. They came into focus for a split second – and then shifted, practically sliding off the page. I had the roaring-in-my-head sensation that I remembered all too well from my schooldays.

'I can't read them. Satisfied?'

'Just give it a go,' he said.

'For God's sake, I don't want to read the stupid book,' I said, and I threw it across the room. It landed awkwardly, the pages crumpling.

Lee picked it up and did his best to straighten them, not saying anything.

'I'm sorry,' I mumbled.

'No, *I'm* sorry, I shouldn't have tried to force you,' said Lee.

'Oh, don't be so *nice* all the time,' I said. 'Why don't you ever lose your temper with me? Go on, tell me I'm acting like an idiot and I'm a totally ungrateful cow and now I've messed up Ava's new book.'

'OK. You're acting like an idiot and you're a totally . . . what was it?' Lee asked.

'Ungrateful cow,' I said, feeling so ridiculous that I started half laughing, half crying.

'Come here,' said Lee, holding out his arms.

I resisted childishly, but he came and grabbed me and whirled me round.

'And I'm acting like – like a bull in a china shop,' said Lee. '*I'm* the idiot, acting like a patronizing git. Oh, Dol, please don't be cross.'

He kissed me and I kissed him back and we ended up slipping

next door to my room and my bed. We were both so worked up it became much more passionate – and as we were both about to come I mumbled, 'Are we flying?'

Lee was past replying, but when we were lying back exhausted, he said, 'What was that you said? I didn't quite catch it, and it didn't seem the right moment to say *What?*'

'I just wondered whether you felt you were flying,' I said, feeling stupidly embarrassed.

He looked at me, his face so close his eyes blurred into one.

'Sort of,' he said. 'Absolutely. So it was like that for you too, Dol?'

I nodded, because I knew he'd be so hurt if I told him the truth. He'd think there was something wrong with his technique, when he was the most considerate lover I'd ever had. It wasn't his fault that I didn't really find it *exciting*.

I lay awake a while that night, trying to work out what was wrong with me. I couldn't sleep on Sunday night either, because I was so nervous about starting at Lavender Hall the next morning. Lee was awake too, overtired from the long drive taking Ava home and missing her terribly.

'I'm so worried Ali and me splitting up is affecting her,' he said despairingly. 'I can't help thinking it's really important for a child to feel utterly secure, with two loving parents.'

'I don't know,' I said. 'Look at Star and me. We managed OK. Well, *she* did.'

Lee sensed he'd hurt my feelings.

'Poor Dol, you look so tense. Are you worrying about Lavender Hall tomorrow? Perhaps I should drive you there as it's your first day? I don't want you getting into a flap and turning the wrong way out of the station,' he said.

'I'm not in a flap,' I said irritably, and turned my back on him. 'I'm *fine*.'

We didn't say any more, both of us fidgeting and wide awake for a very long time.

I felt anything but fine in the morning, racing around getting ready. I put my arty teeshirt on and then immediately pulled it off again because I didn't want Henrietta to think I only had one outfit.

'You're not acting as if you're fine,' said Lee, watching me discard a second top because the sleeves had gone weird in the wash, and then wrinkle my nose at a third because it had a Miffy rabbit motif and seemed more suitable for Ava than me. He was smiling.

'You're laughing at me, aren't you?' I said huffily, now pulling my bootlace so tight it broke in two. 'Oh, *fuck*!'

'It's OK, you've still got enough lace left if you simply re-thread it. Here, I'll do it for you and you finish doing your hair and make-up,' said Lee.

'When have you ever seen me wearing make-up?' I said belligerently, though he'd probably seen me wearing it at least twice. 'I'm Dol, remember, not your wife.'

'Thank goodness,' he said, still managing to stay calm and fond, though I knew I was behaving abominably.

'I wish you'd stop being so relentlessly kind.'

'Oh yeah, that sounds familiar. Much more like my ex-wife. Try sprinkling your protests with a few "gutless" mentions – or perhaps "pathetic".' He was still smiling, but there was an edge to his voice now.

'Oh God, I'm sorry.' I hobbled over to him, one shoe off and one shoe on, and threw my arms round his neck. 'I'm being a total bitch. Yep, cow yesterday, bitch today.'

'Well, I'm getting a bit bitchy now too,' said Lee, giving me a big hug. 'So let's declare a truce and get you to your job.'

He drove me and we arrived at Lavender Hall by twenty to

nine. I thought there would be many other tutors milling about, but the whole place seemed deserted again.

'I'll wait with you until someone else turns up,' said Lee.

'No, it's OK, I'll just mooch around a bit and see if I can find Nina or Henrietta herself,' I said, knowing he was desperate to get back to Mrs Knight's garden.

He gave me a good-luck kiss and drove off, while I wandered towards the back of the house, my knapsack heavy on my back, stuffed with my drawing pad, wads of paper, and every single pencil, brush, crayon and paint I possessed in case Lavender Hall didn't provide enough. As I went through the kitchen garden I heard distant splashing. Was Henrietta having a swim again, even though she was supposed to be meeting and greeting everyone in fifteen minutes? Maybe she needed to calm her nerves too. Or perhaps she'd gone for a quick walk around the pond and had somehow fallen in?

I hurried now, ready to come to the rescue, though from what I'd seen, Henrietta was a strong swimmer and at least twice my size. I rounded the corner and then stopped short, gasping in shock. There was a man wading out of the pool – a slim man with longish dark hair, intense blue eyes, a flat stomach, and deep grooves on either side leading down to another dark tangle around his genitals. He had a light tan – and a mask tattoo above his heart.

Him!

He laughed at my expression, making no attempt to hide himself in any way.

'Hello!' he said, smiling. 'Think of this as your meeting-Mr-Darcy moment – or aren't you a Jane Austen fan?' he said lightly.

I certainly wasn't up to reading Jane Austen but I'd seen Colin Firth in that old *Pride and Prejudice* series. I struggled hard to look cool, though I could feel my face burning.

'You're not wearing the wet white shirt, though,' I said.

He peered at me, then his eyes lit up. 'I recognize you!'

'And I recognize your tattoo,' I said. I stayed staring at it, trying hard not to glance downwards. 'What on earth are you doing here?'

He was grinning now. 'What do you think?'

I didn't have a clue. He had all the confidence of being the Lord of the Manor, if Lavender Hall had such a person, but he was surely much too young to be Henrietta's partner. So was he teaching on the course? Was *he* the beloved boy?

'You were on television once, weren't you?' I asked.

He laughed, reaching for the towel on the bank at last, when he was sure I'd had a really good eyeful.

'Do you really not know who I am?' He said it as if I *should* know. I was irritated by his arrogance.

'Someone from *Love Island*?' I suggested, though I knew it had been some soap.

I thought perhaps he'd be insulted but this time he roared with laughter.

'Oh, you little peach. Do you really think I'm in my twenties? I'm immensely flattered.'

I hated the way he was laughing at me, and made a performance of looking at my watch. 'I have to go. I have a meeting with Miss Yewtree at nine o'clock.'

'Me too,' he said, vigorously towelling himself dry, and then stepping into his underwear and jeans, both pristine white. Most men look ridiculous hopping about on one leg but he managed to look infuriatingly elegant. Who did he think he was? He was acting like the hero of a soft porn movie.

I tried hard to look unimpressed, turned on my heel and marched away. So *was* he another tutor for the summer school? Wasn't he too famous for that? He seemed far too in love with himself to care a jot for the children. What was it with men that they always wanted to show off their dicks?

Star had told me about Freud and his theory that women had penis envy. She had always been much keener on boys than me, but we both still turned up our noses at this ridiculous idea. What woman would actually want an unruly appendage flapping about her front?

It was a relief when I got back to the Hall and saw I wasn't alone any more. A thin, gangly guy in a suit was nervously approaching the door, a long finger extended to press the bell. He wore glasses and twitched them up his nose, reminding me of Oliver when he was a boy. He looked relieved when he saw me.

'Hello! Thank goodness, I thought I might have come too early and didn't know what to do. Are you one of the other tutors?'

'Hello, I'm Dolphin,' I said, trusting him not to mock. 'I'm going to be painting scenery and doing a bit of art with the kids.'

'I'm Morris, the music tutor. I teach music at secondary school too. You'd think I'd have enough of it!' He laughed at himself, embarrassed.

'Still, why not, if it's your passion,' I said. 'Shall we ring the bell?'

Nina came to the door, wearing a surprisingly jaunty navy trouser suit with a red scarf.

'Welcome to Lavender Hall! I think we've met before. I'm Nina, the course manager,' she said briskly, obviously enjoying her current role. 'Do come in!'

Morris and I trooped in, down the long corridor. Other halls like this might have had ancestral portraits hanging on the walls. This one had very large black-and-white portraits of Henrietta when she was much younger. She looked incredibly beautiful back in the seventies, with hair down to her waist and floaty white dresses. She had a blissed-out expression on her face, as if she was having a religious experience – but perhaps she was simply high on drugs. She grew gradually older, posing dramatically on stage, and then morphing into middle age as her soap character. There were at least ten photos of her in the role. It was clearly her heyday.

There were a few photos of Henrietta as an old woman playing cameo parts. The one at the end showed her in a hospital setting with people weeping by her bed as she murmured her last words. She really did look at death's door, her face eerily pale, her eyes looking upwards soulfully. I didn't know how she could bear to display these photos of her declining career, but she was obviously proud of them.

Nina led us into Henrietta's living room – and there she was, the Acting Queen herself, in a splendid maroon gown with lipstick to match, very grand jewellery (gold set with rubies – or maybe coloured glass in gilt?) and Turkish brocade shoes with curly ends.

'Darlings!' she said, as if she was *acting* being a once-famous actress. She'd applied her black eyeliner and crimson lipstick too thickly and with a very wobbly hand. The hand itself was outstretched towards us. Morris took it nervously, clearly wondering if he should shake it or kiss it.

He chose to kiss it, which went down well. I clasped it with both of mine, and that seemed an equally good choice. Henrietta made extravagant conversation about herself and her career as Nina brought in more arriving tutors. It was difficult to remember all their names and specialities: Damian was ballet; Lola modern dance; Ted was a much older guy who wrote plays – or did long ago; motherly Linda did costume design; along with two young blonde women Stevie and Maya. One taught mime, the other singing. Stevie had an expressive face, a lithe body and was dressed in black. Maya had amazing long hair and a beautiful voice. I was certain Stevie was the mime artist and Maya the singer – but bizarrely, they were the other way round.

Damian made the mistake of asking who was going to be in charge of drama. Henrietta sat up straight and rearranged her long scarf, flipping it over her shoulder with attitude.

'*I* am, darling, obviously,' she said. 'And of course, my dear friend and associate who will be joining us shortly.' Then she turned her back on Damian as if he was of no account. 'Well, let us begin! Nina, darling, please hand out the schedules so everyone can look at them before the children start arriving. I've worked on the timetables with immense care so I do hope no one is going to be awkward and want to reschedule.'

My heart started thudding as I looked at the timetable. It was ruled this way and that and peppered with so many words in boxes that it seemed a meaningless puzzle. Thank God 'Art' was a word I quickly recognized. I gradually got the knack of looking up and down each of the days and finding it here and there. I had an hour scheduled for lunch in the middle of the day, but no other breaks. I wasn't sure how my bladder was going to hold out, but decided it might be better not to ask.

Lola and the hapless Damian did have the courage to say that they couldn't possibly demonstrate dance non-stop all day long, and they were in the midst of a heated argument when the formerly naked swimmer came strolling nonchalantly into the room, seemingly unaware that he was a good half-hour late.

'Ah! Joel, darling son!' Henrietta exclaimed, beckoning him towards her, gold bangles sounding like tiny tambourines.

Joel struck a pose, his arms wide in welcome.

'Mother!' he declared dramatically and strode towards her. He kissed her hand, he kissed her all the way up her arm, he kissed the nape of her neck. I stared at them, appalled. He was her *son*? What was he doing kissing her like a lover? But everyone was smiling, apparently enjoying the performance. Even timid Morris was laughing along.

'They're acting, just playing the fool,' he murmured. 'You know. *Heartbreak*. He played Henrietta's evil son. Simon the Scoundrel.'

'Oh!' I said weakly. 'Oh yes. Of course.'

It all slotted into place. I'd never watched *Heartbreak* but I knew it had been very popular in its day. This Joel of the jaunty genitals certainly seemed very popular with everyone here. They all acted like they adored him. Especially Henrietta. She chuckled throatily and shook her head at him, clearly enchanted.

'Behave, you bad boy!' she said, fluttering her eyelashes in a parody of a femme fatale. 'Ladies and gentlemen, may I introduce you to my dear associate, very special friend, star of stage and screen, my much-adored television son, Mr Joel Fortune.'

Joel acted like he had a spotlight on him, striking an attitude. All right, he was sending himself up, but clearly determined to stay the centre of attention. This was the guy I'd actually quite fancied? That I'd even hoped fancied me? He barely gave me a glance now as Henrietta proudly introduced him to everyone. He started working the room, chatting and charming, making little quips, keeping eye contact all the time. He made a big fuss of Maya with her glorious long hair and floaty hyacinth dress, shaking her hand and doubtless discreetly rubbing his thumb up and down the gap between her finger and thumb.

'And you must meet little Dolphin, our artist,' said Henrietta.

I braced myself, putting my hands firmly behind my back. I didn't want him to play that trick again. Plus I was also horribly conscious that my hands had gone all sweaty. Joel simply smiled at me, waving his own hand in the air.

'Oh, we're old friends already,' he said, and I stood there foolishly, unable to think of a single thing to say. By the time I'd pulled myself together he'd moved on to Lola and Damian, both of them looking very keen to make an impression. I pretended I didn't care, decided he wasn't worth bothering about. He was just an irritating show-off – though everyone seemed super-impressed. But then I saw Nina standing at the back, arms folded. She saw me watching her, and she nodded at Joel and rolled her eyes. Then she marched into the centre of the room, coughing to get everyone's attention.

'Shall we get down to business, everyone? The children and parents will be arriving soon. I've just got time to show each of you where you will be working before we gather together to show a united front.'

'Oh, Nina, do you have to be such a bossy boots?' drawled Joel. 'Can't you make us all a coffee first? Please, darling?'

'If you want a coffee, you can make it yourself – *darling*!' Nina snapped. 'Come along, everyone.'

Joel stayed with Henrietta, but the rest of us trooped obediently after Nina. It was a relief to see that everything was beautifully prepared. Morris had his own music room with an upright piano. There was also a grand piano in the large drawing room with the furniture moved to one side and the rugs rolled up so that the dancers could practise. Perhaps Morris was supposed to dash from one room to the other when required.

There were several 'rehearsal' rooms for modern dance and singing and acting, and Henrietta's living room was reserved for giving individual instruction to very promising students. Maya's mime sessions were in the conservatory, and the final performance of the play was also going to be outside on a stage, with an elaborate canopy should there be rain. It was all a bit makeshift, but the rooms were very grand, almost stately-home standard, so perhaps it didn't matter.

We seemed to have used up all the rooms, but Nina led Linda

and me upstairs. She'd been allocated Henrietta's private dressing room, which was meant to be a special favour, but Henrietta's clothes were still festooned everywhere, hanging from door handles, window bars and wardrobes, giving the impression that we were surrounded by multiple Miss Yewtrees.

'I've put you up in the attic, Dolphin,' said Nina. 'Follow me.'

We climbed up a very steep staircase, Nina's large, striped bottom swaying from side to side above me, and went through the door at the top. I couldn't help groaning as I looked around in the dim light. It was stuffed with old furniture and suitcases and racks of clothing. How could we possibly find anywhere to paint scenery and do individual artwork in such darkly crowded confusion?

'Dolphin?' Nina had nimbly edged round the clutter and turned the corner and I followed her, stopping in my tracks at the sight that greeted me. The rest of the attic had been cleared of junk. There was a lengthy skylight above, showing two long tables and some stacking chairs. A generous selection of artistic material was spread out neatly on several trunks and there was even an easel, though it was ancient and listing to one side.

'Will this do?' Nina asked, still puffing a little from the stairs.

'It's brilliant,' I breathed.

'Thank God! I nearly did myself serious damage heaving all that junk up one end while Hen and his lordship were getting pissed together last night,' said Nina.

'Is he staying here, then?' I asked.

'Oh, yes. He makes himself thoroughly at home. I reckon he's banking on it being *his* home when Hen kicks the bucket,' said Nina. 'She's hinted as much. It's her way of keeping him hanging around making a fuss of her.'

I wrinkled my nose. 'That's horrible. Can't you make her see he's just using her?'

'I'm sure she realizes – and doesn't give a damn. She's besotted. Hopeless case. Some women are like that,' Nina sniffed.

'I suppose they are,' I said, thinking of Marigold and her pointless passion for Micky.

'You could say I must be in the same boat myself, because why am I still hovering around her after all these years?' Nina said. 'Anyway, I'm glad this room suits. You'll have to fetch water from the first-floor bathroom, but I'm sure you'll cope.'

'I will!'

Nina smiled at my enthusiasm. 'Do you think you're going to like it here?' she asked.

'I think I'm going to love it,' I said.

18

I was right, I absolutely loved my new job. Initially, I was anxious about the children, wondering if they'd like me. I was fine with individuals, but school memories made me wonder if they'd all gang up on me and laugh at my ideas. But thank goodness they were all keen and friendly, though some were endearingly shy and anxious.

I blessed the good memory I'd developed out of necessity because of my dyslexia. I had eighteen students and I knew all their names and artistic abilities by the end of the first day. My absolute favourite was the youngest child, Miranda. She was a demure eight-year-old with a vivid imagination. When she saw the line of princesses in my drawing pad she started inventing her own, although most of hers had lopsided crowns and wore jeans under their frilly skirts and big boots instead of ballet slippers. She was very much the smallest student. The oldest was fourteen-year-old Adrian, a boy a good head and shoulders taller than me. He had such fair hair it was almost white, and very pale skin. He was very shy and whenever anyone talked to him he blushed scarlet.

I guessed Miranda would be the star of the show, but I thought acting was going to be a terrible ordeal for Adrian. But he was heart-warmingly talented at art, colouring strange ethereal creatures – very pale, very elongated, magical beings that could be his fantasy relatives.

Henrietta had rather overestimated the number of students attending, so I could easily accommodate the older and younger children into one session. I still didn't have to work continuously, so often went to chat to Linda in between sessions. She was busy renovating old costumes before anything new was required.

I liked her a lot, mostly because she seemed reassuringly normal, not tiresomely theatrical. Although she'd worked on costumes all her life, she wasn't a showy dresser. She wore nondescript pastel tops and easy-fit slacks and sandals with Velcro fastenings – real dear-old-nana clothes.

'Do you still design costumes for shows?' I asked her.

'Not much, dear. I used to do lots for telly, even *Strictly*,' she confided. 'That's when I met Henrietta. Do you remember when she was on? She caused quite a sensation at the time, especially when she did the tango – she hammed it up no end, and she was a demon with all those flick kicks. She made a fuss about a couple of her costumes, but I learnt to get on with her. I've more or less retired now – my arthritis has got the upper hand, so to speak – but I can still do a bit of sewing for Henrietta.'

Her arthritis had swollen her fingers into sausages, and she was a bit creaky all over, so she was very grateful if I ran down to the kitchen to make us a cup of tea, or helped ease her up from her chair when she had to go to the bathroom.

'You're such a dear, Dolphin,' she said. 'Your mum must be so proud of you.'

'Mm,' I said darkly. 'I don't think so.' I rarely told people about Marigold, but I found myself blurting out all sorts of things about her to Linda.

'Oh dear, poor soul. Mental illness can be a torment,' she said.

'And poor you, having to cope. Do you have a partner who's a comfort to you?'

I nibbled at my lip, wondering how to answer. 'Well, I've got a very good friend. He's my next-door neighbour actually. We haven't known each other very long, so he's not actually a partner, but he's certainly a comfort to me,' I said.

'That's what you need, dear. My Harry used to be my one and only, though I daresay I took him for granted when we were together,' Linda said sadly.

'Did you split up?'

'Oh, no, he died five years ago. Dropped dead from a heart attack when he was watering the garden. It was such a shock,' she said, tears in her eyes. 'I miss him very much now.'

'I'm so sorry,' I murmured.

Linda patted me kindly on the shoulder.

'Bless you, dear. I still miss him, of course I do, but it was a long time ago. You never quite get used to being on your own, though. You make the most of your new friend next door, dear. We all need a bit of company.'

I'd been used to being on my own, but now Lee had become very much part of my life, despite the short time we'd known each other. He was particularly sweet to me that first Monday evening, rushing home with a punnet of Mrs Knight's raspberries, a pot of double cream and a ready-made meringue from the corner shop to make a celebration cake.

We shared the cake and kissed with creamy lips and I told him all about the children and Linda and all the other tutors.

'They seem quite a nice bunch really. I like Morris the music teacher best, after Linda. There's only one I can't stand,' I said. It was almost true. I still got a little fluttery whenever he came near me, but that didn't mean anything.

'Who's that, then?' said Lee, frowning.

'This actor, Joel Fortune.'

'Not the *Heartbreak* actor?' He pulled a face. 'Ali used to be nuts about him. She could have gone on *Mastermind* with him as her specialist subject. She knew all about his marriage, his long-term relationships, his string of girlfriends. Goodness knows what they all saw in him. He was always swaggering around like he's God's gift to women.'

'Yep!' I said. 'That's him.' Lee had sounded quite heated so I didn't think it a good idea to tell him about the swimming-pool encounter. Or even the first meeting at Artful Ink. I didn't want to wind him up further.

'Henrietta makes a total fool of herself when she's with him. She adores him. He seems to expect *everyone* to adore him,' I said.

The kids hung on his every word and followed him around, and shy Adrian blushed whenever he was near him. The tutors all seemed to think him wonderful too. He'd already made a play for Maya, miming at her from across the room at lunchtime. He was irritatingly good at it. She seemed thrilled, tossing her long hair and miming back at him.

'He sounds sickening,' said Lee. 'Don't *you* start adoring him!'

'Never going to happen,' I assured him. I meant it too. If I was totally honest, I was a little bit annoyed that he'd made such an obvious choice as pretty Maya. They were already murmuring together, laughing at private jokes and wandering off by themselves at lunchtime.

Henrietta noticed too and told Joel she needed to consult with him about their drama sessions over lunch in her living room. Every day. I cringed at her blatant possessiveness, but Joel seemed to think it amusing. He went along with her wishes cheerfully enough, even saying that it was a good idea – but there were obviously plenty of other opportunities to hook up with Maya.

'I can see a romance in the offing,' Morris said to me.

'Definitely,' I said.

Morris sighed. I didn't know whether he was lusting after Maya himself – or maybe Joel? I decided I didn't care. I concentrated on the children instead.

There was a general conference for everyone the next morning, presided over by Henrietta. I wondered if some of the kids might mock her queenly air and flamboyant way of talking, but they all seemed in awe of her. They hadn't been born when she was having her *Heartbreak* heyday, but many episodes of it were still played on one of the more obscure channels, and she'd done several fifteen-second send-up clips on TikTok with Joel that had recently gone viral.

'Now, my dears!' she said, clapping her hands together, her rings banging against each other. 'We've no time to lose. We must decide on the subject of our play if we're going to reach tip-top perfection on Friday week when we have our grand performance. Hopefully you've enjoyed our little taster sessions and your tutors have had time to assess your skills. So – what shall our play be about?'

'Why not a play about a dragon?' Linda said quickly.

This went down well with all the little ones, apart from Max. He'd seemed a quiet little boy in my art class but he'd already disconcerted me by painting a picture of a dead man, using up a lot of red paint.

'Dragons are silly. I want to do something about war, or gangsters, with lots of shooting,' he said, holding an imaginary machine gun and pretending to fire it.

'Yes, who wants to do a fairy story?' sneered Bethany, one of the older girls. 'Couldn't we do a tragic love story?'

'Dragons can be romantic, bonding with maiden dragon-riders,' I said. 'Or they can be super scary and try to *eat* the maidens. And knights sometimes club the dragons with their battle-axes and pierce them with their spears to save the maidens.'

'Clever you, Dolphin. That seems to cover all the bases,' said Henrietta. 'Do you think you could work with that, Ted?'

'Piece of cake,' he said. 'We'll have a prince and a princess as the leads, and lots of knights and maidens so everyone has a decent part. The little ones can be village children.'

I saw Miranda looking downcast.

'Perhaps there could be a very little princess? But a determined little creature who gradually tames the dragon?' I suggested.

Henrietta didn't look too sure this time. 'That's not very traditional,' she said.

'Exactly!' said Joel. 'That's what we need – a modern twist. Brilliant!'

'I think you might be right,' said Henrietta, nodding at him, as if it had been *his* idea.

So it was a done deal – and everyone started concentrating on *The Dragon Play* from that day onwards. I was thrilled that I'd spoken up and grateful that Joel had been so enthusiastic – yet annoyed, too, that he had such sway over people. Still, it meant that Miranda got the part of the littlest princess, which made her practically burst with pride – and astonishingly, Adrian got to be the dragon!

He was forced to audition for the part because he was the tallest. I thought he'd say a few lines in a mouse-squeak – but with a green carrier bag as a makeshift, temporary dragon head he roared ferociously and moved his lanky body in such a threatening manner that he was convincingly scary.

Once all the casting was done, everyone concentrated on the play, though the hour after lunch was considered recreation so the children could choose whichever class they fancied. Whenever they were free, I got my art enthusiasts to chat with me about the scenery. I was at a total loss at first. What should I paint the scenery *on*? What sort of paint? Brushes? I started to panic.

Nina came to my rescue.

'Don't worry, Dolphin, you'll find last year's flats in a corner of the conservatory, behind all the pot plants. And I've ordered in acrylic paint in varying colours, and a job lot of assorted brushes so the little ones can join in. There's several old sheets somewhere too – Henrietta won't want her precious Portuguese tiles getting splashed.'

I took a deep breath. 'So we're doing the scenery painting *in* the conservatory?'

'Well, if you can drag everything up to that attic you're a stronger woman than me. You'd never negotiate those flats up all the stairs,' said Nina.

'But I thought Maya was using the conservatory for her mime classes?' I queried.

'So she is – but if they're any good at mime, they won't disturb you with any chatter, will they?' said Nina. 'Come on now, darling. You'll find a way. We all have to improvise occasionally.'

I did my best. I tried to remember what scenery actually looked like. Marigold had taken Star and me to a pantomime once when we were really small, but I only had the dimmest memory of the stage – I just spent my time wondering why Cinderella's ugly sisters were both obviously men, and wanting to hide under my seat when Marigold started singing along with Cinderella, substituting the word 'Micky' for 'Prince'.

I'd never acted in a play myself, apart from being a donkey for the Nativity in the Infants, and that had been agony because half the class started chanting 'Dolphin is a donkey'. We didn't have proper costumes so I was pretty certain we didn't have scenery either.

I found the Lavender Hall flats in the conservatory and looked glumly at the depictions of a monster alien planet. I tried covering a section with thick white paint, but that made me shake, remembering the terrible day Marigold painted herself white all over to cover her tattoos.

I sat down on a large paint pot, trying to compose myself. The art class peered at me a little anxiously. So did the mimers. Maya was sitting decoratively in a wicker chair, the rounded cream back framing her head like a pale halo. Joel had abandoned his own drama group elsewhere and was lounging in a deckchair beside her, chatting away. The sight of them flirting together didn't help cheer me up.

I hoped they were so involved with each other that they wouldn't notice me – but after a few minutes Joel called, 'Hey, Dolphin, are you OK?'

'Yes, fine,' I said determinedly, jumping up and hoping I looked as if I knew what I was doing.

'Let's see what you've done so far,' said Joel, strolling over. It was obvious I'd done next to nothing. 'Mm,' he said. 'You're splotching that titanium white on a bit thick. I'd thin it down quite a bit or you'll run out of paint. Nina's supplies are always sparse in the extreme, because Hen's running out of money.'

'Thanks,' I said tightly.

'And I'd be a bit freer with the application. You'll be hours just dabbing at it like that,' he said. 'Then once it's dry tomorrow you can get cracking with the kids. I wouldn't risk any spattering techniques, though – those sheets won't give anywhere near enough protection.'

'Thanks,' I repeated, but more grateful this time, because he was really being helpful, and managing not to be patronizing.

'You haven't done this sort of artwork before, have you?' said Joel.

'Nope. As is obvious,' I said.

'Well, you'll pick it up in no time, you're brilliantly artistic. The girl with the blue hair at the studio was doing the most amazing dragon on some young punter and said it was your design,' he said.

So he went back! Was he looking for me?

'Are you going to get one?' I asked.

'I'd quite like one – if you'd do it for me?'

'Sorry. I don't work there any more,' I said. 'But I'm sure Jo would do a good job on you.'

'I'm sure – but she's not you, is she?' he said, slightly lowering his voice.

I glanced over at Maya, who was showing an elaborate tiptoeing mime to the village children cast. I'm sure she was keeping an eye on Joel too. He was smiling, enjoying the situation.

'You're hopeless. You want to charm everyone,' I said.

'Of course I do,' said Joel.

He was so annoyingly obvious – and yet I couldn't help being a little bit charmed myself now. He was actually very helpful, giving me more advice about techniques. He'd apparently learnt a lot hanging around backstage with the scenery crew when he had theatre work.

He was good at mime too, imitating Maya impeccably, often making the children collapse into helpless giggles, but she didn't get cross with him. She'd obviously fallen for him big time. I was determined not to do likewise. I was done flirting with the bad boys, especially as Lee had told me about Joel's string of girlfriends.

Lee had started calling me Bluebell because for a couple of days I came back to the house completely spattered with blue paint, as most of the scenery was sky. The children got bored painting blue, blue, blue endlessly and so did I. In fact, I was so fed up that I started to add a few extras. I took the smallest brush and fashioned a hideous bird of prey with a baby dragon hanging from its beak. I added two young dragons on their hind legs, fighting, and another couple of ancient dragons lying on some rocks, puffing smoke rings competitively, and then several mythical creatures pictured in Lee's *Ancient Myths and Legends* book. I wasn't quite sure who they were, but I painted the man with huge wings flying near the sun, and another handsome dark guy in a short tunic peering in a little pool surrounded by white daffodils. Best of all, sitting right on top of the dragon's lair was the strange man playing his pipes, his goat legs splayed, while white rabbits circled him, bewitched.

'That's Pan, isn't it? He looks a bit sinister!' said Maya. 'And that's Icarus flying near the sun – and oh my God, you've painted Joel as Narcissus, gazing at himself.'

'No, I haven't!' I protested – but when I looked carefully I could see my hand had a will of its own.

Joel came to inspect the painting, inevitably, and smiled.

'I look quite fetching in a white silk tunic, with a garland of flowers round my hair,' he said. 'It's great – but Henrietta's not going to like it.'

'Because he looks just a little bit like you?' I said, crinkling my nose.

'Because it's all too busy for a backdrop. There's far too much going on. It's distracting. The audience will be squinting at it rather than watching the kids act their hearts out,' he said.

I saw he had a point, but I still hoped Henrietta would be impressed. The children all seemed to love these little extras and worked with fresh enthusiasm, covering the grass with a riot of flowers. Miranda added more rabbits because she said they were her favourite animals, though she was careful to paint them well away from the dragon's lair in case it fancied a change of diet.

Henrietta would surely be pleased that the children were all so enthused – but Joel was right. She came hobbling along into the conservatory, leaning heavily on an ebony walking stick. When she saw my lovely detailed backdrop she held up her hands in horror, the stick clattering to the ground so she nearly fell over.

I had to rush to hold her up, while she told me that it wouldn't do at all. It would be far too distracting for the audience, just as Joel had said.

'Really, Dolphin! I thought you'd have more sense than that. Look at all the paint you've wasted! Honestly, what a silly mistake!' she said, reaching for her walking stick. I stepped back warily, though I didn't seriously think she was going to beat me with it.

I was really upset, though, fighting not to cry, especially not in front of the children and Maya and Joel.

'But you must admit, Henrietta, it's a pretty glorious painting in itself,' said Joel, and even Maya murmured agreement.

'Of course, of course. Don't get downhearted, Dolphin. You don't have to create another backdrop – just paint over all these extra figures, especially the ugly great bird holding the baby dragon by one leg. The yummy mummies will think you're trying to give their little ones nightmares,' Henrietta insisted. 'I think we're going to have to tone down young Adrian's performance as it is.'

'But he's incredible!' I said, though Joel frowned to warn me not to argue with her.

'Yes, but I heard one of the little ones say she thought he was very scary,' said Henrietta.

'They *love* being scared!' I said, too worked up to be cautious. 'It's like when your dad plays bears with you and you squeal in fear and yet you're laughing too because you know it's only Dad really.' Not that my own dad had ever played bears with me when I was little, but I'd seen Lee larking about with Ava.

Henrietta looked sharply at me, eyeing me up and down. I waited. Was she going to send me packing already? I wished now I'd held my tongue – but her expression softened.

'Tell you what then, we'll compromise! Adrian can act his little heart out, but when we have the finale with everyone on stage he can whip his dragon head off and prance about to show he's not scary at all. How about that?' Henrietta suggested.

I thought Adrian would rather die than *prance* but she couldn't rush on stage and *make* him perform like a cartoon, so I simply shrugged. Henrietta was smiling now, which gave me the courage to try to save my backdrop too.

'I don't suppose we could compromise a little over my scenery?' I suggested. 'Maybe keep the flowery person peering in the pool, and the goat man playing his pipes? They wouldn't really be too noticeable from the audience, not so they'd distract anyone.'

'You're very tenacious, and I think that's an admirable characteristic. But I'm tenacious too, and the answer is no, absolutely not, they all have to be painted out.' Henrietta hesitated. 'But if you have any spare time over the next week or so, you might like to attempt a similar mural on the attic wall as a memento of our summer school? What do you think?'

'I think that's a great idea!' It wasn't quite the same, and no one would see it, but at least I could recreate it.

Henrietta swept off triumphantly, hanging on to Joel's arm. He turned and grinned at me as he escorted her.

'Is there anything going on between you two?' Maya asked, looking me straight in the eyes.

'Nothing at all,' I said, truthfully enough.

But I couldn't help being pleased that Joel had done his best to stick up for me.

19

On Saturday, I went to see Marigold. She was in the recreation room, sitting at a table with her hands spread wide so that Lettie could paint tiny flowers on her fingernails. They were chatting amicably when I went into the room, but Marigold's expression turned haughty when she saw me.

'Oh, Dolphin! I barely recognized you it's been so long since I've seen you,' she said, while Lettie smirked.

'You know perfectly well I can't come during the week now because I've got my summer job,' I said, trying to be patient.

'I bet you see that Lee every day,' she sneered.

'We're neighbours, for God's sake. Of course we see each other.'

'So why aren't you being neighbourly with him today?' Marigold asked.

'Because he's gone to collect his daughter for the weekend,' I said.

'Oh-oh! I was right. He'll want you to help look after the kiddie. Watch out, you'll end up married to him if you're not careful,' she said. 'I told you, didn't I, Lettie?'

'Yes, you did,' said Lettie.

I hated it that Marigold was discussing my private life with Lettie. She seemed to be cosying up to Marigold, utterly dazzled by her. She'd even inked mock tattoos on her own stick-thin arm.

'Look, we're just . . . in a situationship,' I explained.

'Well, you could have picked someone more exciting. It's not as if he can even do your garden for you, because you haven't got one,' said Marigold, and Lettie sniggered.

I felt like snatching the nail-varnish brush from her and stuffing it up her pert little nose.

'I wonder if I could have a private chat with my mum?' I said instead.

'Hey! Don't talk to Lettie like that, Miss Snippy,' said Marigold. 'Tell you what, Letts. How about you making us all a cup of tea? That would be lovely.'

'OK, Mags,' said Lettie, putting the top on the nail varnish, pocketing it, and rushing off to the kitchen like an eager lap dog.

'Letts? *Mags?*' I said, my eyebrows halfway up my forehead. 'Pass me the sick bowl.'

'Don't be such a sourpuss,' said Marigold. 'She likes us having nicknames.'

'What's the *matter* with you? You'll be exchanging friendship bracelets next and calling each other your BFF,' I said.

'You try being shut up in a psych ward,' snapped Marigold. 'It's good to have a friend. Dr Gibbon is very pleased with us.'

I didn't know which was worse – Marigold off her head leaping into thin air, or Marigold playing besties with a girl practically young enough to be her granddaughter. I could feel myself prickling. Why did Marigold have to encourage her so?

'Is that her attraction? That she's like a grandchild to you?' I asked suddenly, though she seemed to have put her real grandchild out of her mind now.

'Don't be so cheeky!' said Marigold. 'Daughter, maybe. Look how sweet she is to me.' She waved her newly patterned nails.

'What is it with you and decoration? You'll be getting gold and silver teeth next,' I said.

Why was I being so bitchy? Well, I *knew* why. Marigold was implying that Lettie was like a daughter to her – a *better* daughter? I wasn't *jealous*, was I?

I'd gone overboard trying to find special presents for Marigold. I felt in my knapsack and produced the various offerings I'd bought her: a silky green bra and knickers set; a pair of false eyelashes to replace one she'd dropped and then mistaken for a spider; a couple of magazines; and a box of red Lindor chocolates. I'd tried so hard to be imaginative. Surely they would please her? But was I making such an effort partly to outdo Lettie?

To my relief, Marigold cheered up immediately, like a kid at Christmas. When Lettie came back with a tea tray, Marigold showed off all her goodies, and Lettie seemed thrilled for her, though a little wistful.

'Do you get many visitors, Lettie?' I asked.

Lettie breathed through her nose heavily. She looked at Marigold.

'She's taking a break from her family for a while,' Marigold said, her voice uncharacteristically soft. 'They've no understanding of anorexia. They've put so much pressure on the poor girl. It's taken its toll on Lettie and it was too much for her. But you're doing well now, aren't you, chickie?'

I felt all my stomach muscles tense. Marigold had sometimes called me chickie when she was especially fond of me. I glared at Lettie – and then felt ashamed.

'Have a chocolate?' I offered her Marigold's Lindor packet, before realizing this was incredibly tactless. 'Sorry, sorry,' I apologized.

'No, she could have a lick,' said Marigold. 'She's ready to try, aren't you, Letts?'

Lettie didn't look sure, but she allowed Marigold to unwrap a chocolate and hold it out to her. Her pointy pink tongue darted out and gave it the most cursory lick – and then she shut her eyes. She was trembling, her hands clasped.

'It's good, isn't it?' said Marigold.

'It's . . . bliss,' Lettie murmured.

'So try a bite,' Marigold urged gently.

'Maybe tomorrow,' Lettie said.

'Tomorrow, then. Look, I'll put your chocolate back in its wrapper and we'll hide it away for now,' said Marigold.

I stared at her. Where did she learn to be so tactful? I suppose she'd been in wards with other anorexic girls, but she'd never shown any interest in any of them before. Star herself had gone through a serious dieting stage when she was studying for her GCSEs (A* in all ten subjects!) and one Sunday Marigold had tried to tempt her with a roast dinner. She tried very hard, because she rarely cooked properly, and it had actually been delicious. Star had nibbled at a carrot and eaten a spoonful of peas precisely, and Marigold had suddenly picked up the plate and tipped the whole lot over Star's head. Star was furious – especially when I caught her eating a roast potato later on.

'Now, Dolphin, what did you want to have a little chat about?' Marigold said, possibly trying to be tactful with me now. 'Here, Lettie, you have a deck at *Hello!* while we have a natter.'

I started telling Marigold all about Lavender Hall, and how my art classes were surprisingly popular. I so wanted to impress her. I mentioned Miranda and Adrian enthusiastically and she seemed to be listening, but then she suddenly gave a huge yawn.

'Oh, sorry if I'm boring you,' I said curtly.

'Hey!' said Marigold, tapping her lips to hide another yawn. 'I can't help it, it's these God-awful drugs, they're turning me into a zombie. Go on about this school thing you're at. Aren't there any decent men on the staff?'

'Well, it depends on your definition of decent,' I said. 'There's one totally *in*decent guy who swims stark naked.'

Marigold chuckled, visibly perking up. 'I like the sound of him. Why don't you make a play for him?'

'Apart from the fact that he's so clearly bad news, it would be pointless. He's already having an affair with the mime artist.'

'Does he teach swimming, then?'

'No, he teaches drama. He's an actor.'

'An actor! What's his name?' Marigold demanded, interested again.

'He's not really famous. He was in some soap once. Joel something,' I said, deliberately vague.

'Not Joel Fortune?' said Marigold, eyes wide, and even Lettie looked up, blinking in surprise.

'So you've heard of him?'

'Simon the Scoundrel! He was sex on legs, that boy! The soap was rubbish but he was incredible. And now you're telling me you've been swimming with him?'

'Not me! I'd sooner go swimming with a shark,' I insisted.

'So you'd sooner your little codfish, Lee?' Marigold suggested.

'Will you just shut up about Lee! You're a total bitch at times,' I said angrily, and stood up to go.

I hoped she'd protest but she didn't try to stop me. I saw Lettie put her arm round her, as if Marigold needed comforting.

I was the one who needed comforting. I hurried home to Lee and Ava. She was wearing her Princess Elsa dress so Lee had signed up to Disney+ and had *Frozen* on. We watched it together and sang along to all the songs, belting out 'Let It Go'. Then I drew all Ava's favourite characters for her while Lee made tea.

'You're so clever, Dol,' said Ava, helping me colour them in. 'I wish I could draw like you. Look, Daddy's bought me a new picture book! It's *The Gruffalo*. Doesn't he look funny? Will you read it to me?'

She waved a thin paperback at me. I saw the cover. The title. I went hot, remembering that awful encounter with Mrs Harris at Duckies. Of course the character on the front wasn't a bloody giraffe.

Lee was looking over at me, seeing my burning face.

'Shall we read it together after tea?' he suggested.

He was being kind, wanting to help me out – but it made me squirm. I didn't want to look a fool. And I didn't want Lee to treat me as if I was Ava's age.

'I think you're the reading expert. And I'm the one who draws,' I said. 'Shall I draw you your own funny Gruffalo, Ava?' I said.

We drew together until Lee served us tea – an expertly made frittata and fresh runner beans.

'Wait till *my* runner beans come up at Mrs Knight's!' said Lee. 'I'm planning all kinds of veg for next year.'

'Great,' I said, though I wondered if he was meaning we'd be sharing them. He was beaming at me, looking so happy. I turned round from his sink where I was doing the washing up and mumbled, 'Thanks for not pushing the reading thing.'

'I just wanted to try to help but I can see it was stupid of me,' said Lee.

'No, it was really thoughtful,' I said. I gave him a kiss without thinking, and then jerked my head away abruptly, because Ava was staring at us.

'Sorry, poppet, I got a bit carried away there,' I said quickly.

'Don't worry, I kiss Daddy all the time!' she said and blew him heaps. She looked so sweet I had to give her a hug.

She was the loveliest little kid. When I was with her I couldn't help pretending she was mine. It was as if we were a family of three, Lee, Ava and me. Who cared about flying? We were happy together, weren't we?

I felt even happier when I got a message from Oliver out of the blue later that evening. He and Ross had decided to go to Pride in Brighton next week and wondered if we could meet up.

'Oliver and I have been friends since we were little kids. And his husband Ross is lovely too. Perhaps we could all go out for a pub lunch next week before you have to take Ava home?' I asked.

'Or I could do a roast? Though maybe they won't be up for it if they've been drinking and clubbing,' said Lee.

'They're not really that sort of couple,' I said, smiling. 'They're very conventional cosy teachers. I expect they'll watch the parade for a while and then go and find a nice teashop. Oh, Lee, would you really do a roast?'

'Of course. And you can whip up an Angel Delight if you like.'

I pushed him playfully. 'Don't tease! I can't wait for you to meet them. Oliver was so sweet to me when we were at primary school. When we went to secondary school we were in different forms. They were named after planets, Jupiter, Mars, Venus – but my class was the remedial one, Moon, and so we all got called Moonies. Can you imagine!' I said, shaking my head, feeling the stabbing humiliation anew. 'We were the ones that mostly did crayoning just to keep us occupied.'

'Well, it's stood you in good stead, hasn't it?' said Lee. 'Look at you now, teaching art to all those posh little kids at Lavender Hall.'

I laughed. 'You're great at stopping me trudging back down Memory Lane. Well, Misery Lane in my case. But you had a tough time yourself, didn't you, Lee?' I said, remembering he'd told me his mother had died young.

'Oh, so so,' said Lee, shrugging. He looked sideways at Ava, clearly not wanting to talk about it in front of her. When she was in bed and we were having a beer together on the sofa, he told me a little about it.

'I suppose Mum dying affected me most. My brothers were in their teens. They'd left home by the time my dad married again. I never really hit it off with my stepmother. I don't see her now that Dad's died too. End of story.' He said it all deadpan, but his voice was strained.

I clasped his hand in mine. 'There's me always going on about my traumatic childhood, yet yours doesn't sound as if it was much fun either. How come you're so kind and balanced and lovely now?'

'Oh, I can have my moments,' he said with a rueful smile. 'Ali and I used to have awful rows sometimes. I couldn't seem to do anything to please her.'

'Well, she must be an ungrateful cow, then,' I said, winding my arms round his neck and kissing him. I hated it that she'd taken away all his confidence. I felt really protective of him. Did that mean that I was maybe falling in love with him?

I still wasn't sure. We kissed some more and got to the stage when we wanted to creep next door to have sex. Lee cautiously opened his bedside drawer to grab a condom, but Ava woke up and sat up straight in bed.

'What are you doing, Daddy?' she asked sleepily.

'Oh, just looking for a tissue. I've got a bit of a sniffle,' Lee said, and started some very fake sneezing.

'I've got a sniffle too,' said Ava, and she started sneezing as well.

By the time they'd finished larking around and Lee had read Ava several stories to make her sleepy again, the moment had passed and we simply went to sleep ourselves.

20

The second week at Lavender Hall was more intense. Everything was focused on the performance of the play on Friday night. I got the main characters to perform it for me as we finished the backdrop and constructed a reasonably realistic cave for the dragon's lair. Adrian's performance was fantastic, utterly convincing even without the costume. The prince and multiple princesses were all word perfect. Miranda couldn't always remember her small speeches, but improvised so cleverly it didn't really matter.

Henrietta wandered in and out, declaring, 'Posture, darling!' and 'No gabbling!' and 'Expression! You sound as if you're reciting a multiplication table!' at hapless children, but for the most part she seemed pleased. Sometimes she was even moved to clap her hands together so that her bangles jingled.

We managed to get all the scenery finished by Wednesday, so I had a happy time up in the attic scrubbing down one wall for my mural while the children were free to paint whatever they wanted. Miranda painted a big family of rabbits, and I promised that she could paint more on my mural when I'd done the grass.

The pace picked up, children and tutors all at fever pitch by Thursday. Most of the day was spent on a dress rehearsal that went on for ever, until the younger ones were white with exhaustion.

'I think we'd better call it a day, Hen,' Nina said. She was busy working the lights and reading the prompt script. 'I'm so tired my eyes are blurring.'

'Then give the script to Dolphin. We badly need another run-through of the ending, it's as limp as a eunuch's penis,' Henrietta declared.

I don't think the children knew what a eunuch was but they all tittered at the word 'penis'. I felt sick at the thought of prompting them.

'I'm so sorry, I can't read properly,' I began, and saw the surprise on everyone's face. 'Without my specs,' I added quickly.

Henrietta tutted but chose Maya instead. She wasn't a great reader herself. When a child forgot their line she knew the place and prompted quickly, but stumbled over the words, sometimes completely stuck. She carried on valiantly, but her cheeks were burning. I felt so sorry for her, especially when several of the older kids started nudging each other and giggling.

Joel was actually taking part in the play, playing both the hapless King whose princesses were in danger of being swallowed, and the Evil Enchanter. He did a lot of funny business when they were supposed to be having a duel, blundering around the stage fruitlessly stabbing at thin air with his sword, then disappearing, only to reappear immediately, backing on to the stage in the Enchanter's pointy hat, thrusting and parrying for all he was worth.

He'd perfected the role, so that at one point in the play he took the prompt script from poor red-faced Maya and managed it himself. Any child who had dared snigger at her pronunciation was corrected mercilessly now. Maya looked at him as if he was her hero.

Henrietta gave everyone 'notes' – except Joel.

'Magnificent, darling, as always,' she said, smiling at him. Her bright lipstick had worked its way into the little lines around her mouth, and she'd been tugging her hair in exasperation so that it stood up wildly. When she heaved herself upright and struggled on stage to give him a literal pat on the back, her limp seemed more pronounced. Nina tried to help her unobtrusively, cupping her elbow to give her proper support, but Henrietta shook her off and embraced Joel extravagantly.

He raised his eyebrows slightly at us as he peered over her shoulder, but he was charm itself to Henrietta, complimenting her on her direction and reminding her that an indifferent dress rehearsal always meant a brilliant performance. It was a theatrical cliché, but Henrietta acted as if it was a startling revelation and fluttered her eyelashes at him.

'He's such a sweet guy,' Maya murmured to me.

'Yeah, I suppose,' I said a little grudgingly. I still felt flustered whenever he spoke to me. I kept telling myself I didn't really like him. He was too sure of himself, too much of a show-off. All the things I would normally be attracted to . . .

We had to have a second dress rehearsal on Friday morning, which seemed a mistake, because the children were getting heartily sick of the play now, and just wanted the whole thing to be over and done with. They cheered up at lunchtime, when pizzas were delivered to Lavender Hall, with Nina's home-made strawberry ice cream for pudding.

'Now, everyone, find a quiet corner and settle down and have an hour's rest,' Henrietta declared, settling herself on her sofa so thoroughly that several satin cushions slid on to the floor. Linda and I went upstairs. She flopped on to her chair and flicked through a magazine. I went up to the attic, feeling too keyed up to try to take a nap.

I carried on working on my mural. I'd stayed late last night painting sky and grass and it had dried enough now to start the proper artwork. It was such a novelty to draw big. I was so used to inventing tiny designs to fit an arm or an ankle or a back at most, but now I could really extend myself. I deliberately sketched without proper perspective, like a medieval tapestry, drawing small clumps of figures here and there, using the pupils and the staff, with Adrian as the dragon much larger than all the others, his long, scaly tail coiling everywhere in an elaborate pattern. I popped a tiny Miranda in her princess costume sitting on his head, tickling his scaly ear. I drew Joel in his Evil Enchanter outfit walking into the shrubbery hand in hand with Maya. I painted flowers too, herbaceous borders that Lee would approve of, with space in between for Miranda's rabbits.

Linda stomped up the final flight of stairs after an hour or so to see what I was up to. She laughed at my design, and seemed pleased with her own representation, sitting cross-legged and beaming like a cheery tailor, stitching so fast there were six hands flashing through the air.

'You're a clever girl! What a shame it's up here in the attic. I'm not sure Henrietta will be able to haul herself up to see what you've been doing,' she said.

'Maybe it's just as well,' I said, showing her my outline of Henrietta. She was proclaiming theatrically on the roof of Lavender Hall, striking an exaggerated pose, her scarves trailing, jewellery unravelling, one leg kicking sideways in a precarious manner, as if she might overbalance at any moment and fall down into her own lavender bushes.

'Well I never!' said Linda, chuckling. 'You've got her to a T. You're a dark horse, Dolphin. So where are you in this picture, eh?'

'I'm just a representation,' I said. 'That circle there is going to be the pond. See there's something swimming in it?'

'Is it a fish blowing bubbles?' Linda puzzled. Then her face cleared. 'Blow me, it's a dolphin! That's clever! You haven't actually sneaked off and had a swim in the pond, have you? That water looks a bit murky to me.'

'No fear! Especially when I've seen Joel swimming there,' I said, pulling a face.

'Ah! Yes, I should steer clear of that one. I've seen many a broken heart over that young man. Well, middle-aged man now, though he's still got his charms, I suppose. And he's kept his figure nicely,' said Linda thoughtfully.

'And likes to show it off! Don't worry, Linda. I've grown out of falling for bad boys like that,' I said determinedly.

'That's what they all say, dear,' said Linda, shaking her head at me. 'Right, let's get the kids up and ready for action!'

Linda marshalled them all into their costumes apart from Adrian, who had to wait till it was time to go on stage because his dragon costume was so unwieldy and took up too much room.

'And once in it there's no getting out again, not even if you're busting for a wee,' said Linda, making poor Adrian blush, already painfully self-conscious in his vest and shorts. It was a warm day but he was shivering.

'Don't look so worried,' I said, giving his shoulder a pat. 'You're going to be marvellous.'

'My throat's so dry I can hardly talk, let alone do a dragon roar,' he croaked.

I fetched him a glass of water but he would only take the tiniest sips after Linda's warning. I wanted to give him a reassuring hug but knew he would probably die of embarrassment. I reached up and gave him another pat on his hunched shoulder and then went to help Linda with the children's make-up.

They all adored this part, even though they were starting to get nervous too. I made up Miranda, trying my hardest to make her look stunning. I styled her hair carefully and added a few sparkles to her rosy cheeks.

'I look pretty!' she said, peering at herself in the mirror, eyes shining.

'I want waves like that – *and* sparkles!' demanded Bethany, the oldest princess, and the other girls joined in.

I carried on with everyone's make-up while Linda made emergency repairs on split trousers and a bent crown.

Joel had his own box of make-up, and had a complicated job making one side of his face like a King and the other side the Evil Enchanter. I watched, fascinated, as I brushed out waves and sprinkled cheeks. I was at the other side of the room, but he saw me reflected in the mirror.

'I want sparkles too!' he said, in a child's voice.

'You sound like one of those actors in the Haribo adverts,' I said, but I did give the Enchanter side of his face a little glitter around the eye and outlined it more dramatically for good measure.

'I wonder if your make-up is a brilliant metaphor for your personality,' I said, without thinking.

'How come a girl who has difficulty reading knows a literary term like metaphor?' he asked, challenging me with his gaze.

I quivered. He'd seen straight through me. 'I *can* read, it's just – my glasses . . .' I started, and then gave up. 'OK. I can't read properly at all. I'm severely dyslexic. Happy now? Feel free to mock,' I said defiantly.

'You'd be surprised how many actors are hopeless readers. The initial read-through is torture for them – but then they give stunning performances. Dyslexia is nothing to be ashamed of, Dolphin,' he said.

I couldn't make up my mind if he was being sincere or bloody patronizing. I gave him a tight smile instead.

'Ah! I've cracked it at last!' he cried, triumphant. 'I've had a private bet with myself that I'd make you smile by the end of the first session.'

I tried to turn my smile into a glare, but it wouldn't shift. 'So what do you get for winning your own bet?'

'Mm. Maybe that depends on you,' he said.

'Oh, come off it. Stop the cringy flirting, it's not going to get you anywhere,' I said, trying to sound unimpressed. His confidence was so annoying. Yet I couldn't help being flattered. Even thrilled. 'Excuse me, I have another princess to coiffe,' I said, turning away from him.

'Oh my, foreign languages now. So how would you spell "coiffe" then, Dolphin?'

I whipped back around to stare at him. That was so mean! He was deliberately playing games with me. To hell with him.

'Just shut the fuck up, will you?' I murmured in his ear so that Linda and the children couldn't hear me, and went to attend to the next princess. She already had many beautiful braids, so I attached a daisy to each one, and painted her a daisy on both cheeks, which delighted her.

I even persuaded Adrian to have green dragon make-up, though I knew it would be hidden under his splendid papier-mâché head. There, more French, so stuff you, Joel.

Nina came to inspect the children's costumes and did a literal double-take when she spotted Adrian.

'Good God! Is he *ill*? He looks terrible!' she exclaimed. I think she was just joking, but Adrian suddenly roared at her, voice miraculously restored, and she actually jumped backwards.

'Sorry – he's just channelling his inner dragon,' I said.

'Well, he looks ready for a part in *House of the Dragon*,' said Nina. 'Well done, Dolphin.'

'Look at me, Nina!' 'No, look at *me*!' all my little princesses begged.

'Is Henrietta going to come and admire them?' I asked.

'Oh no, she's busy rehearsing,' said Nina.

Rehearsing? Surely Henrietta wasn't going to strut on stage in a surprise cameo appearance? I fervently prayed that she wouldn't.

When the parents had all arrived and I was crouching behind the marquee with the cast, Henrietta swept past us. She was wearing an outrageous gown covered all over with silver sequins, so she looked like a ballroom glitter ball – but her head was held high, her hair swept into a chignon, her make-up extraordinary, her jewellery extravagant, every inch of her an actress.

She was clapped enthusiastically as she went on stage, tottering just slightly in her heels. They must have been agony but she kept her regal air and held out her arms to greet her audience. I worried that she might make a fool of herself, trying to quote poetry and forgetting half of it, but she simply gave an elegant speech welcoming all the parents and assorted relatives, told them their children had been a joy to tutor, and emphasized how incredibly talented they all were, each and every child a total star.

The audience clapped and Henrietta clapped them all in her turn, and then swept off the stage in style. As soon as she was out of their sight she kicked off her high heels. Nina had Henrietta's old Turkish carpet slippers at the ready and she slipped them on with a sigh of relief.

'Bliss!' she said. 'That went well, wouldn't you say? They'll be enrolling their little darlings for the Christmas session before the evening's out.'

Then Morris struck up the overture on the piano and the village children danced on to the stage, singing heartily. They weren't especially talented but they looked so sweet and performed so earnestly that they received enthusiastic applause.

Adrian had to be helped up on stage, Linda deftly arranging his many coils. He gave a low, threatening roar that stopped the children in their tracks. He took a deep breath and positively bellowed, scrabbling after the children, his coils slithering behind him. Some of the audience actually screamed, while others tittered.

'Oh, good for you, Adrian,' I murmured, and from then on I knew the play really was going to be a success.

There were a few small hitches, of course. Little Miranda was so overexcited she forgot her very first line and froze, her hand over her mouth. I clenched my fists, scarcely able to breathe – but she managed to save the day.

'Oh dear, I'm such a forgetful girl!' she said, shaking her head at herself. 'Now, think hard, Princess Miranda. What did you want to say to everyone?'

There was a sympathetic laugh, and a lot of aahing from the audience.

'Oh yes!' said Miranda, and she was off, rushing through her speech and stealing everyone's hearts. I glowed as proudly as if I was her mother.

There was a little party afterwards: juice for the children, wine for the audience, old-fashioned canapés – honeyed sausages on sticks, cheese and pineapple skewered together, triangles of watermelon and feta. It was much better than the cup of tea and biscuit people were expecting, and a shrewd move. Henrietta was not only congratulated by the proud parents – at least a third of them signed up for the Christmas holiday course there and then.

I was pleased to see that Miranda's parents were signing up too. Miranda saw me watching and pulled her mum and dad over to where I was standing.

'So you're the famous Dolphin!' said her father. 'Our daughter's told us all about you! You're her absolute heroine.'

'Well, Miranda's been a joy to teach,' I said. 'I've especially enjoyed watching her create all her rabbits.'

'Can we show Mum and Dad?' Miranda begged. 'The special ones I've done up in the attic?'

I didn't see why not, so I took them into the house and all the way upstairs. It was very hot and airless in the attic and Miranda's father had to stoop so he didn't bang his head. I thought they'd just give the mural a glance and then be on their way. But they stared at it, entranced, even switching on the torches on their mobile phones to see every detail more clearly. They admired Miranda's rabbits – but they loved all my work too.

'Do you paint murals professionally?' Miranda's mother asked.

I stared at her, wondering if she was serious. I was on the verge of laughing and being truthful, explaining it was my first attempt – but something stopped me.

Could I? Maybe specializing in murals for children's rooms? What about all the child-centred drawings I'd prepared a couple of weeks ago that hadn't really been used? Might I make useful contacts for clients from the summer school? Could this be a whole new career?

'I'm thinking of making it my speciality,' I said boldly. 'Might you be interested?'

'That would be marvellous! Do you have a card?' she asked.

'Sadly not with me. But I could give you my details if you'd like?'

'Oh, yes, please! I think Miranda would absolutely adore one in her bedroom,' said her mother. She looked enquiringly at her husband, and he seemed keen.

I sent my name, address and email straight from my phone to his, thanking God that I didn't have to try to write them down, then he took several photos of the mural from different angles.

'I could do you any design you'd like,' I said. 'Though I know what Miranda will pick!'

'Rabbits!' cried Miranda.

'Here's just a few rough sketches for alternative suggestions,' I added, whipping my drawing pad from my knapsack and showing them selected drawings.

'These are really good,' said Miranda's mother. 'Oh, how soon could you do us one?'

'Well, let's find out how much it's going to cost first,' her dad said hurriedly.

Oh God, what shall I suggest? I've absolutely no idea. THINK!!!

'It will obviously depend on the size of room and the detail you'd like,' I said. 'I think you'll find my rates compare favourably with other mural artists. And obviously I have to finish my stint at the summer school first.'

'Well, we'll measure Miranda's bedroom wall and give you some idea what we'd like and then maybe you could send us an estimate?' Miranda's mother suggested. 'Could you possibly start by September?'

'I'd have to consult my diary,' I said grandly, marvelling at myself. 'But I expect I could juggle things to make it happen.'

'Well, that would be perfect,' she said, and she actually gave me a hug. Miranda's dad was more circumspect, but he gave me a warm handshake. It was a wrench saying goodbye to Miranda – but it would be incredible if I really got to paint a mural for her bedroom. When they'd gone I went to the cloakroom and grinned into the mirror, amazed at myself. I even looked slightly different: a little older, more professional, in my element.

'Hello, Dolphin Westward, Mural Artist,' I said, and the woman in the mirror smiled back at me approvingly.

Nearly all the families had gone by the time I emerged. I shouldered my knapsack, ready to rush to catch the half-past train home, but Linda caught me by the arm.

'Hang on, lovie. Aren't you staying for the after-party for the staff?' she said.

'I didn't know there was one.'

'You mustn't miss it, it's the best part. Henrietta won't quite shell out for champagne, but the Prosecco will be flowing, and Nina makes marvellous fruitcake.'

I hesitated a moment. I usually hated the idea of parties, never knowing what to do or say – but this one might be different. I'd give it a try. I could just stay for half an hour and then clear off if I wasn't enjoying myself.

21

I thought it would be one of those parties where people stand around and make small talk. We'd fawn over Henrietta and discuss the play and the children and wonder what the next batch of kids would be like, while sipping fizz out of small glasses and scattering cake crumbs down our fronts.

It started off rather as I'd expected. We all had to toast Henrietta, though she had actually done the least work of any of us. But in ten minutes everyone had drained their first glass, and Nina poured more and then more, and Morris started playing on the grand piano in Henrietta's living room, and Damian and Lola started dancing.

Maya looked at Joel expectantly, but he raised an eyebrow apologetically and walked straight towards Henrietta. She was slumped in her chair, purple shadows under her eyes, her feet spread in her Turkish slippers, but she perked up tremendously when Joel held out his hand. He helped her to her feet, called out to Morris for a change of tempo, and they started dancing to a stately waltz. Henrietta tossed her head coquettishly, and Joel gallantly flirted with her until she tired. Then he settled her back in her chair and called to Nina to get her another drink.

Maya had been waiting somewhat impatiently, fiddling with her hair, and executing little dance steps herself when Morris started playing ancient pop tunes. Joel dutifully joined her, copying her dance steps, and then taking her in his arms and swinging her around until her long hair flew out and her flimsy floral dress spun above her knees. I watched, hoping I didn't look as if I cared. I sipped yet another glass of Prosecco. It slipped down as easily as lemonade.

When their dance finished, I thought Joel was looking in my direction – but then he joined Damian and Lola, the three of them dancing to that old Blur song 'Girls & Boys'.

We were all watching them now as they moved in perfect time, looking ultra cool. Especially Joel. He'd removed all his make-up except for the Evil Enchanter eye I'd drawn for him. It gave him a compelling, rakish look that somehow seemed incredibly sexy.

I wondered if it might be my turn to be his partner next. I went hot at the thought of dancing with him in front of everyone. It was a warm night anyway, even if it was getting dark now. My dress was sticking to me and the hair at the nape of my neck was damp. When Joel, Damian and Lola stopped dancing at last, arms round each other in a circle, all of them laughing breathlessly, my heart started thudding so hard I put my hand on my chest to calm it, spilling half my glass of wine down my front.

Joel saw and smiled. He put his head on one side enquiringly, but I shook my head quickly, feeling a fool. He just shrugged and got Nina up on the floor to dance with him instead. They started doing a wild approximation of a tango, Nina snatching a flower from the vase on the table and clenching it sideways in her teeth. He even went on to whirl Linda around.

The rest of the staff were in a clump dancing together. I felt self-conscious sitting there by myself, so I wandered over to Morris and leant on the piano, nodding along to the tunes. Eventually, I saw Joel approaching out of the corner of my eye.

I tried to think of the right thing to say, but he walked right past me and looked earnestly at Morris.

'I think Nina plays the piano. Would you let her take a turn while you and I have a dance together, Morris?' he asked.

Morris was so startled his glasses steamed up.

'Thank you very much, but I'm totally hopeless at dancing, two left feet, useless, I really can't,' he stammered, playing two duff notes.

Joel sighed theatrically. 'Well, Dolphin, I know you don't seem keen to dance with me either, but to help me save face could you possibly bear to bop about a bit? I can't think of a song about a dolphin to save my life. Something basically fishy, then? "Octopus's Garden"? "Baby Shark"?'

Morris looked unnerved, taking him seriously.

You mustn't take him seriously yourself. Who cares if you've got a damp patch on your front! Everyone's drunk now, and maybe you are too, but what the hell? Grow up! Have a bit of fun!

I laughed. 'All right, I'll dance. Play anything, Morris,' I said, and I held out my hand to Joel.

His hand was surprisingly cool and dry even after all the dancing. My own palm was sweaty, though I hadn't danced at all.

'Slow or fast?' Joel asked me.

'Fast,' I said at once, because I was vaguely worried about dancing cheek to cheek.

'Ah! So you're a fast girl, are you, under that Little Miss Cool exterior?' Joel said, one eyebrow raised.

'Look, do you want to dance or not?' I said, trying to sound light-hearted, though his hand holding mine was making me feel light-*headed*. His Enchanter's eye was gleaming.

'Let's try something with a good beat, but not *too* fast. Do you know "Spirit In The Sky", Morris?'

'We used to sing it in Bible Class while the teacher played the guitar,' said Morris, and started playing.

I'd never been near a Bible Class, but I knew that song by heart. Marigold used to sing and dance to it when she was feeling good. Perhaps the nuns of her past taught it to her? Not likely, because there was such a lively beat, and Marigold did a very bump-and-grind version, swaying her hips in the sexiest fashion. Star and I had often copied her, the three of us leaping about the flat until the woman underneath started banging on her ceiling.

I guessed Joel was expecting me to do a modest little hoppity jive. I'd show him. All the Proseccos were fizzing inside me. I did a Marigold version, exaggerating it if anything. Joel looked amazed, then amused, then got into the beat himself. It was extraordinary; we were only connected by our hands every now and then, when he twirled me round, but we seemed to be dancing in total unison, sensing each other's moves.

It was as if we were in our own world, and it wasn't until Morris finished playing and I heard the applause that I realized everyone had been standing around in a circle, watching. Joel clapped too, and then kissed me. It wasn't a lingering kiss, just a light brush of the lips. It didn't mean anything, just a simple acknowledgement in front of everyone – but it sent me reeling. The room seemed to be whirling round us, and although it was crowded the only person in focus was Joel, smiling at me.

'Well, I think we both need another drink after that,' he said, and poured Prosecco into our glasses.

'Hello?' said a familiar voice. I wheeled around to find *Lee*, standing in the living-room doorway. I gaped at him. What the hell was he doing here?

Had he seen me dancing? Had he seen Joel kiss me? Or had he come two seconds later and simply seen Joel pouring me a drink?

I took a great gulp from my glass, trying to focus, not sure what to do. I started walking unsteadily towards Lee, wondering what to say. He was glancing round at everyone, looking bewildered. Then he looked back at me.

'What's going on?' he asked. He sounded gruffer than usual. Fierce.

'Oooh!' Joel murmured. 'Your guy looks angry.'

Was Lee going to start a row in front of everyone?

'It's a party, obviously,' I said, my chin up.

'I thought there was going to be a play?' Lee said.

'Of course there was a play. And now there's a party,' I said, trying to keep my voice calm. All eyes were on us now. It was as if *we* were the play.

'Why didn't you text me to say what you were up to? I was so worried.'

'For goodness' sake, Lee, I'm not a naughty schoolgirl staying out late. I can stay out all night if I feel like it,' I hissed. He looked horrified. I might have softened, apologized for worrying him, taken his hand, offered him a drink, but I was too furious. How could he embarrass me in front of everyone?

Henrietta heaved herself out of her armchair and shuffled over to us, clinging on to Nina's arm. 'Good heavens, who have we here?' she boomed in her best theatrical voice, looking Lee up and down. He was still in his old gardening clothes, his jeans caked with mud, his boots scuffed. 'Are you a burglar? How exciting!'

She was joking, of course, though it wasn't funny and Lee wasn't laughing.

'Dol's my girlfriend and I'm here to take her home,' he said curtly, and took hold of my wrist. All he needed was an animal skin and a club and he could have passed as a Neanderthal.

People were staring open-mouthed. Joel simply watched, arms folded, evil eye glittering. Morris jumped up from the piano stool and came stumbling over, much the worse for wear.

'Are you all right, Dolphin? Do you need any help?' he said gallantly, though it was obvious Lee could fell him at one blow.

I was so touched and so humiliated and so angry and drunker than I'd realized. The room seemed to be tilting alarmingly now, making me feel sick. Oh God, I was going to *be* sick!

I made a dash for the door and ran to the shrubbery outside, bent over just in time, and was horribly ill. Between heaves I heard voices offering help and Lee saying firmly, 'Thank you, but I'm sure she'll be all right in a minute. Then I'll take her home.'

They ebbed away and I finished vomiting at last, and stood up, gasping and shuddering. Lee took me by the arm and steered me to the van. I wanted to run back inside the Hall but I was too weak now to struggle. He helped me into the front seat and gave me his window-wiping cloth so I could mop myself up a bit. Then he started the van and we didn't say anything to each other the entire journey home. I hunched up in a ball as far as the seat belt would let me, fuddled and furious.

When we got back home, Lee turned the key in the front door and I ran wildly up the stairs, desperate to get away from him and into my room, but I stumbled and fell heavily, banging my knees. I burst into tears – and Lee bent down and tried to put his arm round me.

'Dol? What have you done to yourself? Is it your leg, your ankle? Here, let me see,' he said.

'Get away from me,' I sobbed. 'Don't you dare touch me! How could you humiliate me like that?'

'I'm the one who felt humiliated,' Lee said coldly. 'Seeing you dance like a slut with that creep and then letting him kiss you.'

So he *had* seen me! I'd hoped he hadn't. But so what if he had? I was burning now, my head throbbing as well as my heart. I hated him talking like that, calling me that awful word. I was *dancing* with Joel, not fucking him. I could do what I liked. Lee wasn't my partner, even though he'd called me his girlfriend. We weren't in a proper relationship as such – we'd only known each other a few weeks. How dare he talk to me like that!

'So you think I'm a slut, do you?'

'I didn't say that, I said you were dancing like one,' Lee said. 'How could you act like that in front of everyone?'

'I can act any way I want,' I told him haughtily, fumbling in my bag for the key to my room.

'You're not that sort of girl, Dol,' he said sorrowfully.

'For Christ's sake, I'm not a girl, I'm a grown woman. Can't you get that into your stupid brain?' I hissed.

'So you think I'm stupid, do you? Good to know,' said Lee, his voice rising.

I couldn't be bothered to argue any more. I struggled to my feet, got to my door, let myself in, and then slammed it shut in his face. I cleaned my teeth of the horrible taste of sick and then flopped on my bed, not washing or even taking off my clothes. I lay there, my small room spinning. I kept reliving the last hour. I'd so loved dancing with Joel, I'd thought we must look great together, and people would see I wasn't just shy little Dolphin – but maybe they thought I looked pathetic trying to act in a sultry, sexy way? Maybe Joel had just been leading me on to make a fool of me? Perhaps everyone was secretly laughing at me? Maybe not even secretly, but I'd been too drunk to notice.

Dancing like a slut. How could Lee have said that to me? Maybe he was *right*? Though he'd behaved appallingly and made a spectacle of both of us. How was I ever going to face any of them again? I couldn't just waltz back on Monday and pretend nothing had happened. I loved it at Lavender Hall – but now I'd spoilt it all.

I'd so enjoyed the last couple of weeks. I was good with the children, good with my art teaching, good with make-up, good at getting along with all these interesting, artistic people. I'd made friends, I felt I belonged at last. I'd even got an offer of a brand new job. And I'd danced with Joel Fortune, famous sexy actor, and I'd been pretty sure he was actually keen on me.

Then Lee had showed up and ruined it all.

I started crying then, silent tears of self-pity at first, but I couldn't stop the sobs escalating until I was positively howling, though I pulled the pillow over my head to try to stifle the noise.

Lee must have heard even so, because after a few minutes there was a knock on my door. I ignored it. He knocked harder. Insistently. How dare he act like this! Then he called my name, over and over.

I dragged myself out of bed, and had to stand still for a moment because my knees were sore and my legs were buckling. Lee carried on calling. I made it to my door somehow and hauled it open.

'Oh, thank God, I thought you couldn't hear me.'

'The whole house can hear you. Probably the whole road. Just shut up and go to bed,' I said.

'But you're crying. Let me in, please!' He sounded desperate.

'Just go *away*!' I banged the door with my fist. Now my hand hurt as well as my knees, but it made him go back to his room. I went back to bed. I heard him walking up and down and then putting the kettle on for a cup of tea, and that seemed such a ridiculous old-man action that I hated him all over again.

I don't know how long I lay there stiffly, my head throbbing now, my throat dry, my mouth still tasting of sick. I wanted a glass of water but didn't dare get up because he'd know I was still awake, and it seemed so ridiculous that I couldn't have a drink in my own room that I thumped the pillow, fantasizing that it was his face.

I suppose I must have fallen asleep eventually, because I woke at daylight, hearing Lee showering, getting ready for the long journey to collect Ava. I heard his door shut and then his footsteps stopped, and I knew he was hesitating. I braced myself for him to knock again, but he carried on along the corridor, downstairs until his footsteps faded away. I started to wish he *had* knocked now. My anger had seeped away in the night. My head still hurt terribly and my stomach was churning. I was feeling sick again and had to dash to the loo, only just making it in time.

I sipped water for a while, had a long shower, but still felt so dreadful I flopped back into bed. I lay there, going through every minute of yesterday. It had all been such a wonderful day, I'd been so proud of the children, especially Adrian and little Miranda, and the party had gone well, and the after-party, and the dancing . . . I tingled at the thought of that dancing, how Joel and I had instantly connected and the magic of moving so rhythmically together, almost as good as sex, and I couldn't regret that five minutes, though it must have hurt Lee to see me acting like that with another man.

It wasn't a crime, though, to dance suggestively. It was the way everyone danced. And it wasn't as if Joel was a complete stranger. We were colleagues, and we weren't really being serious. It was just a game, wasn't it? He might have been just leading me on, proving that he could have his way with any woman in the room. Maybe he didn't really want me, he was just showing off to everyone? No, I'd seen his face. He wasn't pretending for a laugh. He was serious. He'd really wanted me – and, if I was completely honest with myself, I had wanted him. So much.

Was that why Lee was so angry? It might not have been just the way I was dancing. Maybe it was the look on *my* face. The helpless attraction.

I flipped over and buried my head in the damp pillow, desperate to go back to sleep again and forget it all, but I couldn't stop thinking of Joel, his eyes, his dark hair, his triumphant smile, his hand as it held mine, his body as he stepped out of the pool, droplets of water glistening on his smooth skin. I imagined him pressing up against me, almost as if he was in the bed with me, kissing me, touching me all over, and then I was touching myself, and when I came I couldn't help crying out.

As I lay there, panting, sated, I thanked God that Lee had gone out. It would have been awful if he'd heard through the paper-thin wall. I felt as guilty as if I had actually had sex with Joel rather than just imagining it. I told myself I surely didn't need to feel bad because we hadn't agreed to have an exclusive relationship, but I knew just how much Lee would mind.

I fell asleep again, and woke much later, at half past twelve. Lee would be back with Ava in half an hour or so. I sat up gingerly and then slid out of bed. The ache in my head had gone, thank God, and I didn't feel sick any more. I had another shower then got dressed and put on a little make-up because I still looked pretty dreadful.

Would I get to see Ava now that Lee and I had had such a row? I suddenly felt as though my heart had been torn from my chest. I'd started to care about Ava as if she was my own daughter. I'd been very fond of Miranda, but my relationship with Ava was entirely different. I loved her. I'd been wondering if I might grow to love Lee too.

If you'd asked me yesterday morning, I'd have said maybe – but I wasn't so sure now. Lee had been so fierce last night, so possessive, so controlling. Would he always act like this if I went off without him? Or had he genuinely been worried out of his mind, picturing me lost in the dark, unable to find my way to the station?

I waited. They were nearly always back by one. It was quarter past now. Perhaps Lee was taking Ava out to lunch today. I checked my phone but there was no recent message – but three increasingly anxious messages sent last night, wondering where I was.

I felt so guilty that I hadn't even bothered to check. It made me fuss more now he was late himself. Half past one. Maybe Lee's ex and her partner had stopped Ava coming? Or had there been some kind of accident? Lee hadn't had a proper night's sleep and had been very shaken up. He could easily have lost concentration on the long journey. Perhaps he and Ava were lying mangled on the roadside right now, with medics shaking their heads over them. It was such a horrifyingly clear vision I clamped my hand over my mouth and rocked to and fro – but then I heard footsteps. The steady plod of a thick-set man, the dancing skitter of a small child.

I ran to my door and flung it open wide. Ava ran forward eagerly and jumped up into my arms. Lee hung back uncertainly.

'OK, lunchtime,' he said, opening his own front door.

'Dol's coming for lunch too, isn't she, Daddy?' Ava asked, clinging to me.

Lee hesitated. 'Of course, if she wants to,' he said off-handedly.

'Well, I'm not sure,' I mumbled.

'Yes, you are!' Ava insisted. 'Please please come!'

'Well, OK then, if it's all right with your dad.'

'Yes, fine,' said Lee, though he didn't really sound as if he meant it. 'I'd better roll up my sleeves and get cracking, then.'

Ava jumped down and peered at him sideways. Lee was wearing a blue teeshirt and his best jeans.

'You haven't *got* any sleeves, Daddy!' she said.

'Yes, I have, my best transparent ones. Mustn't get them messy,' he said, and he mimed undoing the cuffs of his non-existent sleeves and rolling them up past his elbow.

He walked into his room as he did so, and we followed.

'Shall I do mine now?' Ava asked, grinning, and made a beautiful pantomime of her performance. She looked especially cute in a pink-and-white-striped top and blue dungarees with a daisy on the front pocket.

'I love your dungarees, Ava,' I said.

'They're my work clothes. Like Daddy's,' she said proudly. 'My other daddy hasn't got special work clothes, he just wears grey suits.'

I saw Lee wince but he didn't say anything. I said it for him. 'You've only got one daddy, Ava, and he's right here. I expect you mean Phil? Uncle Phil?'

'Mummy says he's my daddy now,' said Ava, though thank goodness she didn't look too happy about it. She went running to her little wooden house and started playing with the mice inside, pretending to feed them all cheese.

'Well, Mummy's wrong,' I muttered, but low enough so that only Lee caught what I was saying.

He smiled at me at last, getting real cheese out of the fridge and a bag of macaroni.

'Are you OK?' I asked. 'You're late back. Traffic?'

'Traffic was fine. Ali and fucking Phil screwed up,' he said. I blinked at him in surprise. It was the first time I'd ever heard him swear. 'They weren't at home. Apparently they'd decided to take Ava on an impromptu shopping trip. Hence the new dungarees. And then they took her for a milkshake. I texted and they said they'd be back in ten minutes. They were actually over an hour.'

There was a pause. I couldn't work out whether we were . . . whatever we were, again. More than friends. Less than partners. He wasn't looking at me now, as he busily grated cheese. I wondered if he was wanting to grate Phil – or me.

I went over to Ava.

'My mice say they want me to make them a garden. Will you draw them one, Dol?'

'I'll do my best. And then maybe we can get you some mustard and cress seeds and grow them on a flannel. They'll make lovely long green grass for the mice to play in,' I offered.

'Mustard?' said Ava, wrinkling her nose. 'That's yellow!'

'No, this is different. I'll start growing it for you if you like, and when you come back to visit Daddy next week it will already have started,' I said.

'And can it have flowers too?'

'Well, perhaps we can have some very brightly coloured flowers, red and blue and purple?' I suggested, thinking I could buy a packet of Quality Street and use the wrappers.

'Oh *yes*!' said Ava. 'You do get good ideas, Dol.' She pretended the mice were all squeaking enthusiastically. Then she said, 'So are you my other mummy now?'

Lee looked round sharply.

'I'm – I'm Daddy's friend from next door,' I said awkwardly. 'Now, I'll fetch my drawing pad and felt tips from my place and we can start on the paper garden while Daddy makes lunch.'

'Macaroni cheese, yum yum. You like it too, don't you?' Ava asked.

'Yes, I do . . . but perhaps it's better if I don't stay for lunch,' I said.

'Of course you're staying, silly!' said Ava, thinking I was joking.

I looked at Lee. 'Yes, don't be silly,' Lee said, but from the tone of his voice I wasn't sure if he really wanted to stay friends now.

We both relaxed a little over lunch, while Ava chatted away. We went out for a drive afterwards to see a special woodland garden open for the weekend. Lee got ideas for Mrs Knight's garden, and Ava and I admired the peacocks wandering around and petted a marmalade cat hanging out in a greenhouse.

'My friend Oliver has a cat just like this one called Orlando,'

I said, and then I remembered with a jolt. Oliver and Ross were meant to be coming to Sunday lunch tomorrow. I wasn't sure Lee would want to cook it now. It would be an enormous cheek to expect it when we still hadn't made up properly.

When Lee came to find us I took a deep breath and mumbled, 'I don't suppose it's still on for lunch with Oli and Ross tomorrow? It's OK, I'll take them out to a pub somewhere.'

'I said I'll do it, so I will,' said Lee in a monotone.

'Well, it's very good of you,' I said.

Lee just shrugged in reply.

'Daddy, can we go and find the café now?' Ava begged.

We had tea and home-made lemon drizzle cake in the conservatory. People looking at us would think we were a happy little family. We were acting like it – but Lee and I were still stilted, both talking to Ava but not a word to each other.

Lee made a prawn stir fry for supper. I tried to make my excuses, but Ava insisted again that I stay. Then we watched *Little Women* on television. Ava seemed to be following it avidly, even though I thought it would be much too old for her, but after a while she climbed on Lee's lap and was mercifully fast asleep when Beth died. I had a little weep, my eyes still sore from last night's crying. Lee was looking at me, and he edged towards me slightly, maybe wanting to hold my hand? But Ava murmured in her sleep and he settled back, not wanting to disturb her.

He rubbed his cheek against the top of her head, holding her as if he could never let her go. He was being so gentle with her. It was hard to stay angry with him when I wanted him to be gentle with me too.

'Are we OK now?' I whispered.

I thought he wasn't going to say anything at first – but then he mumbled 'OK' back. It was hard to interpret his tone.

Ava opened her eyes. 'You're OK, Daddy?' she said sleepily.

'That's right – it's wonderfully OK to have you on my lap, poppet, but my legs are getting pins and needles so I'm going to have to pop you into bed now,' he said.

'That's not fair! I'm wide awake!' she said, but it was a feeble protest.

Lee got her ready for bed and tucked her up. I bent over her to say goodnight, and her arms wound round my neck too. It was such a lovely feeling. I'd enjoyed little stints of babysitting before but I'd never felt as close to a child as this.

Then Ava was asleep and for several very long minutes we just sat at either end of the sofa, me picking at the bobbles on the upholstery, Lee scratching at an insect bite on the back of his hand, neither of us speaking. I had to break the silence eventually.

'We must look like two monkeys in a cage, picking and scratching,' I said.

'What kind of monkey?'

'Well, normally you're a very amiable chimp, very gentle. But you were totally alpha gorilla last night, beating your chest and roaring,' I said.

'With reason,' said Lee.

'Oh, come off it. You were overreacting terribly.'

'You were drunk and flirting outrageously with that actor creep,' said Lee. 'Christ, *him* of all people!'

'You recognized him?'

'Of course I did. I told you, Ali really fancied Joel fucking Fortune,' said Lee.

'Well, I certainly don't,' I said quickly, hoping I sounded convincing. 'It was just a dance. I forgot the Ali thing, though. Now I see why you were so angry.'

'No, I was angry because I'd been so worried about you, and yet there you were, not giving a damn, practically doing a striptease right in front of everyone,' said Lee. 'Didn't you see my missed calls?'

'I've got a perfect right to do a *real* striptease if I want to,' I protested. 'You don't get to say what I do or don't do. I'm a grown woman, and can do what I like.'

'Until it all goes wrong and you want me to look after you,' Lee said.

'That's rubbish,' I said, trying not to think of all the times I'd needed him. 'I can look after myself. Anyway, you *like* to be needed.'

Lee drew in his breath. 'Like you like your mother needing you?'

I felt as if he'd slapped me. 'That's different. Don't you dare compare me to her. I *have* to help her. Who do you think you are anyway, analysing me like Dr Gibbon?'

'Keep your voice down, you'll wake Ava up. And who's this Dr Gibbon and what's he got to do with anything?'

I sighed. Why did he have to be so belligerent now, telling me off as if I was a naughty child?

'He's my mum's psychiatrist. He's very kind and understanding,' I said, emphasizing this. 'Marigold's doing well, for the most part, though she's got fixated on this weird young girl Lettie who hangs round her all the time,' I said.

'Ah!' Lee said.

I waited. 'What do you mean by *ah*?' I demanded.

'Well, if I were this Dr Gibbon, I'd say your nose has been put out of joint because Marigold's found a substitute daughter and is trying hard to make this relationship work as she made such a mess of being a mother to you and your sister,' said Lee.

I blinked at him, infuriated.

'You don't need to look at me like that. Just because I'm scruffy, stupid old Lee and I haven't got a fancy job and I'm a weak sod who lets women walk all over him, it doesn't mean I haven't got a brain in my head to work out the bleeding obvious.'

'If *I* were playing the psychiatrist game, I'd say you're venting all the jealousy and anger you feel towards your wife on to me – when I'm just a friend you've known five minutes,' I said angrily.

'That's all you think we are to each other? Casual friends?' Lee asked, suddenly looking stricken.

'No! Of course you're more than that. I just meant . . . well, it's very early days, isn't it? Oh, Lee, please don't let's quarrel like this, especially when it's all so silly. I don't give a stuff about Joel Fortune,' I said. 'How can I make you understand?'

'You can promise you don't really fancy him,' said Lee.

'I don't! He can be quite sweet at times, but it's all an act. He's actually a bit of a wanker,' I said, though that particular word reminded me uncomfortably of this morning in bed. 'He's a typical actor, totally in love with himself.'

'So why were you dancing with him and letting him kiss you?' Lee asked shakily.

'He was dancing with everyone else before me,' I said truthfully. 'And kissing everyone too, you know what actors are like.' Not *quite* so truthful now.

'So you'll stay away from him in future?'

'I feel like staying away from everyone after that humiliating scene in front of them all,' I said. 'You can't go round acting like that, Lee! You can't order me around and tell me what to do! You're acting very controlling, and it's getting scary.'

'You're not scared of *me*, are you?' Lee asked, sounding incredulous.

'I didn't say that. But look at the way you dragged me off into the car last night—'

'I was helping you because you were drunk!'

'And then here at home you practically beat down my door trying to get to me!'

'I was worried because you were in such a state, crying your eyes out! I wasn't going to *hurt* you! How could you think that of me?' said Lee, and he put his head in his hands.

'Lee?' I wasn't sure if he was just putting it on, but when he sat up again he had tears in his eyes. 'Perhaps we were both acting a bit stupidly,' I said.

'I suppose you're right. I don't usually get all churned up and jealous like this. I'm sorry, Dol. So sorry.'

'I'm sorry too,' I said. 'Sorry you were so upset, I mean.'

'And – and we're still . . . friends?' Lee asked.

'Of course we are.'

We gave each other an awkward hug – but we slept in our separate rooms that night.

22

I didn't sleep well and woke very early, not long after six. I nipped to the loo – and heard Lee moving very slowly and cautiously next door, obviously trying not to wake Ava. Then I heard his door open and close. He paused on the landing, waiting. I stood still, waiting too. Then he gave one very timid knock.

I went to my door and opened it. Lee was standing there in the gloom, dressed in jeans and a teeshirt, but his feet bare.

'Sorry,' he whispered.

'What for?'

'For everything, especially last night.'

He looked so forlorn and miserable that I pulled him into my room. I went to put on the kettle for a coffee and he came and stood beside me.

'Would it be all right if I kissed you?' he said softly.

'Yes, of course.' He was timid at first, giving me a very gentle kiss on the lips. I found I put my hand on the back of his neck automatically. Then we kissed properly and then he was kissing my ear and the crook of my neck and then my breasts, pulling up my nightie so his tongue could circle my nipples.

I reached out to switch the kettle off, worried that Ava would hear it, and then pulled him over to my rumpled bed. I went to cover us up but he gently threw the duvet off, eased my nightie up to my neck and spread my legs.

'Is this all right too?' he whispered, bending over me. I nodded, and he started licking me. It felt so good that I arched my back and opened my legs wider, and pulled the pillow over my head so I didn't make too much noise when I came.

'I think we're definitely friends again now,' I whispered when he surfaced.

'I'm so glad. But I might have to keep on trying this and that, just to make sure we still are,' he whispered back.

We lay there a while, arms tightly round each other, as if we could never let go. Then I eased his own clothes off, edged on top of him, and sat up so we could look at each other all the time we were rocking together. When we were through we curled up, both of us hot and damp and relaxed. I rested my head on his chest now. I could hear his heart slowly steadying. I thought of Joel with his string of girlfriends. Hadn't I learnt my lesson? I didn't want to be one of them. I'd been mad to think there was some magical connection between us. We were both drunk and both good dancers, that was all there was to it.

Lee, Ava and I had a beautiful Sunday morning together. Lee got busy with his roast, and Ava and I acted as his sous chefs. I peeled and chopped and Ava very carefully laid the table, plate by plate, glass by glass, even taking each item of cutlery separately from the drawer to the table. Lee had brought another bunch of roses back on Friday and they were still fresh, in full bloom.

Oliver and Ross were exactly on time, which wasn't a surprise – Oli had always been obsessively punctual when we were children. They arrived looking bright-eyed and pink-cheeked, both wearing black teeshirts, smart jeans and trainers with dazzling white edges.

'Oh, I can see you two had a really wild night,' I joked, when they came to my door. I gave them both a huge hug. If I hadn't known Oliver for ever I might have got them muddled up, because

Ross wore similar round glasses and had the same hairstyle. He was taller and Oli was thinner but seen separately you'd have to concentrate hard to work out which was which.

I took them straight next door, shyly introducing them to Lee and Ava. Oli and Ross were immediately enchanted by Ava. They knew exactly how to chat to her – they were both primary school teachers, after all – and patiently admired all her toys and her new dungarees.

Lee opened a bottle of wine, but Oli only had half a glass and Ross asked if he could have water instead.

'Too much to drink at Pride?' Lee asked.

They laughed. It turned out they'd each had only one lager.

'But we had a great time, and danced a lot, and the Pet Shop Boys were incredible,' Oli said happily.

Ross ruffled his hair fondly. 'Yes, you were totally like a little bouncy ball.'

'I was enjoying myself,' said Oli sheepishly. He glanced at Lee, who had started carving the chicken. 'I'm actually rubbish at dancing, aren't I, Dol?'

'Well, we weren't the coolest kids at the Year Six disco,' I said. 'Me in my witch frock and you bopping about in your shorts.'

'Oh God, those awful shorts,' said Oli, laughing, though he'd suffered agonies at school when his mum insisted that he couldn't have jeans like all the other boys. 'Still, at least you were always great at dancing.'

I looked anxiously at Lee, wondering if he'd make a snide comment about my dancing last night, but he just nodded and went on steadily carving.

'Who'd like a leg?' he asked calmly.

'Can I have the wishbone, Daddy?' Ava begged.

He made sure she got it on her plate and I breathed out slowly, relaxing again. When we sat down, crammed together at Lee's small table, he put his hand on my shoulder and gave it a loving squeeze. Oli saw and smiled.

I pulled Ava's wishbone with her, making sure to hold it at the right angle so that she got the largest portion when it snapped.

'What are you going to wish for, Ava?' Oli asked her, as she waved the bone triumphantly in the air.

'I mustn't tell because then it might not come true,' said Ava. She started whispering under her breath, but she wasn't very good at it, and we could all hear her clearly.

'I wish I could stay with Daddy!' she mumbled, and we all looked at each other. Lee had to blink hard. When we'd cleared our plates and Ava was helping Lee dot strawberries on top of the ice-cream pudding, Oli murmured to me, 'Lee's great.'

I nodded.

'So happy for you, Dol.'

'I know. I'm lucky,' I said. I was, wasn't I? I still tingled from this morning's sex. Lee was being gentle and sweet now. Maybe his behaviour on Friday night was almost understandable? I hadn't behaved in an exemplary fashion myself, had I? And never mind Lee, I was incredibly lucky to have little Ava in my life.

Lee was smiling at me. Everything was fine again – until we were having coffee and Ava was daintily sipping her apple juice.

'We were wondering about getting tattoos,' Oli said, out of the blue.

I stared at him in surprise. I'd never seen them as the sort of guys to get inked.

'What kind? "Love" and "hate" across the knuckles? Popeye the Sailor man? The word "Mother" surrounded by hearts and flowers?' I said jokingly.

'Definitely not "Mother",' said Oli, rolling his eyes. 'Mine is driving me crazy at the moment. Oh, sorry, Dol – I meant she's being really annoying.'

'Don't worry, I know using the word "crazy" is a sensitive issue – but Marigold uses it all the time,' I said.

'I thought you said Dr Gibbon feels she's making great progress?' said Lee.

'I suppose. She keeps coming out with these pat little statements about mental health issues and feels she's ready to leave hospital. As soon as her broken ankle is better she'll be off like a shot with her friend Lettie, thinking she'll be fine. Well, I *want* her to be fine, obviously, but she'll start drinking and meeting the wrong men and get high as a kite and will stop taking her pills and it'll begin all over again.'

I was rather shocked at the words coming out of my mouth. I sounded so cruel and cynical. I poured the rest of the bottle of wine into my glass and then stared at it.

My hand shook and I spilled a little wine. They were all watching.

'Oh God, look at me, I'll have to watch myself or I'll end up in the bed beside Marigold,' I said, trying to turn it into a painful joke.

'I'd swop my mum for yours any day of the week,' Oli said quickly. 'My mum's so sorry for herself and there's just no way we can cheer her up. We see her every weekend – well, except this one – and yet she always makes out she doesn't ever get to see us and goes on about how lonely she is, and tells us these stories about grown-up sons who want their mother to move in with them.'

'God forbid,' Ross said firmly.

'I always thought Marigold was magical,' Oli continued.

'You're not telling me you want to look like her, tattoos all over?' I said incredulously.

'No, no! We just want matching designs, to celebrate our fifth wedding anniversary,' said Ross. 'The traditional gift is something wooden, but we've already got a nice wooden fruit bowl and bookshelves so then we thought about a tattoo to do with wood. Just a little one each.'

'I think that's a great idea,' Lee said earnestly.

'So do I,' I said.

'I know this is a total cheek, Dol, but I don't suppose it would be possible for you to tattoo us now, before we go back home?' Oli asked, his voice wheedling. 'Obviously not here, you haven't got all your implements or whatever they're called – but could we go to the studio?'

'I've always longed to see what they're like inside, but haven't ever had the courage to walk straight in,' said Ross.

I took another large gulp of wine. 'I can't, boys. I'm so sorry.'

'You don't have a key to the studio?' Oli asked.

'I don't work there any more,' I told them.

Oli gasped. 'But I thought you loved it there?'

'I did. Well, most of the time. But there was a huge fuss about me inking an under-age girl,' I admitted.

'You tattooed a child?' Ross asked, shocked.

'Not deliberately! She looked much older than she was and she stole her elder sister's passport and made out she was her,' I said.

'Little minx!' said Oli. 'I'm always amazed when Year Six wear whatever they want in the last week of term. Some of the girls look at least sixteen, all glammed up with full make-up.'

'So what do you do now, Dolphin?' Ross asked.

'Well, I suppose I'm a kind of teacher too at the moment. I do art with some kids at a drama summer camp,' I said. 'We've worked on all the scenery. And we did a mural together and . . .' I let my voice tail away. I wanted to hug the whole mural idea to myself for the moment, in case it didn't come true.

Oli and Ross looked interested, but I didn't want to go into it in front of Lee. We were friends again – with very enjoyable benefits – but it still seemed better to keep right off the subject of Lavender Hall.

'And then?' Ross asked.

'Well, we'll have to see,' I said vaguely.

'If you like doing it, perhaps you could train as a teacher?' Ross said.

'We don't want to condemn her to being boring old teachers like us,' said Oli quickly.

I smiled at him gratefully. He obviously hadn't told Ross that I couldn't read properly.

'We could always set up as team gardeners, Dolly and me,' said Lee. 'She's got a great eye for colour and design. She could be in charge of the herbaceous borders while I do the heavy work. It would be great.'

I stared at him. Had he just thought of this out of the blue, or had he been planning this? Why was I hearing about it for the first time in front of other people? I didn't know what to say, but I didn't want Lee to lose face in front of Oli and Ross.

'That's an interesting idea,' I said neutrally. 'Have you guys got a garden?'

'Well, it's a flat, remember, so no – but we've got a stunning window box. Ross is in charge. He's even got the neighbours asking if he'd do theirs,' Oli said.

There was a lot of wittering about window boxes and plants between the three men. I realized I got bored even talking about gardens, let alone the thought of maintaining one. I drew pictures with Ava instead. I drew another magic garden, with unicorns and flying rabbits and bluebirds, while Ava painstakingly drew three humpty-dumpty figures with big smiles: a big one, a middle-sized one and a much smaller one.

'That's you and Daddy and me,' she said. 'And the baby unicorn's my pet, isn't he?'

'Absolutely,' I agreed, touched.

Eventually, Lee looked at his watch and sighed.

'I'm so sorry – I've got to take Ava back now. We're going to be really late as it is, but I suppose that's fair enough, seeing as they weren't even there when I went to fetch her yesterday,' he said. 'Come on, Ava poppet. Shall we collect up your things?'

'I want to stay *here* with Dol,' Ava protested, making my heart swell.

'I know, but you'll see her next week. Come on, sweetheart.' Lee had to do a lot of chivvying this time, trying to stay calm but firm, but I could tell from the tension in his face that all he really wanted to do was take her in his arms and keep her there safe for ever. I did my best to help him, but she started crying in earnest when he picked her up, and we could hear her wails all the way down the stairs.

'Poor little thing,' said Oli. 'She really loves her dad, doesn't she? And you, Dol.'

'Well, I love her too,' I said.

'She's like your own little daughter,' said Ross.

Oli squeezed my hand. 'You're like a family already, the three of you.'

'Well. Sort of. It's very early days yet,' I said, not knowing whether I was thrilled or alarmed. Somehow both at the same time.

We went to my room to have a cup of tea before the boys had to start their long drive home.

'It's a pity you can't knock the wall through so you could have one big flat,' Oli said.

'I don't think the landlord would be very pleased,' I said.

What about you? Do you want to live in one big flat with Lee?

I looked round my room. It was cramped and crowded with all my toys and trinkets and most people would think it a bizarre home for a thirty-three-year-old – but I loved it. It was mine and a truthful reflection of who I am. I didn't want to extend it and adapt it to make it reflect Lee's taste as well as mine.

So how are you going to pay the rent for your precious room if you can't get another job?

My chest was suddenly tight, so I could hardly breathe. Star sent me money if Marigold got behind on her rent – but I couldn't ask her to do the same for me.

'Couldn't you and Lee move out into a slightly bigger flat together?' said Ross, seeing me looking anxious. 'That's what we did.'

'Well, maybe we could,' I said warily. 'But we've only known each other a matter of weeks.'

'We knew right from the first time we got together,' said Oli.

'Really?'

'Yep. Ross stayed over at mine – and from then on we've never been apart.'

'I'm his first and only,' Ross said, grinning.

'Whereas Ross was a right old tart in his youth,' said Oli.

'But I knew straight away Oli was The One,' said Ross.

I waited until Ross went to use my loo and then whispered to Oli, 'Seriously?'

'Yep. I don't get all this hooking up and then going on to the next and the next. When you find the right one you know, and you simply aren't interested in anyone else. Surely Lee's the right one for you?'

'Well, in some ways, I suppose he could be – but I'm just not sure the spark is there, you know? And oh God, Oli, don't tell anyone, not even Ross, but there's this guy at the summer school, I'm not even sure I really like him, he's got a seriously bad reputation, but I sort of fancy him like mad – well, I *did*. I don't really know how I feel now – and nothing's really happened, but there's just this attraction—'

'Oh, Dol, don't mess things up! Look, all the guys you've gone for before have been hopeless bad-boy types who let you down – right from Rory at school!'

'I know, and I really care about Lee, but I just don't feel that . . . that flying feeling with him.'

'Flying?' said Oli, wrinkling his nose. 'What, feeling anxious and worried that the pilot will have a heart attack or the man beside you looking furtive has a bomb in his bag?'

I punched him playfully. 'You know what I mean. Marigold said that—'

'You're taking *Marigold's* advice?' said Oli, goggling at me.

'Listen, you don't think I'm really *like* Marigold, do you?' I asked desperately. 'Always fixating on the wrong person and making crazy decisions?'

We heard the loo flushing.

'No. You're not a bit like Marigold. You're you,' Oli said firmly. 'And stick with Lee, whatever, promise? I know you, Dol. He's the right one, even if you can't see it yet.'

As Ross emerged from the bathroom, we turned the conversation to other things. When Oli gave me a big hug goodbye, he whispered in my ear, 'Maybe I came on a bit strong. I love you no matter what, Dol, and you have to make your own decisions, OK?'

Oli knew me so well. Was he right? Should I stick with Lee? Maybe the gardening team idea might even work. I tried drawing a real garden, nothing like the fantasy one for Ava, attempting a herbaceous border inspired by the flowers I'd seen at the nursery. I couldn't remember any of their names but I could picture their shapes and colours. I quite liked the effect.

Then I turned over the page and started sketching a dark-haired guy dancing. Somehow, my fingers managed a devastating likeness all by themselves. I stared at the image. I made the eyes look shifty, the mouth a leer, the stance an arrogant strut. Then I tore the page out, making sure there wasn't the faintest imprint on the page underneath. I took the picture and ripped it in half, in quarters, tearing and tearing until it was in tiny, meaningless shreds. I flushed them in small handfuls down the loo until they'd all vanished.

I waited up till Lee got home, and made him a cup of tea and chicken sandwiches and then we climbed into his bed together. I thought of all the passion in the morning, and nestled up to him, kissing him, trying to arouse him, whispering sexy things, but it didn't really work.

'I'm so sorry, Dol. I'm not really in the mood,' he murmured. 'I just keep thinking about Ava and how she cried when I left her. Can we just have a cuddle?'

'Yes, of course,' I said, but I didn't really want cosy affection, I wanted passionate sex again, perhaps to convince myself that Lee really was the right guy for me. I couldn't help feeling rejected, which was ridiculous as we'd had such a good time in bed that very morning. But I knew he was truly sad, so I held him close, gently stroking him. He fell asleep almost straight away, and I lay listening to him breathing, trying to time my own breaths to his.

When his alarm went off the next morning he leant up on one elbow and kissed my forehead.

'I'll be off in ten minutes, Dol. Do you want me to set the alarm again for you?' he whispered, though there was no Ava to hear us.

'Yes. No. I don't know,' I mumbled. 'I don't feel very well. I've got a headache and I feel a bit sick. Perhaps I'd better not go to Lavender Hall today.'

'But it's the first day of the new course. You'll have to go to meet all the children,' said Lee.

'I don't *have* to do anything,' I said, huddling under the covers.

'But I thought you loved going there,' Lee said.

I did – but I hated the thought of seeing everyone after the scene last Friday night. I really did feel sick, probably with nerves.

But I loved this job, I was good at it, I was keen to meet the new pupils, I already had all sorts of fresh ideas bubbling in my head inspired by the dragon in the play. Now we already had the scenery we could experiment with different sorts of art. We could make papier-mâché dragon puppets, we could design dragon lairs, we could imagine what a dragon island would look like, we could draw the contents of a dragon's stomach, we could draw a dragon nursery, a dragon school, a dragon chef confecting lightly toasted delicacies, a dragon flag, dragon jewellery – I could even come full circle and ask everyone to design a dragon tattoo.

I *had* to go. I couldn't let the new students down – and I badly wanted to try out my ideas. I just had to tough it out if the other tutors thought I was pathetic. I jumped out of bed and padded next door to my own room. I went to the loo and peered anxiously down the toilet when I flushed, wondering if tiny paper pieces of Joel Fortune would come bubbling back up the pipes, but not a tiny speck of him materialized.

I settled down and drew various quick dragon sketches, so absorbed that time flew. I had to shower and dress and eat a bowl of muesli in double-quick time, in danger of missing my train. I was going to Lavender Hall, of course I was. I gave myself a hasty glance in the mirror on the wall.

'Chin up! Who gives a fuck about Friday night? This is Monday morning now.' It was the sort of thing Marigold said when she'd had some disastrously embarrassing experience. For once, my mother was a good example. She might be irresponsible, feckless, negligent – but she had courage.

I tilted my chin and marched out my door. My own courage dried up by the time I was on the train. I was shaking when I walked down the long drive. I knew Joel stayed at the Hall. He might be having his early morning splash in the pond. I pictured him dancing around naked, like an escapee from *Saltburn*, the image both ridiculous yet raunchy.

I heard footsteps behind me and I swung round, my knapsack thumping against my back, but it wasn't Joel, it was Morris. His glasses were misted up, his hair was blown awry in the breeze and he'd buttoned his shirt wrong – but he was smiling at me.

'Hey, Dolphin!'

'Hey, Morris,' I said.

There was a short pause. Was either of us going to mention the after-party?

'About Friday?' he said.

I clenched my fists. Dear Jesus, it was starting.

'Do you think I made a fool of myself, playing all those old pop tunes on the piano?' he asked earnestly. 'I don't know anything about modern music, they were all tunes my dad used to play. Everyone seemed to be enjoying themselves, though.'

I had no idea if he was saying this to make me feel better, or if it was truly the only thing concerning him. It didn't matter. He was dear, sweet Morris and he still wanted to be friends.

'You were amazing, and everyone loved them! I think I enjoyed myself a bit too much,' I said, feeling my cheeks burn. 'And suffered for it afterwards.'

'*You* were totally amazing at dancing,' he said.

'Well, I very much doubt I'll be doing that again,' I said, giving a little shiver – though even this early it was surprisingly hot.

Then we talked companionably about the children's performance, certain that no one else would ever be able to better Adrian's brilliant dragon. We were walking quickly and soon caught up with Linda ahead of us, bowed down with bolts of extra material, sparkly pink and blue and yellow synthetic stuff off a market stall, which would hopefully twinkle alluringly under the spotlight. Several of last fortnight's princesses had had difficulty fitting into the ready-made costumes, and she didn't want to embarrass any of the next cohort.

She didn't mention the after-party at all, so I brought it up as I helped her take all her materials upstairs.

'I made a bit of a fool of myself on Friday night,' I said, not looking her in the eye.

'It's happened to us all, love,' Linda said kindly. 'I think I made a tit of myself too, prancing about like a young girl, practically showing my knicks. Still, that's what after-parties are all about. I've seen Henrietta totally legless on more than one occasion, and poor Nina has had to haul her off to bed. Come on then, love, we'd better go down in time for Henrietta's spiel to all the new kids.'

All the tutors were gathering in her drawing room – except Joel. Maya kept looking round anxiously every time anyone came in the room. Henrietta was almost halfway through when the door opened once more.

'Ah, at last!' said Henrietta a little tetchily. 'Children, this is my dear associate, the famous actor and my television son, Simon the Scoundrel – Mr Joel Fortune!'

Joel swanned across the room and kissed Henrietta's hand in a total parody of an actor all too full of himself, and I looked at him with clear eyes. I wondered how I could have been attracted to such a phony. Maya seemed thrilled that he'd come at last, however, and gave him a wave. Joel blew her a little kiss, though he was careful to do it behind Henrietta's back.

I don't know whether he acknowledged me or not because I was determined not to catch his eye. As soon as the welcoming was over, I shepherded my art students up to the attic and chatted to them for a while, and then set them drawing straight away to try to relax them. They seemed a sweet enough bunch of kids, with several cute small girls – but none of them a patch on Miranda.

I didn't really want to go down to the kitchen to face all the other staff at the buffet lunch table, but Linda insisted.

'Don't be daft, dear, you need to get some food inside you. You're ever so pale as it is. You don't want to start fainting in front of the children now, do you?'

So I followed her reluctantly downstairs and there was Joel, filling his plate with food, then nibbling a chicken leg with his bright white teeth, rather like a tattoo flash of a hungry wolf. Maya was by his side, actually leaning into him, so it looked as if they were glued together.

Joel saw me and waved his chicken leg at me. I'd thought I'd ignore him totally, but then I thought that might make him realize the effect that one dance had had on me. It would probably amuse him. So I just gave an airy wave back and then struck up a determined conversation with Ted, asking him his plans for the new play. Then I talked to Damian, who immediately went on about my dancing. He even asked me if I'd had lessons when I was young. I smiled wryly that he thought I'd have the sort of mum who'd take me to ballet or tap but couldn't help being pleased when he said I was a natural. I talked to Lola too, but she wasn't really concentrating on me. She was watching Joel and Maya, scarcely able to take her eyes off them. Off *him*.

That helped me be resolute. I didn't want to join the Joel Fortune Fan Club. Henrietta seemed to be watching Joel and Maya like a hawk too, looking ... amused? Irritated? Envious? She had the actress trick of turning her face into a mask, but her eyes were glittering. Perhaps she and Joel sat together late into the evening, discussing his conquests, while Nina lurked in the background?

It all seemed a bit sad and creepy. I decided I was just going to immerse myself in the course and do my best with the new students. I was pleased that they all responded to my ideas, and we spent the last forty minutes of the session drawing our own dragons.

I stayed behind at the end of the day, pinning their drawings up on the wall opposite my mural. They looked pretty impressive all together like that. I spun round and round, taking in my artwork and their own, thrilled with the result.

'Hey, this is a new kind of dancing! Can I join in?' Joel was smiling at me, head on one side. I'd been so absorbed I hadn't heard him coming up the steps. I prayed I wasn't blushing like a schoolgirl. Luckily the sun was streaming through the skylight making it stiflingly hot up in the attic, so I made a play of fanning myself, hoping he would think I was just hot.

'I'm not sure that's a good idea,' I said.

Joel looked concerned.

'Did your partner stay really angry with you? He didn't hurt you, did he?'

'Of course not!' I said. 'And he's not my partner. We're neighbours. He was simply worried that something had happened to me because I was so late back. He's not usually like that at all.'

'That's a relief! Otherwise I might have been expected to track him down and tell him he was acting like a brute and then he'd likely hit me, because he looks like a tough guy well able to pull a punch, and I'm a cowardly weakling who can't punch a hole in a paper bag,' said Joel.

'Well, that's good to know,' I said, making light of his speech, but actually very touched that he felt he should defend me. And a little guilty on Lee's behalf. 'Lee's strong but he's not the slightest bit tough, truly. He feels a bit of a fool now for making a scene.'

'Quite right too. He certainly wasn't acting like a neighbour. I think there's a bit more to your relationship?' Joel asked.

'It's none of your business,' I said, really getting cross now.

'Of course it isn't. I'm just interested in you, Dolphin,' said Joel. 'You've intrigued me ever since you inked the masks on my chest. I just felt a connection between us – didn't you?'

I shrugged, knowing I really was blushing now. He saw my face was scarlet, and his lips flickered in a tiny smile. 'And when we danced together it was incredible – almost as good as having sex.'

'Stop it!'

'OK, OK – I was just being honest.' He paused. 'Though I really mean it,' he added softly.

'Look, I'd better be going,' I said quickly. My heart was thumping so violently I put my hand up to try to hold it still.

'Are you all right?' he asked. 'Here, sit down.'

So I sat, trying to take deep breaths in the still air. He sat down beside me, so close I could smell his faint lemony cologne and his warm body. He looked at my mural, leaning forward, peering at it closely.

'It's so good,' he murmured. 'Better than the scenery. You've put so much more into it. I love it. Truly. Especially all the birds flying in the sky – and old Icarus, the tips of his wings just starting to melt, his hands clenching as he realizes.'

He was *really* looking at it, spotting details no one else had seen. Did he genuinely love it?

'Do you like my rabbits?' I asked, pointing at Miranda's furry family.

He smiled. 'They're very cute – but I think one of the kids did them. They're sweet. Probably Miranda's work? It was kind of you to let her contribute.'

I smiled at him, happy that he could see the difference between our work and wasn't just paying empty compliments. 'Her parents are thinking of commissioning me to do a mural in her bedroom.'

'Quite right too,' he said. 'Hey, can I commission one too?'

'What would you choose as the subject?' I asked. He must have edged nearer. A strand of his soft dark hair brushed my cheek. It made me shiver, though I did my best to conceal it.

'You think I'll want a bedroom scene, several beautiful girls lounging around, some in slinky robes, some in underwear, some totally naked, all of them gazing at me hopefully,' Joel said, straight-faced.

I burst out laughing, because he was bang on.

'I'm right, aren't I?' he said. 'But maybe I just want one girl, painting, looking over her shoulder and glaring at me, though her eyes might be encouraging.' He reached out quickly and took hold of my hand. He rubbed it lightly with his thumb, the way he'd done before, and I felt little beads of sweat on my neck. I lifted my hair with my other hand to give myself some air, and he came closer still, and blew very softly.

'There now,' he whispered. Then he murmured, 'Is this all right?' and he kissed me very lightly at the nape of my neck, making me wriggle.

'Stop it,' I said automatically.

'I will, if that's what you want,' he said, straightening up and looking in my eyes. 'Really?'

I hesitated. 'Yes. No. I don't know. But—'

'But what? Shall I go now?'

Much as I knew I should, I couldn't let him go. I put my hand behind his head, on his warm brown neck, and kissed him on the mouth. We kissed slowly, softly, but then our mouths opened and we were breathing each other in, and then he pulled me on to his lap and my legs spread either side of his and after several tugs and pulls we were bare-skinned where we needed to be, and as soon as he was inside me we were moving together fiercely, and I couldn't have stopped and neither could he, and we got faster and faster until it was almost unbearably intense, and I felt as if I was flying up in a sky as blue as my mural, straight for the sun, and burning in its flames. He came a second or so after I cried out, and I had time to look at his face and know that I would remember this moment for the rest of my life.

Then he wrapped his arms round me, and we collapsed on our backs on the bare floorboards, shirts under our chins, jeans tangled round our ankles, laughing breathlessly and then relaxed against each other.

I lay on his shoulder, tracing the shape of the masks on his chest. I tiptoed my fingers down his arm, jokingly suggesting he try a full sleeve, an intricate design of calla lilies and lovebirds, with maybe a wolf lurking in among them, wild and hairy with very white savage teeth. Then I saw the time on his watch.

'I'd better get moving,' I said, reluctantly sitting up and trying to get dressed.

Joel sighed. 'Me too, I suppose,' he said, kissing me on the tip of my ear.

'But you're staying here, aren't you?' I asked, surprised.

'I am – but I need to have a shower and get myself dressed for drinks with the Queen Bee in the drawing room before poor Nina serves supper,' said Joel.

'Is that what happens every night?' I asked, astonished. 'I thought you'd be out most evenings – perhaps with Maya?'

'That would be pleasant,' Joel said calmly. 'But I owe it to Henrietta out of politeness – or call it gallantry. And I really do care about the old girl, God help me.'

I took the greatest care going downstairs, and then crept along the corridor to the front door. I glanced back then and saw the kitchen door was open and Nina was staring at me impassively. I gave her an awkward half-wave but her own arms stayed folded.

23

I was fine walking down the drive by myself, staring at the trees above me and the glimpses of sky. My body felt light and airy and open, and I went over our wild encounter in my head again and again, all of me pulsing at the memory. But it was different out in the streets as I hurried to the railway station. I felt so hot and sweaty and I was terrified that I smelt of sex. People seemed to be staring at my burning face and tousled hair, looking disapproving.

Don't be a fool – they can't possibly tell what you've been doing!

And what *had* I been doing? What was the matter with me? I knew perfectly well that I was playing with fire – appropriate analogy. Why had it all been so glorious? Joel hadn't gone through all the careful, sensitive, arousing motions, one by one. He'd just gone for it, and it had been fantastic, the best I've ever had. Was it because he was so caught up in the moment, so obviously loving it? Did we seriously have this mystic connection?

What's the matter with you? Mystic! You and Joel Fortune. You and Maya and a hundred and one girls in the past and almost definitely in the future too. And what about Lee? How is he going to feel if he finds out?

My stomach lurched then, and I felt sick with guilt. We weren't in a relationship, we hadn't known each other long, I should be free to have sex with anyone I chose, and Lee had to realize that was the way of the world. But he was such an old-fashioned kind of guy – a red roses, chocolates, traditional sweetheart. And he was still hurting badly from his wife leaving him.

I knew he was starting to feel really romantic about me. He also treated me like a child at times, which was infuriating – but I couldn't help liking it when he made a fuss of me, cooking for me, comforting me. I'd missed out on proper parenting and it felt so good – although I'd hated it when he'd been overbearing and controlling on Friday night.

Maybe he'd take one look at me and somehow know what had happened? I felt sicker and sicker the nearer I was to home. I tried rehearsing what I might say to him, but the words in my head were jumbled and unconvincing. In spite of everything I just wanted to whisper *Joel Joel Joel Joel Joel* at every step.

Then I was home, letting myself in the front door and running up the stairs. I tiptoed past Lee's door but there was no sound from within. Thank God, he was working late! I let myself in, stripped off my clothes and had a shower, really hot at first, lathering myself with soap twice over, and then an icy rinse to shock me into sense.

I was dry and dressed in clean clothes by the time I heard Lee whistling as he came up the stairs. He knocked on my door, and I went to answer it, hoping I looked casual and friendly – not the slightest bit guilty.

'Hey, Lee!' I said, and he smiled and hugged me warmly. I relaxed a little, knowing I smelt of rose shower gel and the lavender washing powder of my clean clothes.

'Mm, you smell lovely,' said Lee, kissing me. 'I'm all mucky. Give me half a tick and I'll shower.'

The hot water in our house was often temperamental, and I'd

kept my own shower running for a good ten minutes, but he was lucky and came back to my room red in the face, his curls spiralling, in clean clothes too. He'd brought two beers with him.

'Shall we have a drink and a chat before we start thinking about supper?' he suggested, sitting on my sofa.

I wondered if I should try being totally honest and tell him about my attic encounter with Joel, hoping he wouldn't mind too much. Of course I didn't do anything of the sort, though. I described the new students and my plans for the next two weeks, and then the course after that.

'And . . . what about Joel Fortune? Is he still around?' Lee asked, trying his hardest to sound casual.

'Yes, but he was mostly busy with Henrietta, assessing the children's acting ability,' I said, amazed that I sounded so matter of fact.

Lee took a large swallow of his beer.

'Did anyone mention Friday night?' he asked.

I took a deep breath. 'Oh, Linda ticked me off about having too much to drink, but she was only teasing.'

'Nobody mentioned me?' Lee persisted.

I paused, as if I was trying to think. 'No, not really,' I said.

'That's good. I wish I hadn't made such a dick of myself now,' said Lee.

He believed me so easily. I felt a hot flood of guilt, and when he started chatting about his own day, telling me every single strimming, pruning, mowing, mulching detail, I nodded along as if I was truly interested. I even asked a question or two about planting bulbs and vegetables, which delighted him.

'There, I *hoped* you'd get a bit interested in gardening,' he said. 'Tell you what, I'll have a word with Mrs Knight and see if I can show you around her garden sometime. I'm sure she wouldn't mind.'

This was going to be a step too far.

'No, don't. Honestly! I'd sooner wait until you get it all under control,' I said quickly.

'Well, you might be waiting ten or fifteen years in that case,' he said, laughing. Then he hesitated, looking slightly shifty. 'And I'll be starting a bit of building work soon.'

'Yeah?' I said, not really listening because I was wondering if I should offer to cook something for supper. Perhaps it would be easier to get a Deliveroo. Pizza? Fish and chips?

'It seems a bit damp, and needs a lick of paint, obviously, but basically it seems in good nick,' said Lee.

I blinked at him. 'Mrs Knight's house?' I said.

'No! The cottage. The one that used to be the gardener's in the old days.'

'Oh, right,' I said, still not properly concentrating.

'She hasn't actually promised anything, but I think she's considering letting me live there.'

I stared at him. 'Seriously?'

'Well, it goes with the job, or at least it used to. But think, Dol, a whole little house, two bedrooms, my own cottage garden in the front. Maybe I could put a swing at the back for Ava, she'd love that. Or a slide. And I don't think Mrs Knight would object to a small dog – it could keep me company while I work, and Ava's been on about wanting a puppy for ages. Don't you think that would be a good idea?' Lee beamed at me hopefully.

I stared at him, thoughts darting around in my head. He wasn't including *me* in this cottage idea, was he? Surely he couldn't mean it, after only knowing each other a few weeks? Lee and me, and Ava at weekends, though . . . An actual family.

'Well . . . I can see that it might be good for you and Ava,' I said uncertainly.

'It would be bloody marvellous! She could have her own room and I could have my privacy – *we* could,' said Lee.

I looked round my room. I didn't care that it was so small and shabby and eccentrically decorated. It was mine and I loved it. I didn't want to move out. And I was almost certain I didn't want to move in with Lee.

'It's – it's early days yet,' I said as lightly as I could. 'But it sounds a great project.'

Lee looked slightly disappointed, but he was still cheerful enough as we nibbled our takeaway pizza with another beer each, later that evening. He didn't mention the cottage again that night, or the whole week. But sometimes when I looked at him his eyes weren't focused properly and I could tell he was thinking about it.

I thought about it too, on and off. It felt so cold-blooded, but if he really was offering me a place with him, I wouldn't need to worry so much about making enough for my rent. But maybe this mural idea might come off. I had the details of Miranda's parents in my phone. I looked up mural artists on the internet, and felt with the right paints I could maybe do as good a job as any of them.

I tried to read all the information but the words slithered around and wouldn't make sense, and you had to do sums to calculate how much to charge per square metre, whatever that was. I asked Linda at Lavender Hall and she got her tape measure and measured my own dragon mural in the attic.

She scribbled away on a piece of paper and kept coming up with different figures – and we couldn't work out whether we should charge by the hour or day or week.

'And I'm a beginner too, but they're not to know that,' I said. 'Still, I'd better make it as cheap as I can. Shall I suggest two thousand pounds, saying it's a reduced rate?'

'Good idea, love,' she said.

'Linda – could I ask you a massive favour?' I made a huge effort, forcing myself to say the words. 'Would you write the message for me? I'm a bit hopeless about spelling and stuff and I want to sound really professional,' I said.

'Absolutely. My grandson's dyslexic – but luckily they're all clued in at school nowadays,' said Linda. 'Still, you strike me as a very clued-in woman anyway. Apart from one little aspect.' She arched her eyebrows. 'Our Joel.'

'Oh,' I said, wrong-footed.

'Yep. Nina and I have been having a bit of a chinwag. Darling, he's a sweet guy in many ways, but he's not in the market for a long-term relationship,' she said.

'I know,' I said, bristling. 'It's OK. I get him, completely.'

'Well, as long as you do, pet.'

I *did* get him – but somehow I was still helplessly drawn to him. I might have made resolutions at the start of the week to steer completely clear of Joel and leave our attic encounter as a delightful one-off occasion – it wasn't fair to Lee, it wasn't fair to Maya, it wasn't even fair to Henrietta – but I was still bitterly disappointed when Joel didn't come and find me in the attic when the days' sessions were over.

He was friendly in front of everyone, and sometimes I caught him looking at me. He'd give a slight nod then, a little sign between us that he was remembering our encounter too, but we didn't have any private time together at all, not even on the Friday at the end of the first week. I told myself it was all for the best. I paid dutiful visits to Marigold and made a fuss of Ava and pretended that everything was fine. Well, I suppose it felt fine enough during the day, but at night I'd wake up and think of Joel, whether I was in my own bed or Lee's. I'd lie there helplessly, wanting him so much. I'd never felt so easily aroused, so in need of sex.

Lee was working flat out in Mrs Knight's garden to impress her into giving him the cottage, so he was worn out most evenings.

When we did actually have sex it worked perfectly, and he was such a careful and generous lover that I felt satisfied in one way – but still ached for much wilder sex with Joel. I hated feeling like that, because it seemed like I was cheating on Lee. I was extra thoughtful towards him – though my stomach always clenched when he told me I was sweet and lovely and sexy. He said it so sincerely, whereas I was making things up just to make him feel good.

On the Tuesday of the next session I had an email from Miranda's mother. I could more or less make it out, but I showed it to Linda at lunchtime, not trusting myself, wondering if she was just acknowledging my mural terms rather than *commissioning me to start working on it in September!*

Linda read it out to me slowly so I could take it all in – and it was true! I actually burst into tears.

'Hey, hey, lovie, it's nothing to cry about!' said Linda, giving me a hug.

'I'm crying because I'm so happy! They really want me to do it and they're happy to pay me the full amount! She even says they think they're getting a bargain!'

'And so they are, lovie. I'm so pleased for you,' said Linda. 'I'm not surprised at all. You're very talented.'

I cried more then, because she really seemed to mean it. I'd been praised a lot for my tattoo designs, but somehow they didn't really count in my eyes. A mural was real art, though, and I'd loved doing it – and now I'd be paid to paint one!

I practically skipped downstairs to the conservatory with my art class so we could work on making new crowns for the princesses because several had got rather squashed and some of their fruit gum 'jewels' had fallen off. Maya was there, working on a mime class – and Joel was sitting back to front on a chair, giving her suggestions.

'I hope we're not disturbing you,' I said awkwardly.

Maya shook her head and said, 'Not at all,' in an airy manner – but her frown and her folded arms were saying something else entirely. Joel looked round, eased himself off his chair and came over to me.

'Are you OK?' he said quietly. 'Have you been crying?'

I felt a little tremor at the genuine concern in his voice. He was standing very close to me, only one step between us. The slight lemony smell of him made me breathless.

'I'm crying because I'm happy!' I said. 'Remember Miranda? Her parents have commissioned a mural like the one I did in the attic.'

'Ah, the attic!' said Joel, peering at me, and I felt my cheeks pinken.

'Joel, you promised you'd show the children different ways of showing fear,' Maya called, her voice sharp.

'Yes, sure, just coming,' said Joel. 'Well done, Dolphin! I'm really thrilled for you. We should celebrate.'

My breath hitched in my throat. Did he mean that everyone at Lavender Hall should celebrate? Or just the tutors? Or just Joel and me . . . ?

I found myself packing up all the art materials more slowly than usual at the end of the day's session. I could have left them down in the conservatory, but it seemed neater to take them up to the attic. Well, that's what I told myself. I pottered around up there, and then I heard footsteps bounding up the stairs and there was Joel, with a bottle in his hand.

'I've helped myself to one of Henrietta's end-of-session Proseccos. We'll celebrate your success in style. In various ways.' He grinned at me mischievously.

I'd been hoping he'd come up to find me, was already wet with wanting him – and yet I wished he hadn't so obviously taken it for granted that we'd be tearing our clothes off after a couple of swigs of wine.

'Won't Henrietta mind? Or won't Maya wonder where you've got to?'

'They won't know. They think I'm having a nap. Though I've never felt more wide awake.' Joel eased the cork out of the bottle and handed it to me. 'Take a big swig. The only glasses are in Henrietta's drawing room and I didn't care to rummage in her display cabinet.'

I'd swigged from a bottle of beer enough times, but the wine bottle was heavier and I misjudged it. Some of it dribbled down my chin. Joel laughed and licked it delicately, making me gasp, and then took a swig himself. Then he balanced the bottle on a table.

'I can't wait. We'll finish the bottle after.' He started unbuttoning his shirt. 'Shall we?'

I so wanted to say yes – and yet I wanted it to be special and meaningful, not a quick, throwaway shag. I thought of Lee and his serious determination to woo me back. I remembered him coming to my room early on Sunday, so humble, so sweet, so sorry. What was I playing at, willing to betray him so easily?

I hesitated – and then moved away from Joel, while still aching to press myself against him.

'Let's think about it, Joel,' I said.

'What?'

'I just feel uncomfortable. I'm pretty certain Maya will guess where you are. She'll mind terribly.'

'Come on, you don't even like Maya,' he said, trying to pull me closer.

'That doesn't mean I can't feel guilty.'

'Why are you playing games? I can tell you want to just as much as I do. Don't say you're feeling guilty about your caveman guy?' He shook his head incredulously.

'Yes, I am! He'd be so hurt if he knew,' I said.

'It's just sex. And you know how good it was between us. Why waste the moment?' He reached for my hand and did that little stroke again between my finger and thumb.

I'd been on the brink of going ahead in spite of my misgivings – but that practised move annoyed me.

'Don't!'

He stepped back. 'OK, darling, I won't. I'm not going to beg. Here, celebrate by yourself if that's what you want.'

He put the bottle on the floor and walked away, giving that jaunty wave again before going down the stairs. I was left by myself in the attic, pent up, infuriated, desperate, feeling a fool. I wanted to press a replay button and start all over again, but it was too late now.

I had several more swigs of wine but left most of the bottle to go flat. It didn't taste right any more – and I didn't want to drink too much anyway because I didn't want to make Lee suspicious.

I felt foolish and pathetic. Perhaps that's what spurred me on to seek out a printing shop on my way home from the railway station. Nina made sure I was paid weekly so I spent £25 on fifty select business cards with my name, phone and email and the words 'Custom Wall Murals'. I begged the guy behind the desk to check the spelling for me. He was so friendly I hoped he might help me set up my own website if I really made a go of this.

When I collected the cards the next day I painstakingly inked a design on each one: dragons, unicorns, mermaids, fairy castles, Japanese-style anime, dolls and teddy bears, babies, jungles, different animals, including a dolphin leaping. It took a couple of evenings.

'What are all those little drawings, Dol?' Lee asked curiously as we sat together.

I explained my mural idea. 'A painting on a wall?' Lee said.

'Yes, great idea,' he added, but I could tell by the tone of his voice that he thought I was chasing rainbows.

I didn't challenge him, but I became even more determined to show him that I could make a success of my new venture. Oblivious, Lee pored over seed catalogues and plant nursery websites and did his own sketches while I embellished my cards. I suppose it was all quite cosy and domestic, but then I saw he was looking up YouTube videos about how to deal with household damp and rotting window ledges.

'Are you really serious about this old gardener's cottage?' I asked.

'Well, of course I am. Mrs Knight finally told me today that if I do it up she'll let me have it for a peppercorn rent – and it would give me a chance to save up for a proper place of my own,' he said, grinning.

'For you and Ava?' I asked, my heart hammering.

'And you too, if you wanted,' Lee said. He was aiming for a matter-of-fact tone, but it came out painfully earnest.

I hesitated, not knowing what to say.

'Well, like I said. Let's wait and see,' I mumbled.

'Sure, sure,' said Lee.

I was the one who wasn't sure at all. I really didn't want to live in some imperious old lady's gardener's cottage like some poor cap-doffing servant. And I still wasn't at all sure I wanted to live with Lee, though the thought of seeing Ava every weekend was a huge temptation.

I wasn't mad enough to fantasize seriously about living with Joel as an alternative. I knew exactly what it would be like. I'd be staying in by myself every evening, never sure where he was or what he was doing. I felt I'd made the right decision not to have sex with him again – but every time I saw him I couldn't help vividly remembering the bliss of that one brief encounter. I still blushed like a teenager whenever he chatted with me now. He always looked at me mischievously, his lips twitching in a smile, knowing exactly what I was thinking.

I took a bulging pocketful of business cards to the celebration party after the play and forced myself to wander round the proud parents, making a fuss of each child performer, though privately I'd thought them rather a disappointment after Miranda and Adrian and all their friends in the first session.

I wasn't quite bold enough to produce a business card out of the blue, but if a parent complimented me on the scenery or told me how much their child had enjoyed an art class then I produced one of my cards. One father frowned and said, 'I didn't reckon on this being part of a hard sell for arty-crafty stuff,' and I just about died, and prayed Henrietta hadn't heard. But most of the parents were simply lovely and I had two requests for further conversations by the time the parents' party was fizzling to an end.

I'd have stayed for the after-party, but I saw Joel and Maya were in the corner of the drawing room having a row so I steered clear. I had one small glass of Prosecco with Linda and then went home to Lee, though I would rather have gone back to my own room to start sketching potential designs while I was all fired up.

24

Lee was obviously relieved to see me home so early this time. He congratulated me extravagantly on the two possible commissions, clearly amazed. I'd stayed almost stone-cold sober, but he'd bought a bottle of Crémant and then of course we drank it together and ended up in his bed. He made love to me in his sweet, gentle and romantic way, but I couldn't get properly aroused until I thought of Joel and our last time in the attic, and then suddenly I was there, almost on the verge of coming.

Lee went happily to sleep almost straight away, his arm round me. I lay awake for a long time, feeling guilty that I'd fantasized about Joel while having sex with Lee.

Forget Joel, forget Joel, forget Joel. What is the matter with you? Why break your heart when you know he doesn't give a toss about you? Lee loves you. Surely you could learn to love him back?

The weekend was a relief, playing with Ava and making a dutiful visit to Marigold. Dr Gibbon had apparently told her that she'd made such good progress and showed so much insight into her condition that she was likely to be ready to go home soon.

I felt anxious but I was pleased for Marigold, though it was hard talking to her naturally with Lettie there like her shadow. Sometimes they chatted together almost as if I wasn't there. I tried to tell her about my Lavender Hall work and all about the mural I was going to be doing come September.

'That's lovely, Dol,' Marigold said vaguely, but then she and Lettie started going on about some patient throwing their breakfast around that morning, and I felt like a spectator, not part of the conversation. Marigold had her back to me now, simply concentrating on Lettie.

I told myself that I should be pleased that Marigold had made a new friend – but I minded terribly. I dawdled on the way home, not quite ready to play Happy Families with Lee and Ava. Instead, I phoned Star, hoping she wouldn't be tied up with her own little family. Luckily Christopher was fast asleep and Charles was out at a rugby match, so Star could give me her full attention.

'Though I don't see why you're so upset about this Lettie, Dol. She sounds quite sweet. And it lets you off the hook a bit. Maybe you'll be able to get on with your own life now.'

'Yes, I see that,' I said, trying to get my head around why I struggled so much with Lettie. 'It's just I suppose it's because I'm used to Marigold needing *me*, not Lettie,' I mumbled, feeling awkward.

'*I* need you, Dol! I thought I'd found a great nanny for Chrissie a fortnight ago but she was an absolute nightmare, wanting so much time off she was hardly ever there, and bringing her boyfriend back to the house when she was babysitting. *Please* come and live with us. I know you'd be so happy here,' she said. 'You're so good with little children. You love Chrissie, don't you? Plus we could have such fun together. And we've got heaps of friends up here. You might even meet some guy more inspiring than your Lee.'

'Stop it, Star.' But I wavered for a few moments. I *did* love Chrissie – and I loved my sister even more. We might bicker nowadays but we always had such fun together too. I could try to start up my own mural company in Scotland, couldn't I? And Star probably knew lots of well-heeled parents who'd fancy a mural in their children's nurseries and playrooms. But I didn't really want Star to be the fixer, giving advice, telling me what to do. She'd always taken over any of my projects or games when we were children.

It might be the same if I was simply Chrissie's nanny. Star had her own way of dressing him, changing him, comforting him. She'd trust me with him – but she'd be the one in the driver's seat, really. I'd probably still love being Chrissie's nanny. But . . . It was such a big but. I didn't want to be the new nanny. I wanted to be the new *me*.

I went off to Lavender Hall on Monday morning to find there'd been another scene at the second after-party. Maya had caught Joel kissing Lola in the shrubbery and had become frantic, screaming abuse and actually pulling Lola's hair.

'Talk about a cat fight, squawking and scratching! I've never seen the like,' said Linda, her eyes shining at having such juicy gossip to tell me. 'And all the while Joel stayed smirking in a corner. It was just like an episode from *Heartbreak*! Sometimes I think he deliberately acts like a scoundrel because that was his identity for so long. Or he's secretly worrying that he's not a skinny young dude any more and needs to get all the girls lusting after him to reassure himself.'

I couldn't work out whether she was telling me all this as another warning to stay right away from Joel. I managed to shake my head and shrug my shoulders as if I simply wasn't interested but we both knew I was acting.

I felt especially sorry for Maya, who had sent a message to say she couldn't continue the rest of the course. Henrietta was furious with Joel because Maya had been very good at her job. I heard Henrietta shouting at him in her living room but by lunchtime he'd charmed her back into good humour, letting him entertain her with memories from their television time together.

Even so, she insisted that he take over Maya's mime classes as he was the one responsible for her not coming back. I thought he'd protest and try to wheedle out of it, but he was surprisingly obliging. The children found his sessions hilarious. He was great at teaching them, too, encouraging them to do fantastic mimes. Even the shyest, most awkward child found the confidence to preen or sidle or slither.

The weather was hotter than ever, and it felt as if we were all being microwaved in the conservatory. I took my children outside, encouraging them to enhance the dragon's cave with hessian, using some of Lee's old gardening sacks. Joel's kids shared the lawn, though we kept strictly to our own sides. Joel was extra extravagant with his miming sessions and rendered the children helpless with laughter. I had the feeling this was all for my benefit. I did my best to keep my eyes on my own students and their art, pretending I scarcely noticed he was there.

'Your kids are doing some fantastic work,' Joel said, coming up to me eventually.

'Thanks,' I said breezily.

He got nearer, peering over my shoulder at my designs. I tried to carry on drawing, pretending to be oblivious, but I was horribly conscious of his presence. I could smell his wonderful, distinctive scent, hear every breath he took.

'You're doing fantastic work too,' he said softly, and he reached out and touched my right hand. 'It's so weird, you can just move your hand, flex your fingers, and create something beautiful out of nothing.'

'Are you flirting with me because Maya's seen sense and cleared off?' I asked, hoping to sound simply amused.

'Don't tell me I'm wasting my time,' Joel said.

'Definitely,' I said.

'Are you sure?' he said, moving away from me, eyebrows raised. Of course I wasn't sure. If he just stood near me, I felt myself going weak with wanting him. But I hated feeling so helpless, and I was irritated by his confidence. He didn't seem at all bothered about poor Maya. When I ignored him he started cosying up to Lola at lunchtime, and she seemed delighted. Maybe he was just acting as if he fancied her to tease me? Or maybe he really did, and I'd been jettisoned too? The thought made me feel such a fool. I was furious that he might be playing fast and loose with me – and it was particularly embarrassing when Henrietta and Nina and Linda might be noticing. Well, to hell with him. I decided I didn't give a fuck about him any more. How many times did I have to tell myself? I was through, through, through with bad boys.

I had other things on my mind apart from Joel. Both of the second-session parents had got in touch! I went round to their houses after work on two consecutive evenings. The first couple wanted a lily pond mural for their little boy who was obsessed with frogs. That seemed an easy enough prospect. I'd always been a dab hand at frogs at Artful Ink. They liked my sketches. Once I'd measured the bedroom I managed to give them a sensible quote and it was all fixed then and there. I had the whole of September booked, with a herd of unicorns for a little girl's bedroom almost a definite for October. I was so thrilled. Even after I'd deducted money spent on paint, I'd be earning nearly £6,000 for six weeks' work! It would be more money than I'd ever dreamt of! It made me feel so powerful. I wasn't just sad little Dolphin now. When I caught sight of myself in shop windows I had my head up, walking tall. I decided to put Joel entirely out of my mind. And maybe Lee too? Did I really need *any* man in my life now?

By the second week of the course it was obvious that Joel and Lola were an item. Damian seemed to mind and moped around. It was clear he wasn't interested in Lola, though they were close friends. *He* wanted Joel. Every bloody person at Lavender Hall from the oldest to the youngest was under his spell. Though not me. He didn't appeal to me at all any more. I was sure of that. Well . . . almost sure.

This third and final course seemed to slip by ultra quickly. I got to know each of the children very well. There was one girl called Fairy of all things, a plain, sturdy child, though totally adorable. She often sought me out at lunchtimes and confided all sorts of secrets to me. Her mum and dad had recently split up and she was finding the toing and froing between them exhausting and upsetting. It didn't sound as if either of them was making much effort to make her feel wanted.

I felt so sorry for her. If I had a little girl like her, I'd want to spend every day of the holidays with her. I understood exactly what it was like to be a disappointing child.

I knew from her old photos that Star had been a beautiful baby, fair and bonny and advanced for her age. I'd been pale and mousey and nothing like either of my parents, a total changeling child. I knew it was pointless to mind that I'd always been a bit of a letdown, always second best. But of course I couldn't *help* minding.

I tried very hard not to have obvious favourites in my class, but I knew I praised Fairy more than the others – but why not? Her paintings weren't very well executed yet they came direct from the heart. Dr Gibbon would think her picture of a weeping princess with a rampant dragon either side of her, intent on tearing her in two, touchingly significant.

Fairy didn't have either warring parent coming to see her perform in the play. Her mother was flying to New York with her new boyfriend, and her father was too tied up with his work to take any time off that afternoon. They were sending the au pair instead. I was sitting in the same row for the performance. She glanced at the stage occasionally, but most of the time she seemed absorbed in her phone.

I hoped with all my heart that Fairy couldn't see her. When the play came to an end I stood on my feet and cheered, and when it was Fairy's turn to take a bow I clapped so hard my hands stung. I was pleased to see nearly all the staff cheering for her too. Joel usually gave each member of the cast a little box of chocolates afterwards but I saw he gave Fairy a much bigger, fancier box. He could be so charming sometimes, gallant to plain little girls and frail old ladies. He didn't treat women well romantically, having one fling after another, but I supposed he was always honest about not wanting a long-term relationship.

He turned his head and I smiled at him for being so sweet to Fairy. He smiled back and blew me a kiss. I knew it would be crazy to fall in love with him, but I could still like him, couldn't I? I shivered at the memory of our encounter.

I couldn't help thinking that just one more time wouldn't really be such a bad idea, would it? This was the last time I'd be seeing Joel. But no, I wasn't going to go down that route again. I'd blown it. He didn't want me any more anyway, he wanted Lola.

I was determined not to mind too much. I was going to go to the parents' party, circulate around the room, congratulate the children and make an extra fuss of little Fairy. I had to be practical and use this chance to advertise my murals.

So I worked hard, even pressing a mural card on Fairy's indifferent au pair. I praised their children's artwork to every parent there, and blatantly suggested that they might be interested in considering one of my murals.

When I looked up from one of these discussions I saw Henrietta was staring at me with hawk eyes. She beckoned me towards her and I went obediently to her side.

'What's all this, Dolphin? Why are you handing out all these little cards to people?'

She gripped my arm and I was terrified for a few seconds – and then I carefully but firmly detached myself. She didn't have any power over me. My stint with her was over, and I'd done my job well. I knew that and so did she.

I managed to smile at her. 'I'm simply giving a card promoting my artwork to any interested parent. You're a businesswoman – surely you can understand?'

She looked outraged for a moment but then her mask cracked and she actually looked amused.

'My goodness, little Dolphin, are you developing a pair of balls at last?' she said.

She was being appallingly rude, but I decided to weather it.

'Perhaps it's about time,' I said, and then sauntered off. I saw Linda watching approvingly, and I went over and gave her a hug, because I realized just how much I was going to miss her.

'Can we stay in touch?' I asked.

'Of course, dear. We get on really well, don't we? I'm going to miss our chats together.'

'I am too, Linda.'

I was going to miss them all, because in just six weeks they had become my close friends. I went round hugging all the staff while handing out more cards to the parents. I decided to leave before the after-party, still too much in a muddle to want to be around Joel. It might be better if I didn't even say goodbye to him.

But when I started edging out of the room, Joel was suddenly at my side.

'Hey there, Dolphin,' he said, standing so close I could feel his breath on my cheek. It was ridiculous, but my heart started thudding violently.

'Hey,' I said back, trying hard to sound nonchalant.

'Sad it's all over?' he persisted.

'Yes,' I mumbled.

'Sad *we're* all over?'

I was at a loss even for monosyllables. I just shook my head.

'We can still meet up sometimes?' Joel said.

I shrugged, implying maybe.

'I do hope so,' said Joel, looking straight at me with his beautiful eyes. He sounded as if he really meant it. I wanted him so much.

'Come and have a drink anyway,' said Joel. He took hold of me by the elbow and led me to Henrietta's living room. Most of the staff were there, with full glasses. 'Actual champagne tonight!' he crowed, glancing at the labels on the bottles. He went to pour me a glass.

I knew exactly what would happen if I drank too much champagne. 'Er – no, not for me,' I protested. 'I'll just have fizzy water.'

'So you don't quite trust yourself around me, then,' said Joel, teasing.

I stuck to my choice of water and when Joel apologetically went to Henrietta sitting in queenly fashion on her throne, I hurried to join Linda. She was already on her second champagne, making the most of things. She raised her eyebrows at my own glass.

'Wise choice – but it is very good champagne,' she said, taking another gulp.

We all toasted Henrietta and she raised her glass to all of us in grand royal fashion.

'You've all been such darlings!' she said throatily. 'I do hope you'll all come back for the Christmas classes – and then of course there's Easter and next summer. I'd love you all to become my regular tutors, you're a splendid bunch!'

'We sound like grapes!' said Linda, giggling. 'I do hope you come back, Dolphin. I feel like we're old friends now.'

'I'll do my best,' I said.

I gave Linda a hug.

We clinked our glasses together and exchanged phone numbers.

Henrietta commanded Morris to start playing the piano again. Joel swept her an elaborate bow, asking her to dance. She accepted eagerly, fluttering her eyelashes at him, her lipsticked mouth in a coy little smile. She tripped over her long dress several times, already unsteady on her feet from the champagne, but Joel treated her as if she was his dazzling young princess. I couldn't help smiling watching him.

When he'd led Henrietta back to her seat and poured her another glass of champagne, he chatted to her attentively, staying with her until Ted came wandering up to confer with her about the pantomime for the Christmas session. Joel seized the opportunity to dance with Lola, who had been waiting forlornly. She was light and graceful, he was lithe and deft, so they danced beautifully together. It was almost like a dance on *Strictly*, but there didn't seem much connection between them, even though their bodies were pressed against each other. I couldn't help feeling pleased.

Then Damian dared asked Joel to dance, and he happily complied. They looked great together, changing leads every now and then and inventing new moves. It was an even more dynamic success. Everyone cheered at the end. I joined in the clapping, giving Joel a nod of approval.

'Go on, Dolphin, you dance with Joel now,' said Morris. 'Come on, give us all a treat. I'll play "Spirit In The Sky" again.'

'No, no, definitely not!' I protested. 'I've got to go now anyway.'

'I agree, definitely not,' Joel said firmly, which stopped me in my tracks. What did he mean? Was he publicly paying me back for rejecting him that time? Was he really being that petty?

'No repeat performances,' Joel continued. He looked at me. 'We'll do something new. OK, Dolphin? How about . . . "Stay Just A Little Bit Longer"? Do you know that one, Morris?'

'Great choice,' said Morris.

'Well, come on, Dolphin, we'll give it a whirl,' said Joel.

The whole roomful of people started clapping and chanting our names. Even Lola and Damian joined in. I dithered, biting my lip, not feeling as though I could refuse. I could have just this one dance and then rush home. It wouldn't mean anything. So I nodded, Morris started playing, and Joel pulled me into the middle of the room. I wasn't sure the chemistry would work this time. I'd never seen Marigold dance to this – but somehow it didn't matter.

I got into the smoochy beat immediately, and started dancing, mirroring Joel. It was the magic of the music, the joy of dancing with someone so good, so dynamic, so dark. Someone I'd always remember, even if I never saw him again. I might be simply whirling round the carpet in Henrietta's living room, but I was also whirling up above everyone's head, straight through the ceiling, the roof, up in the sky towards the setting sun, flying.

I wanted the music to go on for ever, for it never to stop, for the sun to stay red for ever. Morris extended the song again and again but at last slowed down and stopped. I stood still, wanting to stay in Joel's arms. I wanted him, I wanted him so much, I didn't care about poor Lola watching us, or Lee waiting anxiously at home for me.

Then Henrietta's French clock chimed, and although it was several hours short of midnight I knew I had to leave now.

'I've got to go home. But it's been great working with all of you. Bye, everyone.' I looked Joel in the eyes. 'Bye, Joel,' I said. I gave him a hasty kiss on the lips and then rushed out of the room.

I ran halfway down the drive in the dusk, leaping along, my heart still thudding. Then I heard someone calling me. I didn't have to turn round. I knew who it was. I stopped, clutching my chest.

'No, please, I've *got* to go, it's getting dark already,' I mumbled, struggling to stay calm.

'You forgot your bag with all your stuff,' said Joel, handing it to me, grinning.

'Oh hell, so I did. Well, thanks,' I said, taking it from him, embarrassed that I'd thought he was running after me for any other reason.

'Are you sure you didn't leave it behind on purpose?'

'Of course I didn't! You're utterly amazing! You think every single woman is after you!' I said.

'Then why did you kiss me?' he said.

'I was just kissing you goodbye, for God's sake,' I protested, heart hammering.

'Really? Let's try again,' he said, and he caught hold of me, so that the bag fell to the ground and crayons spilled all over the grass.

I didn't bother to try to pick them up because he was kissing me properly now and I couldn't help kissing him back, our mouths wet and wide, and then his arms were around me and he was steering me back against a tree and we struggled a second with clothing before he lifted me up. I wound my legs tightly round him, and then felt him slide into me, filling me up, and it felt so good, so good. I rubbed against him as he pressed high up inside me. The blood was pounding so hard in my head I couldn't think, my whole body was on fire, so desperate now that everyone could have run out of Lavender Hall to watch and I wouldn't have cared. Nothing mattered but Joel, and we were flying together now, grunting, not bothering to keep quiet, just intent on the sex, nearly there, faster and faster, and it was so good, so much better than anything I'd ever felt before, so that I cried out again and again before we both collapsed against each other.

We slid down on to the grass, and I stared up at the faraway sky through the tree branches and saw the blood red of the setting sun and the silver glimmer of the moon, my body still pulsing with pleasure.

25

Then Joel sat up and gave a shout of triumph, scattering the birds in the trees.

The noise ricocheted in my head. It sounded so gross, so blatant. Literal cock-crowing.

'Shut up!' I hissed. 'They'll hear you back at the Hall.'

He laughed, clearly not caring. Perhaps he *wanted* them to hear.

'So what if they do?'

'How can you be so callous not caring if Lola hears? Especially after you've already broken Maya's heart? You're impossible!' I said, though I hadn't cared myself a few minutes ago.

I knew we were all consenting adults, but it suddenly seemed so sordid. I didn't want to lust after him helplessly and be let down again and again. I struggled to get dressed properly. I was so wet I felt it seeping into my underwear. I'd been so madly carried away I hadn't given a thought to contraception and clearly Joel hadn't either. We hadn't bothered that first encounter either, up in the attic.

What's the matter with you? What if you get pregnant?

I froze as I scrabbled for my crayons in the grass. When did I last have my period? I'd been so caught up in my new life I hadn't really given anything as mundane as a period any thought. I hadn't had it for a while. A long while. I'd last had it when . . . ?

Wasn't it around the time Brian had got rid of me? Later? I started shivering. More than *six weeks* ago? So that meant I was at my most fertile that first time with Joel?

'Oh God!' I groaned, kneeling there on the grass.

'What's up?' said Joel, sounding amused rather than concerned. 'What's this, sudden remorse? Are you praying for forgiveness?'

I burst into tears.

'Dolphin?' He tried to put his arms round my shoulders, but I swiped him away.

'What's the matter?'

'I'm scared I'm pregnant,' I wailed, unable to hold the knowledge back.

'*What?* We've literally had sex a minute ago!'

Why did he have to sound so exasperated?

'I don't mean because of this time! No, from the first time we had sex,' I said.

He gave a great sigh, as if it was all too tedious to think about. I couldn't bear it.

'Don't *sigh* like that! You're the one who didn't take precautions!' I said furiously.

'You're a grown-up, not a little kid! I assumed you'd be taking care of that side of things!' he said.

I'd tried various forms of contraception over the years but hadn't really got on with anything – and it seemed daft to keep on when I mostly wasn't having sex at all. It had been a relief when Lee had always dutifully used a condom.

Are you sure? Absolutely certain?

The only thing I was certain of was that I couldn't stand Joel right this minute, even though he was trying to hold my hand now, actually rubbing between my forefinger and thumb in a gesture that now made me feel queasy.

'Stop that!' I snapped, snatching my hand away. He hung on to me.

'Look, lighten up a little. You're not the first girl in the world to get herself pregnant at the wrong time. If you're sure then all you need to do is take a trip to a special clinic. I'll go with you if you like,' he said, as if he was doing me the greatest favour in the world.

'You're the last person I'd go with! And get *off* me!'

'For Christ's sake, one minute you can't get enough of me and then the next you're all touch-me-not and acting like a crazy person!'

He didn't mean that *I* was crazy, I knew that. But it stopped me short. My head jerked, as if he'd punched me in the face. I was behaving exactly like Marigold. Impulsive, hysterical, uninhibited, desperate for sex, losing all control, feeling as if I was flying – and then tumbling down and down and down.

Could I have bipolar too? I'd worried on and off, but now it was starting to feel terrifyingly possible. I was panicking so much I could hardly breathe. Would *I* end up in a psychiatric ward? And if I really was pregnant, what would be the impact on the baby? Would I be as unreliable a mother as Marigold was to me? What if I passed it on?

I scrambled up, slung my bag on my shoulder and started running.

'Dolphin! Don't turn this into a stupid melodrama! I only want to help you!' Joel called.

'Look, all I want is for you to leave me alone! And – and it's not yours anyway. So you can just relax and carry on shagging elsewhere!' I yelled, and ran harder.

He didn't come after me this time. And I didn't hope he would. I didn't want anything more to do with him now. I knew he wasn't the worst man in the world. I'd sprung it on him and he'd been taken aback. But he didn't really *care* about me. And he certainly didn't seem to give a toss about his child.

I cared. It was *my* child. I found I was walking to the station now with my hands holding my flat stomach protectively. Was it really curled up inside of me, a tiny little hidden creature, *mine*? I'd thought about having a baby before, but it was always a daydream, a fantasy. I'd never felt remotely ready to be a mother. I was always sure I'd never cope. I didn't earn enough money to support the two of us. I wasn't emotionally ready, too much like a child myself.

What sort of mother would I be? If I really did take after Marigold then maybe I'd never manage to be reliable and steady and always there for it, physically and emotionally? She promised she'd never let us down, but she did, again and again. There were those wild and wonderful happy times when she seemed the most magical mother in the world – and awful dark doldrums when she stayed in bed and didn't bother to feed us or tell us what to do.

There was that terrible scary time when Star went off with her father and Marigold and I were left alone and she was possessed with demons who told her to paint over all her tattoos. How could I know how to be a good mother with that as an example? I was stuck being that frightened little girl for ever.

And yet I'd coped even then. I'd phoned for help and got Marigold into hospital, possibly saving her life. I'd carried on and on looking after her ever since. I'd made a name for myself as a tattooist. I'd not given up when I lost my job. I'd found a niche for myself at the summer school and I'd been a success. All the children loved me. And maybe this tiny baby bean might love me too.

I didn't want to take that trip to a clinic. I wanted my baby. I crossed my fingers over my stomach as if physically holding it in place. I tried to imagine it. A child with intense blue eyes and dark hair, charming and confident? I screwed up my face at the thought as I walked into the station. I didn't want it to look remotely like its father. Wouldn't I always be reminded of that wild encounter in the attic? And if I stayed with Lee then surely he'd realize he wasn't the father as soon as the baby was born?

Poor Lee sitting at home, waiting to hear the clunk of the downstairs front door, the pad of my feet up the stairs. If only he hadn't been so diligent about contraception! Then he could maybe be the father? No, he wasn't the sort of man to get carried away and forget to be responsible. I thought back to all the times we'd had sex. Wait a minute. What about the Sunday morning after we'd quarrelled so bitterly about my first dance with Joel? When he'd knocked at my door so sad, so sorry and he'd gone down on me in such a sweet, determined way? And then afterwards . . . I'd climbed on top of him and we'd had sex so he could come too. We'd both been tired and distracted and emotional and *I was pretty sure he hadn't used a condom then*.

Oh, Lee! *Could* it be your baby? The more I thought about it the more sense it made – and the more I felt guilty that I'd had sex with Joel less than an hour ago without a thought for poor Lee.

I texted *On way home, sorry!* – words I could actually manage – and added a whole row of kisses too.

I felt so awful. How could I have betrayed him so easily, especially now I might be nurturing his child inside me? He'd said that he didn't want any more children – and yet I knew him so well. He was an amazingly devoted father to Ava. If I told him I was having his baby, I was certain that he'd be thrilled. He'd never in a million years mention a trip to any clinic. He'd want our baby, he'd want me too, he'd look after us and we'd be a family and I'd have everything I'd ever wanted.

It made such sense. Oli knew me better than anyone, even my own sister, and he thought Lee was perfect for me. Perhaps I'd been a total fool. I knew Lee was a kind, patient, caring, lovely man. We'd had such happy days together. And I loved Ava so much. She'd love being a big sister. At long last I had a chance of being in my own special family. I had to make it happen, for my baby's sake.

I imagined a tiny, gentle Lee-baby, so sensitive, so sweet, a mini-Ava. It was surely what I wanted more than anything in the world? So what had I been doing, fucking mindlessly in the woods with a man who didn't really give a damn about me?

I felt horribly conspicuous on the train home. I couldn't stop wiping my face and brushing my clothes, scared that it was obvious that I'd been having sex. A woman in the same carriage peered over at me and mouthed, 'Are you all right?'

I nodded, trying to smile reassuringly though I probably looked like I was grimacing, because she kept staring at me. I rushed off the train when we got to Seahaven, wondering if I could have a quick wash in the ladies' room in case I smelt of Joel and sex and shame. It was locked, unfortunately, so I ran out of the station to see if I could use the public toilets instead – and ran straight into Lee's arms.

I jumped back, horrified.

'Hey, it's only me, sweetheart! Did you think some complete stranger was grabbing you?' he said.

'But – but I thought you said you were staying at home?' I stammered.

'When I got your text I thought I'd come to the station to meet you. Did you have a good time?' He looked at me properly under the streetlight. 'Have you been crying?' He sounded so concerned.

I wanted to blurt it all out, wanting to confess because I felt so dreadful, but I knew it would kill him. He'd been desperate when his wife was unfaithful. I couldn't do it to him again.

'Yes, I've been sobbing away. It was just so sad saying goodbye to everyone. I hadn't realized how close we'd all become,' I lied, with terrifying fluency.

'Oh, Dol,' he said, putting his arms round me properly, hugging me close.

My stomach clenched, really hurting. Oh no, was my period actually starting now? Or was it just because I felt so guilty? I should be hoping the baby had been a figment of my imagination all along – but the thought of not having it made me realize that I wanted it, no matter what, no matter whose.

'I must have a shower the minute I get in,' I mumbled when we were in the van. 'I was running because I was late and I smell so sweaty and horrible.'

'No, you don't, you smell lovely, you always do,' Lee said, kissing me.

I wriggled away from him as soon as I could, and when we were home I ran into my own room, tore off all my clothes and examined myself. It was all right, no blood at all. I felt weak with relief in spite of everything. I had a long shower, soaping myself thoroughly. I wanted to go to bed now, alone. I needed to think hard about what I was going to do, but Lee had told me in the van that he had our supper in the oven. It would be mean to disappoint him. But was I seriously able to play happy couples with him when I'd just had sex with Joel?

I put on my nightie and dressing gown after I'd towelled myself dry so fiercely that my skin glowed red, then took them off again quickly, in case Lee thought I was trying to be seductive. I put on old, crumpled shorts and a stripy teeshirt, trying to look as dull and unalluring as I could.

'You look so sweet!' Lee said, when I forced myself next door. 'Not much older than Ava.'

I tried hard to smile but I didn't want to play the daddy-and-daughter game today.

I was right about supper. He had a wholesome home-made fish pie in the oven, something I usually golloped up enthusiastically, but now I could only manage a few mouthfuls.

'I suppose you tucked in to all the party food,' Lee said.

I smiled at him wanly. 'I think I'm just too tired to eat,' I said.

'You do look a bit pale. Did it all go well? The kids didn't forget their lines?'

'They performed it beautifully. The parents all seemed thrilled,' I said, trying to look pleased.

'And they liked all your artwork?' he prompted.

'Yes, they were very complimentary.' I was speaking without expression, starting to sound like a Dalek.

'And Henrietta was pleased with you? Did she pay you?'

'Yep, with a fifty-pound bonus actually,' I said. 'And she wants me to do an art session at Christmas time too.'

'Brilliant!' said Lee. 'Though she'll let you off on Christmas Day, won't she? You don't want to miss my turkey.'

'Well, I'm not sure I'm even going to work at Lavender Hall again,' I said determinedly. I knew I couldn't ever risk seeing Joel again. 'I really want to concentrate on building my mural business now. People have shown a lot of interest – but of course I'm not sure how many will actually commission me. Even Miranda's family might not like the mural for her bedroom and want their money back.'

Being honest, I was fairly certain they'd love it, but I just wanted a little bit of reassurance. Lee didn't quite get it.

'You don't really need to worry about money at the moment now I'm at Mrs Knight's. I'm earning way more than I used to so I can always help you out,' he said.

'It's so kind of you to offer, but I couldn't possibly take your money,' I said in a rush.

'Don't you get it?' he asked, pulling me over on to his knee. 'I love helping you.'

I put my hands over my stomach again, trying to keep calm.

'What's the matter? Tummy ache?' he asked. 'Shall I rub it for you?'

Oh God, again with the father–daughter dynamic. 'I think I'll just go to bed,' I said, getting up.

'Curl up in my bed, it's roomier. I'll come to bed too,' said Lee.

No, no, no!

I couldn't possibly have sex with Lee too, not yet, not now. I'd feel too dreadful, too guilty. But I didn't know how to stop him. He got into bed with me, pressing up against my back and rubbing my stomach very slowly and gently, and then his hand slid downwards. I felt myself clenching.

'OK, OK, I'll just let you sleep,' he said, patting my back.

'You're so lovely to me,' I said, trying with all my heart to be grateful. I didn't think I could ever sleep again. If I closed my eyes, I saw Joel looking at me, dancing with me, staring at me, kissing me, fucking me. I felt myself stirring at the memory in spite of everything. I turned over on to my stomach, worried that Lee would sense this. He just carried on stroking my back, murmuring soothingly, oblivious.

I must have slept at some point because I dreamt about babies. I was wandering dazed through a huge nursery of babies in blue and pink cots, looking for my own child. I saw a plump little baby boy with curly hair and rosy cheeks and a nurse held him out to me. He gave me a great gummy smile and I held out my arms but they were slow and stiff and the baby fell right through them and lay wailing on the floor. I stared at it, horrified, and tried to pick him up to comfort him but the nurse pushed me away and lifted him back into his cot.

I stumbled on down the nursery and saw a baby in a pink cot, with several tufts of glossy black hair and amazing blue eyes with long black lashes. I bent to scoop her out, but she started crying. She had a full set of teeth already, very white and sharp and savage. I backed away from her too, and ran on and on down the long ward, and then slammed into the wall at the end.

I woke with a start, still clutching my stomach, and lay awake listening to Lee's soft snoring, his whole body warm and relaxed, with absolutely no idea that I'd deceived him.

I must have dozed a bit, but I was wide awake when Lee's alarm went off. He smiled at me in the early morning light.

'Hello, sweetheart,' he said. 'It's Saturday!'

'Best day of the week because Ava's coming,' I said, as brightly as I could.

'And I've got my big girl by my side,' said Lee. 'Though you're actually such a little scrap of a thing. I hope to God I never roll over heavily in the night – I'd squash you flat.'

He reached out and gently touched my breasts. I held myself very still, trying desperately hard not to pull away.

'I'm flat already,' I said, making a weak attempt at a joke. 'They practically disappear when I'm on my back.'

'They do not! They're beautiful. Just right. Perfect, in fact.' He lent up on his elbow and bent to kiss them. They responded automatically, though I didn't feel in the least turned on. Lee was responding too, touching, coaxing. I did my best to act normally, to open my arms, open my legs, open all of me to him, but it wasn't really working.

'I'm so sorry, I don't think I can – my stomach's still so sore,' I mumbled.

'It's OK, that's fine. I understand,' Lee said, pulling away from me at once. 'Is it your period?'

'Mm – not sure,' I said, hating myself for not being straight with him. He smiled at me sympathetically, and I thought yet again that he was a lovely man, and what a bitch I was being, deceiving him like this.

It was a relief when Lee left to start the long journey to collect Ava. I went next door and had another long shower, wishing there was some way I could scour inside my head too. What had happened to me? Why couldn't I think straight? How had I got myself into this crazy situation? That word ricocheted round my brain.

I wiped the misted mirror and looked at my face. My eyes stared back, strangely bright, glancing this way and that. Marigold's eyes, when she was in a manic phase.

I panicked and phoned Star. I had to ring and ring before she answered.

'Dol? For God's sake, what's happened now? We've only just got Chrissie back to sleep after his early feed and Charles and I are having some private time.'

I could hear him murmuring in the background. Star whispered something back to him.

'It's OK. It doesn't matter,' I mumbled. 'I'll leave you to it.'

'No, don't! I'll only worry about you. Tell me what's up. What's Marigold done now?'

'She's much better, actually. She's going home soon,' I said.

'But not to live with the drug addict?'

'No, he's gone. I got rid of him,' I said, hoping she might be a little bit proud of me. 'I think she might want this girl Lettie to move in with her instead. She's acting like she's her best friend in all the world.'

'Well, isn't that good? Less pressure on you,' said Star. 'I worry about you, Dol, because *you* worry about her so.'

'I worry about me too,' I blurted out. 'Do you think I take after her, Star?'

'Take after Marigold?' Star said incredulously. 'Don't be daft! You're not remotely like her.'

'I *am*. What if I'm bipolar too?' I said, fighting not to cry again.

'Of course you aren't bipolar, you idiot,' she said fondly. 'Whatever makes you think that?'

'I'm acting just like Marigold when she's off her meds. And now I've got myself in a terrible position. I – actually, is Charles beside you? Can he hear?'

'No, he's in the nursery with the baby, trying to settle him all over again. Why, what have you done?' Star couldn't stop the hint of amusement in her voice. She clearly wasn't taking me seriously.

'I've been having sex with this guy Joel as well as Lee, and—'

'Wait, who's Joel?'

'Another teacher at the summer school, Joel Fortune. Anyway, we—'

Star gasped. 'Not the *actor*? He's so hot!'

'Yes, him,' I said impatiently. 'Anyway, I've been having sex with him as well as Lee and now I'm pretty sure I'm going to have a baby,' I whispered.

'Joel's?' Star asked, now agog.

'Well, that's the awful thing. Either could be the father.'

'Oh, Dol, you're hopeless!'

'All right! Don't rub it in. Marigold kept on leaving us at night, shacking up with anyone she fancied. What if I'm going the same way? I couldn't stop myself with Joel, and I keep trying to force it with Lee but I'm just not sure he's really right for me, so I'm stuck – but maybe with a baby!'

'So don't you think the most sensible thing is to have a termination?'

'No! I want it more than anything, my own baby. And don't tell me my period might just be late, it never is, and it's weeks now, and I just *know* I'm pregnant!'

'OK, slow down, I can hardly understand what you're saying.'

'But that's just it, I'm talking too fast and feeling like I'm on fire and I keep getting all these new ideas for designs, they keep on coming, and it's all classic symptoms of a manic phase, you know it is! I'm behaving *exactly* like Marigold!'

'Well, at least you haven't covered yourself in tattoos,' Star joked.

'For God's sake, this is *serious*!' I said furiously. 'Oh, Star, what am I going to do?'

'It's easy!' said Star. 'You move up here and live with us and look after Chrissie and your own baby! We could be one big family. It's the obvious solution. Oh, Dol, do say yes. It would make everybody so happy!'

I thought hard. Would it make *me* happy? It would make things so much easier if I did go up to Scotland. I wouldn't even need to let Lee know about the baby. He'd be devastated if he ever found out there was a fifty per cent chance it was Joel's.

Oli thought I'd be really happy with Lee. Star thought I'd be happy with her. I could try to *make* myself be happy with either of them – but I had tears brimming in my eyes now. Oh God, was I snapping out of a manic phase and falling into a depression?

'Star, I truly think I *am* starting to be bipolar,' I said, beginning to cry properly.

'No, you're not! Your hormones are probably up the creek at the moment. Or your period's late because you've been stressed and now this is premenstrual tension. You'll probably find you'll start tomorrow and you've got in a state for nothing,' said Star, using her special calm doctor voice, which I always found truly irritating.

'Why do you always have to patronize me? Why can't you be more understanding? What kind of a sister are you? What kind of a *doctor*?'

'I'm not a psychiatrist, thank God. Look, if you're really convinced by your totally bonkers bipolar disorder thing, why don't you go and have a chat with Dr Gibbon?' she asked.

'All right, I will,' I said, and I rang off abruptly.

Star phoned back but I didn't answer. She phoned again ten minutes later, and then sent a text saying *Love you whatever* with a row of hearts. Despite everything, she was my own dear Star and I felt slightly comforted. I texted back *Love you too, so much* with a row of hearts as well.

I made myself a rudimentary breakfast and sat sipping coffee, nibbling on toast, looking at my distorted image in the shiny kettle. I even looked mad now, snivelling as I ate. Did Star really think her plan would be best for me – or was she just wanting a nanny to help her out? I longed to be part of a family. My *own* family.

Then I remembered – I didn't just have a mother and a sister. I had a father too. I wondered how he was. Horrible Meg had insisted he wasn't well. Was that really true? We'd never really managed a proper father-and-daughter relationship. But he was still a blood relation and he'd always seemed fond of me.

I flicked through the contacts on my phone and then pressed his number. I waited, praying that Meg wouldn't take it on herself to answer for him again, but after a few rings someone picked up.

'Hello. New Barnes Leisure Pool, the manager speaking. How can I help you?'

It was strange hearing him announcing himself like that on his mobile. There was a hint of pride in the way he said the word 'manager'. I could hear the roar of the swimming pool in the background. He must be walking up and down the tile surround, supervising, whistle at the ready.

'Hello?' he repeated.

'Dad?' I whispered. It always felt so odd calling him that.

'Is that you, Alice? Speak up, love, I can't quite hear you.'

He had two real daughters apart from me, Grace and Alice. Well, I was real too, wasn't I?

'It's Dolphin,' I said.

'Dolphin?' He sounded bewildered. Surely to God he couldn't have forgotten that he had another daughter with such a ridiculous name? 'Hang on, I'll nip upstairs to my office, it's quieter there.'

I waited. I could hear his breath as he opened doors and ran upstairs, light in his sporty trainers. He sounded fit enough. At last another door opened and shut and I heard him give a small *whoof* as he sat down.

'Are you still there, Dolphin?'

'Yes.'

'Sorry about the confusion. Alice is so dotty she's forever losing her phone and dialling me from someone else's number.'

So does that mean he hasn't actually bothered to put a name to *my* number? Perhaps Meg has deleted it altogether? I was tempted to stop the call before I'd even got started, but he was talking again now.

'Well, good to hear from you, Dolphin,' he said, putting on a falsely bright voice. 'When was the last time we were in touch? Christmas?'

So evil-cow Meg hadn't even told him I'd called for help collecting Marigold from Gatwick. But what was the point of bringing it up now?

'Probably,' I said.

There was a slight pause.

'And you're OK, Dolphin?'

'Yes. Well. I just wanted to ask you something, Dad.'

'Fire away,' he said.

'Do I seem anything like Marigold to you?'

'Not at all. I mean, don't get this wrong, you're a very attractive young lady—'

What?

'But your mum was always a serious good-looker, very flamboyant, with her red hair and her figure and all those unusual tattoos,' he said, still sounding a little awed by her.

'I don't mean like her in looks,' I said sharply. 'I'm talking about my personality.'

He considered this for a moment. 'No, not really. I mean, you've always been a quiet little thing. Lovely, of course, but not a bubbly extrovert like Marigold.'

Oh God, this was so pointless. I wanted reassurance that I wasn't seriously mentally ill, not confirmation that I was boring!

'Dad, how did you feel when Oli and I tracked you down? Did you mind desperately that Marigold never told you she was pregnant?'

'Well – it was certainly a bit of a shock – but I wouldn't say I minded. It was lovely to discover a brand new daughter, though of course I already had my own girls,' he said uncertainly.

I was his own girl too, but clearly not just second best, *third* best now.

'Right,' I said, trying to keep my voice steady.

'Look, I'm pretty hopeless at expressing myself, but you do mean a lot to me, Dolphin. I've been thinking, especially since this little heart trouble, we ought to get together more,' he said.

'How would Meg feel about that?'

'Well . . . we could meet up just the two of us,' he suggested awkwardly.

'Lovely,' I said flatly. 'Oh well, I was just checking in. I've got to go now, Dad. Bye.' I rang off and took a deep breath.

I leant against the adjoining wall between my room and Lee's.

I put my hands on my stomach.

'What am I going to do, baby?' I whispered.

Keep me, keep me, keep me!

I knew it would only be the size of a tiny seed, unable to think, let alone speak, but it was just as if it was clamouring inside me, desperate to stay safely tucked in my womb.

'But what sort of mother will I be if I *do* take after Marigold?' I whispered. 'I don't want you to have my sort of childhood. I couldn't bear it.'

I decided to walk all the way to the hospital for my Marigold visit so I could try to clear my head and sort out what I was going to do. I wasn't quite sure how long it would take me so I set off at a fast pace, which quickly turned to a run. Another sign of bipolar disorder – frantic activity, speeding up to an insanely fast pace?

I tried to slow down but it was impossible. I kept barging into people and had to keep offering breathless apologies. I was getting boiling hot now, my teeshirt sticking to me, my shorts rubbing red marks on my inner thighs. I seemed to be burning all over, weaving this way and that, totally out of control. When at last I could see the high tower and the long sprawl of the hospital I slowed down, trying to calm myself and act as normally as possible.

I ran into the ladies' room as soon as I went in the entrance and splashed my face with cold water. I was frightened when I looked in the mirror. Was that woman really me – eyes wild, face screwed up, hair a damp tangle? Anyone seeing me would think I was an escaped patient. Maybe I *would* end up sectioned, stuck in Marigold's ward. I was nearly fifty minutes early so I decided to have something to eat in the basement canteen to see if that helped me calm down.

I walked into the busy room. The psychiatric medical staff had a policy of not wearing uniforms so it was almost impossible to work out who were staff, who were visitors and indeed who were the patients. I hovered in the doorway, the smell of curry turning my stomach, the chatter too loud, the lighting too stark. I felt the whole room slipping sideways, and I had to clutch at the painted white wall to keep upright.

'Hello? Are you OK? Here, sit on the chair and put your head between your legs,' someone said.

Lacking the strength to protest, I did as I was told.

'That's right. Just stay still for a few minutes and you'll feel better.' I knew that tone, that concern. I pushed upwards to see if I was right.

'Hey, head down!' It *was* Dr Gibbon.

'I'm fine now, honestly,' I mumbled.

He was peering at me now. 'It's Dolphin, isn't it? Marigold's daughter?'

'That's me. Come to visit my mum.'

'You're all good now,' he said, patting my back.

'I'm not good at all,' I protested, and started crying. People were staring – truly staring at me, it wasn't just my paranoia. Staring at Dr Gibbon too. 'They think I'm your patient,' I said, then paused to blow my nose. '*Could* I be your patient?'

'I don't think you need a psychiatric doctor just because you're feeling a little bit down,' he said. 'But you mustn't worry so, Dolphin. Your mum's making excellent progress. She can possibly go home next week, just as soon as social services have had a look at her flat and the living arrangements, especially as there's now this plan to have Lettie move in with her. Is that what's worrying you? Here, I'll introduce you to Lettie's doctor.'

He waved to a middle-aged blonde woman at a table near by, who was enthusiastically eating a doughnut with her coffee. She looked surprisingly glamorous in a white silk blouse and black suit. Dr Gibbon steered me over to her table and she waved sugary fingers at us.

'This is Dr Marsden, our anorexia specialist. Marian, this is Dolphin Westward, Marigold's daughter.'

'Hello, Dolphin!' she said, politely ignoring my intermittent sobs. She glanced enquiringly at Dr Gibbon.

'Dolphin's just visiting,' said Dr Gibbon. 'And she knows about this plan of Lettie's to live with Marigold.'

'What do you think about it, Dolphin?' Dr Marsden asked.

I shrugged. 'Well, they seem to like each a lot, but—'

'Ah! We've got a few buts too!' she said. 'Perhaps it won't actually happen. But who knows, they might be a great support for each other.'

'Marigold seems very good at mothering her,' I said. I meant to sound complimentary, but it sounded bitter and I blushed.

'That must be difficult for you, when you've tried so hard to help,' Dr Gibbon murmured. 'Anyway, we'll see how it goes.'

'It's lovely to meet you, Dolphin,' said Dr Marsden. She bit into her doughnut again. It oozed jam over her fingers and she licked it up shamelessly, then smiled at me. 'You look as if you need a spot of food yourself. Here, you two have my table. I must fly.' She gobbled the last morsel of doughnut, downed it with coffee and then dashed off. Somehow she'd managed to keep her beautiful black suit pristine, without a trace of jam or smear of sugar.

'She's so nice,' I said, fumbling for a tissue in my pocket because my nose was running from all the crying.

Dr Gibbon passed me an unused paper napkin and I did my best to mop myself.

'I'm not crying just because of Marigold. I'm crying because I truly need help. *Please* could I be your patient? I'm absolutely certain I've inherited her bipolar disorder and I'm so scared,' I said desperately.

'*I'm* certain you're wrong – but perhaps we could have lunch together as two friends and you can tell me what's going on, and I'll see if I can suggest anything helpful. Let's go somewhere more discreet, not on hospital grounds. Would you be up for a McDonald's? There's one just round the corner.'

'I love McDonald's,' I said. 'It was this huge treat when I was a kid. Star took me there sometimes when she wanted to hang out with this little gang. She was ever so different when we were kids to how she is now.'

'I know. I've heard all about Star from Marigold. *And* her father,' said Dr Gibbon. 'Come on then – McDonald's it is.

'I've heard a lot about you, too, from Marigold,' he added, as we made our way out of the hospital.

'Not as much, I bet,' I said.

'More, actually,' said Dr Gibbon.

I pulled a face, sure he was humouring me.

I still felt a bit sick so I only had a portion of French fries but Dr Gibbon tucked into a Big Mac very happily.

'So, special friend who is definitely not my patient, what makes you think you have bipolar disorder?' Dr Gibbon asked.

'I've recently had all the symptoms,' I said, putting my hand on my stomach underneath the table. 'Can bipolar disorder be hereditary?'

He pondered a moment. 'Occasionally. Like some heart problems. Or some cancers. But it's definitely not a given. And you haven't any symptoms whatsoever as far as I can see.'

'I feel weird. I have heaps more energy. I've got so many ideas, they just keep tumbling out. And I take all sorts of risks, and act impulsively, and get moody and difficult, and – and . . .' I wasn't sure I could come out with it. I looked round to see if anyone was listening, but everyone seemed intent on their meals.

'And?' Dr Gibbon asked, paying me full attention now.

'Can you not look at me when I say it?'

'Sure,' he said, staring resolutely at his burger.

'I have a much higher . . . sexual appetite . . . than usual, and I made a terrible mistake and had sex with this actor guy I've been working with, even though I've been seeing a lovely, kind man at home. He's my next-door neighbour, and he'd be devastated if he found out, but I went ahead and did it anyway, and the very worst thing is that I enjoyed it, even though I know I don't mean anything to the actor guy,' I said, tears pouring down my cheeks. 'But it's just there's a connection between us. I've never felt like this about anyone else – well, not as strongly. Marigold told me that she felt like she was flying when she was with Micky, and it feels like that for me.'

It felt such a relief to be able to tell him what I'd done, though I was boiling hot with embarrassment.

'You can look at me now,' I mumbled.

'Poor Dolphin,' said Dr Gibbon. His face was creased with concern, so that he almost resembled an actual gibbon, but in the loveliest way. 'I feel really sorry for you. Guilt is a terrible thing. I can see it's eating you up inside.'

I was so grateful that he didn't try to brush it off and say it was silly to feel so bad about it.

'Have you told your friend next door?' he asked gently.

'I know I should tell him. But I can't. His wife had an affair and left him. I can't let it happen to him all over again. I think he might even forgive me, but he'd never really trust me. It wouldn't be the same. And I do care about him.'

'Do you love him?'

'Well, I think I *should* love him, because he's so sweet and kind to me. But if I'm honest—'

'Just between you and me?'

'I don't think I do. I suppose I could try and maybe grow to love him, but I don't feel – well, the way my mother still feels about Micky, Star's father.'

'I've heard all about him, many times,' said Dr Gibbon. 'How he'll always be the one she loves – well, maybe *thinks* she loves. So what good do you think this great love has been to her?'

'Well, obviously, it hasn't been good for her at all. But now I'm starting to behave like her.'

'Are you fixated on the actor friend now?' Dr Gibbon asked gently.

'No, I don't think so. I don't expect I'll even see him again. But maybe there'll be other men, lots of men, and I'll break Lee's heart and—'

'Stop it!' said Dr Gibbon, gently but firmly.

'I know, I'm gabbling, talking too quickly, but that's another symptom of bipolar disorder, isn't it?' I said. I lowered my voice. 'Can't you prescribe Lithium for me to stop me acting like this? Or no, maybe not,' I contradicted myself, because I didn't think you could take such a strong drug if you were pregnant. I could hardly get my words out now because my chest was so tight.

'Take some deep breaths. I know, it's what doctors always say, but it works, I promise. In and out. In and out. That's a bit better, isn't it. Now, I'm not diagnosing you because you're not my patient. But as a family friend I would say that it's highly unlikely you've got bipolar disorder. I've dealt with many people who have in my time, and when they're high, very few recognize their condition, not at first anyway. They feel fantastic and at their most creative and witty and delightful and certainly don't see why they should take medicine that slows them down and takes away this wonderful feeling. You've analysed yourself to the nth degree and are certain you're becoming mentally unwell – but does anyone else think you have a mental health problem?'

'I told Star and she thinks I should just lighten up and stop overreacting,' I admitted.

'Well, I wouldn't put it quite like that. I respect you for feeling bad about sleeping with someone else – but regrettably lots of people do that.' He pulled a wry face then and I wondered if he'd ever cheated himself. 'You can be tremendously sexually attracted to someone you know isn't right for you. The trick is to try not to act on it, but I know that isn't easy. I expect you'll feel guilty for a while, but you'll get past it. What have your other relationships been like?'

I played with my fries, trying to lay them all straight in the carton while thinking hard.

'I suppose I've always been attracted to the wrong sort of guy, right from when I was at school. I don't know *why*. I want someone kind and steady who'll always be there for me – and yet now I've found exactly that person, and I can't seem to force myself to feel what I'd need to for him to make it work. I've just fucked everything up. Oh, sorry!'

'I've heard a lot worse. Listen, if we were in therapy together, over a period of weeks, we'd talk about this – well, *you'd* talk – and eventually you'd realize that you want to feel safe and reassured after a pretty hectic childhood and yet, paradoxically, your subconscious pushes you towards dysfunctional relationships because they're all you've known, so they seem like your "safe space", even though you know on a conscious level that they're not. But of course you're not in therapy – though let me know if you'd like to try it, and I can recommend someone. You've got it into your head that you might take after Marigold and have bipolar disorder but I'm sure you haven't got it or any other serious mental illness so far as I can see. You're just a normal, mixed-up human being who makes mistakes like all of us.'

I'd heard every word – but I wanted him to say that again. And then again.

'Do you really mean that?' I asked breathlessly.

'Absolutely. Now eat those fries before they get cold. Marian was right, you do look as if you could do with a square meal inside you.' He took a long gulp of Coke.

'As you're *not* my doctor, can I say that I think you're a lovely man? Or is that transference?'

'You clearly know a great deal about psychiatry,' he said, taking the last bite of his burger and wiping his greasy fingers on his napkin.

'Well, I would do, wouldn't I, having to take responsibility for Marigold.'

'Why do you have to do that?' Dr Gibbon asked.

I blinked at him. 'Well, Star can't, because she's up in Scotland and much too busy anyway.'

'Aren't you busy too? I can't help feeling that you're trying your hardest to be there for your mother all the time, neglecting your own needs. A psychiatrist would say it's a classic case of co-dependency, and maybe *you* need to be needed by her. A good friend would say you've learnt to put Marigold's needs first ever since you were a little girl, and you're still worrying yourself sick about her. She's trying now to look after herself and maybe you should take a step back and let her have a go.'

'I'm not sure it will work,' I said.

'I'm not sure either, but you could both try it? Have a think about it anyway. Put yourself first for once. Concentrate on what *you* want most.' He looked at me earnestly.

'What do *you* think I want most?' I asked.

'Ah, as a friend – *and* a psychiatrist – I would say you have to work that out for yourself. When you get back home, try writing all your choices on a piece of paper. Don't overthink it, just jot everything down. You might be surprised with what you come up with.' He looked at his watch. 'I'd better be getting back now. Would you believe Saturday is meant to be a day off for me, but we've had two urgent referrals overnight and I was the mug to agree to go in to assess them.'

'Three referrals, counting me referring myself,' I said. 'Can I ask just one more question? Given that bipolar disorder *can* be hereditary, even though you think I haven't got it, what about me being able to pass on those genes? Could you promise me it would be safe for me to have a baby?'

He deliberated for a moment. 'There's a small risk, I suppose. But if you did have a baby who had bipolar disorder, would it be such a terrible thing? Some of our greatest world leaders and creative artists have been bipolar. Think *Starry Night* and those marvellous *Sunflowers*. It's pretty certain Van Gogh had the condition.'

'Yes, but I don't want my baby to be so unhappy he cuts off his ear!' I protested.

Dr Gibbon stood up. He hesitated, biting his lip uncertainly. 'Do you think Dr Marsden looks unhappy?' he suddenly asked.

'No! Anything but!'

'Well. Think on,' said Dr Gibbon. 'And she's got both her ears.'

I gasped. 'You're not saying . . . ?'

'I'm not saying anything because I wouldn't ever divulge anything personal about a colleague, and I'm especially fond of Dr Marsden. Who we agree is happy and professional and totally in control, and if she ever needed medication I'm sure she would take it regularly and manage her condition perfectly well.'

I stared at Dr Gibbon, speechless.

'I completely understand why you fear the condition so much, Dolphin. You think you're like Marigold – but you're an entirely different person. People develop bipolar disorder for many different reasons. Yes, sometimes people become mentally ill because they've got an unfortunate combination of genes. But please understand that's just one piece of the puzzle. There are so many other factors in Marigold's life that have contributed to her experience of it. Lots of people with bipolar disorder lead normal, balanced, happy lives – you've just met a shining example. Others don't. But some who've been chronically ill for many years still manage to turn their lives around.' He paused and smiled at me. 'OK, lecture over. Now, are you coming back to the hospital to visit Marigold?' he carried on casually.

We walked back together in companionable silence, and I shook hands with him fervently when we said goodbye. He went into his office and I went into Primrose Ward. I tried to repeat all the things he'd said inside my head, but they were already getting tangled up and distorted. But I felt calmer, I could breathe more easily, and when I got to Marigold's room I went straight up to her and gave her a warm hug. I even managed to give Lettie a quick hug too.

'What's got into you, Dol?' Marigold said.

'Oh, I'm just . . . pleased that you two have made friends,' I said, and I almost meant it.

'We've been planning our flat share,' Lettie said eagerly. 'Marigold says I can have my own bedroom.'

I bristled a moment. There were only two bedrooms, and the small one was supposed to be mine if Marigold needed someone to watch over her. But I hardly ever stayed there – and I certainly didn't want to. Or maybe needed to? So I smiled – and I saw Marigold breathe out in relief.

'Yeah, it's great, isn't it, Lettie?' she said. 'We've been talking it all over. We might even go travelling for a lark, eh?'

I smiled at Marigold fondly. Maybe there was a chance it would really work out for them, though how on earth would they finance all their grand plans? But that was *their* responsibility, not mine. And at least their dream was making them happy now, in this moment.

I spent half an hour with them, trying hard to be friendly with Lettie, and then went home, eager at least to see Ava. She was wearing her cute dungarees again, and Lee had bought her a red toy trowel to put in her front pocket.

'Mrs Knight's invited us to tea,' Lee said proudly.

'Well, that's good. You two have a lovely time,' I said, rather welcoming the chance to think through everything Dr Gibbon had said.

'We three,' said Lee.

I stared at him. I didn't want to go! I had to be honest and tell him. But he was looking so hopefully at me that I couldn't crush him, not in front of Ava. So much for any resolution to try putting myself first!

I hoped that Mrs Knight might be interesting and eccentric, rather like Henrietta, but she was just a pale posh lady in a lilac top and white pleated skirt, her feet puffy in their tight black patent shoes. She said good afternoon to us politely and made a great to-do with the fetching of gilt-edged china plates and cups and two tins, one for cake and one for biscuits. Lee made the tea while she bossed him around, making sure he knew the right number of spoonfuls after he'd warmed the teapot, and then he had to let it 'draw' for exactly three minutes.

He took it all in good part, seemingly pleased to be on such familiar terms with her. She even had Ava running around with ancient lacy napkins for each of us. Ava didn't seem to mind and begged for more 'jobs'. I wasn't left out either. I was commanded to take the lids off the tins and arrange the contents on two bigger plates. The tin contents were a disappointment: a Swiss roll that had gone stale, and dull digestive biscuits.

When we were all sitting down and balancing our dainty plates on our laps, Ava cuddled up close to me on the sofa, as if I was her mother. I knew I'd be a good stepmother. I loved her already – and she seemed to love me. She'd like it if I became Lee's proper partner. He would too. Lee was so good to me in many different ways. We'd settled so quickly into a domestic routine. He could be gentle and kind and comforting when I was down. He'd been bullish and overbearing when he'd seen me dancing with Joel, but he'd tried hard now to trust me not to be playing around. Even though I had been.

I thought of that last time with Joel in the woods and felt a stab inside me, knowing that sex would never be like that with Lee, considerate and determined though he was. But there was no point hankering after Joel again. Dr Gibbon said *I* had to decide what I wanted – but I didn't know! And what about the baby, my baby, my little tadpole child swimming inside of me? I didn't care if it was Lee's or Joel's, it was the one thing I was certain about. I wanted it and I was going to keep it no matter what.

'Dol! Mrs Knight's talking to you,' Lee murmured.

I blinked, jerked back to the present. Mrs Knight was looking at me imperiously.

'I'm sorry?' I said meekly.

'I was saying, what sort of Christian name is Dol?' she enquired. She said the word as if it was some unpleasant euphemism.

I saw Lee looking at me anxiously. I could tell her it was short for Dorothy – a nice, traditional name that she'd likely find acceptable. But why the hell should I?

'It's short for Dolphin, Mrs Knight,' I said, as pleasantly as I could.

'*Dolphin?*' she said. 'What sort of a mother calls her child Dolphin?'

'My sort of mother,' I said.

Mrs Knight looked appalled, but Ava seemed enchanted.

'That's so cool! Dolphins are my absolute favourite animal!' she said, taking a sip of her tea. Then she winced, clearly hating the taste. She pressed her lips together and stirred the cup with increasing desperation, not knowing what to do. I quickly drank it for her when Mrs Knight was fumbling in her bag for her handkerchief. Ava smiled up at me gratefully, snuggling closer. I loved the feel of her curled against me. It almost made this ordeal worth it.

Mrs Knight made no further remarks about my name but she looked down her long, thin nose at me. I stopped trying to make polite conversation and answered her snooty questions in monosyllables. Lee kept giving me anxious glances.

When tea was over and tidied away, we left Mrs Knight to have a 'rest' and went into the garden.

'Phew!' said Lee. 'Sorry she's so hoity-toity, I don't think she can help it. You could have made a bit more effort, though.'

He was ticking me off as if I was a naughty schoolgirl. I hated it, but I didn't want to start a row in front of Ava.

'And why on earth did you tell her your name is Dolphin?' Lee continued, exasperated.

'Because it is,' I said shortly.

'I think it's a lovely name,' Ava said, looking at the two of us anxiously. Lee noticed, and took a deep breath.

'Come and look round the gardens, girls,' he said, as pleasantly as he could manage.

It was a huge, tangled wilderness and after two minutes I was totally bored, but Lee doggedly lectured me about all his planting plans. I tried hard to appear interested, while Ava ran around whooping, pretending it was a magic jungle. The old gardener's cottage was almost at the end, hidden away in a little copse.

'Oh, it's like a fairy cottage!' said Ava, delighted, whereas I was unable to think of anything to say.

It was small and dismal and damp-looking, and when I peered through the grimy, latticed windows I saw old and ugly furniture in the dark, uninviting living room.

'Don't worry, we can gradually get our own furniture. I'm a flatpack demon,' Lee said. 'And I'll paint it in lovely light colours and spruce it all up and make it look like our own special little home.'

My throat dried. I had to tell him outright that I hated the cottage, I hated the overgrown garden, I hated Mrs Knight's dark mausoleum of a house, and I hated Mrs Knight herself. I knew I couldn't live there in a million years.

I watched as Lee and Ava did some digging with their big and little trowels and saw how happy they were together. I was so fond of both of them. I was certain I loved Ava – but I knew I didn't feel actual love for Lee. Was liking him and being grateful and wanting a father figure for my baby ever going to be enough? Could I keep up a pretence for ever?

I put my hands on my stomach again, picturing my tiny, scarcely there baby growing inside me, minute by minute, hour by hour, day by day. It was top of the list that Dr Gibbon suggested I make – and it was a certainty, not an option.

On the way home in the van Ava chattered happily about the fairy-tale cottage and the lovely garden while I stared out the window, not joining in.

'You're very quiet, Dol?' Lee said. 'What's the matter with you?'

I didn't know what to say. The blood pounded so hard in my head that my eyes blurred.

'Well, maybe it's a bit soon to make any major decisions about the cottage,' I mumbled.

'I thought once you'd seen it, you'd fall in love with it,' said Lee, sounding crestfallen.

'*I* love it, Daddy,' Ava said.

'I know, darling. And so do I,' said Lee. 'And I'm sure Dol will too, if she'll only see sense.'

I gulped, anger warring with guilt. He shouldn't have said that to her! I'd never said I'd go there. I *had* seen sense. It wasn't for me. I could pretend, but why should I force myself to go along with Lee's dreams? The old Dol might have tried to get used to it – but it was time for me to stop making compromises.

I didn't want to have an all-out confrontation in front of Ava, though.

'Let's discuss all this later on,' I said. There was just one thing I had to be certain of first. Was I really one hundred per cent certain I was actually going to have a baby?

When we were nearly back in Seahaven, I took a deep breath. 'Could we stop outside the chemist's for two ticks?' I asked.

Lee sighed, uncharacteristically irritable. 'It'll be hell to park there. What do you want? You can use my shampoo or toothpaste or whatever.'

'I want . . . women's things,' I said.

'Oh. Right,' he said ungracefully, clearly assuming I meant tampons.

I needed the exact opposite, of course. I ran into the chemist's and asked for a pregnancy test. Three tests, actually, because I needed to be sure. The woman behind the counter put them in a discreet paper bag for me.

'Could you possibly tell me what I have to do?' I whispered to her.

'There's full instructions inside the package, dear. It's all quite easy,' she said, smiling at me sympathetically.

'Yes, but—' Oh, to hell with the lost-glasses excuses. 'I can't read properly. Could you read them out to me?' I begged.

'Don't worry, there are pictures too. But of course I'll read out what it says as well.'

She murmured the instructions, her voice lowered so that other customers didn't stare.

'Thank you so much,' I said gratefully.

'Well – good luck!' she said.

When we got home, I told Lee and Ava I needed to pop into my flat for a few minutes. Once I was inside my own front door I ran to the loo and did my best to work out exactly what to do, though my hands were shaking so much I nearly dropped the testing device down the loo. Then I waited, trying to block out the sound of Lee and Ava chattering next door. I stared at the space where the lines should come. The test line, the control line. I kept blinking, and then at last I saw the lines. Two distinct lines.

It was true. I was pregnant! Definitely! I felt tears of joy spurting down my cheeks, and realized I knew what I wanted now. Even so, I tried all over again with another test, just to make sure. I had to run the tap so I could squeeze out another spurt of wee, and there was the result all over again. Positive! I had a baby inside me. My baby.

I stowed the unused test away, because I knew I'd feel the need to try again, maybe in the morning. I'd probably be testing away for months until I only had to look down at myself to see I was going to have a baby. My body. My baby.

I washed my hands and stared at myself in the mirror. My eyes were shining again, but with happiness this time. I went back to Lee and Ava, though all I wanted to do was sit by myself stroking my stomach. It was so difficult to try to act normally. Lee and even Ava seemed to be blurred, their voices scarcely audible. I just wanted to commune in peace with my baby.

It seemed so banal and ridiculous to be stuck here making small talk and eating fish and chips for supper. Ava and I sprinkled the mustard and cress we'd grown as a kind of garnish over our meal. Lee took two bottles of beer and a lemonade for Ava out of his fridge.

'Could I please have a lemonade too? I don't really fancy a beer,' I said quickly. Lee sighed as if I was being deliberately difficult.

He was truculent with me, but very loving and enthusiastic with Ava. He kept talking to her about the cottage, asking her how she'd like her bedroom decorated and wondering what sort of puppy she wanted when they lived there.

'What kind shall we pick, Dol? Do you like big dogs or little dogs?' she asked.

'I think it's up to you to choose, darling,' I said, trying to keep my voice steady.

I drew her a variety of dogs, and invented names and personalities for all of them, and added Fido the Van Dog, which made her laugh. She put an arm round my neck and pressed her cheek against mine.

'I do love you, Dol,' she said.

'And I love you, Ava,' I mumbled.

Then Lee took over, supervising a shower and tucking her up in bed and then reading her several bedtime stories. I sat on the sofa, waiting. When Ava had nodded off to sleep he came and sat on the sofa, keeping a small distance between us, his arms folded.

'OK. Let's have this out. Why didn't you try to be nicer to Mrs Knight? I know she's a bit difficult but it's incredibly generous of her to offer me the cottage. I can do it up in a matter of weeks and we can move in. I think it's a fantastic idea. As you saw, Ava's over the moon. It will be a marvellous place for her to come to every weekend, and hopefully for holidays. I can't see why you're not leaping at this chance. Here we are, stuck in these poky little bedsits, with hardly room to swing a cat,' Lee said, barely able to keep his voice down.

'Don't use that horrible expression,' I said. It always made me picture a poor shrieking cat in agony being swung around by its tail by some brute. I knew Lee wasn't a brutal man at all, I knew it was just words, but I still bristled.

'For God's sake, Dol, don't be so picky, I'm just using plain English,' said Lee. 'Look, I'm sorry, I'm trying very hard to be reasonable, but I can't understand why you can't see this is a wonderful chance for both of us. I know you're not the slightest bit interested in gardening, but that's OK – though you could actually make a bit of an effort to try when it means so much to me. You can carry on doing these wall painting things if that's what you want, or do some more art teaching, whatever – just let's jump at this amazing chance.'

It was now or never. Maybe yesterday's Dol couldn't have managed it. I'd have been too scared of upsetting him, wanting to please him, needing to feel he could look after me like a father. But this was now, today.

'I can't, Lee. I can see it's a dream come true for you and Ava. And that's great. But it's not *my* dream. I want to stay here, in my little room next door, because it's mine and I love it. And I want to develop my mural business, and feel free to make my own decisions and do whatever I want. I'd still love to be close friends with you, and spend special time with Ava, but I've realized that I don't want to be in a proper relationship with you. We're both so different and want different things. You've been so kind and looked after me and treated me like a special little girl, but I'm thirty-three years old and I have to start acting like it.'

Lee stared at me, shaking his head, his face screwed up. 'I can't believe you're coming out with all this,' he whispered.

'I'm sorry, I'm truly sorry, I do care about you so much, Lee – but – but it's not enough,' I said.

'It sounds like you don't give a damn about me, or Ava either.'

He glanced over at her bed. Mercifully, she'd had an exhausting afternoon and was already heavily asleep.

I glared at him. 'Of course I care. Can't you see how much I love her?'

'So much so you're willing to break her little heart by not living with us in the cottage?'

This was such a low blow I stopped feeling desperately sorry for him.

'You say you love Ava. What about me? What did you mean, it's not enough?' He reached over and tried to kiss me.

'Please, Lee, don't! *Don't!*' I said, struggling with him.

'I suppose you've still got the hots for the lover-boy actor?' he said, letting me go.

'I'm not ever going to see Joel again. He means nothing to me now.'

'Do you swear that? You haven't ever had sex with him?' Lee asked.

I swallowed hard. 'I swear,' I mumbled uncertainly.

'Don't you dare lie to me! It's written all over your face!' Lee hissed furiously.

Ava half woke at his tone, and murmured sleepily.

'Shh now, darling. Back to sleep,' I called out.

'Just leave my daughter alone,' Lee said curtly, but he'd lowered his voice.

'Oh, Lee, please don't let's quarrel like this, especially over Ava,' I begged.

'You've just been playing games with me all along,' said Lee. 'You've never really wanted me. You've just been using me.'

'No, it's not been like that, please, you know how much you've meant to me over the summer,' I said.

'I *thought* I knew. But I can see I've been a total fool,' said Lee, and then he put his hands over his face and started sobbing.

I listened to his anguished, guttural sounds, utterly horrified, feeing so terrible.

'Please, Lee – I feel so bad. You haven't been a fool, you've been a loving, caring man and—'

'And now you're dumping me, so would you mind getting out of my room, because I can't bear to look at you any more,' said Lee, his face contorted.

Oh God, how had we suddenly escalated into this awful scenario? There was no going back now. I felt so desperately sad – and yet I knew I was doing the right thing for both our sakes.

I leant over Ava in bed and whispered close to her ear, 'Goodbye, Ava darling. I love you so much. I do hope we'll be able to keep seeing each other. Be kind to Daddy, he's a bit sad now.'

Then I stood and put my hand on Lee's shoulder, but he ducked away from me. I went back to my room and went to bed, feeling terrible – and yet relieved that it was over now.

I wondered whether he would come to my room in the morning, but I heard him and Ava going out early and she was saying something about going swimming, so I guessed they were heading to the beach. I felt sad and left out – but knew it was inevitable, and it didn't make me waver in my choice.

I made myself a coffee, picked up my drawing pad and went back to bed. I didn't want to struggle constructing a misspelt list of what I wanted. I did it my way, drawing it all out on a single page. I drew my baby in the centre, in black ink, a small curled-up creature, tiny head against its little knees. I positioned a leg so that it hid the sex – I didn't care if it was a boy or a girl, just so long as it was mine and growing and healthy. It could be bipolar, it could be dyslexic, it could have very rosy cheeks or deep-blue eyes – but it would be itself and I would try so hard to be the best mother it could ever wish for.

I inked a mural behind my child, scattering it with dragons

and unicorns and fairy castles, because this was my new career and I was determined to make it work so that I could support myself and my baby. I knew I'd have childcare problems just like Star, but I wondered if Linda might be willing to help me out. If I had enough mural commissions, I'd be able to pay her a proper wage. I'd make it work no matter what.

Then I drew Marigold and Star, but in brown ink, so I could shade them in sepia, showing they were part of my life ever since I could remember. We were family, and I loved both of them so much. I'd always be there for them if they really needed me, but I couldn't just come running whenever they wanted. It was going to be hard, and I might give in sometimes, but I could still try.

Then, much smaller, in pencil, there was Ava and Lee and Joel – the little girl I'd pretended was my own, the two men I felt for in such different ways, but knew they weren't part of my future. I included a little Dr Gibbon too, because he'd given me the greatest gift I could ever have asked for: a sense of myself.

I inked a little dolphin inside my wrist so that I could look at it whenever I wavered. I was me, Dolphin Westward, and I was going to be just fine, whatever.

Acknowledgements

I'd like to thank my special daughter Emma most of all. She gave me the idea for writing *The Illustrated Mum*, my 1990s book about Dolphin's difficult childhood. We were on holiday together in New York, having enjoyed a marvellous day going to art galleries and shops. We were taking a rest in Central Park, idly people-watching. An extraordinary woman walked past in a very skimpy outfit, showing off her amazing decorative tattoos. She had two little girls with her in dressing-up clothes, staggering along in their mother's high-heeled shoes. Emma gave me a nudge and whispered, 'They look as if they could be characters in one of your books!'

So I wrote about them, totally caught up in their story. The book won several literary awards and was turned into a television drama starring Michelle Collins as Marigold and Alice Connor and Holliday Grainger as Dolphin and Star. The film had a showing at the Museum of Modern Art in New York. I've often wondered whether that distinctive woman in Central Park ever got to see it.

Now I've revisited my fictional characters in *Picture Imperfect* – and it's been the easiest book I've ever written, and in other ways the hardest, because Dolphin, Star and Marigold have always meant so much to me.

The entire team at Transworld have been amazingly supportive and encouraging. My fantastic editor Thorne Ryan has worked so hard on the text and given me praise, encouragement, and tactful suggestions on ways I could improve my book – and dammit, she's always been right! She's been aided and abetted by ultra-helpful editorial assistant Anna Carvanova and meticulous copy-editor Tamsin Shelton.

Dynamic deputy publicity director Becky Short is busy organizing exciting events and interviews and a big tour, where I hope I can meet many special readers. Ultra-innovative Hannah Winter has not only manufactured a travelling life-size statue of me but is organizing posters at railway stations, not to mention more fun TikTok appearances. People might well become sick of the sight of me!

I'm so grateful to Beci Kelly for her imaginative cover design, Hannah Cawse, head of audio, Helena Sheffield, the publicist for the audiobook, Deirdre O'Connell, Phoebe Llanwarne, Rhian Steer and Nina Lewis.

As always, I couldn't manage my working life without Naomi Cooper, my marvellous freelance publicist, who stays calm and cheerful no matter what, and is such fun to travel with. My agents of many years, Caroline Walsh and Georgina Ruffhead, have given me immense support as always, as have all my dear friends, especially Nick White and William Emmett.

Dearest of all, huge thanks to my long-suffering partner Trish, who's listened to me ramble on about this book for many months and given me every encouragement, plus big hugs and chocolates and Crémant whenever I've been flagging.

Jacqueline Wilson wrote her first novel when she was nine years old, and she has been writing ever since. She is now one of Britain's bestselling and most beloved authors. She has written over one hundred books, with total sales of over forty million copies. Her first adult novel, *Think Again*, became an instant *Sunday Times* bestseller.

As well as winning many awards for her books, including the Children's Book of the Year, Jacqueline is a former Children's Laureate, and in 2008 she was appointed a Dame.

Jacqueline is also a great reader, and has amassed over twenty thousand books, along with her famous collection of silver rings.